ICONIC

BOOK ONE OF THE OUTER REACHES

A J GORDON

PETER J ALDIN

Cover Art by Sam Kennedy.

Cover Design by Brenda Mihalko.

PROLOGUE

ADJIRA MO'HALANA MO'NI'MARIAMA had brought the glory of Terranist rule to more worlds than she could keep track of. Her subjects adored her—as they rightly should. Adjira was the Great Kaana, the Foremost of the Okalasi, Bringer of the Light, Mother of the Children of Terra.

But at this moment, she felt neither glorious nor adored. The Kaana simply felt hounded.

She slumped over the dressing table in her bedchamber and murmured soft curses. With her palm upon her read-plate, the device came to life with the warmth of her touch. Adjira's hands were large, and—she could admit this now that she'd fallen into such bleak despair—they were pudgy. But they were always warm, due to her augmented heart and enhanced blood flow. Generations of her Okalasi forebears had possessed long, twiggy fingers, the digits of artists and musicians. Adjira's might have been the same if it weren't for her penchant for the richest foods of the many cultures currently under her rulership.

Adjira's sausage-thick fingers stroked patterns across the read-plate's fingerboard, inputting the code to accept long-range communiqués. Finally, she leaned close to the device's eye and let it study her iris. Then, and only then, did it divulge its secrets. The recording sent by Researcher Chaviss had come from so far away that to even think of the distances involved curdled one's mind. She concentrated on a voice that warbled with digital corruption but remained clear enough for the message to get through.

"Majesty. Good Mother of us all. Full copies of your research are safe within the Haven, and the Haven is complete. Janus has been sent the coordinates. All you need do is command it to bring you here. We are fully functional and, hidden deep within a dust cloud, this world is well-shielded from Martianist probes and scopes. We await your arrival with eager hearts. You are and always will be Empress to us all."

The lights in her bedchamber flickered. The read-plate slipped from Adjira's grip and onto the thick carpet by her toes. The pitch of the alarm that wafted through her open door rose for a few seconds, as did the volume, before one of the more intelligent starship crewmembers decided to snuff the damned caterwauling out completely—at least in her section of the ship. Why, after all, would the Kaana need to hear it?

It was too hard to bend across her full belly and retrieve the reader, and Adjira wouldn't have bothered even if she could manage it. On top of everything else, she had a headache, a product of the noise and the frequently flickering lights, no doubt. Perhaps also due to the stress of the relentless Martianist assault—although she'd never admit that to anyone else.

Who else is there to admit it to? she wondered then. *Not a brother nor a sister left. Not even a damned aunt or cousin.*

More flickering of the lights. One of her Royal Guardians appeared in the doorway, its blocky form dominating the room.

"Majesty."

The voice was artificially deep and normally toneless, but

this time she read some amount of concern in the voice and that single word.

"You want me to flee," she replied.

"Yes, Majesty."

She studied the semi-human a little more closely, recognizing it now as the Guardian commander. She should be excused for not immediately noticing that; they all looked the same, and even sounded the same. If it weren't for the red-and-gold braid looped around this one's thick torso, she wouldn't have picked out its rank at all.

"The attack is getting worse," it added when she didn't respond.

"Yes, the unstable lighting and emergency alarms gave that away," Adjira said and pushed herself upright with a small groan.

"Janus has been trying to reach you."

Her fingers brushed her temple. "I shut him out. He kept prattling and prattling."

"He insists you enter stasis while he attempts to jump the ship. I concur with his opinion."

"If I do that, how am I to make sure my crew won't betray me?"

The cyborg stiffened as if offended, though no emotion showed on its claylike face. "Majesty, there's not a person on board *Iconic* who'd betray you."

She sniffed. "We've lost five ships in the past eleven hours, Commander. One to mutiny—joining our enemy. Three to destruction—that's a kind of betrayal, a betrayal by incompetence. And one to hyperspace as the be-cursed thing jumped away, fleeing its duty, may its crew emerge in the heart of a black hole. I'm *surrounded* by betrayal!"

"Your Guardians continue to shield you with their lives."

Adjira's hands smoothed her hair across her scalp, stroking the area of her skull that covered some of the augments she'd been given. She had only to think it and she'd *have* a shield, a real shield, her own personal energy shield generated by the devices concealed around her body. "If the Martianists cripple and board *Iconic*, I'll need every shield I have at my disposal."

Another sigh. How had it come to this? The glorious and holy Terranist cause brought to nothing, all because her damned father had decided to launch the war a generation early, then had the gall to die and leave her the responsibility of running it and cleaning up his messes! All Adjira had wanted was to complete the research of two centuries, bringing her dynasty's plans to final fruition.

"You know, Commander, if Father had let me do things my way, our armies and navies wouldn't have been merely formidable; they'd have been unstoppable. If we'd launched our strikes against the Augustan dynasty in another twenty years, we'd have been on Tivere within months. The war would be over."

"Majesty, again, I—"

"Yes, yes. I think you're right. Or Janus is. Perhaps we should jump to our Haven and regroup."

"I'm very pleased to hear you say that, Majesty. May I assist you in moving?"

She peered over at it without moving. "And assist me to my pod? To slumber with my harem? I suppose that would be best. If you promise to protect me and protect them."

"Majesty, I've sworn to it, and am designed for it."

With no more effort than a thought, she reconnected the link in her brain with Janus—and felt, rather than heard, the great AI's relief. She said, "Very well. Then..."

A deep shudder ran through the vessel. More alarms pierced the air beyond her door. The commander put a hand to one ear as if listening to an earpiece she knew he didn't wear. The lights dipped. Gravity vanished—or rather, it felt to Adjira like the deck had fallen away from beneath her.

Kaana Adjira would have known some kind of catastrophic event had occurred even if, in the back of her mind, Janus wasn't screaming his outrage and shock.

Admiral Jessata Devota had always thought the greatest view in the universe was the one from her imperial starstriker's bridge. Especially when the *Tibera* was deeply engaged in battle, handing the godsdamned Terranists their asses.

Tibera's bridge took up the highest deck in her superstructure, with windows—real windows, fifty centimeters thick—the entire way around so Devota could march from one side to the other, from one end to the other, and see what was happening around her ship in real time.

The starstriker's main body was a flat diamond with thrusters at both ends for fast reversal in a battle—or for extra maneuverability in the event of a chase such as this one. And what a chase it had been! A running battle that would be sung about for eons, taking place in the void between Earth and the hot world Venus. Mighty ships trading powerful blows as they attempted to outpace and outmaneuver each other. She and her six support vessels—four missile cruisers, a Quintasian gunship, and a turncoat Okalasi cruiser—had whittled down the numbers of *Iconic's* support vessels, losing just two of their own, until the only remaining Terranist ship *was Iconic*.

At first, Devota's senior officers had been petrified that the Terranist fleet was headed for Mars, to scorch it and render it uninhabitable as it had been in ancient days. But that hadn't been their plan at all. If Mars was the second-most sacred world in Martianist ethos, Devota's fleet had cornered their quarry in the gravity well of the *most* holy place of the Terranist cause and identity.

Earth.

Iconic had used the planet's moon to assist in braking hard, coming about into the relatively narrow space between the two celestial bodies. For what reason, Devota couldn't know. Her guess was that they hoped for mercy, hoped Emperor Claudiomo's finest vessels would cease firing with humanity's birthplace hanging there in the background.

As if we care for Earth, Devota scoffed.

Earth's blues and grays shone brightly through the *Tibera's* forward windows, as did its moon, Luna, in the foreground, both reflecting sunlight back at her. Devota was still a long way from the usurper's ship, *Iconic*—not nearly close enough to see it. She had to glance down at her handheld pad for long-range video of the vessel. On her screen, *Iconic* was a tiny artificial splinter suspended in space "beneath" Luna's southern pole.

The Terranist ship's shields flickered on and off, losing integrity in patches. A well-placed nuke could probably destroy it now, if Devota timed it right and slipped it in through the shield patches. The nuclear devastation of the last of the Okalasi usurpers—Adjira—would be a fitting end, all right. But the Imperial Family and the imperial cause deserved better. As did, ironically, the Terranists. Devota had other ideas—an idea given to her by her senior officer's fears for Mars. She had a more... *educational* statement in mind—something not only epic for the recordings, but something that would snuff out any dream of a future "Terranist" empire.

Devota could destroy the rebel Okalasi Dynasty, it's insane cause, *and* its spiritual heart in one fell swoop.

Weapons officers from the various ships in her fleet reported in, announcing the readiness of their weapons and their staff to concentrate their fire upon her order. She exchanged a long look with her adjutant, Captain Gaetius. The man was grinning—actually grinning. And why not? It was Adjira's forces who'd razed his home planet when the loyalist population had unanimously rejected surrender. Gaetius had lost a home and a family to this cow, and to the arrogance of her family's claims to be the true caretakers of humanity's interests and destiny.

Destiny this, you bitch.

She raised her voice, knowing the channels were open between all her fleet's command bridges. "Now hear this. I, Admiral Devota, give this order, and those bound to serve His Excellence Emperor Claudiomo will obey it. Our target is Luna. You may commence firing... now."

Visible through her forward windows, the exhaust plumes of the imperial war machine's mightiest missiles combined with a dozen of its most advanced particle cannons, lancing toward the moon...

This costly twenty-year war had burned whole planets. The arrogant uprising that had cost the Imperium a full half of its territory and left those regions in lawlessness was about to end.

And end it did, in spectacular fashion. Luna's explosion was nothing short of epic, and Devota heard many of her bridge staffers gasp. It appeared to happen in slow motion because of the distance, but the particle cannons had opened deep rifts in the satellite's crust, allowing the missiles access to the core. One-third of the moon broke away as it crumbled into smaller particles, each of which must still have been gargantuan for her to be able to see them with her own eyes from this distance.

The *Iconic* couldn't have dodged such catastrophe, and on Devota's handheld, there was no sign of the Kaana's ship, and nothing on scans when she logged into their readouts.

The bridge had fallen silent, she realized. She'd expected all eyes to be turned to the devastation near Earth, the devastation that would soon impact *upon* Earth, but all eyes were turned to her.

They expected her to say something. So, she said the first words that popped into her head. "The usurper is ended, and our Imperium is safe again."

A great cheer went up. She heard it echoed over comms from the other ships' control centers.

Over the next fifteen minutes, Devota stood at the forward window, watching the continued breakup of Earth's satellite, its broken chunks caught in Earth's gravity well, spiraling in on the birthplace of the human species.

So be it, she thought. *We're no longer beholden to that ancient world. We've conquered a thousand other worlds for the glory of the emperors and the species.*

"Ma'am."

It took a moment for her to notice the quiet voice against the renewed background hubbub. A skinny young man in an ensign's uniform stood nearby, a handheld of his own clutched to his chest.

"What is it?"

"I... Admiral, I don't think *Iconic* was destroyed. See this data here? It suggests the usurper's ship jumped microseconds before the shock front reached it."

"Is this accurate?" Devota studied the device, fighting a sense of alarm.

"Yes, ma'am."

"I see. Your work, Ensign, is excellent." Then Devota pulled her sidearm and shot the man through the head before turning the weapon on his seven bridge colleagues. A shame; a waste. Best of the best, and loyal to the empire, of course, but not sworn adherents to the secretive Cor Fidelis cause, as she was. Such people couldn't be trusted to keep this information to themselves.

Cor Fidelis elements could continue to hunt Kaana Adjira. The rest of the empire had to believe the Kaana was gone. For peace. And for the emperor's glory.

By the time the Marine complement had rushed into the bridge to investigate the weapons discharge, Devota had used the ensign's sidearm to put a hole through the data storage containing the information he'd recorded. "Man went mad. Killed them all before I got him. I think, after all that, he was a Terranist mole."

Damn shame to slight such a loyal, promising young man.

"Get me another bridge crew," she told the Marine sergeant. "We're headed to Tivere."

The data was gone, but Admiral Devota would report this personally and confidentially to the emperor himself.

The emperor would know what to do.

Janus brooded over the great ship and the survivors aboard, one survivor above all others.

Although the Kaana couldn't hear him, he sent her a message, recording it in her stasis pod, hoping it would activate when she was awoken so it would bring her immediate reassurance...

Don't fret, Your Majesty. Sleep well, and be at peace. My systems are severely damaged, and your servants are mostly dead or dying, but I remain. I was designed to keep you safe, and keep you safe I shall. Our first priority is to take you somewhere they won't find you. And while you sleep, I'll utilize all my resources to repair Iconic.

We'll be ready for your revival.

CHAPTER ONE

ALEXIS NALES HEARD VOICES. No one she recognized. *Too rough. Too crude.*

"Foster, she's comin' 'round." A man's voice. She didn't recognize the accent.

A shadow loomed close, but her foggy faceplate allowed little detail. She couldn't move her arms yet.

Who? Where? Why?

Think. What was the last thing... Kaden! she remembered. The *Octavia* had unexpectedly dropped out of hyperspace and was attacked by... unknown. Who'd known where and when they'd be there? Sabotage? Her mind moved on through the jumbled thoughts... *or are they nightmares?* An explosion... *fire, bodies knocked to the deck... pain in my head... Kaden picked me up and put me in a stasis pod.*

Kaden! Her partner for the new Sylvanus Colony on Niviaris. *Where...*

"Hey, cutie." She felt warm, fetid breath on her neck.

Who are these people?

"Foster, things are gettin' really tight here. There's word of a Bukshoga Qlan cruiser snooping in the—"

She heard a distant crackly voice. *Radio? Comm-link? There must be breathable atmo; if they were in suits, I wouldn't hear anything.*

"The Qlan? Those fluxing backstabbers! Thought we had this gig?"

"What've I told you about thinkin'?"

"Okay, okay. We're comin'. We got a raw deal. Not much here to work with, anyhow, 'cept a couple antique space suits—"

Antique?

"Make it quick. Out." Static and silence followed.

"You didn't tell him about the woman," a different voice said from her left. A woman's voice.

"I wanna surprise the cap'n."

"He hates surprises."

"'Zactly. It'll be good for a chuckle."

She heard noises and grunts nearby; another male out of her line of sight.

"This stasis pod's fused to the deck. It ain't movin', Foster. It's too big and... let's face it, it's a relic, like most of the useless junk here. Shit. Even the *Daemon* has better equipment, and that's sayin' somethin'."

"Fine. Just grab the bod. At least we'll prolly get some stellars for 'er at the slave pens."

Distantly, as if numb, Alexis felt her body unstrapped from the harness. Hands on her arms... lifted and... nothing. *Zero-G?*

She blacked out momentarily.

She was on her back. Vague impressions of movement passed her misted mask... moving lights. *Torches?* Everywhere else was darkness. There were no sounds other than those in her immediate vicinity. *No other survivors?*

"Where is everyone?" Her voice felt harsh in her throat, like her vocal cords hadn't been used for some time.

"You're it. We'll hardly make enough stellars to cover costs, let alone a decent profit like the cap'n promised," Foster griped over his shoulder. "You better be worth somethin'."

I'm it? No other survivors of the 134 crew!

"Foster, you dumb shit," the voice of the captain came over their comms. "Maybe I'll cut my losses and dump *you* at Ieoni Orbital with her. Better still, the logs say she's a doctor. She might be a keeper, and you a loser."

Alexis couldn't see them but heard the others sniggering at Foster's rebuke by their leader.

"Frack off, the lot of ya!" Foster spat.

As they jostled her down dark passages, Alexis had a working theory. Scavengers had found the *Octavia*—*Why didn't my stasis pod eject?*—and now were taking her as... salvage? *"We can get some stellars for her,"* the words went through her thawing mind... *Stellars for... me? Selling me? Slavers? How were they out here in the depths of unexplored space? Where was Ieoni Orbital? Where was the rest of her crew?*

As that was going through her confused mind, she started to feel sensations. *The stasis drug's waning. How long was I in stasis?*

When was she?

"Antique space suits..." and, *"it's a relic, like most of this useless junk..."*

"How long?" she croaked, her voice muffled by her mask. Since the voices she could hear were clear—unmuffled—there must be atmosphere. She couldn't move her arms to take her mask off, and no one seemed inclined to assist.

"Hey, the body speaks," the female answered.

She must be the one moving me; her voice is so close. "How long was I out?" Alexis repeated.

"Put it this way, you'd probably be a grandma by now, but not to worry—it's overrated."

A sudden, overwhelming urge hit her. Her stomach convulsed, and she threw up, filling her facemask—

Drowning!

"Shit!" the female swore.

The mask was pulled back roughly, tugging at strands of her jet-black hair.

White fluid floated up and away. Alexis turned her head and coughed again, and more stasis gel erupted from her mouth and nose. She heaved in a lungful of air. And another. She could feel her arms and legs now, but moving was still a chore. *Damn stasis drugs.*

"Stupid bitch!" Foster swore at the other woman. "If she drowns, the stellars'll come outta yer pay."

Alexis lifted her head. Foster was in front—by her boots— leading the way. Blinking through stasis gel-encrusted eyes, she thought he looked like a brute: unshaven, black hair, heavyset. *Probably mostly fat.* Turning the other way, she could see the partner, opposite in looks. Too thin, mousy hair... *been on the fringe too long.*

"Lucky we ain't on the *Daemon*, otherwise you'd be cleanin' up your own stasis puke," Foster growled over his shoulder.

Where are they taking me? The Daemon?

With the face mask off, Alexis recognized where she was: the loading dock of the *Octavia*—or what was left of it. The only illumination was from their suit headlamps, but there were at least four lights showing her the details. There was a connecting tube jury-rigged to the airlock—a translucent, concertina-type tube. She passed scorch marks as well as streaks and splotches on the bulkhead before entering the dimly lit umbilical tube to the scav's ship.

"Welcome to the *Daemon*," the woman behind her said. Her tone didn't sound very welcoming.

Alexis could tell it was a workhorse of a vessel that had seen better days, and as they transported her along the passageway, everything looked mismatched. Again, she wondered how long she'd been in stasis. *"A grandma by now,"* the woman had said.

What was that? Twenty years? Thirty?

As they approached the *Daemon*, the gravity increased. "Krugga, Dennu, take her aft," Foster ordered two hefty crewmen waiting at the end of the tube.

"Frack, Krugga, do your share!" Dennu growled when he tried to lift her.

"I am! This little bit of cargo is damn heavier than she looks." Krugga adjusted his grip on the pod handles.

"I'll send Torg to make sure she's okay," the female said.

"Suit yourself," Foster grumbled as he walked away.

Manhandled roughly onto a flat board down the passageway, Alexis studied the ship. While her limbs were reluctant to obey, her eyes and ears were functioning fine. Over the complaining of her handlers, various ship sounds impinged on her ears—the susurration of ventilation, the whisper of fluids being pumped through piping and conduits, the irregular soft mechanical grinding... *something is amiss there.*

Part of her mind took in other details; twenty-three paces and one left turn before they lowered the stretcher and rolled her unceremoniously onto the deck, where she discovered aft was little more than a cupboard or a small storage area. There were no furnishings, just a blanket on the deck. Krugga and Dennin left, grumbling and complaining, though not a word to her.

Nearly twenty minutes later, after she felt the ship rumble to life, she'd recovered enough to move of her own volition—though everything felt like lead, and there was little space to move. Try as she might, she was unable to get comfortable in the confined area and felt the cramps starting.

Heavy, uneven footsteps approached. There was a brief knock, then the door slid open.

The silver face startled her. *Obviously, I'm still not fully recovered if a droid surprises me.*

"Greetings. I am Torg, the ship's droid, sent to conduct a

medical examination and render any aid, should you require it. Please follow."

Torg stepped away from the door, waiting.

The droid was like most other droids; the silver skin was unusual, but the 185cm standard height was deemed not overly imposing. Those used readily in society had more human skin tones and were attired in clothing. Ship droids were slaved to the vessel and in constant link with it, knowing all aspects immediately. Clothing and cosmetics weren't a requirement as they rarely left the vessel.

Until she had a better idea of what was going on, Alexis had to be on top of her game. If that meant accepting their medication, so be it. *It's not as if they have to ask, and I really need to stretch.*

She stood, using the door frame as support, and gingerly stepped out into the sparsely illuminated passageway.

At two meters wide and three high, it must have been the main thoroughfare through the center of the vessel to be so spacious. The deck was clear of obstructions, with the deckhead used for attaching cabling, pipes, and auxiliary trunking for air circulation.

Why is any of this relevant? At first, Alexis didn't think much of it, but as she was escorted along the passage, more aspects came unbidden to her mind, including the number of doors—whether they were fire doors only or capable of withstanding vacuum.

"That component doesn't look like part of the ship design," Alexis commented as they passed a control panel. It was the little things that stood out; slightly different buttons compared to the others she saw, and the different alloy surrounds. Even the coloring was mismatched.

"This vessel has had a number of additions in its many years of service since its deregistration as a military craft in

4833CY, when it was decommissioned. The additions are not the standard designation for this class of vessel."

"What year is it now?" *I went into the last stasis in 5096.*

"The year is 5122CY."

5122? Twenty-six years? What happened? Where is everyone? Alexis took slow, deep breaths and tried to calm her nerves. Strangely, studying the interior piqued her interest.

"This is a... *Bolide*-class cruiser, is it not?" *Where the hell did that come from?*

"Well observed. It is a Mark 3. The original hull configuration was designed in 4702CY, though not all modifications were an enhancement."

A weird statement to come from a ship droid. "You don't approve?"

"It is not a matter of my approval, though integration has been problematic at times. Here is the med-bay."

She was about to mention the soft grinding she'd heard earlier, but a door slid open silently. Alexis was surprised at the modern, state-of-the-art furnishings within the compartment, compared to what she'd witnessed enroute.

"We have been fortunate in this recent upgrade, however." Torg waved her inside.

Alexis stepped through the door, impressed by what she saw. "Must have cost a load of stellars."

"If purchased at retail, you would be correct."

"This was—Oh. They scavenged it?"

"Several months ago, in Sector 23. Captain Jenna called in a few favors, a few debts. This particular integration was very compatible. Please allow me to demonstrate by reclining on the bed so I can conduct a complete scan."

"An Abbsolin S5?" Alexis recognized the medical array as the same as the one on the *Octavia*. She moved over to it and laid down as requested.

"S8. Things have changed while you have been in stasis for

over twenty-six years." Torg tapped at a small panel. "This could take several minutes. I am sure you have many questions, and I am happy to assist where I can."

"Where was I found?"

"Data files of the vessel class indicate Level 3, near the command deck."

Level 3? I should have been in Level 15... unless. "Was it pod 5?"

There was a pause. "The data does indicate that. Is this an error?"

You bet it's an error! I've had twenty-six years of executive officer subliminal training running through my head. Kaden's training!

"And what Sector?"

"Sector 38."

That made no sense to her. *How far have we expanded in twenty-six years?* "As you say, things have changed. What's the closest star or habitable system?"

"Dioha, an insignificant brown dwarf, is the closest star to our current location, and the nearest inhabited system is Caseex 7, which is still forty-three LY away."

"Sounds like we're far out of the mainstream."

"The captain prefers it that way, until we get a job or find salvage to retrieve."

"Guns for hire or scavengers?" *And I'm mere salvage—less than human.*

"Yes to both, though 'junkers' is the favored name."

"And you?"

"I am neutral. Whether the crew are junkers, researchers, or tourists, I am a droid. Nothing more, nothing less."

Alexis studied Torg as he moved around, considering his design, shape, programmed mannerisms... and his attitude. "You weren't commissioned when they brought this craft online, were you?"

"Another astute observation for a botanist. No, I was not. I was found on a derelict research vessel—the *Argonon*. There was a massive gamma burst, which caused severe damage to the ship, its instrumentation, and the crew."

"You're salvage, too? Not a ship droid?"

"Surprisingly, this craft was running without a droid, just the remnants of an old AI in severe need of an upgrade."

Alexis considered this information from the perspective of the executive officer training she'd acquired. "AI upgrades—or replacements—are only authorized for accredited vessels. It isn't a stretch of the imagination to assume the *Daemon* was no longer an accredited vessel."

"Essentially, you are correct, but the ship is still able to function legally with a ship droid. Using the stellars gained for their share of the *Argonon* salvage, I was more or less integrated with the ship."

"More or less?"

"Some non-life-threatening addons are not compatible for complete integration."

Alexis tucked that information away. *Ship data is always handy to know.* "And what can you tell me about the Sylvanus Colony on Niviaris?" she asked. "You might know it as V-X33B."

Torg took a few seconds to respond.

No doubt correlating with the Daemon's *data files,* Alexis decided.

"I have no record of a Sylvanus Colony. V-X33 is a tri-star system in close proximity to the Shadow Nebula. There is no colony there on record; however, data indicates several uninhabitable high-G planets, of which Niviaris is one."

"We were headed there in the *Octavia*—the ship you found me on." *Or what was left of it.* "What can you tell me about the *Octavia*?"

"The *Octavia* was lost in 5096—or to be more precise, when the last hyper relay recorded its passing. It was decreed 'Lost in Hyper' by Imperial Sector Control. Until now. I will need to amend the data."

"Did you find any more of it? Of the *Octavia*?" *Maybe there were other survivors like me.*

"No. I have analyzed the data from our sensors. The hull scorching and damage is consistent with a plasma cannon. Are you able to confirm any of this, or were you in stasis at the time?"

"I can confirm it, all right. We were in hyperspace. I was awake—as was my partner—when the hyperdrive cut out—"

"How did that occur? *Bolide*-class ships are renowned for superior operational capabilities, which is why it was used for such missions. Even the Mk 3 was superior in many ways."

"I have no idea; I'm a botanist by profession—the power-coupling to the reactor core must have been damaged significantly to override the built-in safety redundancies. That amount of damage could only be the result of a massive disruptor surge. And access to the power-coupling is only for senior crew. Were we sabotaged?" *How the hell did I know all that?* She held her head as it began to throb painfully.

"An enlightened response from a botanist," Torg observed, watching the readings on the screen.

The Abbsolin S8 pinged. In seconds, Torg analyzed the data.

"Your brainwave pattern has anomalies; the Alpha and Delta are within the normal parameters, but your Beta and Gamma are highly irregular for a woman of your age, even coming out of stasis under the circumstances you have experienced. Also, your muscle mass is beyond the normal. You have undergone genetic enhancement, which would explain your increased bone density and muscle enhancement."

"Yes, because the colony's on a heavy-G world." *So, I'm stronger than average. How did I forget that?* "Is any of that bad? The brain function, I mean."

"I do not believe it is detrimental. I perceive your headache and can administer medication."

Alexis nodded. Besides the head throbbing, with the stasis drugs wearing off, her whole body was beginning to ache.

Torg turned, and the comm activated as he continued, "Perhaps further testing could better determine the potential for damage—"

"What damage?" asked a voice on the comm.

"Captain Jenna, this is Alexis Nales of the *Octavius*."

"Is she good to go?"

"Without further analysis, any issues arising due to the long-term stasis will be difficult to predict. Prone to headaches at the least, all normal for stasis removal, but she is fully functional—"

"That's all we need. As long as she's breathing and has all limbs and faculties at the point-of-sale. Sedate her. We'll be in Ieoni Orbital in a couple days with no time to babysit." The link went quiet.

"Charming guy," Alexis remarked, not liking the sound of what she'd heard. "You going to sedate me now?"

"No time was specified, but I will have to afterward. I would like to run through a full analysis, if you are up to it."

"Have I any choice?"

"Not really. My orders were to ensure you are healthy for the sale. To do this, a thorough examination is required."

"Ieoni Orbital; tell me about it."

"I can do so while carrying out the next examination." Again, Torg's silver fingers danced over the keyboard. She felt pain relief as the medication was injected into her thigh. The device hummed, and various arms extended from the base of the Abbsolin bed, moving up and down her body slowly. "Try to remain still and breathe as normal."

The droid then went on in detail about Ieoni Orbital; how it had initially been an outpost for Nommo Solutions, a company mining the local region for twenty years... then when the tilanthium source dried up, the area became far less profitable. The company moved out, selling the old outpost. Now Ieoni Orbital was a hub for general trade.

"Anything else in Sector 38 worthy of note?"

"Not out here. Ieoni Orbital is in Sector 36. The planets there are uninhabitable. They are either too small, too large, or gas giants, and the binary star system is a red and brown dwarf. The only redeeming factor for the sector is location, being that close to a waypoint..."

A description came unbidden to her mind. *Waypoint, a beacon in hyperspace to denote a course correction, generally because of potential disruption to navigation.*

Torg was till speaking. "...and the local Enforcers receive a cut of the profits, so they turn a blind eye to what sort of trade is carried out."

"You do this regularly?" Alexis tried to keep calm. "No doubt slavery is a valuable market here." *I'm about to be a slave!*

"It would appear so to both questions." Torg adjusted the controls.

"And how does that affect your programming? Don't you have a prime directive?"

"I run the ship, and follow the orders of the ship's captain and the authorized crew. I do not injure, nor allow injury to, persons under my care."

"You don't think slaves are injured?" *I'll be one in two days!*

"No one is injured while on this ship. My prime directive allows me to ensure the ship and everyone onboard is unharmed. I have no determination regarding what happens to those off ship."

Ship droids come online the moment the ship systems activate, like a permanent network connection. If the link is broken in any way, the droid is rendered useless and becomes spare parts and scrap. But a new droid can be connected; it's costly, but more cost-effective than losing a ship. A ship without a droid is unable to function safely—or legally—in regulated space.

"What can you tell me about Captain Jenna?"

"That information is classified."

"The crew?"

"That information is classified."

Along with the information Torg could supply, Alexis mulled over what she—*what Kaden*—knew about *Bolide*-class ships.

"Is getting another person's training regimen during stasis detrimental?"

"It has been known to be," Torg replied.

CHAPTER TWO

HE WAS NOWHERE AND NOWHEN.

Adrift in a moment that stretched forever, a moment composed of sensations without meaning.

But the soldier craved meaning.

And in a flash of insight, the scattered memories fluttering around his dislocated mind coalesced into an explanation, an understanding of what was happening to him: he couldn't see; he was cold and slippery, and wet all over. This was awakening. This was...

Decantation.

He sensed his hands and his knees now, supporting him, pressed against something firm but giving.

Ground.

No. Not ground. Decking.

Rubberized decking with tiny holes for draining away the decantation fluids. The darkness would soon lift—or rather, his sight would return. Already, there was a gray smudging around the edges of his vision. Another thing he hoped would soon return was his name.

I should know who I am. A soldier, surely, but...

As he tried to move, one hand slipped across the soft-firm decking and triggered another memory, an old one. Something from home, his childhood. A village in a country on a continent on a planet, all of whose names escaped him. But the chilled air playing across his naked skin was like the air on those mid-summer mornings in the hours before dawn, the time of day when it was cool enough for people to get a head start on their business... and for children to play and bathe where the thick, spongy grass soaked up the dew. A memory, rich and tactile and clear. He could hear the voices of playmates, feel the rasp of the grass, smell the wet earth.

But right now, the soldier couldn't remember his own name.

Sight returned in stages, dim and blurred at first. The flowing air of wherever-this-was raised goosebumps on parts of his body where he didn't want them forming. He heard a hum of voices, adults, crew.

Crew?

The soldier had experienced this many times before—he knew that much—so he put aside anxiety and confusion, remained wobbling on hands and knees. And waited.

Eventually, he could make out the pockmarks in the hard rubber decking a half-meter from his face, and the blurred boundaries of objects and walls resolving and differentiating from one another. He was in a room so long and curved he couldn't see the end from where he crouched. The two walls before and behind him—spacers called them *bulkheads*—were lined with tanks bolted against them or fitted into recesses.

This was a stasis compartment inside a starship or space station, and these bastards had just pulled him out of long sleep. The thin slime congealing on him was tank gel—a blob of it had discolored and set on the deck where he'd puked. Again, a part of his mind reminded him he'd done this before —many times, across many centuries—but it refused to tell him what came next. Between the tanks stood machinery, consoles, pipes, cables, and conduits. A shelf had been provided here and there for clip-pads to rest. A nearby hatchway lay open; out in the passage, a body lay beneath a clean, white sheet. Feet poked from one end.

Five people moved around the compartment near him. He blinked again, then he raised a hand to poke a finger in one ear and scoop out muck. A woman spoke, but the soldier didn't know the language. It sounded familiar, one he'd heard before without ever learning. Recalling more of his own history, he knew there was no point in learning new languages when you lived across centuries. You never changed, while the common languages always did.

A pair of legs passed him, walking away. The woman. She wore a shiny yellow coverall, something signifying her as a technician or nurse. Four identically dressed people milled beyond her. He turned his head the other way and saw that someone else was in the room with him, standing nearby, dressed in a uniform. The uniform was a duty one, gray-on-gray, wide epaulets, no cap or hat. Languages might change—and customs—but the imperial army uniform never did, no matter the locale, no matter the year, no matter the century.

I'm a soldier, he told himself, *and my name is... my name is...*

He studied the exposed skin of his own limbs and torso. His skin was dark, almost space-black, wrinkling ever so subtly in places, the body hair hinting at gray. But where his flesh tone lightened on the underside of his left forearm, it also glowed with a biological tattoo. The bio-tat read:

Cohortis Proselytae
595-CTP
49:12:11:13

His unit, the Specialist Proselyte Battalion.
His service number.

His "lived" age, the biological one: 49 common years, 12 days, 11 hours, 13 minutes.

The 13 flicked over to 14 while he squinted at it.

The man in uniform cleared his throat, recapturing the soldier's attention. This fellow was an officer—the triple bars along one collar attested to that. The officer wore his graying hair to his shoulders, as must be the custom in whatever era this was, partly covering his stiff half-collars. He stood three meters back, staring down with a face like stone. And while the officer appeared to be about the soldier's biological age, no doubt he was a mere *decimal point* of his actual chronological age.

A tremor raced through the soldier's body.

Shit, but it's cold in here!

Since the technician/nurse seemed to have left the soldier to his discomfort, he slapped the floor and gestured sharply at the gray-haired man. The other man certainly outranked him but, shivering violently now, the soldier didn't care.

"A blanket! *Now!*"

The outburst exhausted him. He dropped his head and focused on the small pile of vomited sludge on the deck, riding out a fresh wave of nausea. Someone draped a sheet across him. It wasn't the officer; his gray boots never shifted position. The soldier managed to balance on his knees to free his arms and wrap the sheet tight. He blew air sharply through his nostrils, dislodging more tank-muck.

"*Etwa, keleck toae shoormadshudj,*" the officer told someone in a gravelly voice. "*Taludj nohgeh toh.*"

A flash of yellow suit beside the soldier, and the nurse was pushing something into his ear, the one he'd cleared earlier. He lashed out, knocking her down. "What!" he barked and poked at it. Something slick had reshaped itself to the interior of his earhole. "What are you doing?"

The woman scrambled backward, got up, and hurried away.

"*Lat trujhia*," the officer said to the woman, and then to the soldier, "It's a linguistic interface."

The soldier stopped poking and planted his ass on his heels. *A translator.* "Oh."

"You understand me, yes?"

"Yes."

"Most of your battalion never learned Imperial Common," the man said with a healthy dose of disapproval, "but your files say you're fluent in Imperial True."

"Imp...?" That was the language the officer was speaking now. A second language to the soldier. He took a moment to formulate a response in it. "I speak Imperial True, sure."

"I suppose there's not much point in you learning Common. Unlike True, it changes so much across the eras—and ends up with too many offshoots. You can keep the interface, for the moment, since most of these people don't speak True. A fact that never ceases to irritate me. When we get you suited up— you and your unit—I'll have translator patches assigned to your outfits." The man sniffed and studied him, then lifted a clip-pad to consult it. "You'll be showered and fed soon. You know where you are?"

An image came to him of a vast, irregularly shaped battle station, hyperspace-capable and patrolling the outer edges of a great galactic arm. "I'm aboard a *Maelstrom*-class mobile battle station."

"Excellent. You know *who* you are?"

"I... I'm a soldier."

"Yes. A good one, judging by your reports. It's clear to me why you were awarded a battlefield commission half a millennium back."

"Do I know you? No. I don't, do I?"

The officer snorted softly and let the pad drop to his side. "I should say not. The last time you went under, my father was a zygote."

"I don't know myself. I mean, I don't remember my name." He felt he should be panicked by that, but he wasn't. The room was familiar. The physical sensations were familiar. He'd done this before. He should be safe; he should be fine.

Shouldn't I?

The officer frowned. "Your name is Jabari Maximius."

"Jabari M... M...?"

"Jabari Maximius. Jabari, your birthname. Maximius, your Imperial Service name."

"But Mbaye is my family name." He squinted up at the officer, whose frown deepened. "That's right, isn't it?"

"I've had experience with you Proselyti before. By all that's right, you should have left your family name behind the day you made your oath. Why you like clinging to your past is beyond me."

It all came back then in a rush.

"Proselyti. I... I remember now." The soldier turned his head carefully to the side, gaze settling on a nearby tank the technician/nurses were fussing over. "Our unit, we have d... dispensation. To retain our family names. And to use our forenames as identifiers, our birthnames."

"And praise that particular emperor past for his mercy toward you." The officer's tone undermined the sentiment of his words. He was patently disappointed by the break with protocol. "How old are you?"

"I..." The soldier whose name was Jabari Mbaye checked the bio-tattoo again, because he'd already forgotten what he'd read earlier. That didn't escape the officer's notice, he saw. "I'm forty-nine."

"Well. At least you know where to look."

"I remember we celebrated my birthday during my last mission."

Jabari Mbaye—for that *was* his name—tried to stand, and

failed, collapsing back to hands and knees, the sheet slipping from his shoulders.

"Is he tank sick?" the officer called to one of the technicians in that other language.

Jabari didn't wait for a response. He said, "I'm not. Just takes a moment. Done this a lot. More than most."

More than all the others, last I knew.

Gathering his strength and wits, he caught the officer's eye. "I've never had an officer here when I came out."

"Perhaps I'm as caring and compassionate as the emperor past who allowed you to keep your name."

Jabari straightened onto his knees again. "I don't remember Claudiomo VII being compassionate."

The officer drew his shoulders back. "You might be recovering from your latest bout of stasis, Lieutenant Maximius, but I expect you to check your tongue and the words it chooses."

Getting his feet underneath him, the soldier replied, "That's Lieutenant *Jabari*." He got upright, and this time stayed that way. "Sir."

The officer grunted and checked his clip-pad again. Jabari saw it then; the man's left hand was missing its smallest finger, and the knuckle had long since scarred over. There was also an extra pip on the officer's half-collar, bronze and shaped like a human heart.

Mababu na walezi, he thought, swallowing hard, swallowing a groan. *The one time an officer watches me decant, he has to be a slagging Corfid.*

Clearing more muck from his throat, Jabari was careful to spit it well away from the Cor Fidelis officer. He tried to stand a little straighter, and shifted his gaze to the man's three bars again, but couldn't quite recall what they signified. "May I have the honor of knowing your name and rank, sir?"

"Scipio. And I'm an optio-major." He snapped his fingers at

one of the yellow suits without bothering to look their way. It was the woman Jabari had knocked over earlier. "Check him for me. Is he all right to shower? He's having lingering memory issues."

Staying out of arm's reach, the woman ran a scanner over Jabari. She was shorter than him—much shorter, with stumpy limbs and a skull that seemed flat beneath its covering of short-cropped green hair.

Jabari had to stoop a little to catch her eye. "Sorry about before. Still hadn't woken up properly."

She affected a half-smile but didn't reply. Perhaps she didn't have a linguistic interface of her own. To Scipio, she said, "He can shower, sir. All his bios are back online and settling. No evidence of brain damage."

"But his memory issues..."

"More likely age and the sheer number of decantings he's experienced. It should come back with time."

"Should," Scipio muttered, latching onto that one word.

Jabari's mind latched onto another word the woman had said. *Time.*

I've existed across so much time. Maybe the brain's just not built for that.

The nurse/technician continued for a while in her own language before Scipio silenced her with a curt gesture. "I've been an Imperium warrior for thirty-six common years, Technician, and I've been aboard this *Maelstrom* for thirty-one of them. I think I know the regulations, and why we have them."

She swallowed whatever she'd been about to say and scampered off to other duties.

"It's just," Jabari said, "she doesn't get too many officers down here for decanting. Or too many sleepers who've done it so often and for so long."

Scipio lowered his voice. "Nor do *we* get too many missions like this one. Lieutenant, since you'll be leading your team, it's you I'll liaise with directly. I'll have to trust that your faculties return in full."

"They will, sir."

Because what's the option for me if they don't?

"Get clean and clothed. There are five ratings waiting in the passage outside. Pick one, and they'll lead you to the nearest showers."

"I remember the way now, sir." He clutched his sheet together with one hand while the other reached up to tap his forehead. "Brain's coming back online. As the lady no doubt told you, I'm not as young as I used to be."

Scipio grunted. "Take the rating anyway. Oversee your subordinates once they're decanted and clean. The rating will then take you to the specific chew-room I want you to eat in. You'll be briefed there."

"Thank you, sir."

Optio-Major Scipio started for the door, then hesitated when he saw Jabari hadn't moved. "'Get clean and clothed' was an order, Lieutenant."

"Yes, sir. I'm going."

Jabari shuffled slowly toward the door, finding his balance, though his legs trembled with a weakness born of disuse, and probably low blood sugar. He found the prospect of a solid meal pretty damned appealing. Scipio marched out, turning left along the corridor, careful to step around the body beneath the blanket. Jabari followed him only as far as the dead person and paused there. He glanced up and down the gently curving corridor; there was indeed a detachment of ratings standing against one of the bulkheads, and they stiffened and straightened under his gaze. All were young, their cheeks peppered with acne.

Probably never seen one of us before.

Gods and ancestors, depending on where the hells we are, they were probably born on the Maelstrom.

Carefully, he took a knee and lifted the blanket to uncover a man's head, dried and puckered like a date that had dropped from a palm. The sight wasn't unexpected, but it still made him grimace. He teased the blanket back further to check the man's left forearm: the living tattoo that should have been there displaying his biological age and recruit number was dead, nothing more than a collection of gray dots compared to the lime-colored tattoo glowing healthily on Jabari's own forearm. Dead for some time, then. Perhaps he'd been Scipio's first choice for command. And while the extent of his deformities erased any identifying features, Jabari probably would have known him when the man was alive and well. Cohortis Prose-lytae had only numbered six hundred and eleven at the time of its creation, a small enough battalion for Jabari to know most.

Six hundred and eleven, Jabari thought sourly. *There weren't many of us left the last time I went into the tank. Fewer now with your loss, brother. I mourn you.*

"Tank failure?" he asked the line of junior personnel, the ratings Scipio had lined up at the wall. They jerked and flinched at his question, facing forward and avoiding eye contact, each hoping another would answer. Or perhaps they didn't know the term spoken in Imperial True.

Jabari shrugged; he could always ask the woman techni-cian. Leaving the blanket folded down over the dead man's chest, he touched two fingers to his own forehead, then to the forehead of the desiccated corpse. Cold, it felt like brittle, aging rubber.

In his home tongue of Constantinian Kiswahili, he murmured, "Well met, well played, and well fought, brave warrior. All the way back to Terra, our ancestors honor you. May they take you to their bosom and into their hosts."

Terra, he thought with an eye on the ratings. *These dolts wouldn't understand that name, but if I said "Earth" aloud, it'd be the brig for me.*

The shower could wait. Jabari wound his sheet around his torso, tucking it beneath his armpits to leave his arms free. Returning to the stasis room, he arrived in time to watch another tank disgorge its occupant and send them skidding into a catchment chute at the base. There, they flopped and gagged and writhed while the nurse/techs hovered. When they'd slid the man onto the deck and stood back to monitor his vitals, Jabari saw it was a close friend this time and was glad. The man vomited and coughed, wracked by paroxysms of lung and gut. And Jabari went and crouched before him, waiting for him to look up, waiting for the man's hearing and vision to return. When the man finally noticed him, Jabari raised his voice while putting as much reassurance into it as he could.

"Your name, my friend, is Erkanu Artimus Şahin. Born on New Constantine, like me." He wiped sludge from the man's hair. "And we call you Erkan..."

The meal-room was four meters wide and ten long, with a hatch at one end into the galley, an exit to the passageway at the other. Its walls held viewscreens along with cupboards for stowing plates and cups and cutlery. It was filled with the clatter of tableware and the racket of conversation.

Jabari stuffed noodles into his mouth and held the fork up to the cabin light as he chewed. *Plastic. Apparently, we've come full circle again to "safer" tableware. The decades pass, and the Imperium goes through changes, but all those changes are merely the recycling of things humans have done and said and thought and valued before. What ancient book is it that says, "Wherever stars do shine, there is nothing at all that's new?"*

Erkan nudged him, hard enough to make him swallow noodles prematurely and cough some up again. After he'd finished laughing, Erkan tapped Jabari's fork with his own.

"Plastic, uh? May El Hohim, the creator of humankind, be ever praised, and may the creators of plastic cutlery be cast into an eternal shit tank. Food doesn't feel right on plastic, and it changes the flavors."

"The poor taste is your palate coming online too slowly," one of the women soldiers said.

"Or it's the chefs in this era putting the wrong spices and herbs in the food," said the other. "But, yeah, plastic is shit for eating with."

Jabari sat closest to the exit, with the hatch at his right shoulder. He scanned both sides of the table while the others joked, chatted, and ate. He'd be leading soldiers he knew, liked, and approved of. All but one of them came from the same planet as he, and all were comfortable with him. That was something, at least.

Furthest from him, on the opposite side of the table, sat Tegenwe Acelina Nkoba, a countrywoman. Taller than him, leaner than him, and a hellcat in combat. Like him, she'd had her hair cut back to a thick cap of tight curls across the scalp, keeping it neat and clean. He'd known Tee since enlistment day, so many centuries before. Together, they'd served the Kaanic Terranist cause in the same squad of New Constantinian recruits. While she'd been just one comm-year younger than him back then, Tegenwe was now *noticeably* younger. No lines spoiling *her* perfect skin, no gathering of loose flesh at *her* elbows or throat. No traces of gray in her tightly curled hair. Her one blemish, revealed by constant smiling, was a missing tooth from some combat Jabari hadn't been involved in.

How often have I served while you slept, dear Tegenwe? He snuck a glance at her inner forearm as she stuffed noodles into her mouth. Just thirty-nine now. She'd spent a full decade longer than him in stasis along the way. *Well. That answers that question.*

To Tegenwe's left, Morten Servanus Nils patiently resisted

all attempts to draw or bait him into conversation. Jabari had never spent time with him personally, but he knew of him. While the man was willing to write terse messages on his pad or a comms screen, Morten hadn't spoken a word since the day he'd renounced the Kaana and pledged allegiance to Emperor Claudiomo Augustan. Almost as old as Jabari now, his once-blond hair was grayed and thinned, his brow creased, his cheek bore a bright burn scar, and the nearest ear was missing a chunk of lobe, all of this evidence of being used regularly and brutally by their Martianist commanders over the centuries. Morten was of middle-height with wiry arms and a musician's fingers, and hailed from a planet Jabari had never visited—one of two Terranist worlds the Imperials had scoured clean of life in retaliation for the war.

Beside the quiet man and directly across from Jabari sat Shila Adorantes Teuku. An auxiliary private, "Shill" had worked Jabari's last four missions, all of them under his command. She was good with a weapon, and even better with computer code. While her skin was as pale as Morten's, her hair was blacker even than Jabari's skin. It had grown out in her most recent decades in the tank, but he knew she'd shave it herself soon—most of it, at least. Shill preferred to keep a simple, short tuft on her crown.

Jabari glanced left to Erkan. His friend's big head sprouted a verdant mass of unkempt, uncombed, curly brown hair. Erkan was doing most of the talking—him and Tegenwe, anyway, as if the pair were in competition to get the most words out. Shill seemed as content as Jabari to bide her time, contributing wiseass comments when the opportunities presented themselves.

For whatever this mission was, this would be his team, his and Scipio's. Five, a mere five. The tank technician had said there were twenty-one other Proselyti alive in stasis—all that was left of the once-proud Elite Pure Okalasi Guard battalions, whose fighting numbers in the old days had been five thousand, with support personnel and droids as well. Jabari had checked the makeup of the still-sleeping twenty-one before he'd finally gone for his shower. None of the remaining were officers, leaving him as the highest-ranking member of the Proselyti. The highest of the remnant. And that had made him wonder...

"Ho!" he called, but only Morten paid him any attention. Grinning, he barked louder, "*Ho!* Shut your *ukunuka*-holes, you bunch of Borassan tree-slugs."

Laughter and raised cups acknowledged the insult, but the conversation subsided.

"Now I have you all listening for once," he said, "I want you to look around this table."

"I see trusted friends," Erkan said.

"Trusted warriors," Tegenwe added, agreeing.

"Yes, both true," Jabari told them, "but *look* at us."

A pause while brows furrowed and eyes darted. Eventually, Tegenwe said, "I wasn't going to say anything, but Shill could do with a haircut."

Shill jerked her chin at Erkan across the table. "He needs it more than me. Head looks like an herb garden."

Jabari chuckled before his gaze recaptured everyone else's. "Three privates on that side of the table." He elbowed Erkan gently. "A corporal and a lieutenant on this side. Just five of us. You find nothing curious about that?"

Blank stares until Tegenwe snickered and said, "Someone can't do army math. Two file leaders with only three troopers to command between them?"

Erkan guffawed. "It's gonna be like having one small soup pot with two chefs arguing over what goes into it." Shill joined the laughter, while Morten just stared at Jabari, waiting for the point.

"Actually," Jabari said, "it's more like one soup pot with

hardly any ingredients."

The laughter died away as faces sobered, and postures straightened.

"Small team," Tegenwe said. "So, a stealth mission? Recon?"

Erkan said, "Small unit, simple mission."

"Or a complex one," Jabari replied. "Small numbers are easy to sacrifice."

Shill shrugged. "Maybe they're finally trusting us with something vital."

"Vital," Jabari repeated, lowering his voice to avoid being heard by the nearby galley cook, "such as escorting an officer. And not a Regular."

They fell quiet, absorbing that thought.

"Optio-Major Scipio," Erkan said. "The one you said was watching you decant."

"You said he's Corfid?" Shill angled her left hand, tucking the pinky away.

Jabari nodded.

Shill slapped an imaginary head midair, whispering, "Bloody Corfids."

Morten made a quiet spitting noise.

Jabari leaned back in his chair. "Never had *any* officer watch me wake up before." There was a joke there, but no one made it. He continued, "Non-coms have been on deck, sure, but nothing close to an optio. I suspect he handpicked us."

"As if there's many of us left to choose from," Tee said, continuing to whisper. She shook herself, then scooted along her bench, forcing Morten along until the three on that side bunched together. Louder, she said, "I've met that slagger before, assuming he's the same Scipio. My last awakening was twenty-two common years ago, and it was six months long. Scipio was a junior lieutenant back then."

"Was he an asshole?" Shill asked.

"He tried flirting with me, so there's that. He was pretty terrible at it, too."

"Probably not much practice," Erkan said with a half-hearted laugh, "and not much enthusiasm. Damned Corfids only have eyes for the emperor, not for romance."

"He tries that again," Shill growled, "you tell me and—"

"And nothing," Jabari interjected. "He's an officer, and I'm sure he's outgrown that behavior." He plucked at the patch of hair at the front of his scalp he knew was turning gray.

"Corfids." Erkan put a hand over his heart, then touched his collar, miming the Cor Fidelis sigil. "Bloody true believers. Probably born on this ship. Probably never left it."

"If he's commanding us, we better hope he's left on a *combat* mission," Shill muttered, "at least once."

Tegenwe said, "He was the briefing officer on my mission, that's all."

Erkan grunted. "We can hope he's had more experience since then, but my point is more about this *Maelstrom* we're all still on. It's out here, wandering the Imperium's outer reaches."

"'Peripheries,'" Jabari corrected him mildly.

Erkan ignored him. "Never stopping at a port. Never stopping at a planet. Whole crews marrying and giving birth to other crews, busy undoing everything our Kaan and Kaana did."

"Don't say their names," Shill growled with glances toward galley and passageway.

"I said their titles."

"Even so, Adjira's no longer 'our' Kaana."

"You just said her name," Tee groaned. Shill cursed, realizing her mistake with a dart of the eyes toward the cook in the galley.

Erkan slurped from his water cup. "My point is, these bastards don't learn too many social skills, so I don't want to serve with him."

"And *my* point is," Shill said, leaning in, "he better have learned some combat skills."

They all joined Morten in his silence awhile, lost in their thoughts, until Tegenwe gave a characteristic chuckle, intended to break through the gloom. She never could stay maudlin for long.

"You said this guy's your age now, old man?" When Jabari nodded, she said, "So that's two of you we have to piggyback now!"

Laughter broke out again, along with insults and thrown food.

It wasn't till he'd been hit by his second piece of fruit that Jabari realized someone was standing in the door.

Scipio.

"Attention!" Jabari shouted reflexively, shooting to his feet, bumping the table, and spilling his water cup.

A heartbeat later, the others followed his lead. The optio's gaze raked across them all, as well as the mess they'd made. How long had he been standing there? Had he been outside and within earshot during the entire conversation?

Jabari lifted his chin. "Sir."

Scipio inspected them all a moment longer, then inclined his head. "With me, Lieutenant Jabari."

He moved out of sight. Jabari exchanged an anxious look with the others and followed him.

Scipio stopped a dozen meters along the narrow service passage, feet spread, hands behind his back. When Jabari joined him, he said, "Reports are your team are in good health after decanting."

"Glad to hear it, sir."

"That includes you."

"Glad to hear *that*."

Scipio's stare now leveled over Jabari's shoulder toward the meal-room. "They seem in good spirits, too."

"Of course, sir. We're excited about a new chance to serve emperor and empire."

Scipio's eyes narrowed a moment. Did he suspect Jabari of sarcasm? "You're to report to the *Pleiades-219*. Scout ship, Bay 1105. Departure is in forty-five minutes. Basic kit only. Weapons and other kit will be provided on-journey."

"Briefing too, sir?" When Scipio didn't respond immediately, Jabari added, "It's usual to receive a full briefing before departure. Rest period, combat drills, and fitness training, also. Sir."

"You can rest, train, and build fitness on-journey. And be briefed. Trust me. You'll have plenty of time for all of it."

"Departure time is urgent, sir?"

"Let's just say, we should have left yesterday." Scipio turned heel and headed away. Over his shoulder, he said, "Forty-four minutes, Lieutenant."

"Yes, sir," Jabari said and watched the optio's uniform fade into the gray gloom of the passage. The uniform, he'd noted, was now a travel one, suited for long periods aboard a smallish ship. He muttered, "And we'll see you onboard, I'm sure."

CHAPTER THREE

IEONI ORBITAL

THE TWO ROBUST CREWMEN, Krugga and Dennu, rough-handled her off the *Daemon*.

As they entered the dingy docking area, Alexis decided Ieoni Orbital stank. *Aircon filtration definitely needs an overhaul if not a complete replacement.*

Her "cupboard" cell didn't have the luxury of a viewport. Turning quickly, Alexis managed to get a brief glimpse of her recent ride through a dirty portal. If the interior of the *Daemon* in any way reflected the exterior, she was amazed it wasn't a derelict itself. *Looking at the crew here, it probably was.*

"That's one ugly ship," she muttered. "I thought you *retrieved* junk, not flew it."

"Still far better than where you're goin'," Krugga sniggered as they continued down various dark, odorous passages and stairs to a series of holding cells.

During the transit, her mind again tallied steps and turns, taking in as much detail as possible. Surprisingly, it smelled better here. She also realized she felt heavier. *Feels like about 1.3Gs.*

They passed several people in diverse garb carrying out

various tasks; some in the robes indicative of the typical clothing of the desert worlds, and others in one-piece, body-hugging suits. Some looked weary, dragging their feet.

Near the end of a long, ill-lit passage opposite a bent door, another door slid open, the grinding indicating a lack of lubricant on the door's rollers. She was ushered inside, and the door promptly ground closed.

She heard whimpering and soft talking. It took several seconds for her eyes to pick out the other unfortunates sharing the space; the distances between them implied they were most probably strangers to each other.

At least this is bigger than a cupboard.

Alexis' initial thought was to greet them, but when you were a commodity for sale, "Hi there!" didn't cut it. Finding an empty corner, she took three steps, turned, and slid down the bulkhead, sitting with her legs bent in front of her. She wrapped her arms around her knees as she studied her cellmates.

There were three of them: a couple—maybe a mother and daughter, considering their comparable size differences—and one lone figure. At first, she thought it was a fat kid, but as her eyes adjusted to the darkness, she saw the beard and realized it was a very short but stocky male.

The mother and daughter weren't paying her any attention after her initial entry, but the eyes above the beard of the lone male watched her. She gave a cursory nod, which was acknowledged several moments later.

The only communication was between the mother and daughter, consisting of soft mutterings of consolation.

The stocky male grunted as he stood and limped to the door. Gripping what edges he could, he put his strength into it.

No chance, Alexis thought. Then she heard the creaking of the metal.

After a pause, he relaxed and exhaled, limping back to his corner.

"That was a good try," she said, impressed.

"It's my second cell," he replied in a deep voice. "I'll get there eventually."

Alexis recalled the bent door opposite. "And the leg?"

"The reward for my last efforts."

"How did they manage to capture you?" she asked, wondering, with his strength, how they'd handled him.

"Knock-out gas, initially... and this for afterward." He lifted his beard to reveal a metal collar. "The cowards."

"A neuro-collar? I thought they were banned?"

His chuckle was a deep, low rumble. "Look where we are, lady. Slavery's banned, too."

"Alexis," she said to introduce herself. "I've been in stasis for twenty-six years. Seems like things have changed."

"Not out here. Still, it's better than being sold for body parts. They do transplants, as well." He lowered his voice for the benefit of the child. "And you're not always dead when they do it. I'm Bradyn."

Alexis wondered if, together, they could open the door. She got up to examine it and copied Bradyn's technique. The door responded in a similar fashion.

"You heavy-G, too?" he asked, surprised. "You don't look it."

"Was going to be."

"*Going* to be? Not natural, then?"

"Jeemed for Sylvanus Colony, on a heavy-G world called Niviaris."

"Jeemed?"

"Jeemed... GM-ed. Genetically modified."

"Ah." He shrugged. "We call it corpiforming out here. Never heard of Sylvanus Colony, though."

"Corpiforming?" *Something else to put away.* "Fair enough. Have you heard of the Vladmarin-Xiar system?"

Bradyn shrugged again. "Astronomy wasn't my forte."

"What is?" Alexis resumed her seat against the wall, but closer to Bradyn so they could talk softly.

"Mechanics and engineering."

Handy. "May I ask why you're here?"

"Gambling isn't my forte, either. Too many debts, but too valuable to kill."

"So, they'll recoup by selling you?"

"They hope. Not if I can help it, though. You?"

"I'm salvage, apparently." She saw his quizzical look in the dimness. "I was on a ship that was attacked decades ago. I think I'm the only survivor."

"You did say twenty-six years in stasis. They revived you, and then slaved you? That's gotta suck."

Tell me about it. She nodded.

Time dragged on. Alexis was about to suggest they both try the door again when she heard unsteady footsteps approach outside. It sounded like whoever was out there was struggling; the swearing and cursing got louder until it suddenly stopped.

"Reckon we can jump them?" Bradyn asked, flexing his brawny arms after he stood up.

Alexis was about to agree, then considered the young girl cowering in the corner at the increased noise and the worried look on the mother.

She stood, but shook her head.

Bradyn saw her glance, nodding in understanding. "There'll be another time."

"I'm counting on it." *Hoping, more like.*

The door slid open; the grinding of the rollers had increased. As it did so, Bradyn spasmed, clutching his neck. He gasped and dropped to the metal floor. The child uttered a brief scream and hid her face in her mother's clothing.

Two men—one on the short side, and a slightly taller, thin

man—loomed in the doorway, their silhouettes contrasting with the lights outside.

The thin man had a controller and grinned, seeing the writhing body on the floor. "Hey *dwarf*, we got you a friend," he said as his stocky colleague pulled another neuro-collar out of a pouch on his utility belt.

A third male with long, braided hair came into view, dragging a moaning form into the room and dropping him unceremoniously on the deck. He then turned toward Alexis, brandishing a stun-rod, the end crackling with blue energy.

"Put this on," the shorter man ordered Alexis, tossing the collar at her feet.

"No fragging way." She stepped back, stopped by the bulkhead.

"I was hopin' you'd say that," he said as the man with the stun-rod loomed closer.

She twisted, but too late. Like Bradyn, her body writhed and contorted in pain. Someone was screaming in her head.

When she recovered, the door was closing. The child was crying, and the mother made hushing noises.

"I... I'm okay." Alexis pushed herself up despite the uncomfortable pins and needles in her arms, back, and shoulders. "It's all okay. See?"

The child's sobbing eventually subsided with the mother's soft whispers.

"Must be getting close to market-time," the newcomer groaned. "Anyone posing a threat is getting these collars."

Bradyn helped him to his feet. "Phill, this is Alexis."

The taller man bowed his head. "Phillix Lo, at your service." He then turned to the mother. "My apologies for the language earlier. I was unaware these slimeballs stooped low enough to enslave children."

The mother nodded, remaining silent.

Feeling the new weight around her neck, Alexis ran her

fingers over the device. Like the two men, she now wore a neuro-collar. She noticed with relief the mother and daughter didn't.

Bradyn observed her look. "With her daughter present, they don't see the mother as a threat."

Phillix rubbed his neck, where the neuro-collar was tight. "As I was saying, they're preparing us for market, which is not far away now. I saw several other cells before they stunned me. They're even calling it the 'Surreal Tournament Sale.'"

"Assholes," Bradyn muttered.

A couple hours later, the men returned.

"You know what'll happen if you cause any trouble?" the thin one threatened when the door ground open.

"Yeah, Ollsen, you'll no doubt demonstrate how much of a drocking coward you are again," Bradyn scoffed.

Phillix staggered in pain, clutching his neck.

Ollsen smirked. "What was that?"

Bradyn swore under his breath and helped his friend out the door, where they followed other prisoners. "I hate it when I'm right," he muttered.

"So do I," Phillix agreed with a grimace.

Alexis joined them as they proceeded along the passageway. The other cells were opened one at a time, adding more neuro-collared people to the growing throng.

"What are those?" Alexis asked, pointing to illuminated barcodes on some of the slaves' cheeks.

"Bio-tats."

Her blank look indicated a better response was required.

"Branding. These poor wretches have been slaved before; this is how they know who belongs to who, what their skills are, and any previous rebellious activity."

"Rebellious activity? What happens then?"

"You'll see soon enough."

The group climbed up three levels of metal-grid stairs, and based on the sounds filtering along the passageway, approached a cheering crowd. By the time they entered a large holding pen, there were easily two dozen unfortunates, all about to lose their previous lives to the highest bidder. The thirty-meter-diameter pen was like an arena, situated about three meters below the viewing platform, where all the bidders sat. From there, tier after tier of seats rose in a circle. She estimated the audience held well over three hundred people. Directly above the center of the arena was a massive array of six vid-screens so no brutal, gory detail would be missed by the blood-hungry audience. Whatever was showing was difficult to see from the pen floor.

"See those two over there?" Bradyn indicated with a nod.

Alexis followed his gaze. Through the ambling group of slaves, she saw two well-muscled males. "Yes?"

"Count their fingers."

"There are some missing..." she said after a minute.

"Probably lost toes, too. Punishment for any adverse malcontent. Got to keep 'em in line."

While there were interested glances directed at them, most of the audience's attention was glued to the action above. From the speakers surrounding the area, the sounds of explosions, various projectile and energy weapons, and screams, it appeared the tournament was in full swing.

"Surely they can't all be bidding for slaves?" Alexis asked, appalled at the numbers in the audience. She continued to scan the multitude before locating the people she was after; the reason she was here. Foster's fat bulk was readily identified, and the henchmen to his right were Dennu and Krugga; the woman was there, too, beside another male with a neatly trimmed beard. *Captain Jenna,* she assumed by the way they deferred to him. *My savior. My enslaver.*

When he saw her look, he gave a slight nod and a wink before turning away, chuckling at something the woman beside him said.

That bastard will pay.

"No, not all," Bradyn muttered in answer to her question. He moved closer to speak over the rising tumult of noise. "Once the drocking bidding starts, you'll see at least half those in the front row get up and start haggling."

"Nearly everyone else is here for the show. This is classified as entertainment on this remote piece of shit," Phillix added, referring to the orbital.

Alexis could already see some eager bidders searching for and calculating the best buys as they kept glancing at brochures and scanning the slaves. "We're just commodities to them."

Grim-faced, Bradyn and Phillix agreed.

"We'll need to put a stop to it, then." There was steely determination in her voice.

The two men shared a look of uncertain esteem.

"Easier drocking said than done, I suspect."

"It's Ollsen, that sadistic piece of grunfershit with the controller, who worries me." Phillix motioned surreptitiously with his head to the thin guy they'd met at the cell door. "A touch of a button, and we'll all be floundering on the floor."

Alexis nodded, then indicated the *Daemon* crewmembers in the crowd. "They seem to be deferring to that guy on the end; he must be Jenna, the captain of the *Daemon.* He's the one who found me, and he has the encoding chip to the droid on the ship. If we can get that, we'll have a haven of sorts. That's the only place I have any idea about, unless you have a better idea?"

There was a pause as the two men shared a look; unspoken

words moved between the stocky engineer and his thinner companion.

"Anything we know about here, those that want us know about, too," Bradyn informed her. "There'll be no place to hide."

Phillix nodded and turned to Alexis briefly. "We're with you, whatever transpires."

Alexis was taken aback by the support and confidence. She'd done nothing worthy of any of it. *All I know how to do is grow stuff in a toxic atmosphere.* "Bradyn's mechanics and engineering; what of you?" she asked the taller man.

"IT, nanotech, electronics, and comp—"

"He's a hacker... a coder. If it has a circuit, he can work it."

"And these collars?" She looked at Phillix.

"Easy... given the time and my tools," he replied.

"*I* could probably do something, given the time and tools; what can *you* do better than me here and now?"

Phillix opened his mouth, but stopped, considering the situation.

"Let's mingle," Bradyn advised. "Standing here gossiping, we'll look like we're conspiring on an escape plan."

Which is exactly what we're doing. They moved randomly through the throng. Alexis could see in Phillix's glazed look that his mind was churning with possible solutions.

"Nothing here and now," Phillix admitted finally, "but I don't need to. It's not the collars this instant that's the concern; it's *him*." He motioned to the controller. "Nothing happens with these collars without Ollsen hitting the button. Remove the controller from the equation, and the collars are mere ornaments."

"So then, gents, what can we do to take him out?" Alexis turned her attention to the crowd and their fellow slaves.

The group of unfortunates was from a variety of cultures and environments. Some were aged, potential servants for household menial duties; some were young and strong, potential hard labor. Some were young women...

The noise of the crowd grew. At first, she thought it was the gory demise of another player in the games projected on the massive screens above, but then she noticed one tall, athletic woman in particular arrive in the slave pen.

"Any idea who that is?" she asked, noting the smooth, tight-fitting bodysuit exposing her muscular arms, legs, and abs.

"I don't believe it!" Phillix whispered in awe.

"I guess that answers that. You *do* know; care to enlighten me?"

"It's none other than Sabrya," Phillix said, as if that was an adequate answer. "You know, the Reaper?"

"How about we assume I've been in stasis for over two decades," she grouched, briefly recounting her situation. The woman was clearly known by everyone else, and there was little doubt as to why; not only because of her Amazonian physique, but her stunning looks and sculpted blue, spiky hair was hard to ignore. *Flux, even* I'm *finding her attractive!*

"Sabrya 'the Reaper' Smith," Bradyn whispered, also in awe. "She's a prized fighter—rumored to have been the prime candidate for the Surreal Tournaments finals."

"What happened?"

"No one knows. One minute she's the poster girl for Sector 22; the next, *nada*, as if wiped from the system in a flash."

"So, she's good in combat?"

"*Good?*" Phillix was shocked enough to stare incredulously at Alexis for a moment, forgetting her recent history. "She could take any five of the biggest guys in here without raising a sweat. Maybe even ten."

"She does look tough... but ten? What's her secret?"

"Similar to yours," Bradyn explained. "She's been corpiformed—jeemed—but for combat. Boosted strength, reflexes, and agility for starters."

Phillix added, "Also, subliminal training in gymnastics and martial arts techniques."

"Oh, and don't forget her razor-sharp blade extensions," Bradyn added.

"Which would explain the metal mittens and chains," Alexis guessed.

"Yes. Too valuable to remove, so they block the threat instead."

"Wait." Alexis considered. "Didn't you say these games were the finals between Sectors 17 and 08... where does 22 come into it?"

Bradyn answered, "They lost their chance last month at the playoffs..." He turned to his friend, a look of suspicion on his face.

"The same time Reaper disappeared... " Phillix murmured.

"She threw the tournament?" they said in unison.

"What does that mean?"

"I... I can only guess something big happened to make them lose. They were the favorites to win the games, hands down."

"They drop out, and Sabrya suddenly winds up here," Alexis added it up. "I'm starting to like her. Is she any good without the claws?" She had to raise her voice, as the further violence of the games roused the crowd.

Phillix and Bradyn discussed quietly, remembering to keep milling. After several minutes, they turned back to Alexis.

"Without claws, and against what?"

"Not 'what,' whom." Alexis turned back to the controller.

Eventually, their moving around brought the trio closer to Sabrya Smith. Only a meter separated them.

Her eyes instantly swiveled to them like laser turrets detecting potential foes... and as quickly rejected them as no threat. Her blue eyes moved on... searching...

That hurts. Alexis didn't know why she took offense at the instant dismissal. She saw Sabrya also wore a collar. "Want to get out of here?" she muttered to her.

The eyes under the blue mane drilled back to her, then the other two. There was no immediate answer, just the assessing eyes.

"We need you to take him out; the asshole near the center of the middle row," Alexis directed. "The one with the controller."

The laser-turret eyes swiveled up. If they'd been real lasers, he'd be scorched meat.

"Ollsen. I'd love to take that fragger out. Big time. How?"

Alexis saw the look. *I have no idea...*

"I'll throw you," Bradyn offered.

Sabrya took in his short, swarthy stature. "Helios 6?"

Bradyn nodded, clearly impressed at her recognition of his native world. "Born and bred, fifteenth gen."

"Pioneers." Now Sabrya's eyes showed respect. "Nice, but I need to cover thirteen meters. This orbital has a relative gravity of 1.3; your 6-G strength is still inadequate for tossin' my eighty-two kilos—eighty-six with these shackles—far enough or fast enough—"

"The two of us can," Alexis stated, then made a sudden gamble at the incredulous look. "Assuming you're as good as these two say you are."

The eyes flared briefly at her audacity.

Turrets powered up...

Even Phillix inhaled in shock at her words.

"We'll be fraggin' dead meat if we fail." Sabrya glanced up. "Well... *you* will be."

"Then *we* better not fail. What do you need?"

"These fraggin' chains gone, for starters." There was a clinking of the shackles by her feet. Sabrya assessed the distance and angle to Ollsen. "Two paces for a runup, and you both move to your left a bit... and three paces from the wall. It won't work if the timin' is off."

Alexis turned to Bradyn. "You count to three?"

"I'll manage. I'll need some cover from prying eyes." He moved closer to the fighter.

Sabrya looked at him quizzically.

"You want the drocking restraints removed, yes?"

The fighter acknowledged the glances from prisoners around her, giving a greeting now and then. "This'll be all over soon," she said, encouraging them to move closer.

As they gathered to listen to her, that allowed Bradyn the cover he needed to kneel and grip the chains.

Phillix and Alexis also whispered to their fellow slaves nearby, encouraging them all to bunch up around them and obscure the view from the crowd.

Furtive glances above showed nothing more than a passing interest in the unfortunates below. Anyone suspecting anything either didn't care or was in no position to do much.

Bradyn gripped the chain tightly and pulled gradually. The links contorted and stretched, but not enough to break.

Alexis took the risk and knelt to help. Her added strength was enough to snap the already stressed links.

"That is... surprisin'." Sabrya reassessed her.

"What about your wrists?" Alexis questioned.

"The cuffs aren't long enough for both of you to grip. I'm sure I'll improvise."

Alexis nodded and joined Bradyn, who began to "mingle" closer to the wall, ensuring they were at the location Sabrya had chosen earlier.

Phillix spoke quietly to those nearby, and a few gave Sabrya respectful clearance, moving back from her as she "randomly" strolled about.

Being used to the stares and attention, Sabrya began a

series of stretches, but kept her feet together as if they were still shackled.

Alexis dragged her eyes away from the display to gauge the reaction of the audience; a few men and women were glued to the spectacle of her muscles flexing, but the bulk were too engrossed in the violence and gore on screen.

Ollsen glanced down, eyes darting over them, then panned back to the vid-screen. From the sounds of weaponry, explosions, and meaty thuds, it was a particularly violent part of the game.

Sabrya was also listening to the carnage playing out on the screen. "This is my kinda music. Sounds like this round is about to end. Get ready."

Bradyn stood by Alexis' side, and they turned to face the fighter as if they, too, were in admiration of her physique.

The noise above intensified; the roar of the crowd grew...

Sabrya glanced up and back to them, stepping sideways slightly.

Alexis and Bradyn adjusted their positions, squaring up to her.

The audience above erupted, jumping out of their seats as the games reached a loud and bloody climax.

"Let's fraggin' rhumba." Sabrya nodded.

Together, Alexis and Bradyn bent a knee. "One," they both whispered.

The slaves parted, allowing the warrior room to run.

Sabrya took her two paces at lightning speed.

"Two."

The fighter jumped into their cradled hands.

"Three."

As the pair stood in an explosion of movement, Sabrya leapt and catapulted high, arcing over the wall.

As Alexis swiveled, she saw Sabrya hook the wrist chains under Ollsen's chin as she came down behind him, twisting at the last minute. His head rotated the way she recalled seeing a vid of an owl's head. Sabrya's momentum bent Ollsen back over the chair, further than physically possible without snapping his spine. There was a sickening, wet crunch.

His boots twitched once, then the bent body lay unmoving.

Sabrya reached for the control box and tossed it toward Phillix. She then searched for other targets and leapt away as those nearest started screaming at the sight of the broken man.

"My turn," Phillix said by the wall as he reached out to catch the box. Jostled by the crowd, he fumbled, and it dropped to the floor.

For a split second, a dozen of them, including Alexis, Bradyn, and Phillix, spasmed, falling to the deck as their muscles twitched.

When Phillix looked up through teary eyes, the child was standing in front of him. She held the box. When he reached for it with a shaky hand, she smiled and passed it over.

"*Now*... it's my turn." He crawled to the wall and hunched over the device as the others dragged themselves to their feet.

Chaos reigned above as Sabrya continued to do what she did best: wreak havoc.

Alexis took in the results. Sabrya was selective, merely neutralizing some, but killing those who posed a serious threat, of which there were many. In the fighter's wake, the body count grew.

She's certainly a killing machine.

Jenna's seat, as well as those of the *Daemon* crew, was now empty. She was about to lose her chance at payback.

"Bradyn. Toss me." Fed by anger, desperation, and adrenaline—but mostly anger—Alexis was next to vault over the wall.

As Sabrya had done, Alexis took two paces and jumped, with the expectation of a boost from Bradyn. She stepped into his cupped hands and jumped as he strained and heaved.

"Oof!" she groaned as she smacked into the wall chest-first. The air was forced out of her lungs by the impact, and she barely managed to drape her arms over the railing to keep from falling back.

"Drock, girl. How heavy are you?" Bradyn called.

"Be nice," she grunted, pulling herself up and over the wall.

The crowd was frantic, with people tripping over the seats in their panic to escape the wrath of the blue-haired demon. When they regained their footing, bleeding and holding injured arms or heads, they scurried to the nearest exit. Any other time, she would've felt some sympathy for those in pain, but they were here, partaking in the slavery business in one way or another.

She barely gave the vultures a second thought. While the ensuing chaos hampered her pursuit, it also hampered the security thugs trying to regain some control.

"Meet me at the loading dock four levels down, starboard side!" she called down to Bradyn. "Look for a ship called the *Daemon*."

CHAPTER FOUR

THE FIVE PROSELYTI soldiers assembled light packs in the Q-store nearest to the meal-room. The packs held toiletries, changes of underwear, a multi-tool, and a slimline datapad that could be carried free or strapped to a combat suit's arm. None included personal belongings. They'd long since lost any knick-knacks or mementos from their former homes and previous lives.

Though none of the team had ever been to Launch Bay 1105, years of subjective time aboard the *Maelstrom* had trained them to find their way without seeking directions from data stations or crew. The location markers and arrows painted along floors and bulkheads were brighter than the last time Jabari had seen them—new paint job—but they were exactly the same in detail. The navigation-and-location conventions indicated that this hike across the great hyperspace ark would be in excess of a kilometer long. They started it in cheerful fashion, walking in a tight cluster, trading good-natured jibes, elbow pokes, and head slaps. Even Morten joined in with the latter. The jocularity lasted until they moved through one particular hatchway and found themselves in a broad billeting compartment.

"Shit," Shill and Erkan muttered together.

They faced a hundred-meter march straight through the middle of clusters of off-duty Imperium troopers. Although it was possible none of these youthful Regulars had seen a Proselyti in their lifetime, they'd know Jabari's team for what they were instantly because of the sleeveless tunics and vests revealing their Proselyti bio-tats—and because *Maelstrom* was an enclosed environment that rarely saw strangers or new blood when its marathon patrol route had taken it far distant from major imperial centers.

"Come on," Jabari said and led the way, winding around sets of bunks.

The first faces they passed gawked at them. Before long, they were followed by whispers, then murmurs, then barks of abuse and disgust. Some were in languages he didn't know, but others were rendered in perfect Imperial True.

"Traitor scum."

"Thought you'd bring the whole thing down, but look at you now."

"You're not good enough to lick my boots."

"My dad said you're the worst soldiers he's ever seen."

"Look at the ancient assholes."

"*Blattas imperatricis*."

The last one was becoming the most common. It was the only one that got under Jabari's skin—and one he'd heard many, *many* times over the past seventeen centuries. The phrase meant "the empress's roaches" or "*Kaana's* roaches." Perhaps the reason it still cut so deep was because the Kaana was long dead, along with her efforts on behalf of non-modded, natural Terranist humans everywhere. Or perhaps it was because he and his fellow Proselyti now faithfully served the same empire these buttholes did.

"El Hohim, but this place stinks," Erkan complained loudly.

Jabari hadn't realized the roach taunts had actually stopped him in his tracks until Erkan marched on by and took the lead. Morten and Shill were next to pass him, Shill playing along with Erkan's remark.

"Can't tell whether it's their farts or their breath!" She laughed.

The content of their comments would be meaningless to the Regulars, since the two Proselyti delivered them in Terran True, rather than any imperial tongue. If it allowed them to blow off pressure, Jabari figured it wouldn't hurt. His team was in no danger; the eighty or ninety Regulars in this compartment were under strict orders not to bring harm to Proselyti—nor even to allow it.

Not when we're the Martianist empire's greatest propaganda tool, the originalists who denounced the usurper, who turned their backs on their claims of Earth heritage and genetic simplicity, and their fancy ideas of egalitarian rule.

Someone took Jabari's elbow and got him moving again. Tegenwe. They exchanged a nervous grin as Erkan and Shill took up an ancient ditty comparing the hygiene habits of Martianist emperors to those of dung-bugs and sewer-slime.

"If these cow turds knew our language—" Tegenwe chuckled "—these two would be executed immediately."

"The benefits of being despised. And ancient. And... what the hell is *that?*"

He'd been brought to a halt at the end of a row of single bunks—noncom beds—where an elaborate hologram had flared to life above the closest one. Stylized stars shimmered and spun on an invisible axis; the silver wreath of the Regular Army formed, dissipated, then reformed. Beneath these shapes, the rotating bust of a soldier stared out at the compartment haughtily as text in the Imperial Common font stuttered into being in the empty space beneath the squared, shaven chin. Whispered directly from the holo, Jabari heard the following:

"Fenexxomi Matteus, Second Legionary Corporal, 90th

Imperial Regulars. Medal of Honor for Bravery in the Extreme. Tattoos of High Achievement for Valor Under Fire, Execution of Duties with Extreme Desire, and Efficient Marksmanship. Second Corporal Matteus is a keen spade-ball player and sculptor who likes…"

"Is this a serious thing, or has somebody pranked the *stultum* who sleeps here?" Jabari asked, using the Imperial True word for *idiot*. Some nearby troopers caught it, quitting their muttering, faces darkening.

Tegenwe plucked at Jabari's vest, moving him along. "It's a modern thing. Modern-*ish*. I first saw it on my last mission. This century's younger troops love hearing about themselves and preening for the attention of anybody who comes near them. A little insecure, if you ask me."

"A little weak-minded, if you ask *me*." He caught the eye of a grim-looking noncom who'd sat up to watch him pass and pointed back toward the holo now deactivating and dissipating into a cloud of light particles. "*Putabam nos adoraverunt imperator, non nos.*"

It was a phrase he'd learned and practiced many times, just to irritate Regulars. *I thought we worshipped the emperor, not ourselves.* The noncom narrowed his eyes, then turned on his side, obeying standing orders not to mess with Proselyti—but his shoulders trembled with rage.

Jabari and Tegenwe moved on before the asshole decided, standing orders notwithstanding, it might be worth some hard punishment to achieve a little glory of his own at their expense.

The Launch Bay was like all the others he'd ever seen around this great *Maelstrom*. They never differed in design, only in dimension. This one was of middling size, built precisely to berth the kind of heavy scout ships currently docked there.

There were three of them, all *Meteoroid*-class, fast reconnaissance runners. The vessels had been berthed, belly facing the outer skin of the station so that only a twelve-by-thirty-meter patch of their hulls were visible within the magnetic seal-frame. All three were ready for passengers, their boarding tongues extended to the decking. Only one had two troopers in comfortable green and gray fatigues flanking one of the boarding tongues. Jabari aimed his team toward them.

The pair hailed from different worlds—or at least they'd been corpiformed for different worlds. The man standing left of the ramp was short and skinny, pale-skinned, with large eyes like those of a nocturnal animal. The other was the opposite—face and hands a deep bronze, tall and barrel-bodied, with limbs like the boughs of a tree, his eyes beady like a pig's. His back seemed distended beneath his shirt, as if he carried a backpack beneath it.

The shorter one nodded at Jabari, waving an arm up the tongue-ramp toward the entry hatch. Jabari let the others precede him, and his eye rested on the heart-shaped sigils stitched onto the right arms of the troopers' shirts. Both men were missing one of their smallest fingers.

More damned Corfids, he thought while giving them a polite nod and a tight smile. He let his expression sour as he climbed past them. By the look of those comfortable uniforms, the pair was coming along. At the hatch, he checked over his shoulder; sure enough, they'd fallen in step behind him.

The entry compartment was only big enough for four or five people. Jabari's team had already vanished through the far end by the time he came in. Scipio floated there against a side wall, since the gravity was turned off in the lock so newcomers could transition to a new grav-orientation when they swung into the corridor beyond. Jabari wondered why the hell the empire couldn't make ships that docked nose-in, not belly-down.

He used a handhold to come to a stop before Scipio, pushing his pack gently toward the inner hatch, where he knew it would eventually drift to the passageway deck, where the gravity was on. The Corfid troopers took position at the exit hatch, blocking the docking bay's bright lights, and triggering Jabari's sense of unease at being hemmed in.

"Senior Lieutenant Jabari, these are First Corporals Avilius —" Scipio indicated the short and wiry one, then the hulking one "—and Otho. They'll be my adjutants on mission. They answer to me."

"Understood, sir."

"First Corporals, see that the rest of the team are squared away for their first rest period."

Neither trooper spoke. They brushed by Jabari on their way forward, Otho bumping him hard enough to force him into the bulkhead, where he snatched at a new handhold. He kept an eye on the bigger man as he ducked his head and exited through the hatch. Otho would hail from a world such as Fregor, corpiformed to cope with its arid terrain, greater gravity, and thin air. The bloating on his back indicated an internal water bladder, and possibly larger lungs. Jabari remembered his one trip to the planet, back when he was an adolescent, and his service was to the Kaan, then to the Kaana upon the Kaan's death. He'd only coped with the trip—he'd only *survived*—by wearing a solid-body exosuit. The loyalist Fregorans had fought like demons. That week, Jabari had lost his cousin; in his mind's eye, he saw Sergeant Abowaji's cheeky grin beneath his suit's faceplate, saw it wiped away a moment later by a tracer round, then watched the helmet fill with gore. That had marked Jabari's first ever truly personal setback. The first setback of the Terranist forces. The beginning of the end...

Scipio coughed, snapping Jabari back to the here and now. "A rest period for you too, Lieutenant. It's currently 2300 ship time. Situation update for your team at 0600, then I'll leave it to you to organize drills."

"Yes, sir. It would help if I knew what we're heading into. What our brief is. Can I expect that information at 0600?"

"Information will be shared at the appropriate time, and whenever it's been updated and confirmed. You're in the aft billet with Corporal Erkan. There's a datapad by your bunk. I've sent a handful of mission files to the device. Big picture, all you need to know at commencement is we're headed for an interstellar object, an artifact. It might have artificial gravity; it might not. It may have droid defenses, AI sentries, or corporeal sentries; it may not. Prepare for all those eventualities."

"When you say 'artifact,' sir, you mean a human one, right?"

For the first time, amusement flickered across Scipio's features. "Well, I don't mean aliens!"

"Right. Of course not, sir. I was just making sure we were on the same page."

"If you believe in angels, gods, *or* aliens, Jabari Mbaye, then we're definitely not 'on the same page.'" He shook his head, losing interest in the topic. "Familiarize yourself with the ship. 0600 is breakfast and Situation Update for the team. By 0730, I'll expect you to be busy in the Drill Hall. More questions?"

"None, sir."

"Then I'll see you in the morning."

Jabari spent his first hour of bunk-time lying on his side, with the hand-sized pad they'd provided, perusing Scipio's files. If he'd expected any actual mission details—or even a hint of what they were getting into—he was quickly disappointed. The files were all to do with the ship, its complement of crew and passengers, and inventory lists. Well, it gave him something to read, at least, because he sure didn't feel like sleeping. And if he had, Erkan's snoring in the bunk below would have been enough to prevent it.

The *Pleiades-219* had zero human crew. Apart from the Corfids and Proselyti, most of its functions were overseen by a null-personality AI—a construct he and his team were denied access to. The AI utilized a bevy of tiny maintenance droids to carry out portions of its will—cephalopod-types with seven tentacles, along with tiny simian-form units the size of Jabari's index fingers. One of the simians was quietly refitting a globe in his compartment's ceiling, no doubt spying on him for Scipio.

Two other droids were housed on the ship, and he was given limited data access to them. Far larger than their maintenance counterparts, the combat bots would supplement the mission team. One was a centipede-type recon droid, one-and-a-half meters long, and multi-segmented. The second was a "humanesque" model that, according to the images and specs, was twice Otho's height and width, heavily armored, and brimming with weaponry.

About the optio and his two corporals, there was zero information, except for the electronic confirmation of their presence. While Cor Fidelis troops weren't uncommon in the Peripheries, Jabari had never actually been on a mission with any. In his experience, the fierce imperial cultists were used for political missions, raids that made examples of insurgent populations, execution squads... that kind of thing.

Wazazi na walezi—parents and guardians—slay me now if this is one of those missions.

Perhaps they were just here to keep an eye on Jabari's people.

He tried accessing ship logs, wanting to skim the ship's recent travel records, in case that gave him any clue to where it was going. Access was denied.

Well, they shouldn't have given me Shill, then. He put the device aside, chuckling. Shill was a fine hacker in *any* century. She'd find a way to get the data he wanted.

He flopped on his back and threw an arm across his eyes. He didn't think he'd sleep, since he was too soon out of the tank, there was too much on his mind, and he had a bunkmate who snored like a Rahgbahger ram in rutting season. But what felt like a moment later, his device sounded an alarm to wake him. He was still on his back. The faulty overhead globe had been replaced, the tiny maintenance droid nowhere to be seen.

"0545." Erkan yawned as he swung his legs over the side of his bunk and slapped his own cheeks. "Doesn't matter what time zone my body clock's running on, I've always hated this time of day."

<hr>

Jabari led his group into the ship's four-table mess, a square compartment astern on the upper deck. Most of them wore the sleeveless shirt they'd worn to the ship; Jabari had traded his for a uniform sweater and travel fatigues. The atmo inside *Pleiades-219* was cold, colder than he liked, since he was a child of a hot country who, like all Terranists, had never been corpiformed for anything else.

Food already awaited on the table closest to the door, a gray gruel that would be optimized for nutrition, not for taste. Scipio and his Corfid troopers sat at a different table, finishing theirs, also dressed in travel fatigues.

"Meal first," Scipio said. "Briefing after."

The helping of food was generous, the bowls enormous. Despite its lack of flavor, the Proselyti fell upon it with enthusiasm. The optio and his troopers ate silently, forgoing chitchat. Their presence imposed a dull mood upon the room, and the Proselyti were left to exchange subdued small talk about the ship's temperature, the prospect of hot showers after drilling, the texture of the porridge—and speculation about which variant of animal's milk had been poured on it, or whether the white liquid had come from an animal at all.

As Corporal Avilius carried out steward duties, clearing tables and fetching hot tea from the tight galley, Optio Scipio stood and addressed them with his gaze fixed on a point along the room's rear bulkhead.

"Warriors of the Imperium, you've been awakened into the glorious reign of Emperor Nero XXXIV, and you serve at his pleasure. The mission you're undertaking is one whose parameters and particulars are still fluid. This is due to incomplete intel, with respect to both the location we're deploying to, *and* to what we'll find there. Rest assured that upon arrival at our target destination, I'll know exactly how to proceed in a manner that best suits our emperor's will.

"For the time being, you simply need to know that your every skill and specialty should be sharpened, and your fitness regained in full. Upon arrival at our destination, your team will be led by Lieutenant Jabari, but the emperor has assigned *me* overall mission command."

"The emperor has assigned me..." *That's an odd choice of phrasing,* Jabari thought. Was it modern slang for orders from Imperial Command, or had Scipio actually been addressed by the emperor?

Scipio continued, "My droids and my troopers serve under my authority. Simply put, for as long as we're away from *Maelstrom*, everyone on this scout ship works for me. Our hyperspace journey is expected to take between eight and ten days. It'll be interrupted partway, and I'll explain this in a moment. This stopover may add an extra day or two to trip time. Questions so far?"

A ripple of shaking heads.

Jabari said, "Optio, a 'stopover?'"

"The word was my attempt at humor, because our goal at that location is anything *but* recreational."

"Oh."

"You see, we'll need fuel to complete our journey and return from it. Our *Maelstrom* has operated in a far-flung part of the Peripheries for a decade, moving further outward from the galactic core. This has made resupply for sub-ships difficult. If we'd been blessed enough to be operating out here two thousand years ago, it obviously wouldn't be a problem, because all waystations and settlements were part of one empire—one humanity. Unfortunately, we currently live in a time when the Imperium is still rebuilding to its former glory and working to extend its reach." He sniffed and scratched his cheek, perhaps allowing his gibe at those who'd helped dismantle the Imperium to sink in, perhaps just regathering his thoughts. "Low on fuel, yes, but luckily for us, there's somewhere we can get it that's not far off our intended route. Several days from here."

"And do they like the Imperium there, sir?" Erkan asked him. "Wherever it is we're stopping over."

"No, they don't, which means we're within our rights to *take* instead of *trade*." Shill and Tegenwe shot each other a quick glance, and the optio caught it, prompting him to add, "Any action we take there will be lawful, because the emperor's will is the heart of all law. Besides, the current inhabitants of the Rogers 22 Waypoint are criminals... rascals. They're brigands responsible for a series of attacks on survey vessels in the Zahar Aljamal Reach, among other things. When I say 'series,' I mean nine. One survey ship escaped to tell the tale; eight were lost. That's eight ships with crews of Imperium citizens, scientists, and sailors."

"And we know they're at Rogers 22 how, sir?" Jabari asked. His peripheral vision caught Morten nodding; evidently, he'd been wondering the same thing.

"Automated probe-ships have confirmed the brigands' presence and marked the site for a future military strike. We're hurrying that action up a little, killing two birds with the same stone, as the ancients said. Questions?"

Jabari asked, "We'll have intel on Rogers 22 before we arrive?"

"Transferred to your device while you ate."

"Very good, sir." Jabari glanced down at the small pad, but didn't touch it. Checking it now would suggest he didn't trust the optio. He didn't, and the optio must know he didn't, but that wasn't the kind of thing you did in any military, in any century.

"If there are no more questions, I'll take my tea in my cabin. You have the run of the ship, of course, although you'd need a *very* good reason to enter any systems compartments or the command center—what your era called the 'flight deck.' From here, warriors, you're in Lieutenant Jabari's hands. Your day will be spent drilling. Jabari, my troopers will be joining yours for today's training, if that suits you."

"Of course, sir."

"During drills, they'll follow your orders."

"Very good, sir."

Avilius had just finished setting steaming tea mugs at every place. Scipio lifted his and took it out of the room without further conversation. Avilius moved around his table to set his back to the Proselyti. He and Otho hunkered together, hands busy in a rapid-fire sign language Jabari could barely see, let alone decipher.

"Good tea," Erkan said loudly with a dramatic eye roll that showed just what he thought of the optio's briefing.

Morten pushed his drink away without tasting it and put his head in his hands, retreating into thought.

Shill said, "So, Lieutenant Boss Man. What drills are you delighting us with first today?"

"We, my friends, are beginning with breaching drills in 1.2 gravity first, followed by 1.3, then 1.4."

Groans.

"Hey," Tegenwe complained, "according to the calendar, I'm seventeen hundred years old. Way too old for high-grav combat."

"You're too old for a lot of things," Erkan teased her. She flicked tea at him and laughed.

"Lieutenant's the old bastard." Shill grinned. "You sure you'll be all right for high-grav, *sir?*"

Disapproving of the levity, Otho glared over Avilius' shoulder.

Jabari gave him a wink and a grin.

Don't even think about reprimanding me, Corfid, he thought. *For the rest of the day, you work for me.*

CHAPTER FIVE

ALEXIS PUSHED her way through the panicked crowd and came upon two station security thugs, distinctive in their dark-gray-and-red uniforms. Caught by surprise, she quickly dispatched them with a couple of blows to the solar plexus and smacked their heads together when they doubled over, winded. Her high-g strength was counting much for her success.

A quick look back showed Sabrya dealing with all comers —and winning. *Impressive.*

The nearest exit was a level higher from where she'd arrived with the other intended slaves. Her mind, thanks to Kaden's stasis training, calculated the details she'd absorbed earlier to indicate the route she needed to take to get to the docking bay of the *Daemon*, where she assumed Jenna was heading.

There were elevators, but everyone was clamoring for them; she didn't think Jenna could have had the time to get in one. She picked up her pace and followed the signs for the stairs. The initial holding cells where she'd first met Bradyn had been on the same level as the docking bay for the *Daemon*, with five turns and roughly a hundred and thirty paces through the dim passages separating them. The path they'd been forced along to the arena had involved climbing three levels and traveling another hundred paces. In her mind's eye, she triangulated the various paths she'd taken, then extrapolated that to determine her next route.

Like her, not everyone wanted to wait for the elevator. Alexis stepped to the side and ignored the many vultures from the slave market as they rushed past. She shoved anyone giving her more than a cursory glance. *Do they recognize me?*

Fortunately, no one was interested in going to the lower levels, choosing to go up to the brighter lights and shopping malls in the central area of the orbital.

She began descending as she heard loud footsteps approaching from above.

Reinforcements?

Only after descending two more levels did she stop and listen to the noises of the orbital. The yelling and screaming of the calamity from the arena could still be heard, muted by the distance. Other sounds, however, impinged on her hearing: the pipes and generators of doors hissing open or closed, the general hubbub of life in a completely artificial environment in space. This area was also dimmer than the levels above.

Then she detected the waft of a familiar stench rising from the stairwell; the unique odor she associated with ships docking after weeks or months in space.

"Smelling more like the docking area with each step," she muttered to herself.

That confirmed her calculated path was correct. After descending another floor, she saw Foster lurking below.

Did he hear me, or is he just waiting to see if anyone was following?

None of the other *Daemon* crew members were in sight. Good, all she wanted was the coding card for the ship. *And for Torg.*

Out of sight, Alexis heard Jenna arguing with someone—a crew member. *Who?* Then, *Why do I care?*

She studied the immediate area, noting the symbols for another stairwell further along the passage. Alexis headed for it, recalculating the changed route. As she went down the stairs, two figures appeared below. They ignored her after a casual glance. Dressed in dirty overalls, they were merely workers going about their duties.

Not everyone is a threat. Alexis took a few calming breaths and a moment to deliberate what she really wanted. Apart from not becoming a worker enslaved for the rest of her life to the highest bidder, she wanted a place of safety.

Bradyn and Phillix had agreed there was nowhere either of them would be safe on the orbital. Those who'd come searching knew enough about them to make hiding here pointless—short term at best. And how could they possibly keep Sabrya Smith incognito? *Everyone in the Imperium knows her.*

And that had led her to chase Jenna. It might be too simple a solution, but from Torg's information, possession of the encoding chip enabled control of the droid, and therefore the ship. She wanted the ship for the shelter and maneuverability it would give her. Give them *all*.

And with the ship's data, she'd be able to retrace the path to where they'd found her. Maybe she'd find others. *Maybe I'll find Kaden.*

The raised angry voices ahead made her slow down and approach more stealthily. She didn't recognize the voices, but recognized this passage—the slaving cells were behind her. She picked up the odor of burned flesh and ozone. Part of her mind considered the ability to separate the myriad of smells assailing her nostrils.

Finally, my biology training comes to the fore!

Alexis stopped at a corner, ducked down, and risked a peek.

Jenna was down; a small, balding man bent over him,

blaster in hand. Foster, legs kicking, was up against the bulkhead, held by the neck by some brute of a man.

She didn't hear it, but imagined the sound of vertebrae snapping when she saw the head crick to one side. When he let go, Foster dropped to the deck like a side of grunfer at an abattoir, sprawling across his equally dead captain.

An elevator pinged near them.

With the briefest hesitation, the pair left the bodies and took flight up the stairs.

Bradyn and Phillix stepped cautiously out of the elevator with a handful of rescued slaves. The nearest woman screamed at the sight of the bodies; others put their hands over their mouths in shock or covered the eyes of their young.

The elevator next to them pinged, and another dozen rescues arrived.

"How the hell do we take all of them?" she muttered as she regained her feet. "Two thugs just ran up the stairs." She turned and bent over Jenna, searching for the encoding chip. *Nothing!* "I think they took the chip," she said before realizing they probably didn't know what she was talking about. "The *Daemon's* down there. I'll join you in a few minutes." *I hope.*

Following the two thugs, Alexis bolted up the stairs, hoping her jeemed strength was a match for the brute she'd probably end up fighting. Dodging around the corner to take the next flight of stairs, she found the brute in question on the deck, covered in blood.

Glancing up, she witnessed Sabrya do the impossible, cartwheeling and dodging laser fire. With her final acrobatic maneuvers, the fighter brought her boot up, clipping the bald man under the chin and flinging him back. He flopped over the railing and bounced wetly off each platform, landing hard on the deck she'd just vacated. The background noise wasn't sufficient to drown out the sound of many bones breaking.

"Good timing." Alexis nodded. She pivoted and jumped

over the railing to the short drop below. A quick search of the broken corpse revealed the chip stuffed into his pocket.

"Is that what I think it is?" Sabrya landed lightly beside her as Alexis pocketed it.

"Only if you think it's an encoding biochip for a ship's droid." Alexis noted the fighter's arms and legs gleaming with her exertion. "Impressive work there. All of it." *And still in those metal mittens.*

"It's nice to be appreciated."

"We better get a move on before they realize where we're going and lock down the port."

With a nod from Sabrya, the pair ran down the stairs and caught up with the escapees as they gathered around the *Daemon's* docking bay. The worried group parted when they realized the fighter was with them.

Alexis approached Phillix. "I can only assume you managed to take care of the control boxes. What can you do with this?"

Phillix took the encoding chip from her hands and examined it dubiously. "To be honest, this card has been hacked badly already. I'll be surprised if it works at all, but... give me your hand. I'll need a drop of your blood."

Confused, Alexis complied.

Using one of his cyber tools, Phillix nicked her thumb. As a bead of blood welled, he let it drop onto a section of the card. After another cursory look, he inserted it into the slot on the wall.

At first, nothing happened. Then two lights on the card slot began to alternate flashing red, slowly at first, then increasing rapidly until it was a blur. They went blank, then they flared green as they heard clicking behind the thick alloy. The airlock doors slid open, as did the loading dock doors beyond.

"Well... shit. It worked. Shall we?" Phillix replied.

"That's it?" she asked, incredulous at the minimal security.

"As I said, a botched hack." Phillix retrieved the card and

returned it to Alexis with a grin. "Your Jenna wasn't the original captain, and I doubt whoever he usurped was the original captain, either. All bio-scan requirements have been bypassed, allowing anyone to use it with a drop of fresh blood."

"And *plasma* is a component of blood." *He possesses the plasma chip with my encoding,* she recalled Torg's comment.

"Yes. So?"

"Nothing. Just something I heard recently."

As they were about to board the craft through the loading dock, Torg appeared at the other end.

"Welcome aboard, Captain Nales," he called out.

"Captain?" Bradyn and Sabrya looked at her, meeting her surprised look. Phillix grinned.

"I am linked to the access pad, and indications are, you are now bonded with the chip," the droid said by way of explanation, then took in the group waiting behind her. "We can use the cargo area to house your friends. I can then assess any injuries and take care of them individually in the infirmary."

"Are we able to take care of so many?" Alexis asked as she helped people to a place where they could sit.

"Food supplies will need to be rationed, as well as medicines, until we restock."

Alexis nodded. "Torg, we can deal with this. Are you able to get us out of here immediately?"

"It is inadvisable to depart without proper authorization—"

"Do it anyway. No authorization will be given."

"It is like nothing has changed." Torg pivoted and quickly left.

Orange lights along the orbital's passage began strobing, and Bradyn, Sabrya, and Phillix hurried the last escapees inside.

"I can hear many fraggin' footsteps approachin'," Sabrya called out, turning to face the loading dock.

Bradyn hit the side panel. "That'll hold them until they

work out a bypass." The loading bay and airlock doors closed quickly.

Through a small porthole, Sabrya saw a dozen security guards enter the dock and rush toward the ship. She gave them the finger. "Someone's knockin' on our fraggin' door."

"Everyone, hang on. We will be breaking free of the docking clamps momentarily." Loud bangs through the hull denoted the "breaking free" Torg had mentioned.

Alexis scanned the loading dock quickly, uncertainly.

"Here." Phillix pointed to the wall. "Assuming you're after a comm-link?"

Gratefully, Alexis rushed over to speak with Torg. "Torg, we need to go now!" she said hastily into the mike.

Through the porthole, the orbital came into view as the *Daemon* moved away from it quickly.

"I hope we never go back there again." Sabrya turned away from the view.

"It was a dump anyway," Bradyn added.

"The question is, where do we go from here?" Alexis asked. The group looked unsure. "Not to worry, though. I'm sure something will turn up," she finished confidently.

A couple moments later, Torg reappeared. "I have set course to jump to the next waypoint, and to remain in hyper until we determine our next port of call. This is the protocol set by the previous captain, Jenna. As there was a sense of urgency, I trust it is correct in this case?"

"Um. Yes." Alexis was unused to being addressed as the leader. "I'll head up to the bridge and take a look. Can you see what you can do down here?"

"Of course." Torg turned and immediately began his assessment of the injured.

"Anyone know their way around this tub?" she asked quietly.

"I've seen schematics," Bradyn offered, "but that was years ago."

"More than me. My short time here was in a cupboard, and I was still overcome with stasis sickness. Lead on."

Bradyn used the door Torg had previously. "If it's anything like what I've seen, there'll be a central passageway. Energy cells are in compartments underneath the forward cargo bays, with storage all around us, shuttle dock above, and engineering for the drives on each side of the aft cargo bays."

"It's a cargo ship, isn't it?"

"Initially, they were military haulers outfitted with light armament. But this one—" the engineer looked dubiously at some of the addons "—has so many drocking incompatible parts... I'm amazed it's still flying."

"Luckily, I have a great engineer and an electronics expert on board to keep it together."

Bradyn was silent for a moment.

Alexis thought he was still examining the fit-outs.

"How long do you expect to be on here?" he asked.

She had no idea and said so. "None of this was on my radar. I'm still finding my feet and relying heavily on you all—probably more than I should expect, considering we know so little about each other. No doubt you have families and loved ones to get back to."

"And yours?" he asked as he stopped at a door.

"After so long and that attack? They must be all dead."

The door opened, and they used a lift to get up to the bridge, remaining silent.

"Welcome aboard, Captain," Bradyn said formally as the door swished open. "Drock!"

The bridge didn't look good at all. If anything, it looked worse than the rest of the ship.

"How the hell do they fly this drocking thing?" he wondered, shaking his head.

There were panels missing, exposing the various workings, cabling, and conduits; lights flashing, lights glowing, lights not doing anything; and loose containers of various sizes were pushed up against the bulkheads, unsecured.

"Well, at least Phillix and I won't be bored." He looked around him with dismay.

CHAPTER SIX

ON THE SECOND full day of travel, Jabari left four of the *Pleiades-219's* passengers practicing light hand-to-hand in the upper deck sparring room, and climbed a ladder down to the billet compartments, muttering to himself.

"Refueling stop. Fuel raid more like it. Raiding like bloody common pirates. The *Maelstrom* couldn't fully supply us? This is complete fraugle shit."

He found Shill off-duty and lolling on her bunk with her pad on her chest. Gentle music issued from it. Jabari paused a moment in the hatchway, avoiding notice, taken by the quality of the tune and its performance. It was very close to the music of Shill's home nation, to music that traced its roots down through millennia to the Earth country called Idoneesha.

Noticing him finally, her hand spider-crawled across the screen for the stop icon, but Jabari gestured for her to let it play. The music was soft enough to talk over, and he liked it.

"This must take you back," he said, sitting on the bunk opposite hers.

She turned onto her side, raising herself on an elbow. The

pad slid onto the mattress and stayed there. "It does. Familiar things. Nostalgia."

"Is that bad or good?" he asked. "To be reminded of your roots?"

Shill performed a one-shoulder shrug. "If it centers me, it must be good, right?"

"Right."

"*You* all right, Boss? You look like you could use some downtime and a couple dozen drinks."

"I'm... thinking about something. *Over*thinking, probably."

"Tell me," she said simply. She turned the music off before tapping another icon that remotely closed the compartment hatch.

He gestured to the walls and ceiling, asking her silently if she'd swept the place for bugs.

She gave him a confident nod and a smile.

"This whole 'refuel' thing has me unsettled," Jabari said. "I mean, there's more to it—there has to be. Scipio wants us to believe the *Maelstrom* couldn't spare the fuel for a ship this small? Bloody ridiculous. I mean, it's not a destroyer."

She swung her legs off the bunk and leaned forward on her knees. "Glad I'm not the only one 'round here smelling grunfershit. I know you have to be professional and careful in what you say, and even what you show on your face, but it's about time you brought this up with me. Permission to hack in and do some snooping, sir?"

Remembering the prank she'd pulled on Tegenwe while the other woman had slept last night, Jabari's mood brightened. "Probably a better use of your skills than winding someone's bio-tat a hundred years forward."

Shill pouted. "She started it. Put pepper on my pillow."

"In that case, I approve. Also, it was nice that someone was older than me, even for a few hours." He returned to the main topic. "I'm surprised you didn't already hack in if you're so suspicious of Scipio."

She shook her head. "I do what my leader tells me. I mean, my leader as in you."

"Yes, I got that when you asked permission and used the word 'sir.'"

"You do know you're the highest-ranking officer we have."

"Yes."

"The only officer we—"

"*Yes*, Shill."

Eyes ranging around the walls, she added, "Jabari, you only ever have to say the word, and we'd kill every filthy Imperial we could get our hands on. We'd go out in a blaze—"

"*We're* Imperials," he said quietly.

She sniffed and rolled onto her back, plucking pilling from the mattress above her.

"We made that choice, Shill, to serve the empire so the human race can have peace."

"Yet here we are, off to kill someone again. Probably."

"Probably."

"So, about the hacking. I just didn't want to interfere if there was some other action you were taking."

"Well, I appreciate that, but right now, I'm ordering you to hack the shit out of this ship."

She turned her head, and her grin was back.

"To the extent that it's safe," he added.

"Of course."

He allowed himself a grin, too. "That is, if you think you're up to it."

"Up to it? The AI's bright, but a null personality, so not too bright for me. Scipio's code-walls are as thin as paper. This'll be as simple as a pre-dinner snack."

Jabari climbed the ladderwell again and emerged into the passage by the sparring room. The ruckus of warriors' training rolled out from the large hatchway as he wandered toward it. But when he reached the entry, he saw training was no longer the agenda inside.

Two of the people he'd left there were fighting for real. Tegenwe and Otho. Launching, blocking, and redirecting punches and kicks, coughing ardent, angry curses at each other. Blood dappled the light-blue matting from cuts on their lips, faces, and hands. Both had swelling around one eye, and Tegenwe looked to be favoring one leg. Otho held his left hand tight against his chest, but snapped his right out in a vicious jab that might have taken Tegenwe's head off if she hadn't dodged it.

Meanwhile, Morten and Avilius spectated silently from opposite corners of the room, one eye on the fight, one eye on each other.

Shocked, Jabari grabbed both sides of the hatchway and roared, "Desist! *Now!*"

They did, surprising him. The four soldiers in the room turned to face him and snapped to attention, ingrained discipline reasserting itself at the trigger of a command. Otho stared at him sullenly through one good eye and one that was bloodshot and puffy. Tegenwe's left eye had swollen almost completely shut.

"*What* is going *on?*"

The pair began to raise the arm closest to the other, probably intending to apportion blame like a child would—*He did. She did*—but their arms dropped to their sides without comment, and they dropped their gazes. Otho still nursed one of his hands, and Jabari wondered if Tegenwe had sprained his wrist, or broken it. Given the brute's size, either would be no mean feat.

There was no point in asking mute Morten for a report, so

Jabari turned his attention to Avilius. "Well?"

Technically, Avilius didn't answer to him, but Scipio had insisted Jabari was in command for all drilling and training. The Corfid probably also felt shame at not preventing the melee—or at his partner getting his ass handed to him by a far slighter opponent.

Avilius said something in a singsong language Jabari didn't recognize.

Jabari, like all the Proselyti aboard now, wore a two-way translator patch on one shoulder. It took the device an extra beat to deal with the language, then it murmured into Jabari's left ear, "Heated emotions."

"I'd say that's an understatement," Jabari replied, comfortable returning it in his own tongue.

Avilius switched to Imperial True. "Neither is to blame. The sparring simply provoked adrenaline spikes in both of them."

"These things happen," Tegenwe muttered and dabbed at a bleeding lip. She was lucky. The blows Otho had landed must have been glancing ones.

"Do they?" Jabari lowered his own volume as he heard movement in the passage near him. He released the hatchway and asked her, "They happen, do they?"

She broke eye contact again, and Jabari turned to face Scipio, coming up the corridor. "Nothing to see here, sir."

"Didn't sound like nothing, Lieutenant, from the level and intensity of your shouting."

Jabari had to step inside the room and aside to allow the optio entrance.

Scipio looked the sheepish pair over—the one twice the bulk and weight of the other—and said, "Looks like each gave as good as they got. Otho, does this need to be taken further?"

"No, sir," the big man rumbled, eyes on the ground.

"Tegenwe?"

"No, sir. It's over, and the lieutenant made it clear this wasn't acceptable conduct."

"You shouldn't need him to make that clear," Scipio replied mildly. He offered Jabari a raised eyebrow and left the area without further comment.

"You three males, to the showers," Jabari growled. "Otho, hit the aid room first and see to your injuries." Since the showers and medical station were on this level, he told Tegenwe, "You, follow me to the meal-room, and we'll patch you up, too." He stalked off without lingering to check on their compliance.

He was halfway down the ladder again when he felt Tegenwe on it above him. At the bottom, he watched her descend carefully, avoiding putting too much weight on her left leg.

"Ankle or knee?" he asked when she joined him.

"Knee." She winced. "Might need more than an icepack."

He poked a head out into the passage. No sign of Erkan or Shill. He said quietly, "I can't have you entering battle with a limp."

"We have nanites aboard. Give me some o' them sweet, microscopic robots, and I'll be moving smooth as silk in a day or two." She blinked hard. A second later, Jabari realized it had been intended as a wink, but the other eye was closed over.

He grunted. "Just in time for the 'stopover,' but an ass-damned waste of resources."

"Sorry, Lieutenant."

"Quit the lieutenant grunfershit when it's just us. Let's get you iced and bandaged. When Otho's out of the aid room, we'll get you nanned."

CHAPTER SEVEN

TWO RANDOM JUMPS LATER, they were two hundred and fifty light-years away from Ieoni Orbital and Sector 36.

While Bradyn and Alexis provided what first-aid they could, Phillix kept busy removing everyone's neuro-collar. After the refugees were fed and made as comfortable as possible under the circumstances, the crew gathered in the mess behind the bridge to discuss options. The dinner plates had been cleared from the scratched and wobbly table, and only a tray of protein crackers remained.

The water filtration—like everything else on the ship—wouldn't work to capacity until it was repaired. Only after the water had been boiled was it fit for consumption, and even then, everyone opted to mix it with whiskey sufficient to kill any remaining bugs.

There was a lot of whiskey on board, as well as several pallets of protein bars.

"We can go to Sector 22," Sabrya filled the growing silence as she examined three blades that slid in and out from between her fingers.

Alexis watched, partly enthralled, partly curious. "How...?"

"Nanites." The fighter repeated the process slowly for her benefit.

"Does it... hurt?"

"My pain threshold has been enhanced. Feels like nothin' more than getting' a scratch."

"Sector 22? Will you be safe there?" Bradyn brought them back on topic.

"Didn't you throw the tournament there?" Phillix asked.

"Let's get one thing clear." She turned on the tech, eyes flaring. "I've *never* thrown a fraggin' fight or shirked any challenge or challenger. *They* wanted to make an example of me because of what I did for 22."

"What happened?"

Sabrya took a deep breath then paused. "Another time. Let's just say, I sort of did what we're doin' now."

"But still, will you be safe?" Bradyn repeated. "Will *we?*"

"I'm touched by your concern. Yes, we'll be safe enough there—in most places, I'm fraggin' *persona non grata*, but if we keep a low profile, we'll be fine. Besides, I know a place where we can safely put these people."

"Will this ship be too obvious? I wonder if it's been to 22 before."

"One way to find out." Alexis flicked the comm-link and asked Torg.

"We had brief dealings there thirteen months, nine days, and sixteen hours ago," the ship's droid replied.

"That answers that." She left the link open.

"If I know anything about the mob we left behind, there's no doubt a drocking bounty made public out on the Mesh, soon if not already."

"What's this 'mesh' you refer to?"

"A galaxy-wide system for communications," Bradyn explained. "Think of it like the Grid used by the empire. Theirs is nice, orderly, and heavily monitored. Out here in the

Reaches, it's much less uniform, more of a hodge-podge of networks. The signal fluctuates and drops out, since our setup isn't as rigid—"

"And it isn't fraggin' monitored by the Imps."

Alexis nodded her thanks. "Torg, how many *Bolide*-class ships are there in operational order?"

"Seven on the registry in total. Two each in Sectors 9, 12, and 33, and us."

"Thanks." Alexis turned. "Well, at least we aren't unique."

"Have you walked around this ship?" Bradyn quipped. "I'm pretty sure there's no other drocking ship like this."

Alexis nodded. "Phillix, how can we go about faking the ship's ID?"

"I'm sure it could be done—assuming we have the components. All we need to do is change the transponder code. This ship is ex-military, so the transponder will be encrypted— almost foolproof."

"Is that a no?"

"I said *almost* foolproof. I can do it, of course."

"Make it happen. As for the components, we'll need to make an inventory of the hold. No telling what we have here. We'll compare that with the list you'll make of what you need."

"We could ask our fellow escapees to help. That would cut the time; we don't know their skill set either," Bradyn suggested.

"True. Good point." Alexis stood. "How about Sabrya and I talk to the refugees, and you two can go with Torg. He should be able to help you out with some of the things you find."

Two days after escaping Ieoni Orbital, the *Daemon* reached the planet Plorian, settling on a landing field beside several buildings. Dense scrub bordered two sides, and the other was pasture with cattle that ambled away before resuming their grazing at the other end of the paddock.

As the dust settled, several armed people came out of the nearest building and approached the vessel. A larger man, unarmed and wearing heavy trousers and a sleeveless shirt, stepped forward. Four armed men fanned out behind him, watching the ramp extend and the ship's dim interior.

Sabrya casually strolled down the ramp from the *Daemon* and into the sunlight, dressed in a singlet top and tight shorts scrounged from one of the compartments. The group had gathered the gear from the previous crew and gone through it all to see what was useful and worth keeping.

Alexis had found a shirt and long trousers, as did Phillix. The best Bradyn could find was Foster's clothing, as it was the largest, but being fat wasn't the same as being built for heavy-G. It was tight in some areas and baggy in others.

Anything left of the gear was shared between the refugees.

"You've got a lot of nerve, coming here, Sabby!" the man called out to the fighter. "Half the sector wants you pinned up by your tits, and the other half wants to pin a medal on them."

"Where do you stand?" Sabrya stopped several paces from him.

"Where I can admire your tits from a safe distance."

"Ah, Brutus... so fraggin' crass. It's refreshin' to know you haven't changed one bit. How have you been, you old fool?" Sabrya stepped forward and embraced him in a fierce hug.

"I see you've put on some weight." The last words were a groan as the fighter's embrace tightened.

"Asshole." She let him go and stepped back.

"Besides, I'm a trader now. It ain't good for trade if I pick sides."

"Not pickin' sides? You've changed. What happened to the freedom fighter I knew? The one with humanitarian traits that nearly got us both fragged several times? You even opposed the Surreal Tourney."

"That's all spindrift now. I've changed my ways somewhat." He spat into the dirt and wiped his lips with his thumb. "Are we trading or reminiscing? Coz we ain't got much time to do either."

Sabrya shrugged. "I gather you've heard what happened at Ieoni Orbital." She turned slightly, hearing Alexis and Phillix walking down the loading dock ramp, leading the refugees.

Brutus followed her gaze. "It's all across the Mesh. Everyone with a comm has heard about how you busted up the authorities—"

"They were goin' to make all of us fraggin' slaves!" she vented, then took a deep breath as he looked past her and studied the other passengers. She saw how he reacted to the plight of the refugees. "We need you to take care of these people. I'd like to revisit that 'spindrift' you mentioned. And, yes, we'd also like to trade."

With only faint, nervous mutterings, the refugees milled to the side. They looked around with great interest.

Some have probably never seen real plants and trees, Alexis thought.

Torg stepped out, a pallet of protein bars gliding behind him on a carrier.

Bradyn strode beside him, stopping when he reached Sabrya's side with a tablet. He handed it to her.

"We have a list of items on the ship that could be handy for you, or not." Sabrya in turn handed the tablet to Brutus to peruse. "Our priority is air and water filtration. You'd be doin' us a huge favor."

Brutus examined the tablet curiously. "You know I owe you a favor or two..."

"I wasn't goin' to mention it."

The big man nodded. "We have replacement filters, but

they might need slight modifications to fit your systems," Brutus said after taking a longer look at the *Daemon*. "Though I think it's a waste. You sure that thing is safe?"

Sabrya chuckled. "Safe enough, considerin' our fraggin' limited options. I'm beginnin' to like her odious smell and weird clunks."

"And she keeps us on our toes, too. No boredom," Bradyn added.

"This is Bradyn, our mechanic marvel; Phillix, electronics extraordinaire; and Torg."

Torg's appearance made it obvious it was a ship droid and required no further introduction.

"You captaining this bucket of rivets now?" Brutus questioned her, looking doubtful. "What happened to Jenna?"

"Ha. Not me. Alexis is our captain." Sabrya pointed to Alexis.

Alexis' face reddened slightly at being introduced as their leader. Sure, they listened to her and followed her suggestions, but there'd been no discussion about it.

Bradyn gave her a nudge. "That's your cue."

Alexis stepped forward. "Brutus," she acknowledged him and shook his meaty hand. "Jenna's dead, as well as Foster."

Brutus sized her up, looking her up and down. Whatever his thoughts were, he kept them to himself and simply nodded. "Did you kill them?"

"Someone beat me to it. We think it was the Bukshoga Qlan."

"You sure?" the big trader asked.

"I saw the tattoos," Sabrya affirmed. "It was them."

"Your assistance would be greatly appreciated," Alexis finished.

"I'll do what I can, especially for these unfortunates. As Sab said, I've changed... but not to the extent of ignoring the plight of others. We were in a similar position before; like you, I have a good understanding of what they're going through."

"You also mentioned 'not having much time.' Can you elaborate?"

"Recently, there's been some piracy centered around the region Rogers 22 once serviced. A lot of folks reckon it's randoms, or imperial raids. Either way, everyone's on edge. Personally, that's one of the places I reckon Bukshoga have set up a base. But if there *are* Imps out here, either they or Bukshoga might be aware of your sudden... notoriety. They could be here at any time. With the Mesh report of the bounty, someone's sure to come here hunting for you."

Alexis considered this news. *Bounty?* "What's Rogers 22 again?" she asked.

"It was the waypoint station for this sector, back in its Imperium days. Seedy place now that gets used by a lotta different factions when convenient. Think Ieoni Orbital, but larger and older," Sabrya answered. She turned back to Brutus. "Imp raids? Seriously? Way out fraggin' here?"

He shrugged. "Possibly. Definitely had a report of an Imp scout ship appearing in Lawan System, then jumping out again. Probably just dropping out of hyper to confirm its next coordinates."

"Lawan's a ways from here," Sabrya said thoughtfully, "but it'd be *on* the way here from plenty of their outer systems. What the frag would the emperor's goons be doin' out here? They lost?"

"Can't say. Doubt it, though. They're probably the last of *your* concern, anyway. I doubt they're out to collect the bounty; let's put it that way." He turned back to his men and ordered them to fetch the air and water filters. "You'll find them at the back of Warehouse 2. Check the third row. Green crates."

"That's very generous of you—" Alexis started.

"That crate of protein's worth much more in the right

place." He paused, considering. "Sorry to sound so businesslike. As I said earlier, I owe Sabby, and there really is a risk that hunters will come here. Bad for you, but worse for us if we're caught helping you."

"Understood. We'll get out of here as soon as we can, then. Do you need a hand with anything?"

"Nah. We're pretty self-sufficient." He handed the tablet back. "Most of this stuff is either too big to shift quickly, too old, or too rare. Shit, I don't even know what some of these are, and I used to be an engineer. Maybe find a dealer in bulk scrap metal, and you'll get a few stellars for it all."

Their womenfolk and young had come out during the discussion, once it became obvious the encounter wasn't going to turn violent. They mingled quickly with the refugees and urged them on toward the buildings.

"Please, all of you are invited inside. We can't let you go without a meal of fresh vegetables."

Several minutes later, two burly men carried a heavy green crate out of the warehouse. As they approached the ramp, Bradyn met them and took hold of it. Unsure but encouraged by his words, the men carefully released the heavy load.

"Thanks." With a nod, Bradyn carried the crate by himself.

The pair watched him, slack-jawed, as he walked up the ramp.

"You showing off?" Phillix joked.

"Nope. If I was going to show off, I'd do it one-handed, like this." He adjusted his grip and stance to wave at the electronic tech. "Let's check these out and see what mods are needed."

"Ah... perhaps it can wait. Remember the bit about fresh vegetables?"

"Drock, yeah!" Bradyn placed the crate on the deck at the top of the ramp. "Let's get fed."

The main building's door creaked open as Alexis stepped back out into the bright daylight.

"You two coming? Sabrya's about to eat your share."

"Where to now, Captain?" Torg asked once they'd taken off from Plorian.

True to his word, Brutus had taken the refugees in with a promise to find them suitable housing and employment.

Alexis didn't answer immediately. "Phillix, did you find what you needed to fake the ship's ID?"

"I believe so. I've started already, and it should only take me a couple more hours to tweak it."

"Time we haven't got," Bradyn said as the sensors picked up an incoming ship.

Everyone turned to view the relevant screen. The distances involved were too vast to actually "see" anything, but there was a graphic of a blinking red triangle a few thousand kilometers away. After a couple seconds, the faint, red-dotted line indicating the red triangle's trajectory angled around to intersect their own, a dotted blue line.

"Do we know who it is?" Alexis asked as another blip appeared.

"Drock it!" Bradyn swore as a second image appeared.

Like the first, the second red triangle began to align with their vector.

"Not local enforcers," Torg informed her. "If their signal is accurate, they are merchant vessels. Their relative angle of entry from hyper would indicate a jump from Sector 24."

"Weren't we in Sector 24 recently?" Bradyn questioned the droid.

"Affirmative."

"Too coincidental for my liking," Alexis noted. "Let's get the hell out of here. Torg, what sort of evasive maneuvers did any of the previous captains set in these situations?"

"I can confirm they were all risky ones—"

"And we're still flying. Pick one best suited to this scenario that in your estimation will be the most successful with minimum risk."

Torg paused for a moment. "Everyone should buckle up. Our inertia compensators are not what they used to be."

"What *is?*" Bradyn quipped as he jumped into the nearest seat. The others did the same.

"Add it to your repair list," Alexis advised.

"It's almost as long as the drocking inventory," the engineer muttered.

"No boredom, remember?" Alexis teased.

Torg's silver fingers danced across the keyboard and hovered over the initiator tab.

"Do it!" Alexis barked after checking that everyone had buckled in.

"That is not advisable, Captain. For what I am about to do, I require the utmost accuracy. Certain criteria must be met, or it might fail."

The red blips on the screen were getting closer.

"Can't this ship at least go faster?" Phillix asked, looking nervous.

"Much faster," Torg replied calmly, as expected of a droid, "but in this situation, the fastest speed is not an aspect of the required criteria."

"Pretty sure it drocking is," Bradyn stated. "Phillix, if we survive this, perhaps an overhaul of this bucket of servos and glitches can be arranged."

"I assure you, we are at the optimum velocity for the next phase of the maneuver."

The red triangles had almost merged as one; the distance between them and the blue icon had already halved. Soon, they'd be able to see the vessels on screen without the need for graphics and icons.

Alexis flicked her gaze between the screen and the droid. "They'll be throwing stones at us any minute, Torg."

"Now." The droid flicked the relay.

They all felt the briefest sensation of freefall—minor disorientation, and Alexis' stomach felt like it lurched sideways.

A few of the lights flickered, and the coffee splashed out of the mug as it jumped.

"Is that it—" Alexis gulped as her world suddenly heaved.

The plastic tableware clattered to the deck and slid into the bulkhead. All the lights went dark, then flashed orange, while a muted alarm blared somewhere down below.

An instant later, the lights flashed back on, and everything seemed calm.

Alexis swallowed bile and breathed slowly and deeply until the nausea dissipated. A quick glance around showed her everyone was in one piece, but the floor was a mess.

"We are safe for now," Torg confirmed as he worked at the console until several red diodes on the console stopped blinking. "As you can see, the scanner is now clear of any pursuing craft."

Alexis unbuckled her belt, rose unsteadily to her feet, and checked Bradyn, who was looking a bit gray. He smiled grimly and nodded that he was okay, but there were beads of sweat on his brow.

"What did you do?" she asked Torg.

"I initiated a series of hyperjumps in random directions; we jumped a short distance, stopped, then jumped again. This was accomplished in a matter of seconds. There is much still to learn about the void within 'hyper.' It is theorized with each jump, each vessel leaves a wake of sorts—"

"Like a boat on water?" Alexis now stood beside him and examined the screen.

"Similar, but as the void is 'empty,' it is unknown what the 'wake' is, even now. They termed it a hyper hiccup back then."

"And that was the *minimum* fraggin' risk?" Sabrya had also hopped up. She examined Phillix, who was to her immediate left. He was unconscious, but breathing normally. "I reckon he fainted," the fighter said with a wry grin.

Torg continued, "It was a phenomenon discovered by Captain Xerint'a a hundred and fifty-eight years ago, when evading the Imperials—"

"You evaded Imperials? Aren't they supposed to be top-notch?" Sabrya strode to the other side of the droid. Unfazed by the recent incident, she still moved like a cat.

"Like us all, we have good and bad days. Maybe their AI at the time needed an upgrade?"

"And the delay? You were cutting it pretty fine back there," Alexis asked.

"As the 'hyper hiccup' had been done only the once, and by accident, I had to ensure the same exact conditions were in effect; that being the same velocity, power level, and even the proximity of the other vessels. For all we know, assuming they attempted to follow us as before—which is highly likely—their energy expenditure may have played a part in our success."

Alexis cocked her head to one side. "It worked this time... but Torg—" She leaned over the droid. "Don't *ever* attempt that maneuver again. That's an order."

"Affirmative, Captain." Torg continued to monitor the console. "The procedure has now been erased."

Alex resumed viewing the screen. "Where are we exactly? I'm no astronomer, so I don't recognize any of the star configurations."

"I have installed a subprogram that analyzes the star spectrum instantly upon the completion of any jump." Torg began assessing the data from the sensor array. "I will inform you of that in a few moments."

"In the meantime..." Bradyn got up and pulled a utility belt out of a compartment. "I need to move about, so what better time to check on the damage? What ship systems are you *not* interfaced with?" he asked the droid.

Bradyn's wrist-wrap chimed when Torg's list of the systems arrived a couple seconds later. He glanced down at it, scrolling through the register. "You do what you can with yours, and I'll head down to engineering and see what's shaken loose from this drocking bucket of bolts." He looked at Phillix, drooling slightly in the chair. "When he wakes, if he's up to it, send him down."

Sabrya was already up and picking mugs and plates. "I reckon he's just avoidin' the fraggin' domestics?"

"Possibly." Alexis grabbed a mop to clean the floor of spilled coffee. "But if we do any Crazy-Ivan space jumps again," she directed her voice to the droid, "we'll have another volunteer for domestics."

CHAPTER EIGHT

A VETERAN of a hundred short deployments across thirty-something star systems, Jabari knew most of a soldier's job was waiting.

Knowing that didn't make it any easier.

They'd waited days to reach Scipio's "stopover," and now that the scout ship had emerged from hyperspace, they still had several hours of sublight travel ahead of them. During the journey, *Pleiades-219* would approach the refueling station from below the star system's orbital plane and accretion disc.

Almost immediately, the ship's AI used a network of modified tractor beams to gather and assemble a screen of space rubble, arranging this screen in an arc around the bow. Now, as Jabari tracked its progress on his datapad, the AI sent the screen moving at high velocity, propelling it along a vector that would pass close to the fuel station, but not close enough to trigger any operational anti-meteor defenses. *Pleiades* then dropped in tight behind the rubble screen, hoping to bamboozle the aging station's scanners while it poked a single sensor cable through the rock and ice particles to provide itself with navigation data.

All through this, and for the long journey, there was literally nothing for the soldiers to do. To keep his mind occupied, Jabari paced his cabin, thinking about space station design. In the days of his youth, design had been trending back toward barrel- or carousel-types—giant constructs spun hard to approximate gravity using centrifugal force. The reason for that design trend had been primarily an economic one; such stations were cheaper to build and maintain. And for regions such as the one containing his homeworld, centuries of imperial neglect had led to hard economic times—until the Okalasi Kaan had launched their war.

Space stations, he thought. *Space stations.* They were often more straightforward venues for combat, easier to fight in. But sometimes, they held surprises. In combat, surprises could be deadly.

Leaning on a bulkhead, he called up the file images and text data on Rogers 22. The files showed it was only a little younger than Jabari, commissioned sixteen hundred and eighty-two years earlier, but it wasn't one of the cheaper barrel types. Rather, its engineers had created a central ring station with ten service spokes radiating outward, and the high foot traffic internal areas had been provided with artificial gravity.

There were five terraformed worlds within ten LY of Rogers 22, making it a perfect location to form an "economic cluster," as the empire had called them back in Jabari's day. A terrific region for pirates and crime gangs, and high on the modern empire's agenda for scouting and eventual reclamation.

But this star system was a long, *long* way from the Imperium's core.

And we're going past *it, headed rimward.*

Abandoning the files, he decided to make himself busy in body, since his thoughts kept drifting toward matters that depressed him. For the next few hours, he and his team played cards, kicked a football against a bulkhead, play-wrestled—

whatever they could do to find that balance between readiness and burning off nervous energy. Eventually, with two hours until arrival, the team drifted off into more introspective pursuits: prayer, reading, napping, and listening to music.

Jabari sat in the meal-room now, his head over his datapad, the ship's latest updated images of Rogers 22 on screen.

The station had been placed in high orbit around a gas giant's single moon since the moon was rich with fuel ore. The thing looked its age: worn, mistreated, and damaged. Each of its two-hundred-meter-long radial spokes bore a refueling berth at its end—and two of the berths were missing completely, sheared off by some earlier conflict, or perhaps by meteor strikes during periods when the station was unmanned and powered down. A chunk had also been torn from the inner torus. The torus looked like the kind of circle-buns Jabari's father used to bake, and the damage looked as if someone had taken a small bite. Presumably, that section of the station was sealed off from the area the current bandit occupants used. Apparently, the bandits didn't have the resources to repair it. Just as likely, they didn't have the need.

The ship's AI had labeled the station's fuel berths 1 through 10. The missing ones were 6 and 8. Scipio had identified 7 as their target, since imperial survey probe intel said the berth showed fuel reserves. It had power, but only trace atmo, very little air, and zero signs of recent use. All that indicated the other station spokes provided the bandits with enough for their purposes. Scipio had told him earlier that the station had no small fighter ships with which to attack *Pleiades*, nor did they have runabouts capable of ferrying defenders quickly around to Berth 7. That particular intel had *not* been copied to Jabari's pad, and Scipio had responded stiffly and dismissively when he'd requested it.

More than the waiting, Jabari hated the unknown. He was responsible for his people. He didn't need to be a hyperspace expert to know jump-fuel wasn't an explosion or fire risk; the processes used by hyperspace drives to convert it to energy required nothing as primitive as combustion. So, any hazards within the berth port wouldn't come from fuel. That didn't mean there weren't hazards, though. He perused the files again...

Berth 7 had been created for smaller ships like cargo haulers, migrant transports, surveyors, dispatch ships, or yachts. It comprised a sealable hangar bay that a ship entered at one end via a magnetic shield to keep the atmo inside and smaller space rocks outside. According to *Pleiades'* readouts, it currently had the power the reports had mentioned, enough certainly to maintain the magnetic entry shield. But the scans confirmed very thin levels of atmo inside. As the scout ship approached, Jabari knew Scipio—or more likely the AI—was setting its shields to a compatible frequency to pass on through into the hangar without resistance.

Since even the dumbest, cheapest bandits would own some form of scanner themselves, Jabari sent Scipio a message offering Shill's assistance with fooling those scanners. She could, he wrote, hack their systems the way a Ghrazhni sandfly bite prevented the victim's pain response. That way—just like the sandfly's victim—the station wouldn't know they were there until they were long gone. Careful not to alert the optio to just how adept Shill was, he claimed her expertise was only because the station was roughly from their era, and her coding skills would match its protocols and stylings. Scipio agreed, and Shill was allowed up in the command center to "discuss" the matter with *Pleiades'* AI.

When he felt there was no longer anything to be gained from flicking through the files and data updates, Jabari stood and engaged in a series of stretches. Fifteen minutes after that, Erkan came to get him for fit-out...

Several days ago, the soldiers had entered the scout ship through its cramped belly airlock. Shortly, they'd exit via a drop-ramp housed beneath its "chin." Jabari assembled his Proselyti in the muster compartment behind that ramp.

They'd dressed in comfortable bodystockings underneath their flexi-shell combat suits. The flexi-shells were a mottled gray with matte-black supply pouches glued or strapped around waists, across chests, and along thighs. For this mission, his team had forgone heads-up displays across their visors. Since light would be good, the Proselyti preferred to leave their field of vision uninterrupted. Instead, they'd either wind data-wraps over the left wrist of their suits, or strap their narrow datapads there. They'd armed themselves with Gutpuncher multi-rifles and VF-9 sidearms, loading the handguns with 12mm ballistic smartrounds. Suit pouches held spare mags, aid kits, and patch kits. The multi-rifles held secondary magazines of tiny HE "nub" grenades.

Otho and Avilius joined the Proselyti in the muster compartment. The two Corfid noncoms had kitted themselves out much the same—except for the lack of data-wraps around their wrists and the fact that they'd chosen slim-frame laser carbines as weapons.

Scipio remained in the cockpit after activating the combat droids; the centipede bot and the blocky, humanesque model JT-2090, which he'd nicknamed "Ninety." The hulking human-type had been stored in this compartment for the journey; now it simply waited at the back. A head taller than Jabari, and three times his width, it packed various tools and weapons systems around its thick arms and torso. The crawler had the designation Rec-7. Currently, it perched curled up on Ninety's shoulder.

The team's visors were currently flipped up, allowing Jabari to listen to real acoustics: the rattling of a loose chain as Otho brushed against it, the whir and whine of hydraulics and pump motors, the deeper rumble of the ship, and the mutter of Shill's prayers. A signal came through on his pad. He acknowledged it with the stroke of a finger, then gestured for Ninety to take a position closest to the closed exit ramp. The droid pushed through the small crowd of humans with surprising delicacy for a machine so large.

Facing the others, Jabari said, "Listen up."

Chins lifted. Shill's prayers choked off, and her beads went back in a suit pouch.

"We've separated from the debris screen, and we're on approach, sixteen hundred meters out. AI confirms frequency lock with the hangar bay's safety shield. Scans report 0.9 grav within the bay, and zero bio-signs there, or in the spoke leading up to it. We do this as we simulated it. Ninety goes in first and straight ahead to clear the far end of the bay. My squad stacks left; Erkan's stacks right. The crawler does... whatever it wants to. Zero bio-signs doesn't mean people aren't there or aren't on their way." As if in response to what he was saying, the ship trembled as something powerful impacted its shields. Lights flickered, and gravity went a little sideways for the briefest of moments, niggling at Jabari's gut.

"*Someone's* there," Tegenwe muttered. She had her left hand on her helmet, fingers drumming against the blue daffodil she'd painted on it.

"Automated asteroid defenses," Shill replied.

"There could be droids in that bay, firing outward," Tee added before Erkan whistled and gestured to focus on their leader again.

Jabari consulted his datapad. "Approaching mag shield. Ramp down in seventy seconds."

Despite Erkan trying to keep things on track and serious, Jabari's attention shifted to Tegenwe, and he allow himself a grin as he recalled the tradition she was known for. "Any last words, Private?"

"Keep your language clean, and your shooting cleaner. For the emperor's glory, of course," she added with a nod toward the Corfids. If either suspected sarcasm in that last comment, they didn't show it. Both men pressed fists to their sternums in honor of their revered head of state.

"Lock visors." Jabari turned, lowering his faceplate, and faced into Ninety's broad back. He wouldn't show it to the people behind him—especially not to Ortho and Avilius—but anxiety had his balls in a vice grip; it was making it difficult to fill his lungs.

A hundred missions, he thought. *I've survived a hundred* damn *times. Wazazi na walezi, give me another victory here. Me and my team.*

He forced suit air deep into his lungs, and held it for thirty before release, clamping both hands around his multi-rifle. The weapon wobbled a little in his grip. One of his hands had a tremor—where in the hells had *that* come from? He let go and slapped the fist against his suit, then reapplied his grip. The tremor was gone. Hopefully it stayed that way. Just the adrenaline, that was all.

Last thing I need is stasis sickness.

A mild bump and the brief klaxon bleat in his earpiece announced set down. The globe above the ramp shifted from red to blue, and the green safety field across the ramp housing dissipated with a sizzle.

"Ready!" he barked into his mic.

"*Ready!*" his fellow Proselyti chorused in confirmation. The Corfids were silent.

The ramp shuddered open a few centimeters, as if straining against something, then dropped fast to reveal a long hangar soaked in rusty light. The bay's wide central strip had been left free and clear for parking several ships, although *Pleiades-219* was the only one there. Hoses, bowsers, pipes, and ancient cargo crates cluttered the sides.

Ninety lumbered forward and down, pumping out energy pulses at a target off to his left. Something *zinged* off the droid's head before Jabari took his first step.

The droid fired again, then its voice rumbled in Jabari's helmet speaker, announcing, *"Hostile down!"*

Jabari lurched down the ramp, weapon up, catching sight of a smoking droid chassis sixty meters out across a low gantry. Putting it out of mind, he concentrated on the left side of the bay, knowing Erkan was already at his back and focusing right.

He sprinted away from *Pleiades*, angling toward a single-stacked line of containers half his height. A pedestrian entrance to the hangar was fixed into the bulkhead a hundred meters beyond the containers, a sealed double gate ten meters high and ten wide. He took a position at the containers, and three seconds later, Avilius reached his side. Shill and Morten had hooked back around the ship to guard the other direction. Berth 7's schematics had indicated no exit points along the right wall, and neither Scipio nor the AI were reporting any recent modifications to it, allowing Erkan, Otho, and Tegenwe to focus on the fueling apparatus forty meters off *Pleiades'* starboard hull.

"No contact forward," Jabari reported.

"None astern," Shill reported back.

"Nothing on scans," the optio added from the cockpit. "The hack into their database shows 58 percent fuel reserves in this bay."

And with Shill's coding trick, Jabari thought, *they shouldn't realize any of it's gone until we are.*

He glanced back and could just make out the pale oval of Scipio's face through the canopy. He focused forward again and climbed over the crates before heading for the double access gates. They led, he knew, to a large elevator that might bring hostiles up from the waystation torus if he was unlucky. Much smaller doors stood to either side of that lift, access to a ladder-well on one side, and a smaller staff elevator on the other. Jabari aimed his rifle at the further of the two, while Avilius focused on the closer. As the downed security droid attested, it didn't pay to take chances.

Ninety's broad chassis briefly blocked his view as the droid diverted toward the giant elevator. The centipede no longer perched on its shoulder, and Jabari couldn't see where it had gone. He imagined it was assessing threats further along the lengthy hangar bay, since an area designed to house four or more vessels the size of their scout ship could host plenty of nasty surprises.

A slim welding arm emerged from Ninety's shoulder, where the crawler had been. Beginning at the top of the join between gates, it welded them together. Once finished there, it would start on the smaller hatchways. After that, if it was necessary, the big machine could assist Erkan with the heavier aspects of the refueling job.

A glance across showed Jabari that Erkan's team was still assessing the pump equipment.

"Keep it moving, fueling team," Jabari growled into comms. "Let's not be here longer than we have to."

For a full minute, nothing happened, besides the activity of the droids. Then Scipio barked an alert from within the ship.

"Movement, twelve o'clock!"

Jabari faced down the hangar and away from the ship to see a burst of activity. Manhole covers flew into the air a hundred meters back, the heavy steel discs flicked up like tossed coins. Multilimbed objects boiled out of those holes, dozens of them, their bodies the size of footballs.

"Gnasher droids!" Avilius shouted beside him.

Jabari cursed. The Imperium had decommissioned this design a millennium ago, so either the bandits had found a surplus cache, or someone out here in the Wild Regions was manufacturing the damn things.

From the command center, Scipio reported an estimate numbering in the hundreds.

I can see that, Jabari thought as he poured energy pulses into their midst, leaning his hip against the cargo case for stability.

Avilius came around his right shoulder, joining him in the fight. Ninety rotated the top half of its torso without shifting its thick legs. There was just enough atmo in the chamber to carry the deep *thump* of the robot's anti-personnel cannons to Jabari's external suit mic, competing with the whine of his and Avilius' small arms. Gnashers dropped by the dozen, steaming, smoking, their limbs and pinchers thrashing. But more poured around and over the fallen, spreading wider now, making it harder to target many at once. Three shooters wouldn't be able to stop them all.

Jabari bawled, "Some help here!"

Briefly, the centipede appeared in the midst of the swarm, chewing up and tossing the smaller bots. Knowing the crawler was armored against small arms fire, Jabari forgot about averting his aim, continuing to spray fire along one flank of the bot swarm.

"Engaging!" Shill announced in reply to Jabari's cry for assistance.

Better late than never.

Laser fire spurted from Erkan's position, sporadic because the team's field of vision was interrupted by ship parts and pump stations populating the floor between them and the droids. Soon, the sustained attacks began to prevail; the pile of fallen bots looked like it might outnumber those still moving.

"Where the hype are they all coming from?" someone yelled on comms.

"No idea," Jabari replied, dropping the spent rifle mag and reaching for another. "Looks like we picked the wrong hangar."

Landing anywhere in the Wild Regions had been a gamble, but if the intel was as good as Scipio claimed, it should have mentioned the bandits owning gnashers.

"Above you!" two voices shouted suddenly in Jabari's speaker. On reflex, he danced backward, looking up in time to see six droids dropping from gantries high above.

Atilius remained unaware of the new danger, still picking at stray gnashers on the attackers' left flank.

"Mind your—" was all Jabari managed to shout before all six bots landed on the Corfid.

Their weight and momentum drove the man to his knees, then onto his back. Jabari couldn't turn energy fire on them without risking killing him, so he fast-switched his magazine to hard ballistic rounds. Avilius writhed beneath his attackers, thrashing at them with boots and fists and rifle frame. He let out one blood-curdling cry as Jabari got off his first few slugs. The volley picked one of the buggers off the fallen Corfid, but that was all. A moment later, Ninety swooped in and swept a mighty arm across them, scattering the remaining five to positions on the floor where it could nail them accurately with blaster rounds.

Avilius now lay exposed. On his back. Unmoving.

It was only when Jabari stepped closer that he realized Avilius no longer had a head.

CHAPTER NINE

"THESE WERE RETROFITTED—NOT part of the original construct." Bradyn climbed down the superstructure of the hyperdrives. "Like everything else on this drocking bucket of rivets."

"Is that a bad thing?" Phillix looked at the machinery apprehensively. In the earlier centuries, hyperdrive accidents had been numerous at first, but over time, much reduced. That didn't mean they still didn't happen.

A day had passed since they'd escaped the bounty hunters, and much had been learned by climbing and crawling through the bowels of the *Daemon*—none of it reassuring. Several mechanisms had been completely removed, leaving gaps between other components.

"She's still flying." Bradyn shrugged. "If it was faulty, this bird would have either never jumped in the first place, or disintegrated with all debris scattered through hyper, and we'd be sucking vacuum."

"More like vacuum would be sucking *us*."

Bradyn rolled his eyes. "You know what I drocking mean. Either way, whatever Torg did, this is fragged." He tossed a hunk of damaged alloy onto a nearby bench. "As for those missing bits, damn shoddy work. No doubt military parts taken during the ship's decommissioning."

Phillix nodded. "Wait, I'm sure I saw something like that on our list of cargo." He picked it up for closer inspection, turning it over in his hands. "Not charred, though."

"What, a spare hyperdrive conduit? Don't be ridiculous."

Putting the discolored component down, Phillix swiftly scrolled through the tablet with the inventory and showed him.

"Let's take a look." Bradyn browsed the list dubiously. It was the same list the droid had sent to his wrist-wrap. "How did we miss it?" He tapped the indicated entry, and an image of the unit—or part of it—appeared.

"*We* didn't. Don't forget, the other refugees helped. Then all hell broke loose when we had the bounty hunters on our tail before we left the system. It was probably overlooked in the rush before we landed on Plorian."

Bradyn growled. "A drocking stupid and foolish oversight. Once this is repaired, I'm going through that damn list again myself, item by item. Let's get to the Alpha cargo hold."

Leaving the ship's drive section, the pair of technicians wandered forward along the central corridor, passing several compartments used for cargo of different sizes. An overhead crane, its rail starting from the front airlock, reached all the way to the aft compartments, allowing easy shifting of even the heaviest machinery.

The "hammer" design of the craft was pragmatic, if unorthodox; the bridge, crew's quarters, storage, engineering, and electronics controls were all housed within the "head." It was capable of complete separation if required, complete with its own subspace drives. Individual cargo holds made up the bulk of the vessel's length, with fuel and drives—both subspace and hyper—at the far end.

"Alpha hold—here she is."

"The inventory specified Alpha 2 hold," Phillix said. "That's on the second level of—"

"You do know I've worked on a few drocking ships in my time?" Bradyn looked at the electrician.

"I... of course. Just a habit of mine."

"Hmmm. This could be a tedious trip," Bradyn muttered as he started up the ladder.

<hr>

"So, not a whole hyperdrive unit." Bradyn walked around what was left of a similar-looking drive. Even with the inventory, it had taken thirty minutes to locate the part in question. "I'll take this unit apart and scavenge what's needed. It should fit, even though it's a newer version."

"Perhaps that's why it's here? Why the rest of this junk is here, as spares for all the other bits of kit. Look at this place. Other than the hull—as far as we know—there are so damn many addons, it's sort of hard to work out what was here originally."

"Drocking tell me about it!" Bradyn waved his arms about. "It's not what many would do, but it makes sense—if you have too few stellars to buy, but enough storage to hold it all." Bradyn eyed the other parts while he was here. "I haven't had the time to go through every crawlspace, but we better."

"We?"

"You may realize, not everything on here is drocking mechanical." Bradyn slapped him lightly on the back, sending Phillix stumbling. "Sorry." He helped him up. "Electronics, my boy. I'm wagering the components Torg isn't interfaced with are also addons, and that's where you come in—you and your gizmo."

"I'll have you know, this *gizmo* as you call it, is a state-of-the-art prosthetic hand and forearm designed specifically for my craft." He showed the range of built-in devices.

"Exactly. Gizmo. That wasn't a criticism." Bradyn winked and walked to the stairs. "I'm surprised they let you keep it if it was worth so much. Would it cover what you owed? You could've avoided drocking slavery."

"It would have, but the biotech makes it uniquely compatible with my DNA only. Besides, very few people knew about it, unless I showed them." Once the devices were retracted, the arm looked like a normal arm. "I've been very secretive about it."

Bradyn nodded in approval. "Let's get back and report to Alexis. Tell her the good news."

"You like her as a leader? As our captain?" Phillix asked as they made their way from the storage compartment tucked in behind the command section.

Bradyn shrugged, considering an answer. "She's likable enough. She listens to people and makes a decision—not always what she wants to do, though. And she's stepped up to take the position. You want it?"

"Me?" Phillix balked at the top of the ladder.

Bradyn barked a deep laugh. "It's okay, Phillix. I wasn't putting you up for consideration. Like me, you prefer to be working with your hands—or hand," he jibed, "not ordering others. Different strokes and all..."

"What about Sabrya?"

Back in the main corridor, they strode the short distance forward to the lift to take them up the three levels to the bridge.

Bradyn tapped the button. "She doesn't seem interested and would sooner slice the head off anyone she was vexed with, which tends to reduce crew morale. I think she's right where she wants to be. Not quite in charge, but not fighting for faceless, corrupt sponsors... again."

Alexis and Sabrya were on the bridge under Torg's guidance, familiarizing themselves with the various controls. They were looking over the navigation console when the desk beeped.

"That would be the finalized survey results." The droid called the data up on the computer monitor. "It would appear the exact required conditions of the previous hyper hiccup were not met. I can only assume this was an anomaly with the pursuing ships' drives, as everything on our end was in spec: velocity, gravitational forces, angular momentum, approximate distance of the other craft, and the amount of power delivered to the drives before cutout."

"How fraggin' reassurin'. Even droids have to blame others," Sabrya commented.

"Simply stating facts—"

"That looks like the Perseus Arm." Alexis referred to the map displayed on the nav console. The indicated area showed thousands of stars, highlighting the more prominent. When a star icon was tapped, relevant details popped up in a sidebar, including a short history, if known. "And I was supposed to be —" she expanded the map "—there."

Sabrya and the droid looked closer.

"The Vladmarin-Xiar System? What's there?"

"Sylvanus Colony."

"That was three decades ago? Never heard of it. What about you, Metalhead?"

"The Vladmarin-Xiar System is a tri-star system, but there is no indication of a colony, or in fact anything other than some barren, high-G exo-planets. It is in close proximity to the Shadow Nebula—cosmically speaking."

"Yes, that's right." Alexis zoomed in to check the data of each of the three stars in the system: V-X33A, V-X33B, and V-

X33C. "Niviaris is orbiting V-X33B." Nothing regarding terraforming appeared, let alone any mention of a colony.

"There's plenty of references to the discovery of the system back in 3999CY."

"We are 170 lightyears from where I intended," Torg confirmed, "and 186 from the V-X System. Coincidentally, this area puts us closer to where you were found." The droid manipulated the chart by spreading his hands above the surface. Built-in sensors noted the hand movement and enlarged the indicated area when he pointed to where a blue icon blinked slowly. "This is our current location." He then moved his hand to another area, and the map centered itself. "And this is where we found your pod's signal." He tapped the screen.

A brief note appeared, detailing time of visit and what was found.

5122CY, July 20. Found debris after weak emergency signal detected. Vessel name *Octavia*; very few remnants. Must have been adrift for years. Salvage was basically worthless. Bodies in stasis pods found.

"It says 'bodies.' I thought I was the only one?" Alexis went pale. *Did they leave someone behind?*

"The only *surviving* one is more accurate," Torg stated.

Sabrya punched the droid's shoulder. "Good one, tinpot."

I need to go there and find out who... Alexis controlled her emotions. "Was any of this signaled to authorities?"

"It was not a priority of Captain Jenna, nor the previous captains, to notify authorities of any of his activities, unless it was to claim a finder's fee."

Alexis leaned on the counter, breathing deeply.

"You all right?" Sabrya asked, moving closer to her.

"Increased heart and respiratio—"

"I wasn't askin' you," the fighter snapped at the droid. "Don't you have a ship's system to probe?"

Torg stayed silent.

Alexis nodded. "I'm okay." She straightened her back and paced around the console, thinking. "That's, what, almost... 73 LYs away?"

"72.67 lightyears," Torg corrected.

Sabrya looked surprised. "That's accurate guesswork... for a fraggin' *botanist.*"

"It's complicated." Alexis stopped beside Torg. "Can this ship get there?"

"Get where?" Bradyn said from the elevator as he stepped out.

As Phillix exited, there was an electrical short-circuit, causing the lift doors to slam closed.

"Crap!" Phillix jumped forward to avoid being squashed, bumping into the stocky engineer. He lost his balance, but Bradyn reached quickly out to steady him. They both turned to see the elevator open and close several more times.

"You better fix that with your gizmo before it takes your other arm off, or worse, mine." Bradyn grinned at Sabrya and Alexis.

Muttering under his breath, Phillix began investigating the fault as the others grouped around the console. Alexis told them where they were, where she wanted to go, and why.

"I understand completely why you'd want to go there." The engineer scratched his face. "It's possible, but only after repairs and adjustments. Until then, the hyperdrives are offline."

"Traveling at subspace speed, it would take us over a hundred years to reach the nearest planet," Phillix muttered from the elevator door.

"You can fix it?" Alexis asked Bradyn hopefully.

"I can try. Apparently, this tub is hauling spare parts in the cargo holds." He showed her the item on the inventory. "Right under our drocking noses."

"That seems... fortunate. How long will the repairs take?"

Bradyn shrugged. "With Torg's assistance, it could be done in a week or so."

"A week?"

"Now she's talkin' like a botanist." Sabrya smiled to take the sting out of her words.

"We aren't talking about servicing a land skimmer, here." He shook his head slowly, like talking to a child. "Hyperdrives are a very complex piece of kit. The only reason I'm even attempting to do it is I've worked on one of these before, years ago, but it wasn't this model."

Alexis chuckled. "Sorry. Of course. I'm sure you know what you're doing. What if Phillix helps?"

"Then it'd be two weeks."

"I heard that," Phillix grumbled from the elevator.

"Nice one." Sabrya chuckled with Bradyn. "All those spare parts—is that what Brutus meant by old relics?"

"Reckon so. Looks like the junk here has been scavenged over time to retrofit whatever was needed, adapting what they could."

"Hence why the stuff is still here and not traded—"

"Or spaced."

"I can confirm, once this vessel was decommissioned and then subsequently purchased, many of the captains utilized this practice. At the time, there were few spares available for this particular craft, so they reverted to extreme measures and began scouring space, starting with areas of previous battles. Understandably, the findings were rare, but once a piece of cargo was found, it was stripped to its basic components; anything usable was stored, and anything else was sold. Nothing was wasted."

Once the elevator was repaired, Phillix joined them by the nav console and scrutinized it.

Torg continued, "No opportunity for gaining a few extra stellars was missed until Captain Jenna came along. He didn't have the same outlook. His method was more... direct and violent."

"We call it stealing. How many captains has the *Daemon* had?"

"Nineteen since its purchase, but it was not always called the *Daemon*. In keeping with imperial naming conventions, the original name was Latin, in this case the *Malleus*. The first non-military owner was Lord Darke from Augustus 4 in Sector 19; he changed the name to *Daemon*. He was a nobleman, though minor, and not overly popular. I believe he named the ship as a bit of a joke regarding his name, though my understanding of humor is limited. That was back in 4988CY, before my time—"

"Before your time? You weren't fraggin' commissioned with the ship?" Sabrya asked.

Phillix nodded. "I was wondering the same. You have too many blank periods of time leading to inconsistencies in the data you provide."

As he had with Alexis, Torg explained that his initial inter-facing with the *Daemon* had occurred well after the decommis-sioning. "I joined in 5005, during Captain Xerint'a's command."

"How long was the *Daemon* derelict before she was purchased?"

"Let's do the math," Phillix offered. "Officially decommis-sioned in 4702; Darke had it in 4985—two hund—"

"We can count." Bradyn yawned.

Alexis cleared her throat. "The ship is 420 years old; it was derelict for 283 years until Darke bought it; Torg has been on her for 117 years."

"Okay." Sabrya stood up and faced her. "First off, you know far too much about captainin' and ship things for a fraggin' botanist, and then you start doin' astral navigation in your head. What aren't you tellin' us?"

"Easy, Sab—"

"You know, don't you?" Sabrya turned to the engineer.

"My ship, the *Octavia*, was attacked twenty-six years ago," Alexis started. "I was knocked unconscious. Someone—probably my partner—put me in his stasis pod. He was the assistant XO."

The fighter turned back to listen, her irritation at the engineer forgotten.

"You had command officer subliminal training all that time?" Phillix shook his head. "Your head must be *pounding*."

"I'm coping."

"That explains why it's easy for you to take charge." Sabrya relaxed. "And your partner?"

"I lost him. Everyone I knew." Alexis looked down to study the charts again.

"Sorry," Sabrya said softly, then looked at the others, at a rare loss for words.

"It was over two decades ago." Alexis shrugged.

Torg was standing motionless, like a droid. Bradyn had leaned against another table, looking down at his feet.

"Did they remove the original AI?" Phillix asked, breaking the growing silence.

"From here?" Alexis said after a deep breath. "They would have. No way the military would allow any of their AIs to get into civilian hands. Same with armaments and classified systems."

"Which explains those drocking missing sections we found." Bradyn shared a look with Phillix.

"Back then," Torg added, "much of the decommissioning process was done via contractors, keeping military personnel available for deployment, and not tied up in mundane tasks."

"Contractors! That explains the shoddy work," Bradyn grouched. "No one thought to bring in another drocking AI?"

"No doubt too expensive to fit out," Phillix suggested.

"But they had enough for Torg? High-grade ship droids aren't cheap."

"Who said anything about high-grade?" Sabrya joked, relieved the awkward moment was now behind them.

"I was not purchased; I, too, was salvaged." The droid told them of the research vessel he'd been found on.

After a swig of water from her flask, Alexis cleared her throat. "Back to the business at hand; there are bounty hunters after us, and we're sitting demoleans—even if we're over a hundred lightyears off course. While the hyperdrive is being repaired, we have the opportunity to change the ship's name and ID again. Anyone got any ideas?" She glanced around at the blank faces.

"How about *Hammer*?" Bradyn suggested.

Alexis looked unsure. "It does resemble one..."

"If I may suggest, *Malleus* is Imperial True for hammer."

"You like that name?" Alexis asked the droid.

"Considering its configuration—and Bradyn's choice—I felt it was apt, and you did ask," Torg replied.

"He has a point," Phillix added. "I'm comfortable with it. Sort of coming full circle, renaming it after all these years. Besides, I think it's bad luck to rename a ship once it's been commissioned."

"You didn't strike me as superstitious." Sabrya looked at him in surprise.

The electronics technician reddened, more out of embarrassment than anger.

"Phillix," Alexis turned to the electronics tech, "since you've fixed the damned elevator door, that's your next task; changing the transponder code and anything else that would identify this vessel as anything other than the *Malleus*. Torg might be able to help, if there are any military protocols still embedded in the system." She focused on the itinerary again, only vaguely recognizing some items. "I should take a closer look at all this. Maybe there's something there from the *Octavia*. I was still out of it when they found me. Maybe they grabbed other stuff I don't know about." She had no clue if they did, but anything would be better than nothing. *Surely there were other salvageable items.*

Is that it? After an hour, Alexis finished climbing around cargo hold Charlie 2. A few items—too few—were secured to the deck. She noticed a section of a maneuvering thruster had scorch marks indicating intense heat.

"Torg, can you see this?" She had activated the cam on her datapad and brought the piece into range.

"I can," Torg confirmed a second later. "You may not recall, but when we first spoke, I had established through spectrographic analysis that the damage was caused by a plasma cannon."

She nodded, remembering. "And you're sure everything salvaged from the *Octavia* was brought to this storage unit?"

"I am absolutely certain."

Alexis signed off, sat on the edge of the escape pod she'd found, and held her head in her hands. Even though the incident had happened over two decades ago, it had only been a week for her, subjectively. It was still too new, too raw... She wiped her eyes as she heard Bradyn climbing up the stairs to join her.

"Any luck?" he asked. If he saw her tears, he didn't comment.

"Just these." She sniffed and indicated various components of a dark alloy. "And this escape pod has the *Octavia* emblem on the side."

"Empty? I mean... any sign it had..."

"No body, you mean? It looks pristine. Unused."

Bradyn looked abashed. "Sorry. Stupid question."

She shrugged.

"That looks like unusual damage." He picked up the scorched component. "No fire did this. Probably a plasma cannon or similar. See the slag on the edge? Your ship was attacked."

"That's what Torg said. Great minds and all..."

Bradyn grimaced. "Now I'm thinking like a drocking ancient tin can."

"Or he's thinking like a human."

"Torg, how long do you estimate it'll take to jump there?"

After a couple tedious days spent going over the items in the holds, Alexis had ventured to the bridge after supper. Phillix was already there, working on a console, with Bradyn looking over his shoulder. "No one else checking the inventory?" Alexis asked rhetorically.

"Forty-nine hours and thirty-seven minutes," the droid answered. "We should be able to do it in one jump."

"That seems pretty quick." Once again, she examined the star charts on the nav consol.

"Much of the hyping is done in small jumps until a region is known and charted. Only then would a larger jump be advisable. I am confident in the calculations for several reasons: the hyperdrive is in far better condition with Bradyn's work, our tarrying here has enabled me to take precise readings of the local space, and we've been to this destination before."

"Any idea why Jenna was way out here? Is the area of any significance?"

"There is a cache of a fragmented recording mentioning a battle in the vicinity." Torg highlighted an area roughly 3LY further rimward of the area where she'd been rescued.

"A battle for what?" Alexis studied the area, finding nothing of enough importance to warrant a battle. It was void for many lightyears.

"That is unclear, as the one record is incomplete. Either no further transmissions were received, or it was redacted. From the language and idioms used, the most experienced historians feel it involved an imperial ship, or ships, but nowhere else is such a fleet ever mentioned."

"I'm assuming the former. If the record was redacted, I doubt there'd be any mention of an imperial fleet, especially involving a battle they lost," Alexis noted. "And who were they fighting way out here?"

"You mentioned historians. How old is it?" Sabrya asked. She'd been on watch and was taking the opportunity to do pull-ups on a ladder. "Where did this fraggin' record come from?"

"There's a cache? From pre-decommissioning?" Phillix's interest picked up.

"I thought everything military was removed?" Sabrya said.

"Shoddy contractors," Bradyn surmised in disgust. "Wouldn't know a drocking backup drive from a hyperdrive."

"To answer your question as to the age, we are looking at anything from fifteen hundred to two thousand years ago."

Bradyn whistled.

"I'm curious how they managed to work that out, considering the record's so fragmented. Was it a corrupted file? Perhaps if I could access it, I might be able to reveal something else." Phillix was leaning forward in his chair.

"I can forward you a copy if you wish," the ship's droid offered.

Phillix shook his head. "A copy will only record what you have. I want to find what you *haven't*. I'll need the original, if there's any hope of digging into the corrupted data. In fact, I'll need the actual cache—analyzing the original hardware could also reveal something vital."

"Captain?"

Alexis was engrossed in the charts until Sabrya nudged her. "That's you."

"Will you grant authorization for Phillix to access the original cache?"

"What? Of course," she said after the briefest consideration. "As far as I'm concerned, we're all in this together. We have different backgrounds, experiences, and knowledge bases; anything and everything could be pertinent to our survival. Everyone here can have access to whatever they need."

"Great." Phillix rubbed his hands together. "Torg, if you could point me in the direction of the cache location, I'll get straight to it."

"You sure you don't want to join us in crawling over every component in the holds?" Alexis asked. "We still have Charlie 3 to Delta 4 to go."

"Actually... no." Phillix grinned as he headed to his cabin, a gleam in his eye.

CHAPTER TEN

"IT WAS SHIT INTEL. It was a shit mission. This is *all* grunfer-shit." Tegenwe was the only one up and pacing around the sparring room, and her thoughts continued to spill out of her head in a muttered stream.

"What are we *doing* out here? This is hell. This is our gods-damned hell. Assigned to centuries of punishment for the sin of wanting a better galaxy for all humans everywhere. While the Kaana may have been ruthless, at least *she* knew how to equip and prep her armies properly. The Okalasi knew how to do intel."

They'd been speeding away from Rogers 22 for four hours now, returning to the jump point. They were showered, fed, and dressed again in their travel fatigues. The other Proselyti sat in a rough circle in the middle of the square room's blue matting. Shill chewed her lip and watched Tee pace. Morten hugged his knees, resting his head on his arms, demonstrating just how supple he was, even in middle age. Erkan had been as silent as Morten since the short battle in the fueling bay, his face set like stone.

And Jabari—well, Jabari had watched a man lose his head

right in front of him and had nearly been overrun, too. Jabari found himself in a very bad mood, indeed.

Tegenwe poked Morten with a toe as she passed him. "Give me something, brother. You gotta be as angry as me. You gotta have something to say about this. That could've been your head chewed to slag back there. Or his. Or his. Or hers..." She pointed.

Grudgingly, Morten uncurled and performed ten terse signs before dropping his hands to the mat.

Shill translated, "Whatever emperor is in power, their commanders always send *us* to do the worst jobs."

"Fah!" Tegenwe spat, maintaining her angry pacing until it brought her around the room and close to Jabari. "We're one shooter down, and we're not even at our target destination. If this is the emperor's mission, why didn't the *Maelstrom's* commanders fuel us properly to begin with?"

"That's the big question in my mind."

Jabari's quiet words silenced Tee, and she stopped to face him. He glanced toward the room's sealed hatch. No one could hear them in here—Shill had made sure of that by frying the compartment's bugs—but it always felt risky, saying things like that aloud.

He continued, voice low and teeth clenched, "It's mind games and misinformation. Scipio wants us to believe the Imperium *still* hasn't recovered enough to fuel its scout ships fully. He wants us to think the *Maelstrom* couldn't spare the resources—even though it's the 'emperor's will.' *And* he wants us to believe the landing on Rogers 22 was fuel related. I absolutely don't think it was."

"What other reason would he have for stopping there?" Shill asked. "It's not like we took anything but fuel."

"Didn't we?" Jabari narrowed his eyes at her. "You're the coding specialist. You don't think it's possible that while we were out there, distracted by gnashers, he was sitting in the command center hacking Rogers' computer core for something?"

"Intel," Tegenwe growled. "The gut-maggot wanted intel."

"*Fresh* intel," Jabari agreed.

"Bastard knew what we were headed into," Erkan murmured, picking at a spot on the mat.

Jabari took a long breath in and out, leaning back on his hands. "Maybe, maybe not. He probably took a calculated risk."

"With our lives."

"No argument there."

Tegenwe snorted derisively. "Then the idiot lost one of his own damned Corfids in the process."

Jabari nodded. "But he got his data. Data he couldn't get from anywhere else, apparently." He caught Shill's eye. "You know what to do next."

"I've been doing it every spare moment I have, boss man. He's got the AI wired tighter than I expected. But I'm close."

"Close isn't close enough. Get it done."

She scratched an ear. She seemed about to say more when the hatch unzipped into the bulkheads, and the man himself stood there. Scrutinizing their guilty expressions, he said, "A strange place to find you all. Especially when you don't seem to be sparring."

Belatedly, all those sitting rose and faced him at attention.

Jabari asked, "How's Corporal Otho, sir?"

Scipio hadn't moved from the passageway. He placed his hands behind his back and said, "If you're asking whether he's upset or angry over the death of a comrade, he's not. Corporal Otho is perfectly fine. Corporal Otho understands the sacrifice required, and the sacrifice Avilius made. What happened, happened in service of empire and emperor."

"Yes, sir."

"I came to tell you your courage under fire didn't go unnoticed. Nor did your efficiency in getting the ship refueled. I've ordered Otho to take a prolonged off-duty period, and I want the rest of you to do the same. You've earned a full thirty-six-hour break from drills and exercise, and new commendations for your records."

"Very generous, sir," Tegenwe said. Her tone was professionally neutral, but Jabari caught the tremor in her voice as she fought her emotions.

If Scipio heard it, he ignored it. He said, "We'll hit the jump point soon, so we press on." For the next few minutes, he lapsed into a long discourse about the importance of bolstering "civilization."

The longer the optio spoke, the harder Jabari had to fight down his mounting rage. His team, he knew, fought their own hot emotions.

He interrupted, "Sir. A word outside?"

Scipio froze midsentence, then said, "With me."

Rather than allowing the conversation to take place in the corridor, Scipio took Jabari along it, down a ladder, and into his tight, sparsely decorated cabin. There, he finally faced his subordinate.

"Yes?"

"Sir, your intel on the waystation was wrong. It didn't allow for the possibility of so many enemy droids in such close proximity with such rapid response capability."

"That intel was the best at hand. I was forced to rely on stealth probe scans. After all, out here, we *are* beyond the reach of normal—"

"'Out here' and moving *further* out," Jabari interrupted. "Further from reliable intel and support. Sir."

Scipio lifted his chin. "What of it?"

"Our mission takes us into dangerous territory."

A quiet snort. "What mission doesn't?"

Jabari could think of plenty but didn't list them. The question was a sidetrack, a deflection. "We're professional soldiers,

Optio. We want to do things properly, with decent resourcing and decent prep. I hate to put it this way, sir, but I've been alive a lot longer than you, and I've experienced—"

For the first time, emotion darkened the flesh across Scipio's cheeks and drew his lips back from his teeth. "You've been *alive* longer than me? Is *that* what you said, Lieutenant? You were perhaps about to explain that you're more experienced than me. A veteran. Check the inside of your forearm. Check your tattoo. You've been around, *subjectively*, about the same amount of time as me, biologically speaking. If you think you know about *professional* preparation for battle, well then, so do I. If you think you've seen action, so have I. There are actions, and campaigns, and entire *wars* that began and ended while you slept through them. Slept! Of those campaigns, I fought in twelve. And yes, all came *after* Private Tegenwe was returned to stasis the last time." He lifted the edge of his tunic to reveal a band of pale-skinned belly. "You see this burn scar? A trophy of the Mahemo Economic Uprising. The slight imperfection in my right eye? That's because it's low-grade cybernetic augment. I left the real one back on Kingston Prime, after a mad god-lover skewered it with a dirk."

Jabari kept his shoulders back and his fists hidden behind him. "Sir, I'm merely saying that successful military missions *aren't* successful when they lose the operatives involved in them. They require careful preparation, careful organization, well-rounded resourcing, and support. I'm not insulting your—"

Scipio cut him off again, his teeth clenched as he spoke through them. "And I'm saying we're as prepared and resourced and *organized* as we can be under the circumstances."

"We left the *Maelstrom* without sufficient fuel."

Let's see you defend your lie, you slagger.

"Because our commanding officers deemed that fuel was needed elsewhere, and we could resupply en route."

"En route to *where?* Optio, we don't even know what our objectives are."

"You'll be briefed as you need to know. As I already told you."

"That's highly irregular in any century. You gave us a day-and-a-half's break from drilling, but we don't know what we're drilling *for*."

"You're prepping for eventualities. High-G combat, zero-G combat, hatch breaching and compartment clearing, ship-to-ship dives, droid engagement..."

Jabari wasn't getting through—he really wasn't—but he had to try. The welfare of his people depended on it. So, he tried a different approach. "Sir, we just lost Avilius. If you're the only one onboard with knowledge of the mission's parameters and objectives, what happens if *you* die?"

One of Scipio's eyes ticked momentarily. The real eye. "That something you've been prepping for, Lieutenant? That what you were all discussing in the sparring room?"

"Of course not! I merely..."

He paused a moment while wondering if this was the reason Scipio was keeping his intel from them, to keep himself alive. Was the man scared a crew of Proselyti might murder him and steal his ship?

"Sir, in seventeen centuries, has any *Proselyte* ever given cause for such a fear? We've sworn fealty to empire and emperor. I've personally proven that loyalty on many, many occasions. What other life do we have, apart from serving the human race, and creating peace again for the galaxy? I want this mission to be successful—but I also want my soldiers to return alive. That's the only reason I'd like better intel on what we're facing and why."

As quickly as he'd heated up, Scipio cooled. He side-stepped, dropped into a chair, and crossed one leg over the other. "Your requests are noted. I've no intention of throwing your lives away, if that's your concern. It does the empire no good to squander well-blooded troopers. The one thing I'll tell you now is, we have several more days of travel ahead."

Ah, Jabari thought with a spark of realization. *The data he got from the waystation confirmed our destination.*

"Meanwhile," Scipio continued, "I expect you to follow orders. From the point at which your rest period is over, your standing orders are to maintain your fire team at combat readiness."

Jabari straightened his back and stared over the officer's head at the wall. "Yes, sir."

"I expect you've already decided the next drills will be anti-combat-droid ones?"

Jabari ground his teeth. "Indeed, sir."

"Excellent thinking. Anything more?"

"No, sir."

Scipio rotated the chair to face a table and opened a paper book there, the Cor Fidelis holy book *Cor ad Imperatores Pertinet.* Jingoistic fraugle shit, the whole book. Jabari had picked up a copy from a dead Corfid's kit once and read the stupid thing in the days he'd had to wait for evac.

Scipio said, "Then you're dismissed."

On his way back to the sparring room, Jabari decided he was getting tired of useless conversations with the optio.

But what choice do I have? I'm a soldier. He's my commanding officer.

"Oh, I have choices," he muttered as he climbed the ladder.

If it came to that—and despite what he'd told the optio—the man wouldn't be the first CO in history to meet with an unfortunate accident.

CHAPTER ELEVEN

AFTER HOURS of climbing over and through the ship to become more familiar with it, Alexis ventured back to the galley for a break and some food. She grabbed one of the nutribars and headed to check on the bridge with a flask of water.

"How's it looking out there? No bounty hunters pinging us?" she asked as she stepped quickly out of the lift. Phillix did a good job at repairing what he could, but after seeing the state of some of the ship's other compartments, she was doubtful of how long the previous ad hoc repairs would last.

Torg was manning the control panel and, as a practice that was becoming habitual, Sabrya was doing chin-ups in the corner, preferring to use the bridge to conduct her exercises.

"Our sensors are not detecting any other traffic, if that is what you mean. I would immediately notify you otherwise."

"Good news. Is that because of the ship's new transponder ID?" Alexis asked. *I better remember to thank Phillix for that.*

"Not in this case. Apart from our remoteness, the ship's transponder is switched off. We only use it when approaching an orbital or planetary body."

"Why's that?"

"The previous captains were reluctant to let their location be known, except when absolutely necessary. That is the protocol currently in place."

"Now that we're no longer the *Daemon*, we have nothing to hide, so change it back to proper protocols," Alexis ordered.

"Isn't the transponder ID also partly for navigational safety?" the fighter asked.

Alexis looked at her with a surprised smile. She'd known soon after their departure from Ieoni Orbital that Sabrya felt out of place. Phillix was an extraordinary tech, and Bradyn did amazing things with machinery that had already seen hundreds of years of work and abuse, but the famous bringer-of-death and creator of mayhem, known to some as the Reaper, felt like a burden on a spaceship.

"What? Did you think I couldn't fraggin' read?" Sabrya said upon seeing her look. "Since I'm a loose wheel here with no particular skills other than rippin' heads off people, I've been goin' through the manuals. Got to earn my keep." Sabrya finished her exercise and strode over, wiping her body down with a towel. "Nothin's free." Her tone dropped lower on the last words, and her eyes briefly took on a distant look.

"You've already earned it." Alexis put her hand on Sabrya's bare shoulder, noticing the exudation of oily sweat. "We wouldn't be here without your special skills."

"You are correct," Torg answered her previous question. "Once the AIs detect our signal on waystations in range, they will insert our trajectory into their navigational logs. That data is instantly relayed to adjacent waystations, which in turn ensures safe passage for other ships jumping in or through the system." Torg deftly manipulated a keypad. "It is done. The new *Malleus* ID is now available for interrogation."

"Isn't the role of a ship's droid to make sure the ship is safe and adherin' to all intergalactic safety regulations?" Sabrya questioned. "Nobody wants to collide with another ship in hyperspace."

"Or anywhere for that matter," Alexis added.

"You forget, I am not technically a ship's droid, and I am interfaced with only a minimum of the ship's systems. Besides, at the velocity a spaceship travels, it is such that we would not be aware of any collision."

"Listen, Tinpot, that's not the fraggin' point," the fighter said.

"Hey, Torg, I need a break," Alexis intervened. "Are you able to continue this inventory for me? I'm sure Sabrya and I can manage here."

"Of course, Captain." He took the tablet from her and made his way to the elevator, his left leg dragging slightly.

Captain. She'd have to get used to people calling her that one day. "Remind me to ask Bradyn to look at Torg's knee," she said to Sabrya.

"Sure thing, boss."

Alexis continued to chew her nutribar quietly.

"Got to finish my set." Sabrya stood, tossed the towel on a chair, and proceeded to do more chin-ups. She noticed Alexis watching her. "I'll go crazy if I don't keep in shape."

"Your shape's fine," Alexis said unthinkingly until she heard Sabrya chuckle. "That was a compliment, not an advance. How did you get into it? The Surreal Tournament, I mean."

"Just unlucky. Wrong place, wrong time," she said vaguely while exercising. There was no strain in her voice.

"Is that oily sweat part of your enhancements?" She wiped her hand on the discarded towel.

"Enhancements? That's a funny way of puttin' it." She dropped to the floor and collected the towel when Alexis handed it to her. "I wasn't asked. It was a means to an end that helps me survive in the tourney."

"Sorry. I have no idea about you. Didn't they use clones in the tourney?"

Sabrya dabbed at her face. "Tell you what, we'll go head-to-head with push-ups. If you can keep up, I'll tell."

"Really? I'd be lucky to do five."

"Didn't you say your genetics were modified for high-G?"

"True, but that's raw strength—pushups are more for stamina."

"Your call."

Alexis thought about it for a moment. "I guess I could do with some exercise. It's been a couple decades since I did anything physically demanding."

"Except throwin' my weight over a four-meter wall into the crowd."

"I had help, and we were all fueled by adrenaline."

They found space on the floor. Alexis mimicked the positioning of Sabrya's arms.

"Straighten your back," the fighter instructed. "You're not a bridge. Ready? One... two..."

At first, Alexis' timing was off and slow, but she picked up a rhythm and continued at the pace set.

"Forty-nine... fifty. Not bad, Captain."

"I'm surprised myself. Is that it?"

"Sure. Unless you want to go again?"

"I'll pass." Alexis rolled over onto her back and breathed heavily. "Does that mean I get to hear your story now?"

"Some. I need a drink first." The fighter flipped up and headed for the galley. She returned shortly and leaned on the nav console. Alexis was up and checking the control panel. Sabrya took a swig and started. "My father wasn't the best educated, but he was a good brawler and wrestler. When he didn't have a bout—which was once or twice a tenday—he worked shifts at the mines. Mum was very ill with Schneider Disease, and medical issues put us in debt. The wrestlin' didn't cut it, so my father worked double shifts, even did time in the spaceport, but it still wasn't enough..." She paused as she swallowed more water. "Bills were due. They were goin' to take me, put me to work—"

"Surely not in the mines?"

"That would've been preferable. No, this was sex work."

"Oh. How old were you?"

"About thirteen. Anyway, when they fraggin' grabbed me, my father fought them. He did a lot of damage, too, but there were six of them. They beat him up bad and took me away."

"And your mother?"

"She died a month later, so I heard. It's common. Some get by; some people are more susceptible to it. That's why we were in debt. Anyway, I still managed to put three in hospital—"

"At thirteen?"

"Dad taught me some fightin' techniques. Long story short, considerin' my attitude, they decided I was more suited to conflict, so they trained me as a fighter instead. If I wasn't any good, there was always the original plan—or so they thought. I trained hard with one thing on my mind."

"Revenge?"

"You bet. Two years after they took me, my backer and I came to an understandin' on the proviso that if I'd fight in the tourney, he'd release me so I could find each of the thugs and exact my revenge." She stopped to see the look of shock on Alexis' face. "My dad died of his injuries. I had no family to go back to. As far as I was concerned, I had nothin' to live for and nothin' to lose. I was definitely not goin' to the sex farm. I was prepared to die and take as many as I could with me. It's surprisin', the risks you'll take when you've lost everythin'."

"Did you escape?"

"Escape? Are you kiddin'? I was still a kid... and I'd made a promise. Then my trainin' got really serious. I was taken offworld to a fightin' camp, sort of a school to train for the tourney. There was big money in it—for the fighters as well, if they survived."

"Don't they use clones in those games?"

"They do, but the very last round is flesh and blood. With the weapons we use—well, you've seen it. It's brutal and bloody. All the early rounds are to work out the other fighter's techniques, their weaknesses."

"Don't some of the others have prosthetics? I saw one with a laser saw attachment…"

"If you're not killed outright, and if they reckon you're good enough, they patch you up if it's viable. By then, we'd agree to anythin'. The crowds love it, and it's slightly better than dyin'."

"Slightly better?"

"Yeah. Apart from the adulation, we might get another chance at guttin' the guy that did it to us."

Nutribar forgotten, Alexis finished it and washed it down with a drink. "What are your plans now? More revenge?"

"Maybe. See what crosses my orbit. This is as quiet as I've had it for years. Besides, fightin' is all I know."

"If you like it here, maybe I could train you up…" Alexis suggested.

"For fraggin' real?"

"Sure. I mean, I'm not exactly qualified myself, but twenty-six years of subliminal training has to count for something. You seem to have an aptitude, from that bit of reading the manual."

"Got to help out—"

"Exactly. I mean, I guess I could just let Torg do it if you're not interested."

"You'd do that? Teach me?"

"Sure, why not? If you do it, then Torg could also help Bradyn and Phillix."

Sabrya pulled a face, considering. "I could probably get the hang of helpin' here."

"Great. I can send you some more files, and you can sit in

and see what we do up here... which isn't all that much, considering most of it's automatic until there's a problem."

"Sabrya reports we're almost there. What is it you hope to find once we drop out of hyper?" Bradyn was finalizing the inventory and cross-referencing what they had with the list of items needed for repairs. "From the records Torg supplied, Jenna scoured the place pretty thoroughly."

Alexis sat on a crate and wiped her brow. She gazed around the medium-sized cargo hold of Delta 6—the final compartment on her list, and one the droid couldn't access because of his faulty knee. "I'm sure he did, but Jenna was only looking for salvage—something useful, or to gain a few stellars. I'm after anything that can give me a hint to what happened to the *Octavia*. Did we strike back? Were there any remnants of the attackers? That sort of thing."

"The *Octavia* was armed?" Bradyn showed interest in that information. There was another question on his lips when they heard Phillix's voice over the comm.

"Captain, you might like to get up here."

"What is it?"

"Something that could change everything for us."

"Like what?" she asked, but there was no reply. "Damn."

"Mind if I tag along?" Bradyn asked.

"You should know you don't have to ask." Alexis pocketed her tablet and strode the few meters to the ladder. The engineer followed her through the ship to where Phillix had been holed up for hours working on the comm. It was beside the junction of the command section and the bulk of the vessel.

Phillix glanced over his shoulder as the first head rose through the open hatch. "You didn't think to bring Torg?"

"We saw him on the way." Alexis climbed up and stepped further inside to make room for Bradyn. She had to stoop, as the compartment was low and narrow. "The faulty servo in his leg prevents him from accessing several sections, specifically those with ladders. It's been like that for decades. Spares are hard to come by, and no one previously gave a toss about a droid. Which reminds me, Bradyn, are you able to take a look at it?"

"I'll add it to my list, but the fault could be electrical." He turned to Phillix. "Did you manage to analyze that recording?" The swarthy engineer squeezed through the hatch. Seeing the cramped conditions, he decided to sit on the hatch lip, his legs dangling through the opening.

Phillix sat cross-legged on the deck, working on his tablet, which was linked to a wall panel. The crawlspace only had service lighting every three meters. It was dimly lit, but his torso was illuminated by the glow from the tablet, giving him an eerie aspect. Thin cabling connected his prosthetic arm to a communication relay panel on the bulkhead.

"Not completely, but it's old," the tech confirmed. "So far, I've found fragments of metadata, which does confirm the date as circa 3470CY." Phillix stopped tapping the keypad and pointed to coding on his tablet. "And there's several references here to 'Iconic.'"

"Iconic? What does that mean?" Bradyn asked, unable to see the coding from where he sat.

"I don't know yet; I'm still trawling for more data. It's capitalized, like a proper noun... I can only assume it was a ship or a base of some importance."

Alex sighed. She had more urgent things to do and not much time to do it. "Yes, well, that's fascinating, especially getting that date, which you could've relayed over the comm, but how is that changing everything for us?"

"It isn't." He picked up a torch and pointed it at some conduit overhead. A section had been removed, revealing cabling. "That will, though."

Everyone looked up to the light on the deckhead. Like the bulkheads on either side, cables, conduit, and various forms of pipework stretched its length, disappearing along the crawlspace in both directions.

"Fascinating," Alexis repeated, but her tone indicated it was anything but.

"It *is*. That's an AI-specific data connector."

"So? We know the *Malleus*—thanks for changing the ID, by the way—we know she had an AI. I've seen conduit like that in some of the other crawlspaces—"

The tech put down his tablet, swiveled on the floor, and spoke to them earnestly. "The cable is live!"

"Live? So, it has power? I must be missing something." She looked to the mechanic for assistance.

"You're suggesting there's an active AI on board?" Bradyn hazarded a guess.

"Maybe not the core AI, no, but a node. And a node has AI infrastructure and programming. It's also a place an AI stores data and uses as backup in case of emergency."

"If a section of the ship is severely damaged, can the node act as a surrogate AI?" Alexis asked.

"Yes. I think the *Malleus* still has AI capability."

Alexis took a deep breath. "Now *that's* a game changer."

"How is it no one's drocking found it before?" Bradyn queried.

Phillix shrugged. "Torg probably would have, if not for his dodgy leg; no one else probably knew what they were looking at."

"It's not connected to anything?" Alexis asked, moving closer to look at the data cabling.

"Nothing we're using. If it is, whatever it is has been either dormant or running automatically for centuries." Phillix looked at Alexis, eyes wide like an excited child finding his Nameday gift. "Do you know what this means?"

"Sure do. It means someone with the requisite expertise is going to have to crawl through the guts of the ship to locate it. Thanks for volunteering." She slapped him on the shoulder. "And good job. That's your new priority. Ancient records—regardless of the historical significance—can be put aside for the moment. Let me know when you find it." She turned toward the hatch.

Bradyn started making his way down the ladder, chuckling at the dismayed look on Phillix's face.

After several frustrating hours searching the ship's database for references to either the *Octavia* or Niviaris' colony, Alexis stood, stretched, and made herself coffee before retracing her way back to the bridge.

Surprisingly, Sabrya had finally gone for a few hours' sleep, and while Bradyn said he was going to work on the hyperdrive, she suspected he slept there as well, favoring the engineering space over Foster's cabin. There was a sort of solace in being alone on the bridge.

"Phillix, anything to report?" Alexis asked over the comm after sipping her drink.

It was a short period before Phillix replied. "Preliminary diagnostics confirm it's part of a functioning AI, but it's been dormant all this time. With all the butchering carried out in the last several hundred years, it's been severed from the systems we're currently using."

"Can that be rectified?"

"It'll take time. One system at a time, but we'll need components—more spares, more data cabling."

"Do you think we can find them among what we're carrying?"

"I doubt it. Definitely not on the inventory. Maybe we can work with a few compatible connectors, but without cable, it's pointless."

"I gather the data cable is a specialty item."

"Yes, to carry massive amounts of data at lightning speed."

"If only you'd joined us earlier, you'd know exactly where to get your spares. I'll leave you to it," Alexis said. "Don't forget to eat and sleep."

"Yes, mum."

CHAPTER TWELVE

"I GOT IT," Shill said. She perched on Jabari's bunk, making him sit up and move his long legs out of her way.

"You got what?"

"The data you wanted. Answers."

"You did?"

Her expression tightened. "You'll love this."

He groaned and scooted straighter. "When you get sarcastic, I get worried. It usually means *you're* worried." He frowned as one of the multi-limbed maintenance bots resembling a squid entered the room. It carried something, a tiny vial or bottle.

Shill lifted her face toward it and held out one hand, palm up. "Thank you, Greasy."

The bot stopped above her and released the vial to drop precisely into the middle of her palm. Then it scurried away.

The vial contained a clear liquid. "What's that?" Jabari asked, then gestured to the door. "And... *Greasy*?"

"I've been tinkering with some of the bots, too. This," she added, pocketing the vial, "is hooch. I got it to steal from Otho's quarters. All mine, though. My steal, my hooch."

Erkan muttered imprecations from his bunk above them.

"You have been busy," Jabari told her.

"Well, it's not like I haven't had the time."

"All right. Tell me what you discovered."

"First of all, you were right about Scipio mining intel from Rogers 22. Lots of fresh station files there to trawl through, some of them in a dialect not even the AI understands. But the really interesting stuff is Scipio's personal files. They include journal entries where he's kind of talking to himself and thinking things through." Her face relaxed into a smile. "No one else to talk to, I guess."

"What's he talking to himself about?"

"Many things, but the most relevant is the stuff about that refueling stop. You said at the start of this mission that he told you it had something to do with an artifact. Well, it was the bandit syndicate that first found out about it, according to whatever spy network Scipio's tapped into out here. That syndicate's way more widespread and powerful than the optio led us to believe. Anyway, they recently received an alert from some source they couldn't identify, and it was imperial spy probes that picked it up from *them*. Actually, it was Corfid spy probes."

"He's *journaling* about this? Like my younger cousins used to do about boys?"

"Well, he might be laying down information to create reports to his superiors. It's not clear. Most journal files ramble. A lot."

"All right. What else?"

"One reason we were sent to Rogers 22 was to give him a chance to validate the intel and ensure it was current. He wanted confirmation that the 'artifact' hadn't shifted position, *and* whether or not the bandits had tried to board the damned thing. Which they haven't, so far, because they don't understand the signal, and they've probably got other things to do besides visiting some distant star system where no one lives. No short-term money in that, and too much risk."

"But Scipio knows what the artifact is, and why it's important. His files tell us that?"

She screwed up her face. "The files don't tell us what it is."

"Damn."

"But they do tell us the other reason Scipio didn't hang around the *Maelstrom* long enough to fuel up properly."

"Oh?"

"The *Maelstrom* commanders knew nothing about his mission. He's out here without their say-so."

Jabari scratched at his short, wiry hair. "He's rogue."

"He's off his leash, that's for sure. I found evidence of three 'what-the-hell-are-you-doing' messages from the commanders he simply ignored, and now he's blocked their signals."

Jabari stopped scratching. "All that crap about the emperor's will…"

"It might still be real." She touched her pad to his, transferring files. "Read the journal entry I've relabeled 'Big Hero.' Scipio thinks he's doing what the emperor would want him to."

"Corfids are all crazy, but what if he's psychotic?"

Erkan's face appeared over the side of the bunk. "What do we do about this?"

"I'll confront him about it," Jabari said. Then, "Or maybe I won't. Maybe this doesn't change the mission. I'll have to read these files." He pulled the tablet onto his lap.

Not much slag-damn else to do around here.

"Doesn't change the mission?" Erkan slid off his bunk and thumped to the floor. "If he's rogue, we have an opportunity. A huge one."

"What opportunity?" they asked him in chorus.

"The *Pleiades*." He took a step toward the nearest bulkhead and slapped it. "We steal it."

Jabari growled, shaking his head wearily.

"Are you crazy?" Shill added in a stage whisper.

"We could be free," Erkan said, eyes hard.

"Free," Jabari repeated. "Free to do what? Go where?"

"Go *here*." He waved his arms around him. "The Wild Regions. We're outside the Imperium. So, we burn these Corfid assholes, take their ship, and find a new home. Out here. The empire'll think we disappeared on mission. You said it yourself: Scipio's rogue. We all vanish, the *Maelstrom* commanders won't be surprised."

"*You're* losing *your* mind."

"Come on. No more ass-damned stasis. No more ass-damned fighting for the empire."

"And they'll hunt us," Shill said. "A bunch of Proselyti who outnumber the Corfids aboard just happen to go missing? They'll hunt us down for sure."

"Out here?" he scoffed. "Let 'em try."

"Erkan." Jabari got off the bunk and got eye to eye with his colleague, his friend.

Before he could say more, Erkan raised a hand, still defiant. "I know we're leaving lots of sisters and brothers behind, but I don't think they'd mind us doing it. I'd be happy if it was five of them who got the chance."

"You think you're the first of us to consider escaping, brother?"

Erkan squirmed. "No, but—"

"You know why none of us have, don't you?"

Erkan's defiance broke down as his fantasy dissipated, and reality reasserted itself. He turned away.

But Jabari went on. "We swore an oath to the Imperium. We break that, we become deserters and—"

"All right, all right," Erkan mumbled.

"—and they'll kill an equal number of Proselyti. Just decant five of them, drag them to an airlock, and vent them. Record the whole thing."

"I know, I know. I'm sorry."

"The poor bastards who get vented won't even be told what

they're dying for, but every Proselyti decanted afterward will see that video, or hear of it. And they'll know who's responsible. You want that as your legacy?"

Erkan pushed off the bulkhead. "All *right!* It was a stupid idea. The Imps'll probably slag a couple Terranist settlements, as well. I *get* it. I don't wanna hear any more."

Jabari put a hand on the man's shoulder. It trembled beneath his grip. "Brother, it wasn't a stupid idea. Freedom is never a stupid idea. But fantasizing about freedom is one thing—discussing it seriously is another."

"Yeah," Shill said, rising and punching them both in the arm. "And if Scipio really is rogue, finishing the mission might give us enough dirt on him that the emperor will *reward* us for it. And maybe some of our sisters and brothers, too."

"Sure, maybe," Jabari said and returned to his bunk, stretching out again, "but we have to survive it first."

CHAPTER THIRTEEN

ALEXIS HUNCHED OVER THE NAV-CON, perusing a file containing everything Jenna had recorded, which wasn't much, apart from finding her pod in a scattering of wreckage. As Torg had said previously, the area had been raked over quite thoroughly.

She shook her head to wake up. Her jaw cracked with a huge yawn. An idea came to mind, but no doubt Jenna would've done the same thing. She ran through the location data of the few items the ship had detected when he was in charge. Only one item had been located since they'd dropped out of hyper over a day ago. They got close enough to ascertain it was the wreckage of a ship, but nothing they knew of, and nothing resembling the *Octavia*.

"It might be a completely different piece," she mumbled. She programmed the comp to cross-reference its previous location—if it had one, and assuming it was known—to where it was now. From that, she'd be able to determine drift and trajectory, thereby backtracking to its source.

"We might have something, Captain," Torg said.

A faint beep impinged on her awareness.

"Any idea what it is?" She strode over quickly to where the droid stood by the main control panel. She opted to take the seat; leaning over the console put a twinge in her back.

The scope showed an intermittent blinking red dot on the extreme edge.

"It is very weak," Torg noted, adjusting the control to enhance the image.

"Can we increase the gain on the receiver?" she suggested.

"I have the video gain set at max as it is."

She studied the data as it updated. "No velocity to speak of, therefore no trajectory or bearing."

"It does seem to be stationary," Torg confirmed. "Shall I set a course toward it?"

"That looks to be... thirty-two K klicks?"

"Closer to thirty-*five* thousand kilometers. We will be there in two hours and forty-five minutes."

"And nothing at all found otherwise?"

"Other than that portion of debris you were studying, nothing yet, but as the area we are now in is very close to where we first located wreckage, it would be prudent to continue at our current velocity for another five hundred kilometers to be clear of any obstruction. I have also logged the wreckage we just found."

"I certainly don't want to find the *Octavia* or salvage by running into it." She stood and wandered back to the nav console. "Good work, Torg."

"Unnecessary, Captain. It is all programming."

"Any luck with that AI yet?" Bradyn had joined Phillix in the crawlspaces in his search for data cabling.

"Yeah. Sure. It's up and running, doing a complete diagnostic of the entire ship."

"Seriously? That's fant—" Bradyn stopped, seeing the tech's body shaking with mirth. "Asshole."

Phill chuckled. "Anyway, I found where it is, but I'll need you or Torg to assist me in gaining access. It's in a small, concealed compartment."

"You can't access it? Don't tell me there's a locking mechanism you can't hack!"

"Nah. It's a completely sealed section. If there is a lock, it can only be accessed from the inside. If I can hook up to it, perhaps I can work on it, but for that I need more AI data cabling and the proper connectors. I'm hoping if those slack contractors missed the AI, they might have missed cabling in other sections."

"And perhaps another AI node?"

"Who knows?" Phillix grunted as he crawled around a tight bend. "Wouldn't surprise me."

Bradyn had an even harder time attempting to negotiate the tight space, and he regretted volunteering to assist. "Maybe I should go check out the node you mentioned. Where is it exactly?"

"About thirty meters from where I was working on that ancient message."

"And how's that going?" Bradyn had to stop. There was no way his bulk could get through. His other concern was how to get out if he continued.

"You'll recall the captain said this now has priority."

"Uh-huh... and she'll sic Sabrya on you if you don't listen."

"That's why I'm not touching it. Now, as I was saying, thirty meters beyond the comm panel, and it's on the roof in the left-hand corner."

"Deckhead," Bradyn said as he backed out the crawlspace.

"Be nice."

"No, the ceiling, it's called the deckhe—"

His last words were cut off by a loud *bang* followed by a violent shudder.

"What the frack was that?" Phillix called. "Was that the hyperdrive again?"

"Doubt it. We'd be vaporized."

They could hear an alarm in the distance.

After a moment of shocked silence, Phillix began backing out as a hatch several meters in front of him snapped shut along the crawlspace, and amber lights flashed. "We've got depressurization!"

"Drock! Where? How?" Staggering to the floor from the low access hatch, Bradyn managed to get back to the main passage, where more amber lights flashed.

Alexis' voice rang out over the comm, "We've got a hull breach starboard aft quarter, Delta 5 hold."

The distinctive sound of the droid's limping gait sounded in his ears. Torg appeared from a cross-passage. "I will seal this section off," he said as he rumbled past.

Blast doors separated each section. The droid hit a large red tab, and the massive door dropped with a *clang*. "I will enter Delta 5 and repair what I can," Torg said over the comm.

Looking through the thick glass viewport, Bradyn watched the droid activate the next blast door, then go swiftly through the protocol to depressurize his section; that way he could enter the hold where the hull had ruptured. The droid entered and closed the door behind him. With nothing else to see or do, Bradyn pivoted and ran toward the command module.

"Going to the bridge," he called into the access hatch as he passed.

Moments later, Phillix emerged, barely seeing the receding bulk of the engineer before he entered the stairwell. With quick strides to the blast door, he peered through the window, but there was only empty passage and another blast door. Strobing red lights indicated it was now a depressurized zone. He turned and followed Bradyn, grabbing his tool bag from the crawl-space entrance on the way.

"What happened?" Bradyn asked the moment he entered the bridge.

"We aren't sure y—" Alexis stopped as the *Malleus* was struck again. Only the vibration was felt; there was no sound. "Starboard aft again." She finished scanning the panels as lights flashed red.

"Is it debris?" Bradyn asked.

"Nothing detected."

"Well, something's out there!" Bradyn vented, noting the fighter wasn't in her usual spot doing her exercises. "Where's Sabrya?"

"Getting familiar with the engineering section," she continued before Bradyn complained. "Torg, can you hear me?"

"Affirmative, Captain," the droid replied.

She sighed with relief. "Report. What can you see?"

"The hull has been struck by what appears to be some form of energy weapon."

"What?" Alexis and Bradyn asked.

"I cannot determine the type of energy until I conduct a complete—"

"That doesn't make sense. There's nothing out there." Alexis stared out the viewport. The space around the ship was empty. She leaned close to the scanner, adjusting the control to zoom in. "Wait... Bradyn. Look at this."

The engineer was already by her side and squinted at the screen. There was a brief rippling effect. "A glitch?" He looked outside, but it was clear of any vessel.

"What did I miss?" Phillix rocked up behind them, panting slightly from the exertion of the stairs. "Where's Sabrya?"

"Nice to know everyone misses me," Sabrya said over the comm.

"Getting familiar with the engineering section as part of her new duties as XO," Bradyn grumped, then added softly, "I hope she doesn't touch anything."

"I heard that. You're fraggin' lucky I'm stuck back here," the fighter muttered.

"Keep safe." Alexis stepped back to allow the hacker some room. "Phillix, what's your opinion of that? And don't tell me it's a glitch. Not after what's happening."

Phillix mimicked Bradyn, looking long and hard at the screen.

"It..." He paused. "There *is* something there... possibly shielded somehow..."

"Shielded?"

"Something to prevent being seen or detected."

"Stealth tech? Out here?" Bradyn stared at the hacker as if he was crazy. "Imps are the only ones who can make that tech work, and it's not this good. And what the drock would they be doing with it out here, anyway?"

"*We're* out here." Alexis moved closer again, unable to see anything out the viewport. "Tell me more," she encouraged the reticent technician.

"It's been conjectured for several centuries now that better stealth tech might be developed—a field that prevents any emissions: no light, no radio, no thermal, no radiation whatsoever. Many attempts have been made, but it's been dismissed as fantasy."

"And you think this is it?" Bradyn queried dubiously.

"What, like we stumbled on a secret test site?" Alexis asked.

Bradyn shrugged and shook his head. "We stumbled onto *something*. Not a test site, though. Surely there'd be a cordon of military craft fending off approaching ships."

"It wouldn't even come to that. A simple subprogram fed to

the local waystations would prevent ships from straying anywhere near here," Phillix explained.

"If not a secret test site, then what? We've received no communication at all."

"That would give the game away—" Phillix started.

"And blowing a drocking hole in our hull didn't? Torg? What's happening out there?"

"I am at the edge of the breach. There is—brace yourselves!"

Another hit; another shudder. More lights flashed, some red, some amber. "I'm just glad the ship is big enough, and the hits are far enough away not to lose a life," Alexis grumbled.

"So, I don't count, then?" Sabrya queried. "That last hit was close. I'm goin' to check this area, compartment by fraggin' compartment."

"Affirmative. Report back ASAP."

"There is a vessel of some description out there," the droid noted.

"You can see it?" Alexis sounded exasperated. She jumped into the chair and began maneuvering the *Malleus*.

"Where are you going?" Bradyn asked.

"Away from whatever's shooting at us. We're being hit on the starboard aft, so we turn to port. Keep talking, Torg."

"The vessel is hard to see, and then only for a moment when the energy weapon discharges. I can, however, confirm it is using a plasma cannon."

"Plasma cannon?" Phillix echoed. "Why are we still in one piece after three hits?"

"From visual analysis of the beam, the weapon appears very weak," Torg answered.

"Warning shots?" the tech speculated.

"But why? We'd have continued to cruise past if they hadn't fired. We'd be none the wiser." Alexis continued to manipulate the controls. Subliminal training was one thing, but she still needed to feel the physical aspects as well.

"Maybe they don't know that."

"Torg. What's the damage?" Bradyn asked.

"In Delta 5 hold, there is a rupture approximately 17.34 square centimeters low in the bulkhead. The second impact struck slightly higher, but the rupture is half the size. The third impact is higher and further aft. I am unable to ascertain damage at this point. There is no evidence of a loss of cargo, but there is slag residue; some of the cargo was struck, thereby blocking potential damage to the ship infrastructure."

"Another reason having all this salvage is a good thing." Bradyn smiled grimly.

"You're starting to sound like the previous captains." Alexis chuckled. "I'd much prefer their stealth tech, or whatever it is, and not get shot at all. Torg, any idea why the plasma beam is so weak? Is it damaged?"

"From my limited observation of the beam's appearance and the rate of fire, I would estimate the power source is almost depleted. This may also be the cause of the diminished stealth capability that is present. I will repair these two breaches, then check engineering. Also, I believe we are now out of their range."

"Affirmative," Alexis finished, having put twenty kilometers between them before she slowed and turned the ship around to face the area they'd come from.

"With the spread of these 'glitches,' I reckon there are several of them," Bradyn observed, pointing to the minute pixels on the scope when they appeared.

"What, several ships with simultaneously depleting power supplies? Surely that's extremely unlikely? Phillix?"

"Hmm?" The tech looked up from the scanner. "Yes, unlikely—virtually impossible. No, it's one vessel." He lowered himself to the deck and slid underneath the console.

"One ship?" Bradyn scoffed and began a quick calculation.

Alexis beat him to it. "Over five kilometers in length."

Bradyn continued to run the numbers. When his eyes widened, he looked out the viewport in disbelief. "I've worked on spacecraft for three decades across seven sectors. There is no vessel of such a size in existence."

"And yet, here it is." Phillix was lying on his back, working on the underside of the scanner.

"Sort of." Alexis stood beside the engineer, looking down at Phillix's legs, his thin ankles showing. *No socks and ill-fitting pants.* She shook her head to concentrate. "What are you up to?"

"I'm adjusting the gain on the scope from the receiver. Maybe it'll reveal more of the vessel or whatever it is out there."

Alexis nodded. "Fine," she answered. After staring outside for many minutes, she said, "I can't see a damn thing."

"Captain, I have remotely accessed the nav and input the data from my observations," Torg informed her.

She looked down at the scanner. A red icon blinked directly in front of them. "You're sure it's there?" she asked, frustrated.

"Something certainly is, and the location is accurate to within several meters, and relative to account for our new position."

Bradyn resumed sitting and sighed. "Lucky us, I guess. With only one gun firing at us, it confirms your theory of one vessel. I would've thought if there were several craft, then surely more would fire." He considered for a moment after seeing Alexis' nod. "Assuming it's where it is, how close were we, and at what angle did we pass?"

Alexis checked their flight path log. "At a guess, we were less than five klicks out, and our trajectory had us passing over it."

"And still only one gun fired. Surely a ship that size would have several batteries of weapons."

"Meaning there are no weapons on this side?"

"None functioning—or their sensor capabilities are null on that side."

"Or the power is simply depleted, as Torg suggested."

"Food for thought."

"5.35 kilometers!" Phillix crowed.

"What?" Bradyn shifted in the chair to face him.

"That's how long it is." He winked at the engineer. "I had to confirm those numbers."

"Look—and this is to both of you—you can doublecheck every damn thing I do, but this isn't a game. I'm not competing with anyone. I keep having to remind you, I've had two decades of command officer subliminal training to fall back on. I didn't choose any of this. If you want the job, it's all yours..."

Looking remorseful, both men remained silent.

"Need a hand, boss?" a familiar voice came over the speaker. "I'm pretty good at settlin' arguments."

"No, I don't believe I do." Alexis watched the sullen men.

"Good, because we need Bradyn in engineering."

"Why's that?" the engineer asked, rebuke forgotten.

"Because the last hit did somethin' back here, and I don't think it's fraggin' good."

CHAPTER FOURTEEN

SITTING AT THE CONSOLE, Alexis looked over her shoulder as the lift doors snapped open. The droid hobbled in, his leg seeming much the worse for wear.

"What happened to you?"

"Some difficulty with the ladder. The knee servo is now only 23 percent efficient."

"I've added it to Bradyn's growing list. I'll see that he gets to it, when the opportunity arises, as a priority. We need you, so for now, you need to take care."

"It was essential to keep the ship safe. I utilized sections of an internal wall—non-structural, of course. I can confirm there was only superficial internal damage in Delta 5, as the salvaged components took the remaining energy bolts." The droid stood like a statue beside her right shoulder, leaning slightly due to the damaged knee. "Now that the air pressure has returned, Bradyn and Phillix are checking the damage to the hyperdrive."

"Excellent. And good work, Torg." She returned her attention to the conn. "I've been running some numbers... here, check them and see if they're correct. Then you'll know what my next plans are."

The droid scanned the tablet. "I concur."

"Good. Phillix increased the sensitivity of the scanner—"

"If he has, then any incoming signal of a normal power level will potentially damage the circuitry."

"I guess, being as remote as we are, that's a risk worth taking. Phillix assures me he has enough spares to repair it if there are complications. I'm not letting any chance go by to overlook a stasis pod, so we're concentrating on locating very small or very weak emissions. I'd be dead if you hadn't found me." *Surely someone else survived?* "And if it wasn't for his mod, we could have missed the new data we now have."

"New data?" Torg examined the scope image, where one orange and one red icon blinked consistently. As the ship circled the mysterious vessel, the orange blip was gradually being positioned between them and the red blip.

"While you were repairin' the hull, we detected some more debris," Sabrya said from her usual corner, where she was resting after her exercise. Once the techs had arrived in engineering, Alexis had called her back to the bridge.

"Is it the *Octavia*?"

"Could be. We'll find out soon enough. How are our spacesuits?"

"That is one thing the previous crews maintained fastidiously. We have six, and they are all in excellent condition."

"You checked?"

"I always check them after the crew finishes."

Alexis filled the droid in on the current situation. "Considering where and how we were struck, we have a couple theories: that the stealth vessel has only one active weapon, or the sensors on this side aren't functioning. We were only fired upon when we were moving beyond its location, not when we approached—which strikes me as pointless."

"And since we're here and not under fire, I reckon the captain is right."

"I concur," the droid agreed.

"I'm also keeping the debris between us and the vessel as cover, just in case." She arced the *Malleus* around so it was facing the mysterious vessel and the debris. "We're almost in position." On the scope, the orange and red icons were now in line with their projected trajectory. She then nudged the joystick. Incrementally, the distance between the *Malleus* and the orange icon decreased. A slight adjustment of attitude angled the craft lower and ensured the bulk of the debris was still between them.

Sabrya slinked up to the viewport silently. "Hard to see an unlit chunk of metal in this dark."

Alexis nodded, concentrating. "Look for what you *can't* see; dead ahead, and slightly below the bridge level, you'll see the stars beyond blackout. I'm aiming for that shadow."

The fighter picked a spot in the suggested region and stared, waiting. "Hey, would you look at that! You were fraggin' right."

"Doubter," Alexis grumbled as she edged the ship closer.

A soft buzz and a red light blinked. "The sensor readings say we're a hundred meters out." Bringing the ship to a stop relative to the debris, she visibly relaxed.

"Who's goin' out?" Sabrya asked.

"Try to stop me," Alexis stated. "If it *is* the *Octavia*, I'll know it for sure. I'll probably need an engineer, so that means Bradyn when he's ready. Sabrya—" she turned to the fighter "—happy to sit in the seat for a while? Torg will be here, too."

"Sure," Sabrya said confidently. "I'll make sure chrome-features doesn't do anythin'."

"Bad news, Captain," the engineer reported in. "The hyper-drives are completely out of commission now."

"Frack it! And nothing to repair it?" Alexis spun out of her chair and paced the bridge.

"Regrettably, no. We were too damn lucky before to have

anything. Both Phillix and I have doublechecked, and there's nothing in our holds to replace the slagged sections."

Running through her training, she found nothing in her knowledge base to fix a broken hyperdrive, other than, 'keep the crew busy.' "May as well meet me in the airlock. We're going for a walk. Phillix, want to keep working on that AI?"

"Sure thing, Captain."

"Nice, compliant crew you have there, boss." Sabrya grinned.

"Have you done this before?" Bradyn asked as he helped Alexis don the space suit, after he'd ensured all the seals were adequate. He had no doubt Torg was capable of carrying out his duties, but how long had it been since he'd checked them?

"Once, in training," *decades ago,* "but not in real space."

"Yah. Well, it's like riding a hoverboard—once you've done it, you never forget."

"We'll see. When I turn purple, I'll blame you."

"As will I," Sabrya said over the comms.

Bradyn doublechecked that her air supply was turned on before he lowered the helmet. "Once I seal this, check your comms."

Alexis nodded, looking grim as the clear head covering was lowered.

"And stop holding your breath." He chuckled, seeing her through the plexiglass sphere. "Can you hear me?"

"Affirmative." She nodded, her voice coming over the speakers in his suit's neck fixture, where each helmet sealed.

"Right, now me." With his massive frame to cope with life on a high-G world, it was a tight squeeze, but he managed. "Good thing these are so flexible." He showed her how to doublecheck the other safety procedures, then placed his own helmet on. "Comms check."

"I hear you." She gave him a thumbs-up.

Bradyn nodded. "Sabrya, we're ready to go and about to depressurize."

"Roger," she replied.

The airlock went from white to flashing orange as depressurization began, and then a solid red once it was complete. The engineer fixed her tether, then his own to an anchor point outside the airlock.

After a quick glance, Bradyn hit the glowing blue button. The airlock door split down the middle, and both halves retracted swiftly.

"After you, Captain."

She stepped through the threshold, seeing the void for the first time.

Bradyn moved to her side. "It's a magnificent sight," he whispered in awe.

They both remained there for several minutes, taking in the vast emptiness of the void.

"You guys okay?" Sabrya's voice cut the moment of tranquility.

"Yeah, sure," Alexis acknowledged. "Just taking a moment."

"She's a spoilsport," the engineer muttered.

"A spoilsport with a vengeful countenance—oh, and the airlock override," Sabrya responded.

"I know of several maintenance hatches..."

Alexis cleared her throat. "Surely you wouldn't leave your boss stranded?"

"We have two hours before reserves kick in, but I'm sure she'll get over her peevishness soon enough," the engineer said.

"What peevishness?" the fighter asked.

"See?" Bradyn winked at Alexis. "Forgotten already."

Alexis merely nodded as she studied the area in front of them. "Can you see it?"

"You mean the darker nothingness? Sure. Would've been too easy if there was a local sun to light things up."

"Let's go." Without another word or prompting from Bradyn, she took a controlled leap, more of a dive, toward the large chunk of debris. "Too bad there are no external spotlights on the *Malleus*. Sabrya, make a note of that." Alexis activated her suit light.

"Roger, boss," the fighter back in the command seat replied. "I'll get Torg to check if there's something in the inventory."

The unknown chunk of wreckage was too far for her suit light to illuminate, but a dim circle appeared and gradually became more defined as her momentum brought her closer. It was joined by another circle of light as Bradyn closed in.

"Any idea yet?" he asked as the debris became clearer. Based on its sheer size, it was undeniably part of a spacecraft, not drifting cargo. "Maybe it's part of the other ship—the one that shot at us—broken off in some fight long ago. We don't know why it's here or what happened to it."

"Not yet."

They stopped several meters from it, careful to avoid any obstruction that could puncture their suits.

"See that opening?" Alexis pointed to a darker square. "When it comes around again, I'm going in. Bradyn, you stay out here and hold my tether, otherwise we'll both get tangled, and none of us will get back." She handed him her lifeline.

Bradyn clipped it to his belt as they waited for the debris to rotate.

"Here we go." He turned her and gave her a gentle nudge when the opening returned. Pushing her sent him back slightly from the rotating mass. "Make sure you keep a good grip."

"I'm on," she said, more to inform the crew of her progress, then she looked back. The wreckage turned ponderously, making the lone figure of the engineer, with the *Malleus* in the background, appear to rise. It wasn't long before he was out of sight. Alexis turned and climbed the few meters to the opening she'd seen earlier.

"Anything?" Bradyn asked several minutes later.

"It looks like an airlock. Not sure why it's open, but I'm going in."

"Mind how you go," Bradyn cautioned again.

At this stage, nothing on the surface indicated what she was looking at, other than a section of a spacecraft. *Then again, I have no real idea what any section of the* Octavia *looked like, only the overall shape.* She said as much to Bradyn.

Once oriented to the deck, Alexis used her mag-boots and walked, slowly, further into the interior. With immense sadness and some relief, she recognized some sections.

"This is—was—the *Octavia*." She walked slowly around the area. She gasped when she found a body floating in a corner. She recognized his name badge; Grodan was one of the engineering crew. Down the dark corridor, her light stabbed several other bodies floating in the dark.

"Alexis..."

"Captain?"

"Huh? Yes?" She had no idea how long they had been calling.

"You okay?"

"I'm fine, just—" Tears trickled down her face as the body floated in front of her. Part of the suit had snagged a lever, holding it in place. Tentatively, she reached out to turn the body to face her.

Not Kaden. She sighed in relief. Whoever it was, he looked serene in death.

"We have company. Another ship's entered the area."

"How long ago?" Alexis reluctantly dragged her eyes from her fellow crewman. They were stinging, but there was nothing she could do about that. "Frack, turn off our transponder!"

"It's way on the other side. Torg says it has a similar signature to one of the bounty hunter ships... Wait. It's gone."

"What do you mean? I'm coming in."

"It's back again!"

"What's happening?" Alexis had deactivated her mag-boots and was pulling herself along the passageway toward the airlock. "Is it just the one, or more?"

"Whether by intention or not, the vessel dipped into the shield, then back out. It is too early to ascertain if it was intentional, but it is now slowing and turn—"

"Frag. There's somethin' else out there now! Definitely another ship appeared! It's movin' to intercept the first one."

———

"What the flux is happening? What's their range?" Alexis asked the moment they both returned to the airlock. She needed something to push the image of the frozen body from her mind.

Bradyn hit the pressurization button the moment they reentered the airlock. While they waited apprehensively, they coiled the tethers, then stowed them.

"Dog fightin' at the moment," Sabrya answered. "Energy discharges, but no idea about any damage. They're about five hundred klicks out."

"Do we even know who's after us? There were at least two ships chasing us back in Sector 24, and they weren't fighting each other like these two are."

"Other than fraggin' bounty hunters for escapin' Ieoni Orbital's slave pens? Maybe whoever had Jenna killed, and Brutus mentioned local enforcers... reckon they'd be chasin' us?"

"Local enforcers out here? Nah, they wouldn't have the drocking resources, but the criminal gang that killed Jenna—the Bukshoga Qlan—it's highly probable they'd be keen to follow up." Bradyn helped Alexis out of her vac-suit the moment they got the green light. "Did they see us?" He directed his question to the command center.

"Can't say. They are, however, fraggin' preoccupied," Sabrya informed.

"Either way, I don't want to be here when whoever wins comes looking." Alexis opened the inner airlock door once they were both unsuited. "On our way!"

Leaving the vac-suits on the bench, Bradyn followed in her footsteps as she climbed the stairs, disdaining the wait for the elevator.

***

"We still hiding behind the big ship? What happens if one of them comes over to this side?" Phillix asked when he joined Torg and Sabrya. He'd been in the bowels of the ship, continuing his search for data cables, and had difficulty finding an exit.

Torg made sure all comms were linked, so no one missed out on the conversation.

"Oh, we're not hiding *behind* it, we're going into the cloaking shield!" Alexis called.

"Into?" Phillix asked, looking apprehensive.

Sabrya explained, "While you were fraggin' lazin' about in the crawlspaces, that bounty hunter arrived and disappeared through the field. No idea whether it was meant to or not, but that grabbed their attention. As soon as they realized what had happened, they spun around to investigate, then the other ship made its appearance. Pew pew."

"Who are *they*?" Phillix asked as the two ships whipped across the window. "Where did they come from?"

"Other than from another fraggin' direction, no idea, but they're fast and angry. Definitely military."

"The point being," Alexis cut in as she entered the bridge, Bradyn close behind, "as we've witnessed, we can enter the cloaking field safely. Any further developments, Torg?"

Now everybody was on the bridge, waiting apprehensively as the two strange vessels danced around each other.

"From their speed, angle, and elapsed time, I estimate the cloaking shield is projecting approximately a hundred meters from the vessel's hull, at the very least."

"What happened to the scanner?" Alexis asked, noting the usual display was blank. "No red icons. No green glitches."

"As I indicated earlier, with the increased sensitivity, all it took was an emission from one of those craft to blow the circuits."

"Frag." Alexis moved between Sabrya and the droid, looking through the viewport. Flashes of energy indicated the ships' positions, though the ships themselves were too far away to see with the naked eye. "If we haven't been detected, great. If we have, we'll have to work something out."

"I guess it'll give us more time, at least." The tech licked his lips nervously.

"Find any data cable?" Bradyn asked to take his mind off the other ships.

"Hmm? Yes. About thirty... thirty-five meters of it. Why?"

"I'll give you a hand to collect it."

"What. Now?"

"Why not? There isn't much we can do here at the moment,

and it'll keep us busy and out of their hair." He nodded to the
two women hunched over the console.

"Won't they need us when we get closer?"

"We're going in real slow," Alexis replied, speaking over
Sabrya's chuckle, "and the cable could be of great importance.
We'll call once we know what we're dealing with. Promise."

CHAPTER FIFTEEN

JABARI HAD BEEN SUMMONED to the *Pleiades'* command center. He came to rest just inside the compartment, feeling the puff of air against the back of his shirt as the door closed behind him.

"Optio?" he prompted when Scipio didn't immediately acknowledge his presence.

The lights in the small room had been dimmed. Scipio sat stiffly in the command chair against the helm and the forward glass that curved around the ship's bow. Idle maintenance bots shifted slowly across the ceiling, trading positions. They brought a childhood memory to the surface, of Jabari and his father watching a cluster of bats nestling in for their sleep period. Otho occupied the only other chair in the room, squashed in to Jabari's right. The Corfid glanced at him with mild dislike and returned to tapping his stylus against a screen.

Scipio motioned him forward, then pointed through the curved windows. "We're here."

Jabari took up position at the optio's shoulder, frowning. There was nothing visible but the starfield—not from his angle, anyway. And from where he stood, the stars were sparse: some of those impossibly distant twinkles were possibly nebulae or entire galaxies. Jabari knew what he was looking at. "Sir, we're on the very edge of the spiral arm."

"Indeed, we are."

Jabari's gaze dropped to the holo-chart by the optio's knee. Nothing in it: no planets, no waystations or other habitats, no gun platforms or other ships. The holo-field was a blank sphere, a lime-green haze with *Pleiades-219's* tiny white dot dead center. "*This* is our endpoint, sir?"

Scipio allowed himself a smile as faint as the holo-chart's field. "If you're thinking we're in the exact middle of nowhere, you're absolutely correct, Lieutenant. Nevertheless, there's something out there." He passed his hand through the holo, making it flare.

"You mentioned an artifact, sir," Jabari allowed himself to muse aloud. "We... don't appear to be in a star system, so it can't be part of a settlement or an outpost."

"Keep going."

He leaned over a display board. There *was* something. "Scans read a broad spread of artificial debris, with its leading edge two hundred meters ahead of our position."

"Yes."

"Ship debris. Small particles. None of them bigger than... than my bunk. We want something among all that?"

"No."

His frown deepened. "Sir, if our target's larger than a ground bus, we must still be a long way out from it."

"Well, that remains to be seen." Scipio shared a wry glance with Otho. "Literally."

Jabari shifted, growing impatient with the games.

Scipio noticed. He said, "Our orders are to capture what's out there or—in extremis—destroy it."

Orders, he thought. *You lying dog. You're making this up as you go along.*

"But *what's* here?" Jabari passed his fingertips through the side of the nav-holo, making it flare again.

"It's time for the details I promised you. Three times since the year 5088, our *Maelstrom* detected a distress signal. A *ghost* signal... from a ghost ship. It would appear for a moment, then snuff out. The first time was, as I say, thirty-four years ago. A curiosity—and a signal so faint, it was impossible to judge the distance it had crossed to reach our sensors. It appeared again twenty-six years ago, long enough and strong enough to indicate our great carrier had moved closer to the source—or it to us—and clear enough to judge direction, but again, not enough for distance. Then nothing, for all that time. Until fourteen days ago, when it was picked up by a Cor Fidelis probe. The probe vanished shortly afterward, and we presume it was shot down. But first, it was able to record both direction and distance, and FTL-transmit that to the *Maelstrom*, before we relayed the message to Cor Fidelis Command. This message narrowed the location of the signal to a region five hundred and forty million cubic kilometers in size."

Jabari winced. "Reasonably large search area, Optio."

"Tight enough for our emperor to order an exploratory mission. On our way, we've had two items of intel that narrow it further. The first was a piece of pure luck when, during our sojourn on Rogers 22, our AI routinely trawled data from the waystation's servers and came across a report. A report about a colony vessel vanishing somewhere close to the volume of space we'd been directed to."

Jabari pressed his nails into his palms, thinking, *Pure luck? Lying dog.*

"And the second item, sir?"

"The second was a return on an investment. You're aware we not only send probes out to the rebel territories, but maintain feeler cells throughout them? Another word for those cells is *spies*. Our spies gather information as well as spreading it." It was his turn to brush a hand through the nav-holo. "When one of them discovered a Bukshoga Qlan crew had marked this area for recon, she placed a tracking transponder onboard their ship. Our arrival nearby has triggered that tracker."

"Bukshoga Qlan? What's that? A settlement? A scavenger faction?"

"One of this sector's biggest crime syndicates. Outlaws hugging the fringes of the empire. They love the Wild Regions. Their proclivities are drug running, prostitution, salvage, and resale. All the staples. Also bounty hunting—which is their term for slave-trading. We curtail their activities whenever opportunity presents itself, to prevent their reach from extending further into our territory than it has."

"You hope this group will lead us to the ship we're looking for, but, sir... it's been thirty-four years since the first distress signal. Whoever triggered it *could* be long dead. Unless... you think they're in stasis?"

"Actually, that's our suspicion, but the ship's arguably more important than any occupants."

He got it then, heart beating a little faster. "The reason *Pleiades* can't detect it is it's masked."

"Cloaked, yes. Solid deduction."

Jabari looked from nav-holo to display board to Scipio. "From all our sensors? *Imperial* sensors?" He heard himself gasp then; he couldn't help it, because the explanation that came to mind was simply crazy.

What ship can block imperial scans? It can't *be... hers. No, of course it can't be hers.*

Confirming Jabari's thought, Scipio said, "A Terranist capital ship, yes, left over from the civil war, making it as old as you, my *Proselyte* friend. And if your beloved Kaana has come to mind, Jabari, please put her from your thoughts. You and I both know it's not the *Iconic*; that ship was pulverized the day before you were captured."

The Iconic *was pulverized when the great bitch Admiral Devota exploded the moon it was passing, a moon with ninety thousand inhabitants on it. That atrocity was the only way the Imperium could overpower the Kaana.*

Forcing a neutral expression, Jabari couldn't refrain from correcting the optio. "No one was captured. You refer to the day before we *surrendered*. Sir."

Scipio fussed with the controls of the data board closest to the nav-holo. "Semantics, Lieutenant, and hardly a cause for pride either way."

Jabari cleared his throat. "You believe we're close to a remnant of one of—" He almost said *our*. "—her fleets. We're here to capture the stealth tech. That's why you wanted a team with Terranist genes?"

Scipio straightened, returning his gaze. "In case the thing uses gene detectors. Not much point in Otho or me trying to deactivate defenses encrypted by Terranists."

Jabari turned his head, facing the void outside. "Gene detectors might no longer be functional, sir, nor any defenses the ship had."

"The bloody stealth shield works fine," Otho muttered from his station without looking their way.

Scipio nodded. "It's as the corporal says. Safer to have you go in, Jabari."

Jabari's thoughts began to spiral, memories of his former devotion, the glorious decades of Terranist victories, and then the crushing setbacks. He was trying to form a statement or a question, anything to snap himself out of it, when Otho spoke again, this time with more energy in his tone.

"There it is again, sir! Thirty klicks off our port bow, thirty degrees elevation."

Scipio twisted forward, staring slightly "up" from their position. Jabari leaned into the glass, following the officer's gaze until he saw the blue tail-flare of a ship's sublight thruster. In the blink of an eye, it vanished again, leaving him to wonder if it had been his imagination.

Scipio obviously didn't think so. "I'd call that confirmation. That's our Qlan ship."

Jabari checked the display he'd checked earlier. "It's vanished. Nothing out there, sir."

"Because those idiots have found the stealth field, and they're playing around with it like Lydian musk seals diving in and out of the sea—testing its boundaries and properties." Scipio dropped into his command chair. Interfacing directly with the ship's AI, he said, "*Pleiades*, target the vessel's last location for intercept."

"Engage or hail, sir?" the ship asked in a quiet, emotionless voice.

"Engage."

Like moving through an invisible black veil, the *Malleus* disappeared through the nothingness. Hidden beyond, the most stunning ship they'd ever laid their eyes on appeared. It was clear the original color of the ship had been white. If there'd been a nearby sun, the viewport would have dimmed from the reflected light, but now, it looked like it had been through hell—evidence of being struck by objects large enough to have obliterated the *Malleus*, but merely scouring this leviathan.

Initially too stunned to speak, the two women on the bridge stared in wonder at its sheer size. Their angle of entry through the shield brought them over the top of the ship's bow. Gradually, they navigated along its port side, moving slowly toward the rear.

As they cruised along the side of the behemoth vessel, it filled the viewport. Sabrya had to lean forward to view the top.

"What's that?" She pointed to a darker area near the front of the massive ship—one of the many signs of damage marring the once-white hull—but while most of the damage had been on the top starboard side, this particular damage was on the opposite side.

"It... appears to be wreckage of some description. Look, there are other parts."

"More of the *Octavia*?" Alexis guessed, seeing signs of more impacts. "Can you enhance the screen?"

"I can." Torg adjusted a dial, and the view enlarged, but not enough to identify the debris. "It looks as though the bulk of *Octavia* penetrated the hull in a collision. Though damaged, the hull has a 58.4 percent similarity to that of a *Bolide*-class vessel."

Hoping for something conclusive, Alexis stared at the view as the *Malleus* cruised along the length of the ship. Several irregular structures, large and small, drifted and tumbled in the blackness.

The droid's silver fingers were tapping a keypad rapidly. "I am detecting a myriad of energy spikes throughout the vessel; while they are very weak, there is a slightly larger area midships, and a small but more powerful one toward the rear—possibly the power plant of the field generator, and I deduce that single spike is the plasma cannon. From what I can gather of the configuration, there are two hangars toward the rear on both sides. They are also showing weak energy spikes—other craft, I believe."

"What are those?" Alexis enlarged the on-screen image and pointed to a series of faint, thin lines.

"From their spacing, I would expect them to be internal atmo-fields." Torg continued, "I can confirm the vessel is 5.37 kilometers in length, and .8 of a kilometer in height, with a width of 1.5 kilometers at its widest part. Computer estimates it to be 2.5 million tons."

Alexis gasped in surprise, enough to take her eyes away from the floating debris.

"That's fraggin' *big!*" Sabrya swore, glancing at her.

"Probably bigger than most colonies' entire fleets together," Alexis agreed in awe. She studied the new vessel through the viewport. "You mentioned hangars? Let's go to the nearest one."

Torg toggled the joystick used for close-in maneuvers.

"This would make a fraggin' awesome scape for a Surreal Tournament."

"Well, we know that's never going to happen."

"True. Brutal, bloody, and gruesome as they are, they had some absolutely glorious venues."

"No doubt gloriously destroyed, with all that firepower and explosions."

"And they were well-compensated. Many of the areas chosen were marked for some form of redevelopment. We did them a fraggin' favor."

"You have any regrets?"

"Shit, no, but I fully intend to revisit those worlds when I'm on holiday."

"You think we'll get holidays, or even time for ourselves?"

"One needs to stay positive, or else they're fraggin' dead—meat for the grinder."

"I'll remember those words of wisdom." Alexis turned to the droid as a large open area came into view. Inside were several small craft. "Looks like you were right. It's a hangar, and open to vacuum. The atmo-field is down, and there's no gravity. Some of the craft are up against the hangar deckhead."

"What are they? Personal transports?" Sabrya guessed. "They don't look like anythin' I've seen before."

Alexis shrugged, deep in thought, then pointed to a fresh exchange of plasma cannon blasts above them as the two fighting ships flashed past. "Torg, can you explain to me why the cloaking shield allows light in, but not out?"

"What do you mean?" Sabrya asked before the droid answered.

"The shield stops all forms of radiation and emissions from going out, yet look." The captain pointed needlessly. "We can still see the stars. And while it's dimmer, we can see those ships. If the shield worked both ways, we'd be in total darkness, and we'd see nothing 'outside.'"

"If I could explain it, there would be a high probability I could devise such a device myself. Maybe at full power, it is different."

"I take it you have no answer?"

"Correct. Not with the current data available."

"We could do very well out of this—if we fraggin' survive," Sabrya murmured with her face turned to where the dogfighting ships had been moments earlier.

"Where's that positivity gone?"

"Frag! You're right. I've rested too long and need exercise to energize my nanites." The fighter promptly dropped to the deck and began a series of push-ups.

When she wasn't exercising on the bridge, she was either using the larger cargo holds as a parkour training ground, or doing sprints up and down the central corridor. Alexis had seen some of her free-running and was amazed at her agility and the distances she could jump.

"Let's hope somethin' interestin' happens soon!" Sabrya moved to the corner to commence a regime of one-armed pull-ups.

Torg had stopped the *Malleus* alongside the massive vessel in front of the hangar.

"I assume we can't land in there. It isn't tall enough." Alexis studied the opening. "Could we back it in? Do we have anchor grapples or mag-lock pads?"

"Reversing is more problematic, but we *can* enter. The ComCen is not fixed in place, but adjustments to the inertia dampeners and grav-field generators will need to be made."

"What do you mean? It rotates?"

"Affirmative." Torg made the necessary reconfigurations, then walked over and opened a panel on a subsidiary control console. "Would you care to do the honors?"

Alexis looked unsure as she moved closer. "This wheel controls the alignment of the ComCen?" She laid her hands on the rim.

"It does. There are one hundred and eighty notches, so you have the option of going port or starboard. I would advise to do it slowly; it has been a while, but I am confident we will remain intact."

"Intact? You better explain that to me."

"As you will be aware, the command center is able to separate from the rest of the ship. I am not detecting any signs of alarm or malfunction, so I am confident we will not separate."

"Right." Sabrya moved closer to watch, sweat beading her brow. "No fraggin' pressure."

"Correct. Space is a vacuum," Torg replied blandly.

She hit him on the shoulder. "Idiot Tinman."

Alexis rolled her eyes and began turning the dial clockwise gingerly.

Looking outside, she saw the view change accordingly. The side of the white vessel, previously parallel to the deck, was gradually becoming perpendicular. Taking Torg's counsel, over five minutes passed before the ComCen was horizontal. Alexis was unsteady for a few minutes and leaned on the console until her middle ear compensated.

Torg and Sabrya showed no effects.

With the main scanner out of commission, Torg analyzed the other display's data screen as it scrolled up. "Referencing those minuscule energy spikes, that one is potentially the plasma cannon—it is in the correct area. This could be the generator for the cloaking shield." He pointed to a slightly larger spike. "And I dare say this is the ship's main powerplant."

"With the energy depletion, and assuming no one survived,

there'd be no need for gravity or atmo. I'm going to assume, therefore, there'll be no functioning life-support systems. What are these?" Alexis was looking at a regular pattern of glowing dots within the larger central area.

"From their size and arrangement, it could be stasis pods with residual power. If so, that would explain why the area still has some power; the AI would be shunting what power it could to maintain stasis pods. I will know more once I interface with a workstation."

"You think you can do that?"

"I will take some of Sabrya's positivity and estimate there is a probability of success."

"That is... unusual for a droid. Tell me, before you were brought here, what was your function on the *Argonon*? What was the *Argonon* researching?"

"Black hole phenomena. They were testing a theory regarding black holes and white holes. By sending a specific signal into it from various vectors, it was hoped one of the myriad of waystations throughout the known galaxy would detect it, and thereby prove their existence.

"When we first met, you recall, I indicated I was running at 67 percent capacity. That was not just an indication of my malfunctioning leg servo. I was partially affected by the gamma outburst. I believe that is also why I am unable to fully integrate with some systems."

Alexis sighed. "You're an asset now, but if we can get you to 100 percent, you probably wouldn't need any of us. That reminds me, we did have a couple droids on the *Octavia*. I didn't see them myself, but if we find more sections, we might be able to do something."

"I look forward to being able to function fully and serve where I can. Would you care to take the helm for docking?"

Alexis paused. *Flux it!* She reached the controls and held them gently. *I'm a botanist, not a fragging spaceship pilot.* As she concentrated, a calm came over her. Subliminal training kicking in? As she gently toggling the joystick, the ship gradually turned head-on to the hull, then with a slight nudge, edged closer as she negated any lateral drift.

Torg read out distance and velocity. "Fifty meters, forty... we can reduce speed to five meters per second. Twenty meters..."

With the gentlest pull on the controller, she slowed the *Malleus* to five meters. A quick view through the various external cams showed the *Malleus* was positioned correctly.

It was just a matter of drifting in steadily.

There was a distant screech of metal on metal. It was painfully long.

Sabrya checked the cams. "It's one of the other runabouts, wedged between us and the hangar roof."

"Any damage, Torg?"

"Nothing I am aware of."

"I'll go check," Sabrya offered.

"No. I'm stopping." Alexis manipulated the controls until all indications showed the *Malleus* was stationary.

"Have we got mag-locks or grapples?" Alexis asked.

"Not for this particular alignment."

"Maybe the wedged ship will be enough to keep us from drifting."

"It will have to do."

"What was that noise?" Phillix's nervous voice came over the comm. "Run into space banshees?"

"Why would your mum be here?" Sabrya quipped.

"Nothing to worry about," Alexis snapped before anyone came up with another witty reply. "We've docked. Let's meet back here on the bridge in fifteen." She flipped off the comms. "I'm hitting the head."

Feeling flushed, Alexis went to her quarters to wash her face and take a quiet moment to get her thoughts together. Navigating a spaceship through uncharted space, avoiding bounty hunters, and landing on derelict vessels had never been a consideration for a doctor of botany.

The vision of the body floating in the darkness overwhelmed her.

It wasn't him. Is he just drifting in space? Where is he?

Apart from the sight, she had trouble coming to terms with Kaden's training taking over more and more. It wasn't *her*, yet she—her mind—took to it as if it was natural. "Like it or not, until I get to a planet and my hands into the soil, this is the way it has to be." *And I'll bury you and our people.*

By the time she returned to the bridge, everyone was gawping at the view from the various external cams. Several minor displays showed different aspects—the view above and below, as well as both sides. Being so close, the main viewport just showed a bulkhead of the hangar.

"You got pretty close," Bradyn pointed out.

"Pfft. Meters away," Alexis scoffed. She moved over to the nav console, dissolved the space graphics, and brought up a schematic, not much more than a vague, gray shape. "This is a rough representation of the ship." She pointed to the small, glowing areas. "Now then, Torg believes these are the remaining powerplant and shield generator, and this is the plasma cannon. The larger area could possibly be living quarters, and these could be stasis pods."

"Stasis pods? You mean someone could be alive?"

"That remains to be seen. We have no idea how long this ship has been out here."

"If it was a recent secret project, there's no way the power would be depleted; it would take centuries," Bradyn stated. "Also, a vessel of this size with cloaking is unheard of. Not in any histories I've watched or read."

"Saying… what?"

"Either—I can't believe I'm saying it—it's alien, or much older than anything ever found before."

"Preliminary analysis of the configuration of this vessel and the smaller ships in the hanger indicate a very high probability of human design; therefore, not alien."

"And there's nothing in any fraggin' histories about aliens, either," Sabrya muttered. "Why're we even discussin' that?"

"Which leaves us with an ancient *human* leviathan," Bradyn said. "Who could build something so massive? No individual sector could ever do it… not even the empire builds ships this massive, except for their *Maelstrom*s."

"No doubt we'll find out once we get in there. There's little to no atmo, so it's suits until we get to that central area. In time, we can work something out. Our priorities are to see if there's something to repair our hyperdrives and examine those stasis pods. Chances are—assuming there are pod survivors—we can gain more information," Alexis finished.

"What about the other ships?" Phillix asked, eyes darting uneasily. He scowled at the now-defunct scanner.

"We can't do anything about them, so while the situation may change any minute, let's not get distracted. We'll deal with it if and when it happens."

"Does anyone else think it coincidental that, out here in such a remote section of the galaxy, three ships arrived at the same time?" Sabrya questioned.

"Our arrival here aside, two of the vessels are bounty hunters and would appear to have followed us—so not so much a coincidence there, though they must have an AI to have tracked us so quickly and accurately. As to the third ship—that *is* a quandary. Its swift interaction with the bounty hunters so soon after it arrived would indicate it was here already, waiting," Torg answered.

"Or pursuing them?" Phillix suggested.

"Why not fraggin' attack us, then, when we first arrived?" Sabrya asked.

"I have no data," Torg answered. "I can only deduce they did not attack because they did not scan us."

"Good. Bradyn and Phillix, your job is to deal with the hyperdrive repair."

"On a ship like this, I doubt very much anything will be compatible." Bradyn rubbed his chin.

"Try. If our drive is shit, we'll need something; otherwise, we're stuck here. Sabrya and I will find these stasis pods. Torg will stay here and monitor both, as well as trying to interface with the ship."

"You think it's wise to split up?" the tech asked.

Alexis remained calm, hoping to allay Phillix's fears. "For now, on a derelict ship, we can perceive no internal threat, but I'm not discounting at least one of those other ships coming in for a closer look. We know the bounty hunters are aware of this ship, and us; and based on their actions, the other ship is now, too—if it wasn't already."

"I will monitor your progress and the local space within the shield, and update you with any further developments," the droid stated.

"Questions?" Alexis asked. "Okay. We still have four unused vac-suits."

"I will also check the two recently used suits," Torg suggested.

"I'd rather you see what you can do about the scanner. That has priority." Alexis nodded to the droid. "We'll grab the suits and head to the loading bay. Each one should be good for two hours, so freshen up, do what you need to do, and we'll meet down below in ten minutes."

CHAPTER SIXTEEN

A KLAXON SOUNDED in the scout ship's corridor: action was imminent.

Jabari's team would hear it no matter their location. Scipio waved him to the side of the cabin, where zero-G grips had been fixed to the bulkhead. Jabari repositioned himself and watched a sprinkling of blue and white stars wheel into view beyond the window, in the direction of the invisible ship.

Ships, he corrected himself.

There was no sense of motion, of course, but he knew *Pleiades* was accelerating toward the target location. The scout ship sent a probing slash of laser light ahead of itself.

There was still nothing out there.

And then there was.

A ship. *Comet*-class, from the looks of it, orange and white. A blocky corvette that reminded Jabari of a pistol without the grip. It pushed up and to *Pleiades'* starboard. He got a good look before it vanished from sight, evading them. One gunnery turret had been visible on top, swinging his way, and the thing would have a missile battery or a secondary turret beneath. Small flashes across *Pleiades'* shields were the result of an accurate stream of kinetic cannon pellets, every pellet the size of a human fist.

As *Pleiades* came about, the Qlan ship returned to view, an orange oblong within a blue shield-haze. Its deadly hail of kinetic rounds became visible because every fifth or sixth round was a tracer to assist with manual aiming. The fact that they were aiming manually told Jabari volumes about them—and how poorly their ship was performing. Scipio sat as still as stone with a smirk on his face. This wasn't an engagement he expected to lose.

The corvette whipped around and over while *Pleiades* sent daggers of coherent light chasing after it. The starfield beyond the ComCen windows wheeled and churned as *Pleiades* came about. Jabari told his brain there was no way he'd be tossed from one bulkhead to the other, but its older, more primitive parts overrode the logic, clamping his hand on the wall rail while the ship torqued about to stick with the corvette.

Gods, I hate space combat... Shit!

His grip tightened, and he repeated the curse word aloud as the gray-white hull of another ship—an *immense* ship— appeared before them like a wall. Even Otho barked in surprise.

Pleiades' AI calmly murmured, "New vessel detected," as it banked up and away from the barrier.

Scipio actually laughed. "I see that." With uncharacteristically wide eyes and a wide grin, he turned to Jabari. "I told you there was something here."

Both hands on the wall rail now, Jabari ignored him and watched through the forward window as the *Pleiades* rotated to put its topside toward the huge ship, giving the impression of flying sideways along a towering cliff face of metal alloy.

"Portside edge of the hull," Scipio announced, as if he'd read the focus of Jabari's thoughts. "We'll be past it in a second, but this ship is *huge*. Over five kilometers long..."

Jabari remembered well that the Okalasi rulers had produced three ships of that size. All were on record as destroyed, including the one containing Kaana Adjira.

"Reacquired," *Pleiades* announced, and Jabari caught sight of the Qlan corvette corkscrewing up toward the edge of the starship's upper hull.

A ruby lance from *Pleiades'* laser cannon scored a direct hit, and the corvette's blue shields tinted bright yellow before it vanished over the starship. *Pleiades* braked and vectored to follow.

Scipio laughed. "Shield's overloading."

"I saw that," Jabari muttered, too low for the optio to hear.

They came over the lip of the starship's portside hull, *Pleiades* spindling to place the giant ship "above" them so Jabari could watch it through the cabin windows where they curved overhead. All three men stared across a subtly curved frame that was largely smooth, with the occasional protuberance.

And suddenly, they were staring at the fading orange bloom of a fuel explosion, and an expanding cloud of smaller ship debris. The corvette's remains.

"What the—?" Scipio started to say as *Pleiades* jinked to avoid a collision with it.

Then something struck the scout ship's shields, injecting so much energy into them that they turned opaque. Another klaxon rang out overhead. For three more seconds, the men flew blind within a brightening shell of overloaded shield until those shields collapsed. A half second more of black sky and gray hull, then they were hammered by a titan's fist one more time. The ship's lights failed, replaced instantly by red emergency lighting.

"Grapples!" Scipio screamed at the AI. "We can't lose this—!"

Through the bulkhead, Jabari felt the triple bump of the grapples firing. The view through the glass swung around again as the cables snapped taut. *Pleiades* lurched to a stop before arcing around and toward the massive hull. The impact sent a jolt through every surface of the ship, resulting in a momentary loss of inertial dampening.

Jabari's head struck the wall. When the stars cleared from his vision, he was still standing, and the cabin lights were coming back on. *Pleiades* bobbed on its tethers, rotating slowly as the grapple cables no doubt twisted around each other. But the great starship hull outside appeared stationary, meaning they'd latched on securely.

"What happened?" he asked, the ringing in his ears dulling his own voice.

Scipio didn't answer immediately. His hands flew over the helm displays, calling up data. Eventually, he spun his chair Jabari's way, his expression dazed. He started something in a raspy voice, then had to clear his throat to make himself intelligible. "That damn ship out there is almost completely nonfunctional, except for its cloak and one almost-depleted plasma cannon. Damn our luck! It took out the Qlan vessel before turning on us."

Jabari thought, *And you couldn't anticipate disruptor cannons* before *we got up close to it?*

Scipio must have read the thought on Jabari's face. "Perhaps you think me impulsive, giving chase to the scavengers."

The word *reckless* came to mind, but Jabari kept it to himself and let Scipio continue.

"Nevertheless, we're where we want to be." Scipio gestured toward the great ship's skin as it slid into view again. "And we're minus our only competitors."

Competitors. Interesting word choice.

Several icons blinked on the comms screen as the rest of the team called in, requesting an update. A "what-the-slagging-hell-just-happened" update. Anticipating what his commander would say next, Otho levered himself from his chair and was halfway to the door before Scipio had said it to Jabari.

"Prep your team to dive across to our target vessel, Lieutenant."

Queasy and angry, and trying not to show either, Jabari unwrapped his fingers from the handgrip and took a moment to get control of his legs and his sense of balance. He dabbed a finger at the sore spot on his head.

"What ship is that, sir?"

"It's an old Terranist ship, with old Terranist tech, that's wanted by our emperor. That's what we *know*. That's all you need to know at this juncture. And *this*," he added, leaning back in his chair, "is your test, my *Proselyte* friend. Who do you serve? What's your purpose? How do you want your story to end? Your former Kaanate is dust. Our galaxy is in chaos, with the true empire unable to bring peace and order to it all.

"When your battalion swore allegiance to the Imperium, you all said it was to serve the human race and revive that peace and order. It's taken you seventeen hundred years so far to fulfill that purpose. With this mission, you might give our liege exactly what he needs to reunite our scattered tribes. You do that, Jabari, then you and all of your remaining troopers can retire, showered with Nero XXXIV's gracious rewards. Or will you continue to waste my time and try my patience by asking pointless questions?"

Jabari met the Cor Fidelis officer's stare for the longest of moments. Then, slow and steady, he raised one hand in a precise salute. "My team will be ready for boarding in twenty minutes, sir."

With Sabrya insisting on leading, Alexis, Phillix, and lastly, Bradyn stepped out of the airlock into the hangar. Pausing briefly, Sabrya's headlamp swung around the darkened area. Some equipment and crates were still strapped securely to the deck to one side, while many items drifted aimlessly within the hangar confines. "No doubt a few items were struck when we docked, so be wary. We don't need fraggin' cracked face shields."

Another insistence was the bulky weapon she carried, found in one of the previous crew's quarters. The charge was full, but it looked old and ill-treated.

"An early Gutpuncher. Who the frag thought it a good idea to bring such a powerful weapon onto a spaceship? I just hope this old thing doesn't blow up in my face. What about you?"

"This will have to suffice." Alexis brandished a shock prod. "It's about the only weapon I've had any experience with."

"I have a pry bar and other tools," Bradyn said.

"All I need is my hacking... gizmo," Phillix added with a shrug.

Sabrya shook her head as she moved in, trying to hide her disappointment at the lack of any real weapons. "Probably for the best, or you might shoot one of us." She stopped at the nearest door, partially open.

The compartment looked to have been used for storage. Like in the hangar, many crates were secured. Some were individual, while some were stacked two or three high. A few crates were drifting—broken free of damaged tie-downs.

"Maybe more for our inventory?" Phillix suggested, pushing one of the drifting crates away.

"No drocking way." Bradyn grimaced at the thought.

Alexis spoke up. "Concentrate on the current task."

Sabrya's voice cut the chatter through her helmet comms, "I can see a doorway ahead and to our left."

Using the various crates to push against, the group made their way to the indicated door. Moving gracefully, the fighter arrived before the others, slung her rifle, and attempted to force the sliding doors apart, but they weren't budging.

"Bradyn. You're up." Alexis motioned her XO to move to the side, allowing the swarthy engineer access.

He shrugged off his backpack, extracted the small pry bar, and forced it between the seal. With a bit of effort, he managed to create a gap. The long-dead servos were no match for his prodigious strength. Once he got both hands between them, they parted within seconds.

No words were heard, but some guttural sound came through the speakers. Sabrya drifted past, one blade raised.

"It's really just technique." He winked at the fighter as she turned and checked the area beyond.

"All clear." Sabrya slid through the gap into the darkness. "No, wait." She kicked off into the darkness. "There are several bodies."

They followed and grouped up around the doorway. In both directions, a wide corridor stretched beyond the reach of their headlamps; opposite was a white wall, broken intermittently by vertical grooves. All surfaces had a minimum of obstructions to mar their otherwise smooth façades. Down the center of the long passageway, they saw the drifting corpses Sabrya had spoken of. There was also a series of walk-easies stretching off into the darkness.

"I suspect those dark lines on the bulkheads are for blast or fire door tracks," Bradyn suggested.

"We entered port, just aft of midships," Alexis said. "The stasis pods—or what we think are stasis pods—are situated closer to the center. You two head aft and see what's what."

"Here." Sabrya handed Phillix a marking pen. "Leave a trail in case you get lost."

With nods, the two men moved aft along the corridor, pulling themselves along the railings of the walk-easy.

"We'll need to find a cross passageway to get to the center," Sabrya said.

"Only one way to find it. After you?"

"Of course." The fighter pushed off and glided effortlessly through the darkness like she was born to it. Admiring her skill, Alexis bumbled along, gliding several meters behind, matching the speed, if not the grace. *Too bad subliminal training didn't cover this.*

Every now and then, they had to dodge or push past bodies. Checking the walls as they glided along steadily, they found a door after a few minutes. To one side, above a panel of buttons similar to a keyboard, their headlamps lit up a plaque.

"Can you see this, Torg?" Alexis moved her head so her cam showed the script on the bulkhead.

"Affirmative. It looks to be old Terran in origin. Please move back so the whole plaque is in view for context."

"Terran? From... Earth?" Sabrya helped Alexis move back and steadied her.

"As to the origin of the vessel, I cannot say for certain yet, and there were a number of Terran worlds populated by Earth's descendants. This text is in Terran True, and it will take a moment to translate."

"Did the old Terran worlds have better tech than we have today?" Alexis asked.

"Someone obviously did." Sabrya kept swiveling her head, checking the corridor.

"You think someone's going to sneak up on us?"

"Nope, I'm watchin' to make sure someone doesn't."

"Torg, can you see any other energy spikes?" Alexis asked the droid back on the ship. "Anything at all?"

"The data is sporadic, bu—can make out Ph—ix... Bradyn continuing aft... —wards engineering, and you both. From what I can tell, you are now closer to what I believe to be the stasis pods. I still see six small dots equidistant. Other than—pl-sma cannon, there are no other energy -pikes.”

“See? Nothing to worry about.” Alexis punched Sabrya’s shoulder lightly.

Sabrya reflexively pushed her leg against the bulkhead behind her to offset the force of the impact of the punch, otherwise she’d have been knocked into a slow tumble. “Other than comms breakin’ up.”

“Please kee- still, Captain. Thank you. Translation complete,” Torg said a minute later. “It reads: *‘To have comm–d is to have all the power you will -ver need. To have all the power you will ever need is to have the emp— in the palm of your hand. My han- wields that power, and as long as I sh-ll live, the empire will remain mine and mine alon-. Any person swearing fealty shall have my et—nal blessing; any person who opposes... is a dead person walking. Everlasting life to the Empire of Earth! Kaana Adjira mo’Halana mo’ni’Mariama— Foremost of the Okalasi, Bringer of the Light, Protector of All.’*”

“Deep,” Sabrya quipped. “Sounds like the testosterone-fueled ramblings I heard from my first Surreal Tournament conquest. He died screamin’.”

“Meaning what, exactly, Torg?” Alexis queried.

“The initial part is a quote from an emperor named Tiberius. He was an early Roman emperor on Terra. Unless the translation is incorrect, it then becomes a mix of quotes.” He paused. “This is from the inaugural speech of Kaana Adjira, the last of the Okalasi. That dynasty ruled for III years until her defeat. Her internal rivals—many of whom died mysteriously, in quick succession—stated she was verging on insanity, citing unofficial and horrendous experimentation, though they didn’t specify what that experimentation involved. Official records indicate the Kaana’s dynasty ended with her reported death 1,706 years ago, along with the destruction of the Terran moon when the flagship—the *Iconic*—was destroyed by Martianist forces."

"Seriously? How accurate are these records?"

"As ac–rate as the Imperium archives allow."

"Ha. Exactly," Sabrya scoffed. "History's written by the victors. The emperor would say whatever he needed to keep control; his historians would say whatever they needed to keep their heads."

"If this vessel is as old as that, then it was way before the current emperor or imperial historians had any say in it."

"Separate, independent historical archives exist that detail the devastating impact the attack on the moon had on Terra. Apart from several large chunks eventually drawn into Terra's gravity well, the planet's axial tilt adjusted by 2.6 degrees, and its tides were greatly affected. That led to massive flooding in many inhabited areas, as well as seasonal changes worldwide."

"So, your sayin' Terra was fragged. Got it. Ancient history."

"Wasn't there something in the messages you and Phillix worked on mentioning something about a vessel called the *Iconic*?" Alexis asked.

"The me-sage tha- wasn't a prio-ity?" Phillix said over the comm.

"Yep. That one. Guess what?"

"Now it's a priority?" the tech guessed.

"Smart man." Sabrya laughed.

"The discovery of the Kaana would certainly be a thorn in the emperor's side," Alexis mused. "Imagine what the historians would say."

"Fake news, fraggin' disinformation. I doubt it'd get much traction, and anyone believin' it, let alone spreadin' it, would be dead meat." Sabrya's visor was misting with her exertions.

"That doesn't bode well for us, then," Alexis commented.

"One quote means little. For all we know this ship—

massive as it is—could be one of several in her fleet. Who's to say she's here?"

"I can't imagine anyone—even an empress—having more than one ship this size."

"Fair enough. If we do find her, we simply won't tell anyone. It would attract attention we just don't fraggin' need. Keep it as a story for your grandkids."

As if I'll be having grandkids! "What about those on the other ships out there?"

"If they don't know who we are, we're safe. If we're lucky, none of those ships will survive, but if they do come on board, we'll just have to deal with them."

"Speaking of which, what's happening out there, Torg?"

"Captain, I have managed to repa-r the scanner as ordered. The readings show both ships sus-ained heavy damage; the one I recognized as the bou— hunter has been destroyed. The unknown craft impacted this vessel and vanished from scopes."

"Vanished? Exploded?"

"No indication of explosion. I am getting no signs of their drives. One conclusion is that they sustained damage and are drifting in the large vessel's shadow, unable to navigate."

"Let me know if anything changes."

"Roger, Capta—"

"After we check out these stasis pods—if that's what they are—how about we find the source of this stealth field? That tech alone would make us all fraggin' millionaires. Maybe we could even take this ship as salvage?" Sabrya suggested.

"Sounds good, though I don't like our chances. We're too few in number to crew a ship of this size, and with the power depleting, how long do you think the shield will last? But one thing at a time. Let's get through here first and see about these pods."

"Here, hold this." Sabrya handed her the rifle. "Ever used one before?"

"Are you kidding? With my botany training?" Alexis laughed, clipping her shock prod to her utility belt and swapping it for the rifle. When she held the weapon, she gripped it like a veteran and automatically checked all the controls, switching through the multi-rifle's options adeptly.

Sabrya swore, "So how the hell does a fraggin' botanist know how to do that?"

Alexis sighed. "Damn subliminal training, I suspect."

"Full of fraggin' surprises." Sabrya swore again and turned her attention to the sliding doors. She extended her rippers, forcing them between the seam, and managed to grip the doors. They started opening, but it was slow going.

Alexis was about to help with her superior strength, then thought better of it, deciding showing the fighter up wouldn't improve her morale after Bradyn had made short work of the other doors.

"E—use me, Captain," Torg said. "I was run—ng through the data from the message Phillix was working on."

"And?"

"While there is more data to correlate, I was cross-ref—encing it with the historical archives. It says the Kaana's flagship is the *Iconic*."

"The one you said was destroyed along with the Terran moon?"

"Affirmative."

"You're saying this is the *Iconic*?"

"Affirmative," the droid repeated.

"Yep. We're dead meat," Sabrya vented. "What did I tell you about the fraggin' victors rewritin' history?" She used her ire to fuel her muscles. The doors grudgingly slid open wide enough for the two of them to move through. She moved back, not looking pleased at the time or effort it cost. "Too much downtime! Somethin' better happen soon before I completely lose the nanite effect."

"Good work," Alexis praised, noting the frustrated look on the fighter's face as she handed the weapon back.

Sabrya sighed. "Thanks, but you—"

Anticipating where the conversation was going, Alexis put her hand up to silence her, then reached out and tapped her arm control to cut the audio to the others.

Sabrya continued at Alexis' nod. "You know as well as I do you could've done it quicker."

"What would be the point? There's no rush, and I know you enjoy the exercise."

"Still, thanks."

"Sabrya. Like I said to the boys, I'm not interested in any pissing contests. You have such great skill at what you do. I could never hope to match any of that. But if you want help, I'm there." She switched back to full comms as they moved on.

"Captain," Torg interrupted. "Fresh analysis of hull vibrations leads me to conclude that the unid—tified intruder ship somehow attached itself to the vessel after it was damaged."

"Well... flux it to hell!" Sabrya swore, continuing to move ahead.

"You guys hear that?" Alexis asked.

"They ar- out of comms range. Phillix believes it is a curse word from her Sur-eal Tournam-nts," Torg informed them.

"Tell him he's a—"

"What I mean is," Alexis explained, "tell them our priority has changed. See what Phillix can do about life support... gravity, air... whatever he can."

"He will do," Torg replied after relaying the information. "In fact, Bradyn says zero gravity has helped their progress, and they are very close to the power plant."

The comms went silent for a few moments.

"I have boosted the signal as best I can," Torg announced.

"There's bound to be a direct connection to the AI from there. I'll see what I can do." Phillix was audible, though scratchy and faint, and he sounded more excited than he'd been for a while.

"Phill, make sure you warn us if you're switching gravity on. I don't want to faceplant, crack my helmet, and die of asphyxiation," Alexis said.

"And you know what I'll do to you if *that* happens," Sabrya warned.

Phillix didn't reply.

<hr>

The two women continued, making their way toward the center of the ship.

"Is it just me, or are we comin' to a more populated area?" Sabrya asked after some time, pushing past several corpses frozen together. She studied them briefly; they'd died while hugging.

"Definitely more." Alexis brushed bodies and debris aside, sending both tumbling slowly to the other side of the passage. The image reminded her of the dead crewman on the wreckage of the *Octavia*. She shook her head in annoyance, but Torg interrupted her thoughts.

"Captain, I see several n-w energy spikes; one is quite powerful, but there is another that seems weak or intermittent, barely registering. They are some way out from your position."

"Fraggin' boarders from the other ship?" Sabrya hissed in excitement.

"They are coming from the same area where I believe that ship latched on to the hull, but I do not believe they are human," Torg informed them. "Understand, I am not picking up heat signatures, I am detecting energy emissions only. If they were human, and I was sensing heat signatures, the integrity of their vac-suits would be compromised."

"Droids, then?"

"A high probability."

"More than likely armed and sent out to scout for threats." If possible, Sabrya became even more alert—tense, but relaxed with it. She adjusted her weapon setting. "No doubt someone will be followin' at some stage."

"I will be unable to detect them by heat signature in that case," Torg advised. "And before you ask, your suits have trackers. You have made good progress. The pods are a matter of minutes away, but it looks like you have to go up one deck."

"On it." Sabrya started looking at the deckhead for hatches or stairs.

CHAPTER SEVENTEEN

BECAUSE THEY'D HAVE the two bots as backup, most of the team decided to arm themselves with slim-framed laser carbines, which were easier to manage than the bulkier multi-rifles. Otho and Erkan were the exception there, preferring the heavier, more versatile weapons. By the time the team was ready to dive between vessels, Scipio's menagerie of maintenance bots had repaired *Pleiades'* maneuvering thrusters enough for the scout ship to stabilize itself on its trio of grappling cables. That would make the crossing less precarious.

"Looks like someone was here before us."

The others followed Tee's outstretched arm as she leaned out the open hatch ahead of them. Over a thousand meters away, another vessel was embedded in the hull, two-thirds of it jutting out at a severe angle.

"Looks like an old Bolide-class," Shill said as they all leaned out with her.

"Collision?" Erkan asked.

"Maybe they didn't have grapples." Tee chuckled.

"Luckily they didn't make a boom-boom," Erkan added, "one ship hitting another that slagging hard."

"Both ships were probably dormant," Shill speculated. "Plus, didn't anyone tell you that starship builders tend to make them out of non-flammable stuff?" She reached out and brushed an alloy bulkhead with one glove.

"Focus on the mission," Jabari ordered and pointed over at the mammoth ship's hull.

One at a time, the soldiers made the dive. The blocky combat bot Ninety went first, with the centipede bot curled around one leg, followed by Otho. Those two caught and secured the others as they landed one by one against the great starship's hull. No turrets were visible from their position, and Jabari thanked his ancestors for that.

Their combat suits' grav-boots drew them toward the nearest surface and anchored them there, allowing them to walk across the hull into an empty docking berth with a platform lift set in the middle of it, exposed directly to vacuum. It took Ninety a full ten minutes to carve a portal through the lift floor using a fine laser, creating an entry to a wide goods airlock lit up by the droid's spotlight beams.

By contrast, the human troopers avoided using flashlights. Their suits certainly included helmet lamps, but the ostendo "render-tech" built into their visors was far superior and more versatile. With its ability to scan for various forms of radiation and the bounce light of multiple wavelengths, ostendo digitally rendered the data in visual form across the inside of the visor. And it wouldn't give them away to hostiles like visible light would.

The equally thick blast door between the airlock and the internal compartment beyond it had been slid partway into the bulkhead at some point in the past. The resulting gap would be wide enough for all to squeeze through—although Ninety would have to hug his various weapons modules close. As the flexishell-suited humans gathered to one side of the airlock, the centipede slithered down Ninety's chassis, raced across the deck, and vanished through the doorway. Moments later, it began feeding video to Jabari's HUD from two different camera angles.

The chamber beyond was a cargo hold large enough to accommodate the entirety of *Pleiades-219*, with an open staging area closest to the airlock, and rows of storage fixtures toward the back. Many of the fixtures had tilted over or worked loose. Steel and plastic detritus drifted through the middle of the gravity-less compartment. The crawler nosed its way past a piece of something indistinct as it continued exploring the area.

"No life signs," grated the centipede's metallic voice through his helmet speaker. "Commencing second stage recon."

Perhaps because Shill didn't have the centipede's data stream on her HUD, but had heard its update, she asked, "What's that thing's name again?"

"Rec-7," Tee replied before Jabari could. "Thing gives me the creeps."

"Won't be so creepy if it takes out any defense protocols before they kill us," Erkan replied. "Minds on mission."

Since nothing of concern had shown up on the crawler's feeds, Jabari said, "Ninety, you're up."

The big droid pulled his arms and modules tight and sidled through the gap. Jabari imagined hearing, from the far side of the door, the sounds of gun muzzles and extension arms extending and locking back in place, and servos whirring as the guns searched for a target. Despite his combat suit having exterior microphones, there was, of course, no air to transmit that sound.

He let the bots search for a full minute longer, then waved Morten and Erkan to the cargo hold opening. Morten went left, Erkan right. Another signal, and Shill followed Morten. Tegenwe shadowed Erkan. Jabari tapped Otho's shoulder to move out ahead of him and then followed. According to his briefing files, this era's protocol was for squad leaders to bring up the rear. *Much rather be leading from the front. Maybe "leader" doesn't actually mean "leader" in this era's languages.* Scipio remaining behind in *Pleiades'* ComCen made that seem more likely.

Jabari caught up to Otho as the Corfid took a knee just beyond the gap. The cargo hold was just as Rec-7's vidfeeds had indicated: tall, wide, deep, and littered with floating crap. While Ninety and Rec-7 continued out into the sea of floating trash, Erkan and Tegenwe fast-marched toward the corner fifty meters away, hugging the wall, brushing debris from their path with their left arms. Jabari kept after them.

"Joining stack," Shill announced, indicating she and Morten had found nothing of note or concern in the other direction and were coming up behind Jabari.

"That's our direction," Jabari confirmed as Erkan stepped out from the wall to point questioningly across the vast chamber toward the jumble of toppled and floating racking. "We've come in at the uppermost deck, slightly to starboard, and closer to the bow. We'll cut across this deck and find a way down to explore the belly of the beast."

"Prefer to keep heading forward, boss," Shill grumped as she headed out after Erkan. "Usually, monster ships like this housed life support and stealth systems up that way."

Without comment, Tee's visor turned Jabari's way for just a moment before she, too, followed Erkan. Was she wondering what Jabari was wondering? Whether there were stasis pods back there containing important people from their era? Whether there were surviving Terranists in them?

Keeping pace with the others, Otho rumbled, "Optio wants us to explore the middle of the ship."

"Optio did say that," Jabari agreed, tone neutral. He signaled Morten to hang back and pair up with him while they trailed the rest of the group. "And Optio is listening if he has objections to a change of plan. The bots can search the center.

Shill has a point: we'll go forward first, see what we see, and come back this way if it's pointless."

After a moment, Scipio's voice crackled to life in his helmet. He simply said, *"Agreed."*

The human members of his team wended their way through the maze of fallen and floating storage fixtures, while the droids vanished in other directions. Within minutes, they were out of the cargo bay and into a passage. Jabari had to admit, as much as he didn't like working with combat bots, he felt more and more vulnerable the further he moved away from them. Ninety and Rec-7 had proven themselves valuable in the skirmish on Rogers 22, and the arterial cross-corridor out of the cargo hold was dark, freezing, and empty. His nerves were jumping. His heart rate and blood pressure were up. A slight tremor had started up in his hand.

He took the next few minutes of uneventful travel to modify his body response through cognitive reframing, telling himself that he was born for action, that this was action, that this mission had seen all the firefights it was likely to, and that moving forward would be nothing more than explore-and-report. This was a dead ship, and there were no hostiles on a dead ship. He was further reassured by the thought that the Qlan hadn't even landed here before it was blasted out of the sky. *No doubt what happened to that other wreck.*

Through the shell of his suit, he heard and felt the *click-clunk* of his grav-boots against the deck plating as the team pushed on through passages patched with frost, speckled with tiny particles of frozen gases, and barred by the occasional floating body someone would have to nudge aside or push toward the ceiling. They dropped down the center of a multi-deck stairwell, passing a single body and a floating datapad along the way, exiting several decks lower onto a square pedestrian concourse. Tables and benches were welded to the floor in a dozen places. Planter boxes that had once held ornamental garden beds now saw those plants frozen and crumbling, while clods of soil floated around, resembling peppercorns. From the center of the concourse, travelators vanished into tunnels through the bulkheads, headed forward and aft, port and starboard. They were powered down. Elevators had been placed along three of the walls. Their doors and call buttons didn't respond to touch.

"Decisions, decisions," Erkan muttered. He brushed frost from a wall plaque that explained in Terran True which compartments the elevator ran to.

"Still headed forward, boss?" Tegenwe asked. She'd moved further away from the group, scrutinizing a corpse who'd somehow wedged itself between a table and a bench.

All the corpses they'd seen so far had been badly damaged by the severe cold of deep space, but their uniforms were recognizable as Terranist military and Terranist civilian support staff. Jabari wondered if he'd known any of them. Tee glanced at him meaningfully again.

"Forward," he confirmed. "We float-fly along that conveyor tube rather than walking. Save time that way. No suit thrusters; save your fuel. You all hear me? Suit thrusters are to be used sparingly as per procedure."

"Yes, boss," a couple muttered.

"Not like last time. I'm looking at you, Shill."

"No, boss."

"No, you won't use them, or no, you're not listening to me?"

"I hear and obey, boss."

"All right, good. Shill, you're leading the way. You get a power reading, we investigate. You read nothing in the next twenty minutes, you can guide us to the most likely area to investigate for life-support control."

"You want to float-fly," Otho growled. "What if the power returns? Fragile bodies like yours'll fall straight down and break a bone."

"We've *got* suits on," Shill muttered.

Tegenwe's face was invisible behind her visor, but even in a combat suit, she managed to communicate outrage through her body language as she stepped closer to Otho. "Fragile bodies?"

The shoulders of the Corfid corporal's suit rose a little, hunching with those of the body inside it. "Not modded like mine. A fact. I meant no disrespect."

"Sure sounded like disrespect."

Otho turned square on to her. "You'll keep your distance from me, Private, if you know what's good for you."

Before Jabari could intervene in the quickly escalating argument, Shill did. She held her data slate in front of Otho's helmet, interrupting his line of sight. "Fresh data from Pleiades, guys. New scans show some power on this ship. Apart from keeping the cloak on, and keeping that damn cannon up there operational, there's energy trickling from place to place, as if the ship's keeping itself from fully dying. Like it's hibernating, but a lot of it's pooling in an area up that way." She pointed to the forward travelator tube.

"All right, then," Jabari said. "That's our direction."

***

Following Shill as she followed the live scans from *Pleiades,* they exited the travelator tube via a station set in the portside bulkhead. Jabari was the last one out; the other soldiers had spread along a new passageway, their weapons angled in various directions. The corridor appeared to be for pedestrian traffic only, narrow and low-ceilinged. It was carpeted, the frosted pile crunching beneath his boots. The passage stretched three dozen meters in each direction from the travelator tube before hooking left either way you went. The walls and ceiling had been decorated with murals, tapestries, and ornate cornicing. All of it looked as if it would crumble at a touch. Several doors were set in the wall opposite the travelator exit—hinged doors, from the looks of them, all closed. When Jabari glanced back at the travelator tube, he gasped to discover the exit he'd come through was gone, or at least undetectable. He ran a glove across the surface where it had been and found it smooth.

"Meld-tech," he whispered. "Godsdamned meld-tech."

Expensive tech. Rich person's tech. Intended to hide the ugliness of things like maintenance hatches and transit stations. Recognizing the need of a passenger to pass on through, a portion of the wall had simply "dissolved," then seamlessly reprinted again to fill the gap. There was obviously power around here, enough to create the doorway and seal it behind them—although it seemed like the power had faded enough that the meld-tech couldn't repeat the performance as he stroked the surface. He hadn't seen the likes of it since—

"Boss?"

He dropped the hand, blowing out a breath to clear his thoughts, and faced the helmet with the blue daffodil.

"Orders?" Tee asked gently.

"Move on."

"Doors?" Erkan suggested from along the corridor, nodding at the set of them along the wall.

"Doors," he confirmed.

With his back to the vanished transit exit, he watched Otho and Morten head right and set the cutting lasers in their suit arms to the two doors in that direction. The women took the two doors opposite. Erkan stomped toward one end of the passage, scouting.

A knot still held Jabari's gut in a vice grip. When he'd been a young man—a *very* young man—he'd traveled on a ship that was nowhere near this size, but that had some of the same interior features. This reminded him strongly of that time, arriving through the jump point to join the Battle of Eradia, only to receive news of the Kaana's death and the end of the war. He, along with half the people on the ship, had surrendered. The rest hadn't been as smart, leaving on attack transports for the nearby planet. They'd dragged out the war another day and a half until every last one of them were slaughtered—as well as fifteen thousand non-combatant collaterals—for no gain whatsoever.

Three of his people had left the passage while he'd been reliving a past almost two millennia out of date. His right hand was twitching, a tic in the palm working his index and middle fingers.

Tegenwe was still burning through her door. Over comms, Shill muttered something about food.

"Reports," Jabari ordered.

"Storeroom," Otho said and came out his door. Morten appeared from the next one along and made the hand sign indicating, Same.

"Galley," Shill reported. "A big one."

Finally finishing cutting, Tegenwe kicked at her chunk of door, sending it into the room beyond. She poked her rifle inside, then her helmet. "Meeting room. Table. Four chairs. Holo-projector. Bodies. Actually... more like mummies." She turned from the sight to face along the corridor.

"Anyone else got bodies?" Jabari asked. A chorus of no's. He asked Tegenwe, "Military uniforms?"

"Yup. New Constantine insignia. Might be our cousins in there."

Jabari tapped a mural on the wall. "On *this* deck? I don't think any of our cousins made it this high up the ranks."

Tegenwe pointed, and Jabari glanced at the artwork he'd just tapped to find it *had* shattered and crumbled, the pieces drifting closer to his suit.

"That was probably worth millions," she said.

"Yes, to traitors," Otho interjected.

There were some light grumbles on comms about the way

he'd ruined the mood, but Corfids weren't known for their sense of humor—or for appreciating art—and were especially impervious to the kind of dark humor that kept other soldiers sane in the face of horror and threat.

"Art is art; it doesn't take sides."

Jabari swept away the small cloud of mural particles and coughed for attention, heading off further squabbling. "Otho, Morten. Scout around that corner. I'll follow you. Shill, Tegenwe, catch up with Erkan. Maybe we'll meet around the—"

He was interrupted by Erkan's voice in his helmet. "Um, I think maybe you all wanna come join me."

All five soldiers in the hallway startled into action at the edge in his voice, powerwalking in his direction.

Jabari asked, "Trouble?"

"Not... hostiles. Just... come see."

Jabari saw, all right.

And it was something a part of his mind had half expected and dreaded.

Erkan's passageway ended in a gilded door that hinged outward. He'd left it swinging free and poking back into the passage. Because Shill and Tegenwe preceded Jabari into the room beyond, it was their gasps and mutterings that first alerted him of what to expect. The room was no ordinary ship cabin. The outer room—a small antechamber—was three meters across with a double door that opened into a stateroom ten by ten meters in dimension. The larger room might have belonged to the ship's captain, except that Jabari had never known *any* warship to devote this much space to even its most senior officer's quarters. Nor this much opulence—wood paneling around three of the four walls, some kind of soft cushioning on the fourth, an oval table and chairs center-cabin, a desk and dresser against one side, a long wardrobe along the opposite, and a bed wide enough for three Othos.

The cabin abounded in colors that age and cold temperatures had barely faded. Some of the colors were interpreted faithfully by his ostendo-vision colors, while his HUD described the others. For example, it told him that the thick carpet scuffed by the three soldiers who'd preceded him was a rich carmine.

Four fat pillows had been knocked from the bed to the floor beside it. It hit him then: the room had gravity! Apparently, it had maintained gravity for all these eons. The table and chairs sat in a neat position, and all objects rested on the floor or other surfaces.

The two women stopped a few steps in. Jabari strode past them to where Erkan stood by the table, staring at a huge plaque fixed to the wall above the head of the bed, rimed with frost, but still legible.

"It can't be," the Proselyti corporal murmured. His helmet turned Jabari's way. "It can't be."

Jabari's pulse hammered in his throat, and his brain tried to insist that his eyes were lying to it, but he knew what he was looking at. This was a room he'd seen on videos—he and several billion other Terrans. He knew what it was and where he was now.

Jabari was standing inside the Terranist flagship *Iconic*.

He was standing in the personal stateroom of the Kaana.

CHAPTER EIGHTEEN

THE HUGE BED'S headboard bore an ornate plaque, positioned to catch the eye of anyone entering the room. Its inscription was familiar to Jabari:

*"To have command is to have all the power you will ever need.
To have all the power you will ever need is to have an empire in the
palm of your hand.
My hand wields that power, and as long as I shall live, the empire
will remain mine and mine alone.
Any person swearing fealty shall have my eternal blessing; any
person who opposes me is a dead person walking.
Everlasting life to the Empire of Terra!"*

*Kaana Adjira mo'Halana mo'ni'Mariama
Foremost of the Okalasi, Bringer of the Light, Protector of All.*

Erkan was staring at Jabari, though neither could see the other's face behind their mirrored visors. Did he want Jabari to say something? What could anyone say upon such an astounding discovery?

The Kaana's ship!

The Iconic*!*

Interrupting the moment and jolting Jabari from his shock, Scipio's voice blared in his speaker. "You've found it? Are there stasis pods, Otho? Is she there? Team video is scrambled, but I still have audio. Why is no one speaking? Report!"

Otho appeared to shake himself. Perhaps he'd been as stunned as the Proselyti. Perhaps he hadn't expected this any more than they had.

"No pods visible," Otho said, and entered the stateroom, where he stormed about, kicking chairs over, and pulling out drawers. "She's not in here, sir."

Morten had dropped into a crouch just inside the stateroom door, helmet bowed in introspection. Shill had dropped the data slate she'd brought along, and was now tapping furiously at the data panel on her suit's right forearm.

Tegenwe made a hand signal behind her back, where only Erkan and Jabari would see it. Jabari and Erkan joined her on a team-only frequency laid over the excited prattle of the two Corfids, a frequency Shill had shielded from Scipio's eavesdropping.

"They're here to find her body!" Tegenwe gasped.

"I can't believe the *Iconic* survived!" Erkan replied. "How the hell'd it escape from close proximity to a godsdamned moon explosion?"

Oblivious to them, Otho was asking Scipio, "Where do we head next, sir?"

"Keep searching that room. Tear it apart if you have to."

"With pleasure, sir." Otho ripped the drawer from the desk and smashed it against a wall.

"She may not be on the vessel at all, of course," Scipio added, "but any clue you can find... Anything..."

While Tegenwe and Erkan continued yammering to each other, Otho disassembled aspects of the empress' chamber in a determined act of political and historical blasphemy.

And Jabari's thoughts churned.

They want her as propaganda. Dead or alive, they want her body as a theater prop. This horror never ends; it'll never go away. They kept us alive, hoping for this day, for our final humiliation. And I'm just standing here, taking it, watching this dead-eyed ox desecrate her most sacred stateroom. They'll parade her ship and her tech and her corpse for all the trillions to gawk and marvel and sneer and cheer the latest of the beloved Martianist emperors, the wolf who keeps them all in peaceful squalor, the wolf who keeps them all as sheep. And we, we Proselyti, are the biggest sheep of all. We've served our enemy. We've bared our throats to the wolf. We've dishonored our Kaanate, our Kaana, our Queen, our Defender and Light—

Jabari screamed.

His scream was the eruption of every gram of pain and shame and rage Jabari had suppressed through all the subjective years since he'd surrendered. A scream building for seventeen hundred actual years.

It filled his helmet with raw white noise.

It blotted out the others.

When he was finished, when he ran out of breath, his throat burning in the aftermath, he stared out from his suit at a ring of immobile spacesuits, women and men silenced by his outburst. Jabari's ears rang, but in the room beyond—and in his commset—there was nothing but shocked, dead silence.

"Optio Scipio," he said, voice hoarse and ragged, "you brought us here to recover the Terran empress. You brought us here to *rub our noses* in our disgrace."

When Scipio replied, his tone lacked any trace of empathy. "I needed you here in case the *Iconic* wanted to register your gene scans, or even your Terranist voiceprints, if it has those on record. How else could we disengage any operational internal defense protocols? Or unlock any stasis pods we found?"

"*Her* stasis pod. The only pod you want is hers."

"If it turned to out to be her ship, well, of course it was."

"Lies," Jabari said. "Our lives have been based on lies ever since capitulation, and you're still lying. You don't need our DNA prints or voice records. You just want someone here to placate the Kaana if she's alive, someone who could talk her into surrender the way *we* were talked into it."

Across the chamber, Otho remained frozen in place, his blast rifle shouldered, and the drawers of a magnificently sculpted clothing unit clutched in each hand. His body language lacked expression the way Scipio's voice lacked heart.

Jabari faced the Corfid corporal, using him as a focal point for his next words, seeing him as an embodiment of Martianist rule. "We've done everything we were asked to do, faced death for many emperors, watched our sisters and brothers carved to pieces beside us, or die silently from tank failures. We humiliated ourselves by changing our allegiance to another empire, but we won't do this. We won't dishonor ourselves this way. We won't defile her ship for you."

"You swore an oath," Scipio replied evenly. "Remember the stakes—"

"We Proselyti are descendants of Earth," Jabari said and heard his voice quaver as he mentioned the forbidden name. "We serve the *people* of the empire; we serve *the human race*, as did our Kaana. If you revive Adjira, or if you parade her corpse, you'll only inflame tensions. You'll plunge our galaxy into greater conflict."

"Jabari, you're no political scientist. Your opinions are worthless. Your rank is lieutenant, but you're a grunt and always have been. An ancient grunt with ancient ideas. You're also relieved of command. That now passes to Corporal Otho."

Otho's thick voice grunted in pleasure. He let the drawers drop to the carpet.

"The hells it does," Jabari growled. "This mission is over."

"Private Jabari, I repeat, you swore fealty to the August Line, the Imperial Family whose lineage traces back to Holy Mars. All the other Proselyti in stasis swore the same."

"And before that, we swore fealty to the Kaana Adjira, and the Kaan before her."

No one else spoke. No one else moved. Otho was actually growling, low and quiet, a guard dog readying to pounce.

From the distant scout ship's command center, Scipio snarled, "Think carefully about what you're saying, and about your next words."

"I've had seventeen hundred years to think. I'm tired of thinking. You're right, I'm a grunt, a soldier, and I see things very simply. I already broke one oath when I surrendered to the Imperium. It's not so hard to break another, now that we know it was based on a fallacy all along, because the empire lied about Adjira's fate."

Scipio snarled a retort, but Jabari wasn't listening. He turned a full circle, seeing his reflection in the blank faceplates of his colleagues, wondering at the thoughts going on behind that glass. "I won't speak for the rest of my team, but for the first time since I left New Constantine, I'm home."

"As close to home as we can get," Tegenwe murmured before Scipio could reply again.

The frozen tableau had held since Jabari's scream. It was broken by another bellow, this time from Otho.

"Traitors!" He brandished his melon-sized fists at them.

"Traitors to you, maybe," Erkan said, "but not to the *true* empire."

The big Corfid shouted again and swung his blast rifle around to pump two ballistic rounds into Jabari's suit.

Because his boots had automatically powered down, the

rounds hit Jabari hard enough to knock him off his feet. He was aware of more shouting over comms and the staccato flash of rifle fire. When he raised himself up on his elbows, Otho was down, with limbs spread and weapon hanging free from its sling. The Corfid's suit smoked from several ruptures. Erkan and Shill moved to stand over the fallen Cor Fideli. Erkan kept his weapon trained, while Shill used a knife to slice through the man's rifle sling and toss the weapon aside. Tegenwe and Morten knelt by Jabari's side, running gloves over his torso, checking his suit integrity.

Jabari grinned hysterically at them, though they couldn't see his face behind the tinted visor. "Are we having fun?"

Tegenwe *tutted* at him over comms. "Glad you can joke. Lucky for you, he had his weapon dialed down for some reason, and your armor held. You won't be using anything in these equipment pouches, though." She patted the ruined pouches, then she and Morten helped him up and settled him on his feet. His rifle had slipped from his shoulder to the carpet.

"Get that for me?" he asked Morten, then with Tegenwe, he stalked over to Otho.

Scipio hollered in their comms, demanding an update. Jabari tapped at his wrist controls to lower the volume, ignoring it. Morten handed him his rifle.

"He's still alive," Shill told them, poking Otho with her boot. "Might last an hour or two."

"Already lived too long," Tegenwe said.

She positioned her rifle, pointing sideways across the line of Otho's face, set the muzzle against the beveled edge of the Corfid's visor, dialed the aperture to a fine one, and activated it, slicing off a flap of visor plate as big as Jabari's hand. The suit's internal pressure pushed the flap out to reveal the big man's face, exposed to vacuum. Otho's body bucked, his thick arms heaving, while Erkan and Shill stood on his hands, using their weight to keep him pinned. Jabari and Tegenwe caught the dying man's attention, and Otho's face contorted with defiance and pain, even as it frosted over from the ultra-low temperatures of the chamber. His skin turned blue, and capillaries showed dark in his eyes.

Jabari told him, "You hurt a lot of innocent people to get to where you are. You Cor Fideli always do."

Unable to hold his last breath any longer, Otho expelled it in a cloud of vapor, which quickly turned to crystals. Much of it froze while it was still in his mouth. For a moment, he gulped at nothing, straining to fill his lungs. Then his face seized up in a rictus of hate and agony—and remained that way.

"What have you done?" Scipio kept saying in their suit speakers.

Jabari decided it was time to round off the conversation with the man.

"What have we done, Optio Scipio? What we've done here today is told you and your emperor to well and truly go slag yourselves."

Around him, four helmets nodded in agreement.

"Oh, Optio?" Tegenwe added. "Otho's death makes it two lives your mission has ended unnecessarily."

The pause was long enough that Jabari began to wonder if comms had been terminated. When Scipio spoke again, his voice held its normal, controlled smugness.

"Wrong on two counts, traitors. They didn't die unnecessarily—for my mission will achieve a mighty moral and technological victory for our Imperium. And it won't be only two lives that are ended."

Someone snorted in amusement. Jabari thought it might have been Shill.

He said, "Your threat is a toothless one, Optio. We don't think you have any orders from the Emperor himself. You're either a liar in that regard, or you're simply delusional. Your mission isn't authorized, is it? When you return to the Maelstrom, you'll be arrested, and no one will care about the five Proselyti who didn't make it back. In fact, they'll think you executed us to cover up your game. They might even think we died trying to bring a rogue officer to heel. From experience, those Peripheries commanders trust you Cor Fidelis assholes about as much as I do. And even if you do return here with a larger detachment, we'll have jumped the *Iconic* someplace else."

Three of his people made questioning gestures at that. He replied with an elaborate shrug—maybe they could pilot it, maybe they couldn't, but as Tegenwe had said, they were now as close to home as they'd been in many centuries. They were standing in a ship that had defied the Imperium's best attempts at destruction. If they died here, they'd die in solidarity with their cause, and in defiance of Martianist arrogance and Martianist rule.

Scipio snorted. "Even if that were possible, you don't have the time. I don't need to travel back and seek reinforcements. I'm going to show you all the reach of our emperor's power. One of you is about to die, and that'll give the remainder an opportunity to live."

Helmets turned to look at each other. Jabari's turned toward the door. No one was out there in the anteroom or the corridor beyond.

Scipio continued, "When I've killed your colleague, the survivors may choose to repent and complete this mission, following my orders to the letter, before returning to live out long lives in an imperial prison. But at least they'll have life."

"And how do you plan to kill one of us, Scipio?" Jabari asked. He kept his voice level while hastily motioning Morten to check the entryway. Had one of the combat bots followed them? Or did Scipio have a plant among them, a spy? His attention slid across his fellows briefly before he dismissed the thought as ridiculous. These were Terranists. These were *friends*, brothers and sisters all.

"I have a failsafe card," Scipio said, "set within all your spines, and I believe I'll use it on the one I've heard complain the most since decantation. Say your goodbyes to Private Tegenwe."

The whole team turned to face the helmet with the blue daffodil. Jabari felt his jaw drop open as Scipio's threat became clear. His heart rate spiked. A chill ran down his cheeks, his neck, his throat.

The empire had placed explosives inside them.

Or acid cartridges.

And Scipio was about to trigger Tegenwe's.

"Tee," he said.

She slapped her hands uselessly across her suit, as if she could claw through it and remove whatever they'd put inside her.

But when Shill laughed, all of them froze again, Tegenwe included.

"You should... see yourself!" Shill managed through the guffaws. She mimicked Tegenwe's frantic suit-slapping. "Only... only thing funnier to see would be Scipio's face!"

Jabari caught on. Nothing had happened to Tegenwe. Nothing *would* happen. "You deactivated his devices?"

Controlling her laughter only when Tee punched her hard in the arm, Shill explained, "Yeah, about eight minutes into the trip, after I discovered his dumb little bioweapons. But I made 'em look like they were still functional."

"You bloody amazing, incredible little bitch!" Tegenwe giggled.

Shill giggled, too, and asked, "So how's it feel, Optio, sir? Doesn't look like the emperor has that much 'reach' after all."

Self-control fraying, the optio replied, "I'll have five of your comrades decanted and executed for this. Belay that—I'll have them all executed!"

"But you could always do that," Jabari told him, feeling the truth of it, acknowledging something that had always trickled dread into the back of his mind. "Any of you could, at any time you decided, and none of us could ever stop you. But we five can stop you from doing *this* one thing, Corfid."

Scipio lost all his composure now. "You idiots! I have two combat bots aboard! Once they've dealt with you, I'll still complete my mission! I'll find her! I'll—!"

Jabari muted him, saying, "Fly back home, little bird. We're finished with you." He cut comms from *Pleiades-219* completely and watched the others tap at their comms panels to follow his lead.

In the aftermath, the team lapsed into stunned silence, processing everything that had just happened. Shill moved across to a wall panel and inserted a data spine from her suit glove. She tapped out something on her wrist panel. Light flared from glowing lines along the ceiling and walls. She removed the data spine.

With the lights back on, the team slapped at more controls on their upper left arms. Jabari did, too, and his ostendo melted away, the visor becoming transparent. For the first time in two hours, he regarded the faces of his team as they regarded him. Erkan grinned, as did Shill when she joined them again. Tegenwe chewed her lip, nostrils flaring as she took long, deep breaths. Morten's expression was grave, introspective.

"Well, sisters, brothers," Jabari said. "We've sure done it now."

"We're free," Tegenwe said. "Free to stick it to Scipio and all those Corfid slag-suckers. For as long as that freedom lasts, it's sweet, sweet, sweet."

"You said we'll fly the ship away," Erkan said, sobering. "How we gonna do that? Shill, can you fix it?"

She shrugged. "Can try."

"One thing first," Jabari said. "It was Imperials who made me a lieutenant, but you heard him demote me, and we're not exactly part of their army anymore. We make our own decisions from here. We either vote on a new leader, or we decide to have no leader. No leader beside her majesty, I mean." He glanced at the plaque on the wall. "Gods, could she actually be *alive* somewhere on this ship?"

"Or somewhere not on this ship?" Shill added.

"Good point."

Erkan straightened, clearing his throat. "I'm voting on keeping a team leader, and that's you, my friend."

The others stiffened in their suits, too, adopting formal postures.

"Yeah, I vote for you," Shill said. "You're older than us, so that should make you wiser, right?"

"Seem to know what you're doing," Tee said and winked, "so far."

Morten saluted with the ghost of a smile quirking his lips for the first time Jabari could remember.

"It's kinda great, making our own decisions again, ain't it?" Erkan said. "I could get used to this."

Without warning, gravity stopped working. Several objects, including Otho's corpse, began floating gently upward, testimony that *Iconic* was moving in some fashion. Jabari thought, while grateful that his boots had automatically engaged, *The ship was probably already moving slowly through space, drifting before we boarded.* The room's light strips dimmed. After a few seconds of that, gravity returned, and the lights returned to full brightness. Objects settled against surfaces. Otho thumped onto the floor.

"What happened?" Jabari asked.

Shill did something on a wrist panel, then shrugged. *"Not sure."*

Jabari glanced at the wall board she'd been fiddling with earlier. "Something you did?"

"Not me. Might be that *Iconic's* systems are randomly cycling on and off again, or there's some wear and tear interrupting flow that the ship had to circumvent."

Jabari's boots remained powered on this time, evidence that the suit itself didn't trust the environment. He powered them down manually, thinking it might be a good idea to save the suit's batteries. "All right. We have two immediate goals. Short term, get this ship moving, and get life support online in some area where it's useful for us. I don't want to live in this suit any longer than I have to."

"Longer term?" Tegenwe asked.

He looked toward the plaque above the bed. "Long term, we find out what happened to the Kaana."

Jabari's next command decision was to send Tegenwe, Shill, and Morten further toward *Iconic's* bow. Although Scipio had blocked access to *Pleiades'* servers, they still had their saved files on the great ship, including schematic scans and energy readings. Shill was convinced useful systems centers would be found that way. Something was using a trickle of power up that way, and if other occupants of the great ship were surviving, and were hostile, three would be better than two in a firefight.

Ancestors, if you hear me, Jabari prayed, *please don't let there be a firefight. Please protect my people.*

There was another compartment showing up as a low-level power user, back the way they'd come, but a few decks lower— an area *Pleiades'* files surmised was a pod room. A stasis pod room. The first of them would be his and Erkan's destination.

"Don't like splitting up this way," Tegenwe complained before they parted.

"But you did vote me leader. So, do what I say, Private."

She growled and didn't move. Morten and Shill waited patiently for her by the exit.

Jabari added seriously, "Two groups can cover more ground, and it puts our chicklings in two nests, so the raider monkeys don't get them all. In other words—"

Tegenwe stopped him with a raised palm. "I come from the same bloody country on the same bloody world as you. I remember the saying and its meaning. And, hey... you're the ones heading toward the combat bots."

"Don't remind us," Erkan muttered. He was stripping anything useful from Otho's suit: spare mags, backup recyclers, nutrient tubes, and the other multi-rifle, which Erkan strapped diagonally across the back of his own suit.

Jabari reached out and touched Tegenwe's shoulder lightly. "Go. You've got more ground to cover, potentially."

She narrowed an eye at him and strode out into the service passageway, taking her partners with her. When she was out of sight, he could still hear her quip, "Typical damn leader, taking the shorter journey for himself."

"The power's gone to his head," Shill replied.

"Long-range comms silence," Jabari ordered them. "Close channel only. Don't want Scipio finding a way to eavesdrop."

"Go get—" Tegenwe started before she cut the channel.

Erkan came to stand where Tee had been, slipping a fistful of nutrient tubes into one of Jabari's thigh pockets so they bulged out the top. He found a chest pouch undamaged by Otho's blaster fire and put a recycler in it.

"Little intimate there, Corporal," Jabari joked, using the close channel he'd ordered the others to use.

"Just looking after the guy who's got my back if things go guts-out." He met Jabari's gaze. "We're checking out those pods?"

"We are, at least the compartment that showed up on

Scipio's scans." On his data panel, he brought up the best-guess map file he'd been working from before Scipio had cut live data updates. The location he wanted was maybe two decks down from here, and six hundred meters on a diagonal vector toward the starboard hull. In reality, it'd be more like a kilometer of weaving around bulkheads and conduit channels.

Jabari tapped his fingers against the recycler Erkan had just given him. "Let's move, brother. We won't have air forever."

CHAPTER NINETEEN

"CAPTAIN, I have managed to locate some old schematics for the *Iconic*—"

"Now you t-ll us!" Phillix muttered. "Took you l-ng enough."

"Until twenty-eight minutes ago, I was unaware this vessel was the *Iconic*."

"While we've been bumbl-ng about trying to find the powerplant," Phillix complained. "Remind me to give you a complete system over—"

"Check your arm screens," Torg continued. "The pods should be behind the next bulkhead to your right."

They were closer to the centerline and halfway along a corridor that stretched almost the entire width of the ship. Every now and then, they crossed atmo-shields; when they entered a compartment with air, they stopped to replenish their tanks. The air was stale, but better than asphyxiation.

Looking to their right forearms, they saw the layout of the vessel displayed on the small screens. Quick manipulation with their fingers enlarged sections and moved the image in any desired orientation. There was a pair of sliding doors a few meters ahead.

"Captain, the smaller of the energy spikes just changed course and appears to be closing in on your location," Torg warned.

"Frag. How soon, and where exactly is it?"

"Difficult to be precise, as I've noted several anomalies between the schematics I have and what I see from your mov—"

"Get on with it!" Sabrya grouched.

"Approximately two minutes."

"What the flux!" Sabrya forced open the sliding doors. "Get in here!"

Alexis didn't hesitate and stepped through the opening. Anything that made Sabrya worry was definitely a threat. "Is it bad?"

"If it's merely a security droid... meh... it'll be a pain, but if it's a combat droid, it could be very bad, especially as we only have one real weapon." The fighter followed.

Once Sabrya had stepped through the doorway, Alexis started to close them. A dark, insectoid head lunged through, but was snared in the narrowing gap. Gnashing mandibles scissored a finger's width away from her face. She imagined the sound of them as they opened and closed.

A primordial cry erupted from her lungs as she turned her head away in shock.

"Flux!" Sabrya leapt closer, pulled Alexis back, and before the crawler came through completely, fired the gutpuncher point-blank, the energy blast shattering its head and fusing the next section. *You said two fraggin' minutes!* she swore at the ship's droid as she stepped back.

"That was an approximation only," Torg replied.

Alexis, now more composed, studied the droid. Four segments of it had squeezed through the door before it jammed. What she could see was shaped like the centipede varieties from a hundred worlds, only much bigger, its segmented body painted a matte color to avoid reflecting light, every second set of legs ending in sticky gripper digits, while the odd pairs looked as if they could cut and slash.

"Needless to say, you'll lose whatever those mandibles latch onto," Sabrya told her.

"You've seen one before?" Alexis asked.

"A couple years back. They're tricky little shits."

"Seemed easy enough to deal with." Alexis' shrug was lost in the suit.

"You think so? Keep watchin'," Sabrya suggested. As she was speaking, parts of the ruined head of the crawler floated nearby, but the next segment of the body began reforming another set of mandibles as if from thin air. "It's another form of nanotech. You destroy one section or one feature, and hey, presto, new section."

"Not so easy, then. How do you kill it? That's all I care about."

"A girl after my own heart." Sabrya's chuckle sounded deep. "There's a couple of ways, but you have to get the whole thing at once; a real hot forge, vat of acid... tossin' it into space, or maybe crushin' it under a press."

"Little chance of anything like that at the moment." In disgust, Alexis jammed the shock prod through. Flashing brighter than the light from her headlamp, the area lit up with sparks as the full dose charge sent a web of electricity coursing over the crawler's body. The droid froze, and the nano replication stopped.

"We'd better go. That's only a temporary fix." Sabrya quickly scanned the compartment they'd entered. It was large, with dozens of rows of tables and bench seats stretching into the darkness.

"I see we found a mess hall." Alexis followed the fighter's gaze.

More writing in ancient text along the bulkheads.

Together, the two women kicked off, pulling themselves across the ceiling by light fixtures.

"That crawler can twist on itself in an instant," the fighter continued. "It has razor-sharp jaws, and those slasher-legs are like scythes. The one I saw a couple years back wrapped around a guy like a scarf and cut right through him. Very messy in zero-G."

Alexis studied her screen. "Torg, you said this was where the stasis pods were."

"Where are we, and why?" Sabrya also looked at her schematic, but it didn't correlate exactly with what they could see.

"I cannot be certain the vessel has not been modified since these plans were issued. We are talking more than seventeen centuries."

"So, no stasis pods."

"Evidently not there. You are close, possibly the next compartment to your left, toward the centerline."

"Torg, remind me to rip your head off when we get back," Sabrya hissed.

"Analyze any data you can find and let us know," Alexis ordered the droid.

"Affirmative, Captain."

Halfway along the bulkhead of the mess hall, they spotted a door.

"Well, that's good news." Alexis pointed to her arm screen. "We're almost on the centerline of the ship. It shows there's a passageway and another chamber through there. That should put us exactly in the center, where important pods are supposed to be."

"If we don't find the pods, when we get back, I'm makin' some permanent adjustments to our fraggin' droid," Sabrya commented. She handed Alexis her weapon before turning and driving her blades between the door seals. "Maybe we can find a droid on this ship to replace it."

"You've just put holes in your gloves," Alexis pointed out.

"I'll fix them in a minute." The fighter grunted with the effort, but soon there was a sufficient gap between the doors to allow egress for the two space-suited women. Beyond was a very short passage. The entrance at the other end was an iris door with eight curved segments. The whole section looked different from what they'd seen during their travel. The bulk-heads were a different material, and the door was large and circular. "This could be tricky," she said, studying the door's seals.

"Phillix, any chance on power yet?" Alexis asked.

"Possibly. I'm making some prog-ess. Where are y-u exactly?"

"Torg? Are you able to patch our locations through to the arm screens?"

"Stand by."

While waiting, Sabrya opened a pack on her utility belt and removed the tube of sealant, quickly applying it to the finger-tips of her gloves before she lost too much air.

A minute later, they saw four green blips displayed on their arm screens; two were near the center of the ship, and the other pair further to the rear. Apart from the distance, both were situated on the centerline of the vessel.

"Everyone should be receiving the data now," Torg said.

Alexis looked at the scale, still daunted by this ship's sheer size. "You're over fifteen hundred meters away!"

"It's all relative. Once I'm in fully with the AI, I can be virtually anywhere." A panel next to the door glowed faintly, and the overhead lights flashed on. Some sections sparked and dark-ened immediately after a brief flaring. "How's that?" the tech whiz asked.

"It's an improvement." Sabrya tapped what she guessed was the "open" button on the panel.

The segments of the iris door opened a fraction, then froze. A puff of mist gushed out due to an imbalance in air pressure. After a kick from Sabrya, the iris scissored open completely, sliding into the bulkhead to reveal a short corridor and another circular door, this one with a couple of recessed windows.

"Good work, both of you."

"This looks like—"

"An airlock?" Alexis finished.

They examined the door and beyond. The view through the windows revealed a large, oval-shaped compartment. Wide strips in the deckhead roughly a meter apart spread a diffuse glow throughout the room. Unlike other areas with floating, frozen corpses and debris, this room was pristine and untouched. Spaced along one curved wall stood three stasis pods like nothing they'd ever seen before; the other wall was identical. At the far end was another circular door. The door frame was elaborately decorated.

"I think we found it," Alexis reported.

"I wonder why this section was sealed off from the rest of the ship?" Sabrya scanned the room warily. "What's so special about it... other than its fraggin' weird decor?"

"They certainly did things differently a thousand years ago." Alexis tapped a panel with two illuminated buttons: one green, the other translucent and blank.

The door behind them irised shut, and the overhead lights strobed slowly.

"Repressurizing." Alexis checked her HUD.

When the pressure equalized, the strobing reverted to a steady, diffuse glow, and a burst of mist from nozzles in the deckhead shrouded them momentarily.

"And that would be decontamination, I reckon." The fighter shrugged.

Once the vapor had been sucked out through the vents in the deck, the interior door irised open readily.

"We have gravity." Sabrya strolled to the nearest pod to scrutinize the occupant while Alexis walked over to the one opposite.

Doublechecking her HUD and arm screen to verify that it was safe, Alexis retracted her faceplate and breathed in the cooler air.

"I... he's... fraggin' *pregnant!*" Sabrya said after taking a long look. Inside the pod was a semi-naked man, a translucent bio-skin covering him from neck to feet to regulate temperature and muscle stimulation. What her eyes lingered on was the translucent, bulging abdomen.

"That appears to be an ectogenesis—an embryo outside a uterus," the droid explained. "In this case, there is an artificial uterus. It has occurred several times throughout history."

"These ones are pregnant, too." Sabrya leapt across to check the other pods before moving to Alexis' side. "It's not new tech or anythin'... male pregnancy has been goin' on forever."

Dragging her eyes away, Alexis crouched to examine the side of the pod and the digital reader displaying the occupants' vitals; text scrolled rapidly along the bottom of the screen, too fast for her to read.

"Correlating the data from what I can see from both your cam feeds, the fetuses are identical females," Torg announced. "All indications are that their source cellular tissue came from the Kaana."

"Like fraggin' clonin'?"

"Affirmative."

"Shit!"

"What is it?" Alexis glanced to where Sabrya had turned.

In the bulkhead above the pod, a sliding door revealed a cavity where a large, humanoid male stood with metal plating visible below the skin, protecting vital organs. His muscles were ludicrously enlarged, and he was clothed only in leggings. Tubes and wires from his facemask curved around to his back.

"Is that prototype jeeming? It's gross." Alexis screwed her face up at the disfigured male.

"We have freakish Guardians protectin' these... other freaks," Sabrya said as a niche appeared next to each pod.

At first, the unnaturally muscled figure stood like a statue, then as it slowly powered up, the human-looking eyes glowed, and he began moving and flexing his massive arms. The bulging muscle, with implanted sections of armor, made it look quite formidable, but by the way it was moving, encumbered.

"See. It's impractical. Those muscles are so excessively enlarged, it looks like they can barely move. Not quickly, anyway." Sabrya leapt up, using the mass of the figure to control her momentum. She pivoted and pushed the blades into its overly thick neck. Out of reach of its flailing arms, she worked at sawing through the tubes and wires before ripping its head off. She turned her head away at the spurt of hydraulic fluid and blood, but it sprayed over her faceplate. "No wonder they're so ugly. They're fraggin' cyborgs!" Sabrya retracted her faceplate so she could see.

The remainder of the body shuddered and slumped in its harness, as immobile as a statue, like it had been for the last seventeen centuries.

"*And* you've just put holes in your gloves again."

Sabrya shrugged. "Damned reflexes. We should've just blown his head off."

"I'm hea–ng your way," they heard Bradyn call out over their headsets.

The guardian opposite, looking almost identical to the headless one, was also in the throes of activating—they all were.

"At least your nanites will be happy." Alexis noticed how

quickly Sabrya's movements became. *And to think, I thought she was fast before!*

"Frag the nanites. I'm happy!" Sabrya hurled the head and leapt after it a moment later.

Having a few seconds longer to power up, the cyborg across the compartment was alert enough to deflect the head before jumping down. It began lumbering across the room.

Sabrya met it halfway, twisted, and stomped her heel into its chest, leaving a sizable depression where she broke its ribs. Her momentum equalized with the cyborg's. Its boots slipped on the trail of blood.

Like a cat, she twisted and landed on her feet, while the broken cyborg dropped in a heap, writhing on the ground. She stepped over and drove her heel into its throat before it could recover.

The four remaining Guardians, now fully activated, emerged from a niche behind each pod, looking for the reason they were woken. Eight orange, glowing eyes behind their masks turned toward the two intruders.

"This isn't good." Alexis raised her multi-rifle, quickly selected a setting, and fired—or tried to. She tried again. "Shit." She quickly ran over the settings as the cyborgs moved ponderously closer. "Everything looks okay! Why?"

"Weapon suppression field. Frag it."

"What?" Alexis moved back, putting some distance between herself and the nearest Guardian.

"I've encountered this in a tourney. The sponsors thought it funny, loadin' us up with state-of-the-art weaponry, then shovin' us into a scenario where none of it worked until we took out the generator, but we were too busy fightin'. I reckon they don't want to risk the pods with wayward energy blasts."

Alexis continued to step back, deciding the best use of her weapon right now was as a state-of-the-art club. "You hearing all that, Phillix?" She leapt forward and swung hard at its head.

"I'll see wh-t I -an do," was his reply.

The approaching cyborg raised its arm to block the attack, but while the weapon broke, so did the arm. Its eyes now glowered red.

"Okay. I'm thinking red eyes are bad." Alexis ducked a wild swing that would have stove in her helmet.

While the cyborg was focused on Alexis, Sabrya leapt over, drove her blades deep into its back, and ripped her arms down savagely. Alexis dodged sideways to avoid the swinging arm before the glowing eyes went dark, and the guardian toppled. From the lacerated back, she saw exposed muscle and bone, while a mixture of blood and a greenish fluid oozed over the deck.

"This is great! My nanites are crankin', and I haven't had this much fun in weeks!" Sabrya stepped back and prepared for another attack. *This shouldn't take too long.*

One of the cyborgs on the floor twitched and reached out, locking its hand around the fighter's ankle. While not very agile, its grip was like a vice.

Sabrya stomped and pulled, but she was stuck like a wild animal in a trap. Groaning in pain as the pressure increased, she reached down, stabbing and slashing its sinews and muscle fiber. "Frag you!"

Alexis had also seen the movement and jumped over. She landed on its arm and shoulder, feeling the bones break, then pried the fingers apart to free the ankle.

"Looks like your boot's still intact," she said after a brief examination. "How's the foot?"

Sabrya leaned back against a pod in agony, only nodding. Sweat beaded her face, either from her exertions or the pain. "It'll take a few minutes for the nanites to repair," she gasped.

"That's a few minutes we don't have." Alexis stood, facing the oncoming Guardians, and came to a decision. "Phillix. Shut the gravity off."

"The grav-ty? You s-re?"

"Do it! Now!" she ordered vehemently. Alexis ran, jumped, and twisted at the approaching attacker, slamming her boots into his abdomen and chest, copying the fighter's technique.

Caught off guard, he flew back against one of the stasis pods while flailing his arms for balance.

"You surprise me, girl." Sabrya nodded in approval.

"Me, too."

A light started flashing red on the small screen on the side of the stasis pod.

"That brute just cracked the pod cowling. The seal's broken. See the air leaking out?" Alexis pointed to the vapor seeping through the now-frosting glass. The readout showing the occupant's life signs dropping rapidly.

"That's not fraggin' good, either."

"What, the— Oh." Alexis followed Sabrya's gaze.

The far door had irised open. Five more Guardians, not as freakishly muscled, but far more agile, trotted through the door. Beyond, they glimpsed another pod.

"Phillix!"

"Look out!" Sabrya warned.

Phillix, in the company of Bradyn, had eventually made his way aft to locate the node where he hoped to begin work on the ship's AI. He anticipated that, while ancient, the AI needed to control all facets of this ship would be an amazing one.

Bradyn started searching the area for spare parts or something to replace what they needed. "I don't expect to find anything, though," he said. "Big and beautiful though she might be, after a millennium and a half, I doubt anything will be compatible."

By that stage, Phillix had started working on the keypad,

familiarizing himself with the ship's systems. The first thing he did was arrange for the area to have gravity and air.

The gizmo, as Bradyn called it, was far more than some addon tool. What he hadn't revealed was that it allowed a direct neural interface—that's how he could code so well. When he was *inside* a computer, it was much easier to work.

Still, while Bradyn was around, he worked the way he normally did out of habit. In most cases, it sufficed. It didn't take him long to realize how complex this task would be. As he began to decipher the code, he was constantly interrupted to turn lights on, turn gravity on, then off, then the lights again, then open and close doors.

"How can I work under these conditions?" he muttered to himself for the hundredth time. He always found it difficult to integrate with people. Simple things to him were complex to others, whereas he was confused and at a loss to understand why people found things he considered mundane so fascinating.

Even before his formal technical training, Phillix saw patterns and revelations in obscurity, and he thrived on it. Getting the neural implant—painful, dangerous, and prohibitively expensive—had been his savior, though it had ended up with him being broke and sold into slavery... almost.

Data flows, computer coding, and matrices made the gloom of existence worth it. He could see the matrix—the wonder and beauty of its symmetry and complexity. That's what set him apart from everyone he knew, and while he felt alone, if his solitude meant delving into this, he'd embrace the solitude willingly.

Yes, he got on well with Bradyn, mainly because the engineer had a deep understanding of mechanics, and in that regard, they could converse on the same plane. But where Bradyn was enthralled with everything mechanical, he was more enthralled with the esoteric—the unseen things.

Sabrya was the sort of person he dealt with dozens of times a day. Brutish, in your face... simpleminded. Kill or be killed. If it wasn't understood, it was stupid. Deep inside, though, he was jealous of her popularity, her confidence, and marveled at her abilities. That was something he'd never hope to attain, so he shunned it and stayed within his shell.

Alexis was another story. She might not understand him, but at least she treated him as human and acknowledged his capabilities. She accepted him for what and who he was and gave him the tasks she knew he could do. He'd seen the effects of stasis sickness before; her quick recovery from recent tragedy was astounding to him, and her ability to cope with all that had occurred in a week surpassed him. He was keen to look into the subliminal training that seemed to dominate her actions and thought processes, thinking if he could gain a better understanding of reprogramming a human mind, a computer, even an AI, would be even easier.

At first glance, he knew this AI was going to be fascinating. Yes, it was almost two thousand years old, but it had remained pure and unadulterated for all that time. Once this ship had completed the emergency jump, no extraneous influences had existed to mar its perfection. It had remained alone, drifting... and over time, it had evolved into the beautiful thing it was now.

The urgent call to cut gravity again immediately stopped his train of thought. His companions were in trouble, and while they had their differences, they were relying on his help. He had to concentrate on them more, then they were fine again and leaving him alone in his solitude.

Back to the matrices... what was the AI trying to hide? He found out early enough it had been given the name "Janus." *What was that... the Roman god of transition? Of beginnings?*

Bradyn returned from his exploration of the engineering section. "She's just as big and beautiful on the inside," the big man announced on his arrival. "A lot of stuff here that's surprisingly advanced, even for us today, but there's nothing here compatible with the *Malleus*. I'm going to help the ladies. Looks like they could do with some."

"So soon?"

"Dude, it's been almost an hour."

"You do what you're good at, and so will I," Phillix responded absently. Once Bradyn left to go help the captain and the fighter, he took his opportunity.

***

She dodged too late, and the air was knocked out of her as a cyborg lashed out with a punch to her chest. Alexis cartwheeled back as the room plunged into grav-free darkness. *Now he fluxing does it!* she swore to herself.

Automatically, the suit's headlamps turned on. As she tumbled back, weightless, she saw glimpses of some of the other Guardians, also flailing about the chamber.

She grunted when she hit the far wall at an angle.

"You okay?" Sabrya asked from the semi-darkened room.

"I think so," Alexis wheezed.

Sabrya cruised closer. The light played over Alexis' suit, revealing a tear. "It ruptured your suit, too."

Hissing at the effort, Alexis looked down to see the small gash.

"And your ribs?" the fighter queried. "That was a hard hit."

"Maybe a cracked rib. You?"

"The loss of gravity eased the pain and evened out the odds. We're fraggin' lucky these freaks haven't been modded to work in zero-G."

When the artificial gravity was cut, the cyborgs floated wildly, colliding with each other or the bulkheads.

"Maybe whoever created them was overconfident?"

"Or just fraggin' insane."

Bradyn's voice cut in over the chatter. "Can you both make your way back to the mess hall?"

"Why? How's that going to help?" Alexis asked, as she looked around to orient herself. They were now several meters from the entrance.

"There's an access hatch to the maintenance shaft I'm using to get to you. I'll be there in a couple minutes."

"What? How—"

"You'll see. Meet me in the aft corner. Port side."

"Right." Alexis turned to Sabrya. "Get your ass out of here."

"You first!"

"That's an order, damn it!"

"We'll go together."

"Hey, Phill! Can you override the airlock?"

"Airlock n-w?... umm—"

"Work on it, but don't override until I say so!"

All they heard in response was muffled grumbling, "... cut this... acti–ate th–"

Turning to the airlock, they pushed off cautiously. While Alexis made sure they were on target for the airlock, Sabrya watched for the glowing eyes of the Guardians to pinpoint their location. It looked like they were pushing or pulling themselves along the deck or deckhead, making use of anything they could get their hands on.

"They're comin'." Reaching the door, the fighter gripped the frame, pivoted up, and placed her feet on the opposite wall, horizontal to the deck and above the exit. She was now lying along the deckhead. Activating her boots was awkward with her injured ankle. As Alexis drifted by, she pulled her up and closer.

"Turn your headlamp off," Sabrya said as she deactivated hers, "and your arm screen."

"My headlamp?"

"There's method in my madness. Trust me." Sabrya guided her boss into the furthest corner against the deckhead. "There's somethin' out there we've forgotten."

Inky darkness surrounded them.

"The crawler?" Alexis said after a momentary pause. "Flux."

"See how that word sort of rolls off the lips?" The fighter chuckled. "This is a long shot, but..."

"Oh ca-tain, I'm ready t- o-erride the ai-lock at y-ur command."

"Faceplates!" Alexis remembered and closed hers, then gripped the decontamination nozzles for support. "Do it now!" she ordered Phillix.

Holding tightly, they felt a vibration through their boots as the door mechanism within the bulkhead worked against the pressure differential.

Alexis felt Sabrya's hand tense on her shoulder as the first pair of glowing eyes shot past less than a meter away. The first cyborg, one of the over-muscled ones, was too big to fit through the gap, and the others slammed into him. Like meat in a mincer, he was forced through. The decompression slowed as the gap clogged, sealed by cyborg bodies.

One of the Guardians at the rear tumbled closer and somehow sensed the two women lying along the deckhead. It reached out, its clawing fingers brushing Sabrya's suit.

The fighter lashed out with her razors, shredding his arm. His screams were drowned out by the roar of explosive decompression as the door suddenly snapped open. The remaining Guardians disappeared, along with the remaining air.

They waited, not daring to breathe in the darkness.

"Make sure you cover that rip," Sabrya reminded her.

"Look who's talking. I've got one tear; you still have six. Or is that twelve now?"

"A comedian. I may as well leave my blades extended and seal around them."

"I have a tube of gelseal if you need it."

They spent a few minutes applying sealant to each other's leaks, and then checked for more.

"You ladies okay?" Bradyn asked. "I think I'm at the correct access hatch, if these schematics are accurate."

"Don't enter the mess hall, Bradyn," Alexis ordered. "Phillix?"

"Let me gu-ss, r-activa-e t-e airlock?"

"If you don't want us to asphyxiate."

"And -ave Bra-yn in charge? No thanks," the tech answered.

"I'm hurt," Bradyn mocked. "Besides, we know Sabrya would be next in line."

"Not fraggin' likely." Sabrya shifted positions and looked out as the airlock door remained open.

"The door is ja-med," Phillix sounded desperate.

"Torg, are you detecting any spikes in the mess hall?" Alexis asked.

"Several, but weak, and I am unable to ascertain what is what," the droid declared.

Alexis copied the fighter. They peered into the hall from each side of the circular door. "It was too good to hope they'd wipe themselves out." A shaft of light from the distant entrance was all that lit the large room. From that, she sighted vague drifting shapes, and... "Are those blood globules?"

"Probably, mixed with hydraulic fluid... and body parts. Several weak spikes could be damaged cyborgs, or it could be several sections of that fraggin' crawler," Sabrya added.

"Regardless, we'll have to think of something soon before we run out of air."

"Phillix, can you manage the lights?" the fighter asked.

"You sure?" Alexis sounded dubious.

"Gravity-free might have been an advantage with the cyborgs, but the crawler can still maneuver, and it can detect us in the dark," the experienced fighter explained. "The lights will make our odds 40/60 at best. If it's only damaged cyborgs in here, we can finish them off, and then we'll know we're safe."

"And we'll be in deep shit if it's both the cyborgs and the crawler."

CHAPTER TWENTY

GONE WAS the gravity of the Kaana's bed chamber. Gone also was the light. Plunged into the pitch black of dead ship sections, Jabari's enhanced ostendo vision tinged everything with yellows, grays, greens, and blues, rendering the environment "visible" again.

He and Erkan were intent on the compartments *Pleiades* had guessed were pod rooms. It took them twenty minutes to reach the service corridor leading to the first of their target locations—twenty minutes of pushing through frozen, floating corpses and other detritus, burning their way through locked hatchways, detouring around a collapsed section that was probably open to space, and zero-G climbing and gliding. Forty minutes without contact with the rest of their team—since he'd ordered long-range comms silence to thwart Scipio, if the asshole had stuck around. Besides, there was nothing to contact them about; they'd rendezvous back at the Kaana's stateroom later.

Finally, the pair exited a ladder tube into one end of their targeted passage. The corridor was sealed at this end, with its fire door down. It was difficult to tell at this distance, but it appeared to Jabari that the far end was open. Still enhanced in mild ostendo colors, it stretched a hundred meters before them, the walls and decking segmented at intervals by more fire door tracks. There was less debris here, and fewer bodies. The smooth, unadorned walls of the corridor were punctuated by a handful of hatchways at either side. All appeared open. Jabari doublechecked his map file. "It's one of these."

Moving shoulder by shoulder, nudging floating crap aside or up toward the ceiling, Jabari peered through the hatchways to their right, while Erkan did the same to their left. Some had wall mounts with nothing attached, and they had no way of determining their purpose. Others had empty bunks with frozen blankets and personal items drifting around them. The data panels by these hatches remained blank, so there was no indication of the function the rooms had served. Jabari noticed the uniforms on the corpses for the first time.

They served soldiers, probably.

"Getting weirder," Erkan commented as he gently moved a dead woman through one of the hatches. "These bodies are messed up by vacuum, but they're not as decayed as the others we saw."

Jabari grunted. "Still alive more recently, although 'recently' could mean five centuries, or ten. Did you notice, though? The uniforms are from our time."

"Everyone here was Terranist. No jeeming or other modding. It really is her ship. I can't believe it."

"Something damaged *Iconic* badly, something like a moon exploding near it. These people might have come out of stasis every few centuries to attend to things—same as the Proselyti. Except the last time *they* came out, systems failed completely and killed them."

"Which means... the ship jumped here by itself?"

Although Erkan wouldn't see it, Jabari made a musing face for a moment. "Why not? We had pretty smart ships."

"Smart, all right," Erkan agreed. "Some of them were damn sassy, too. I was once on this..." Seeing Jabari had frozen in place, Erkan copied him. "What?"

Jabari kept his voice low and pointed with his weapon. "That door." The next one on his side was a wide one. There was no matching hatch on the opposite wall. This one was partly open, showing a gap of thirty centimeters or so. "We've seen them open, and we've seen them shut, but we haven't seen them like that. I'll pull; you cover."

He moved to it, shouldering his weapon. Erkan had Otho's multi-rifle slung, and his own in hand. He came over and stood with the weapon at the gap, while Jabari wrapped fingers around the handle. The door moved more easily than he'd expected, rolling into the bulkhead and locking in place. He moved through and to the left with his back to the wall. Erkan took up a matching position on the other side.

Feeling his mouth drop into an 'O' of surprise, Jabari heard Erkan say, *"Huh."* They dropped into matching combat crouches.

The compartment was a mess hall, square, forty meters to a side. Metal tables and chairs in neat rows had been welded to the decking. Strewn in a slowly spreading cloud across the far third of the area was what looked like cushion stuffing. Jabari's HUD briefly tagged a lot of it in blue with an icon denoting organic matter—and not just any organic matter...

Minced human.

He tracked the direction it had gradually spread from: an irised door two-thirds of the way along the left wall, and open.

Someone got sucked through a pressure differential. Explosive decompression. Nasty. And....

"It's fresh," he told Erkan. "Still cooling."

Floating behind the mess of particles came a group of misshapen bodies, none of them wearing vac suits, and all of them still as warm as the minced person. From within that irised door, a line of lighter shading showed against the HUD's general green. There, then gone, then flashing through the gap again.

"Lamplight," Erkan said. "Think it's Ninety?"

Their close-comms frequency had also been provided with Shill's blocking code to prevent eavesdropping. Jabari felt safe continuing to transmit. "Ninety's too big for that door. No lamp, either. He uses thermal imaging, tachyon scans, EM pulses, ultrasound..."

"Sometimes you impress me, my friend."

"So, impress *me* by telling me who the hells it is, if it's not the droid."

A moment later, the question was answered when two intact, space-suited humans stepped out through the circular hatch. The strangers' continued reliance on lamplight indicated they wouldn't detect the Proselyti unless they played the beams directly across them. For the moment, he could continue observing unnoticed.

"Look like scavengers?" Erkan asked him.

Jabari glanced at his HUD's zoom icon and blinked three times to trigger it. The vision in his visor lurched forward, so he could study the pair up close. Women, judging by the body language and sculpted suit design, and they were pretty banged up, suits patched in places with a gel sealant. One held a rifle. Or... no. It *had* been a rifle, but it was broken now. Whatever they'd done in that side room, whoever they'd fought, they'd completed it hand-to-hand. Hopefully that meant she was out of ammunition.

In response to Erkan's question, he replied, "That's no uniform they're wearing."

"Civs, but looks like they been fightin' close quarters—with whoever got chewed up through that hole."

"Ya think?"

Erkan huffed a laugh. "Get slagged, Lieutenant."

"Back at you, Corporal." He zoomed his faceplate vision out, then moved his hand to an arm panel.

"I'm skimming for their suit frequency."

"Me, too. Race ya."

It took a good ten seconds for his comms to locate the women's frequency and overlay it across his and Erkan's. One woman's voice was deep for a female, curt and abrupt like Jabari's original training sergeant. The other one called her "Sabrya," and Sabrya called her "Alexis." Alexis had a voice like the soft autumn breezes of New Constantine, a voice Jabari immediately labeled feminine. He had no idea what language they spoke—it wasn't Imperial Common or any of the trade languages he'd heard over the past millennium—but the combat suit's translator interpreted it without trouble, so it must have been a Peripheries language familiar enough to the Imperials.

"Challenge 'em?" Erkan asked him.

"Let's stay low and let it play out. We don't confront unless they threaten us."

Erkan made an unhappy noise. "Procedure is to make 'em stand down before we treat 'em nice."

"Imperial procedure."

"In that case, all right, then."

"Plus, we're a surprise to them. Let's see how this pans out."

As he continued watching from his hunched position, Jabari wondered who the women had confronted in the side room. Who'd been crushed and minced through the iris? Decanted Terranist troopers?

A new knot twisted in his gut. If, in some bizarre twist,

they'd awoken Kaana Adjira from stasis, and *her* body parts were floating along there, Jabari would kill them both. Slowly.

Just then, lighting flickered on, interrupting his thoughts. Jabari crouched lower, curling in as much as the combat suit would allow. But the two women had other things to focus on than him...

"Where the flux is that crawler?" Alexis slunk back into the corner, discarding the broken weapon, and feeling for her shock prod.

"You still w–nt lights, C–tain?" Phillix asked.

"Did we not just say that?" Sabrya answered, annoyed.

The lights flickered in both the oval room and the mess hall. While the oval room became fully illuminated, the mess hall had patches of darkness where the overhead lighting had been damaged. Globules of fluid drifted aimlessly; a few hit the bulkhead near them, merging with the smears already there.

"No sign of the crawler yet, but it could be hidin' or reformin' under these fraggin' tables, or in the shadows. Stay here." With a delicate jump, Sabrya floated toward the center of the large room.

Alexis tested her rib injury while following the fighter's progress through the various illuminated areas, waiting apprehensively when she disappeared into the shadows, out of reach of her headlamp.

A flash of blue lit up the area briefly. Then Sabrya appeared, heading back. "That answers that question; all the cyborgs are down, and the crawler's in several sections," she said.

"If that one droid can slaughter all those cyborgs, we'd better get out of here and come up with one of those plans you mentioned to destroy it once and for all."

"A strategic withdrawal," Sabrya agreed, brandishing a shock prod. "From one of the elite cyborgs," she explained.

"How about a strategic withdrawal through this access hatch?" Bradyn suggested.

They turned to see him hanging upside down from the aft corner.

"Don't worry, there are atmo-shields all along this shaft. Phillix says it's a hardwired failsafe, as the shaft runs down the centerline of the vessel. They'll be the last things to go, even in a catastrophic power failure."

"Good to know." Alexis pushed Sabrya toward the new hatch, then followed on foot. "How did you get here so quickly?"

"You'll—"

"Captain," Torg interrupted. "I'm detecting a spike moving near you!"

Alexis pivoted on the spot, discarding the broken rifle. She had her shock prod ready, desperately searching.

"Above you!" Bradyn warned, pointing. He dropped out of the hatch and kicked off the bulkhead.

Looking up, Alexis spotted a couple sections of the crawler detach from the deckhead, aiming directly for her.

"Flux!" Sabrya twisted in the air, managing to turn around, but her feet had nothing to push off of; no amount of agility or enhanced strength could propel itself by will alone in a grav-free environment. She continued to drift further away from her captain.

Suddenly, she was propelled forward by an immense force.

"Probably the last time I'll get to push you around," Bradyn said from where he braced himself against one of the solid tables. "Phill, we'll need the gravity back on in a sec."

"I haven't pr-perly ass-ssed that sect—"

"Do it anyway!" the engineer grouched.

As the crawler glided closer, Alexis twisted to the side and zapped it with the shock prod. It was a glancing blow, as the prod slid off the smooth, curved surface of the droid. It darted toward the deck, where it quickly slid under a table.

The room plunged into darkness again as the gravity came on.

"Frag!" Sabrya grunted as she dropped. Reflexes kicked in, and she landed in a roll, coming up hard against one of the many tables bolted to the deck.

Three sets of headlamps flashed on, and the beams swept across the area.

"Lights, damn you!" Sabrya spat.

Whatever the tech was saying was incoherent in his panic.

"Sabrya, look out!" Torg warned .

The fighter felt it the instant it touched her boot. Without thinking, she kicked it as hard as she could with her good foot. A section of crawler connected solidly with her boot, but by torchlight, there was little chance of spotting where it landed.

From out of the darkness, there came a flash of intense light —an energy weapon discharging near the meeting of mess hall and corridor. The beam dazzled them and transformed a table into a smoldering, glowing glob.

"Who the frag is that?" Alexis exclaimed.

Two more beams of light scythed across the darkness as the pair turned toward the source. The illumination of their lamps showed a spray of red mist from over by the corridor entry, where someone's blood had sprayed into the vacuum.

"What the *frag*?" Alexis repeated.

The lights finally blinked on.

"Did that work?" Phillix asked.

While he was still getting used to the newcomer who'd dropped through a ceiling duct—a thickset male who'd shoved Sabrya into the air—Jabari heard a word from one of the women that chilled his blood.

"...crawler..."

Rec-7?

If the damn thing was in there, they had problems.

It was then that the screaming began over comms, and Jabari realized all the problems were Erkan's.

CHAPTER TWENTY-ONE

EVEN WITH ITS deeply ingrained military conditioning, Jabari's mind locked up with shock and overwhelm. So much was happening, so much input...

The three civilian suits active around the chamber. The subtle tugging at his limbs and his weapon, signifying that grav had activated in this section. The sinuous form of the centipede bot as it snaked up and across a table, leaving a slick of gore in its wake, avoiding the energy beams he was firing at it.

The devastation and desecration of Erkan's suit near him.

Erkan. His comrade, his friend. His brother.

But the ingrained training had flicked that inner synaptic switch, focusing Jabari. It sidelined grief and shock, compartmentalizing the storm of information and issues facing him. Right now, everything was about Rec-7. The centipede bastard that had come out of nowhere, wrapping itself speedily around Erkan's chest and shoulder like a sash. It had snapped his multi-rifle in half and sawn through the man within seconds, using nanotech to refine its pincers and cutting legs into edges so keen, they could slice through armor. He'd fired on it from close range—probably hit Erkan, too—sent the bot fleeing...

He tracked its movement as it scurried between tables, avoiding his laser fire, no doubt reassessing the situation before mounting another attack. Jabari squeezed off a final burst, vaporizing a cubic meter of frozen human remains before superheating another table and chair so they dissolved into glowing slag. His wild firing had managed to nick the bot across a rear segment. It vanished into one of the holes he'd burned in the wall. Why in all the hells had it retreated? The energy from his weapon would do little more than cause it the electronic equivalent of pain, maybe scramble its thinking.

Perhaps the damn thing *was* hurting. Perhaps these strangers had already damaged it before he'd arrived.

Not enough to save Erkan...

With Rec-7 temporarily out of the picture, Jabari maintained his combat focus, kept his rifle angled toward the droid's bolt-hole, and avoided looking at his friend's ravaged body as he sidled closer to the woman and the man near the circular side door. The other woman, Sabrya, had managed to bring herself down near them, moving in protectively. They were smart not to venture far from that irised hatch, where they'd have shelter if the bot returned. It also kept them away from the fallen Guardian bodies, and the mass of chewed-up human remains strewn across the tables and floor, where the fresh gravity had dumped it all.

Hooking into their comms frequency, Jabari relied on his suit to translate his words. "Identify yourselves." Since his suit translator knew their language, it could be trusted to make his words understandable to them.

The smaller woman, Alexis, raised her arms, indicating it was she who replied, "If that crawler's your enemy, we're your friends."

The concept of *friend* stabbed at Jabari's chest, constricting his throat despite the combat focus. He pushed on. "You're scavengers? Not members of any armed services?"

Another voice snorted, and the taller, beefier woman turned her shoulder to him, scanning the room, squatting to peer under tables.

What the slag? Who turns their back on an armed imperial soldier? He spared a glance at the hole where Rec-7 had vanished. *Someone more worried about that.*

"It'll take time we don't have to explain who we are," she said dismissively. She held a shock prod, as if that would keep a centipede bot at bay for long.

The smaller of the pair stepped between Jabari and her colleague, tapping her chestplate. "Alexis. That's Sabrya and Bradyn. You are?"

He hesitated, but with one bot skulking nearby, and Ninety potentially alert to his location, he had to agree with the bigger woman: there wasn't time for dragging things out.

"Jabari."

He was close enough now to see their faces through their visors, and his HUD told him there was light in the room again. Jabari powered off his ostendo and unmirrored his faceplate so they could see him, too.

Sabrya rose from her crouch and pivoted slowly, sweeping the room for threats like a trained soldier. She said, "That's an Imp suit, but Jabari's not an Imp name, and standard Imp procedure is to make us relinquish our weapons, even ones this shitty. So, you might be the scavenger."

"As you said, there's no time for long stories." He checked the direction Rec-7 had gone, turning his shoulder to keep Erkan's remains out of view, then pointed his rifle at the airlock. "What did you find in there?"

The two women in unison pointed to the human stew that had dropped from midair.

Jabari clenched his teeth. "What *else*?"

Alexis gestured in conciliation. "Stasis pods. Some weirdness in them. You can go see, but first we have to—” she pointed toward Rec-7’s bolt-hole “—you know.”

“The other bit’s still around here, too,” Sabrya growled.

Jabari tensed again. “The other…?”

“We damaged it. We jammed it in the main door and zapped it. The head and another segment came off, but they’ve morphed into a smaller version, and it’s still around here somewhere.”

Despite the danger, Jabari had to get into that stasis room. That was the whole reason he’d come here, the whole reason Erkan had just died in front of him. He had to see. The likelihood that *she* was there was greater now, because he’d noticed a faded motif on the mess hall’s rear wall. The emblem of the 9th Okalasi Battalion, the Kaana’s personal strike force. This hall had been for the detachment’s use, a detachment that would only have been stationed to protect her majesty.

“Those men you killed in the stasis room,” he said, finding it harder to bear down on his anger, his rage, “they wore insignia like that?”

The women glanced at it.

“*Nope,*” Alexis said. She sounded genuine. “They were cyborgs, if that helps?”

He narrowed his eyes at her. “You mean mechanically enhanced?” Now that he was looking at the carnage without ostendo, he could see that some of it *was* mixed with liquid of a weird blue color, rather than just the reds and browns of human gore.

Hydraulic fluid. Guardians.

“Yes,” Sabrya said. “Can we talk about the crawler and gettin’ the frag out of here?”

“We’ll leave when I say we leave.”

“So, you are an Imp after all,” she groused. “Fraggin’ jackboots, the lot of you.”

Alexis made a musing sound. “He’s not acting like an Imp.”

She dropped the shock-prod and ventured closer, showing her empty hands. "Jabari, I promise you, we're not bad people. We're not your enemies. What's happening here is the latest in a long series of bad things happening to us, and you, you just lost your colleague. I lost someone recently, too. I have some idea what you're going through."

"I'm not going through—"

"We were attacked by those cyborgs. It was self-defense... and regrettable. But if that bot returns—if both parts of it return—we'll need to defend ourselves again. I figure you have the same problem as us. Now, it didn't look like your weapon did much more than scare it away for the moment. Sabrya says it's hard to kill—"

"Fraggin' truth, it is," Sabrya growled.

"So maybe we should work together."

Jabari considered calling in his remaining teammates. Shill and Tegenwe were smarter than him. They could solve this problem, sharp thinkers as they were. But maybe it would be better to keep them in the dark, keep them separate. Keep them safe.

Besides, he wasn't ready to tell them about Erkan. He wasn't ready to acknowledge it himself.

"All right, we'll find a way to put this bot down together."

If we survive that, I'll decide what to do with you.

He sidestepped, keeping the Sabrya woman in full view. "You. Sabrya. You said the centipede bot is hard to kill? What do you know about it? *How* do you know about it?"

She only spared him a brief turn of her helmet as she continued her vigilance, slinking like an animal on the prowl. "How could you not know about them, wearin' that uniform?"

"Quicker we kill it, quicker it's done. So cut the spindrift and tell me what you know."

Her sniff of irritation was clear over the speaker. Then she said, "It's a form of nanotech where you have to destroy the whole thing, or it'll keep comin' at ya. We'll need a very hot fire, a lot of acid, crush it under a shitload of pressure, or we'll have to toss the fragger into space."

"Damn," he replied. "Not much chance of any of those in here."

The man, Bradyn, cleared his throat at that and said, "Actually, I saw something that might do the trick." He jerked his thumb over his shoulder, indicating something past the hatch he'd emerged from. "Something back there."

<hr>

"Good luck," Alexis told Bradyn as he peered down at her from the ceiling hatch. Sabrya had helped him climb back up. The mechanic gave Alexis a wink, but even with his expression washed out by his interior helmet lights, he looked nervous. She didn't blame him.

As Jabari prepared to join the engineer in the maintenance shaft, he caught Alexis' eye. "You don't kill anyone else you find in that room. You don't interact with anyone in there until I get back."

Standing a few meters back, Sabrya bristled. "Depends on whether they try to interact with us—and the way they interact."

"You heard me."

"I'm just hearin' fraggin' static." Sabrya actually took a step toward him. "You seem to be under the delusion that we're under your control."

Alexis placed a hand on her arm. "We'll do our best, Jabari—I'm assuming you're here for someone in stasis?"

His head snapped toward his fallen comrade, then snapped away. "We came here to investigate that room. I'd like to complete the job without further bloodshed, if that meets with your approval."

"It does," Alexis said, talking over whatever Sabrya was about to say. "We'll tread carefully, I assure you. And... good luck."

She flinched when Jabari fired his weapon across the room without warning. Sabrya's augmented reflexes put her in front of Alexis in the same instant.

"You see something?" Alexis asked the soldier.

"Baiting it," he replied, giving Sabrya a long-assessing look. Then he passed the laser up to Bradyn before leaping up with the help of his suit thrusters. Alexis kept watch on the room until both men had disappeared from view.

"I should have fraggin' gone." Sabrya pivoted and strode purposefully to the area where the other soldier's body lay in a pool of congealing blood and organs.

Alexis groaned, bending over to peer under tables. "Shouldn't we be, you know, getting out of here?"

Unperturbed by the suggestion, the urgency, or the butchery, Sabrya rolled the top half of the soldier's body over and slid the intact imperial multi-rifle out from under it. Alexis wondered for a second why the man had carried two of them.

Sabrya crowed, "Fraggin' yay!" A moment later, she brandished a fat pouch of spare magazines to go with the weapon. Flinging off the gory remnants, she hooked it under her utility belt and returned to her captain's side.

"I see your ankle's better," Alexis noted.

"Improvin' by the minute but kickin' that crawler earned my suit another air leak. We need to get through the airlock, and soon."

"Exactly what I was suggesting." Alexis smiled. "Phillix?" she called, relying on comms.

"I he-rd, but I'm uns-re whether the ai-lock door w-ll respo-d after the ov-rride." Phillix sounded unsure, and sheepish.

"I'm confident you can do it," Alexis reassured him.

Sabrya rolled her eyes.

What? Alexis mouthed silently.

The fighter grinned, shook her head, and strode toward the airlock, then balked and stared up at the ceiling hatch.

Jabari was back there, leaning upside down the way Bradyn had earlier, but with his rifle in hand. "Got it working?" he asked, and it took Alexis a split second to realize he was talking to Bradyn, and not looking at her.

On comms, the mechanic replied, "Do Barunti sheep have six legs? Get your drocking ass in here and hang onto something, and I'll fire it up."

"Not until we have company." Jabari fired a sustained burst along the side wall of the mess, snarling curses his suit couldn't seem to fully translate.

"What's he yelling for?" Alexis asked, moving to join her friend.

"Apart from testosterone overload? Probably transmittin' directly at the crawl—" Sabrya started to say, then found herself preparing for an attack as a long, dark shape eeled its way from the far wall, then up it, then along the ceiling toward the open hatch.

"Hey, Imp, that thing's bits have reconnected into one... fraggin' bit," Sabrya warned.

Jabari had already withdrawn. "Copy."

Sabrya grabbed Alexis' shoulder and dragged her into the oval room. There was a pause while nothing happened. She hissed, "Gadgetman, pull your hand outta your pants and close the damned iris!"

"I gath-r it hasn't cl-sed yet?... so, it's bad."

"This inner door and that other door should be okay." Alexis pointed to the second room. "Phillix, give us a couple minutes, then try the other doors. We'll have to use this first chamber as an ad hoc airlock."

"Yes, capt-n," the tech replied.

The two women picked their way across the outer room, avoiding the streaks of blood and other fluids on the deck.

Sabrya stopped in her tracks.

Alexis was a few paces ahead before she realized. "What is it?"

"That shit is wrong on so many fraggin' levels."

Disconcerted at the tough fighter's reaction, Alexis followed her stare with a feeling of dread.

The cowling of the damaged pod, already weakened by the earlier cyborg impact, had blown loose with the depressurization. A gruesome mess coated the pods. The external womb had ruptured, leaving the remains of the fetus visible.

"That's not intestines..."

"Frag. Not like any bowels I've seen before... that's a fraggin' tail!" Sabrya spat in shock.

"I ha-e it now, Capta-n," Phillix said.

"Move it." It was Alexis' turn to urge Sabrya into motion, grabbing her shoulder.

They were only too glad to turn their backs on the abomination. They reached the entrance to the second chamber with a few strides.

The inner chamber was the same size as the outer one, its walls also curved, but that was where the similarities ended. While the previous one was bland and devoid of any decor, this chamber was lavishly furnished. Colorful tapestries—which had hidden the cyborg niches—were now ripped and strewn on the floor. The one and only stasis pod lay in the center of the chamber.

Via her earpiece, Alexis heard the sounds of the ruckus up in the maintenance shaft above her, but the men needed to concentrate, so she refrained from pestering them with questions. *Bradyn will update us when he can.*

"How's your air?" she asked Sabrya instead.

Sabrya was examining the rupture in her boot and cursing

quietly. "I doubt we have enough sealant for that. I've got about six minutes left."

"Six minutes! You should've said something."

"Would it have made any difference? It is what it is. The nanites are good for a bit longer."

"Phillix?"

"Six m-nutes. I -eard... working on the door now."

Sabrya huffed. "I bet he's thinkin' of activatin' it in about seven minutes."

"I heard tha-, too."

"Get on with it, then," Alexis retorted, letting some of her angst slip.

"Stand clear," they heard a few seconds later.

The door to the chamber spun closed. Through the small window, they saw the inner door of the previous chamber also spin closed.

"Press-rizing now."

"I'll take any sealant you have left." Sabrya slid down the bulkhead as the atmosphere in the chamber was restored. Alexis joined her, dropping a gel tube in her lap, and watching her arm viewer. "77 percent... 83 percent... 96... done." Satisfied that the air had been restored, she lifted her faceplate and tentatively inhaled. Cooler it may have been, but it had a faint, unpleasant aroma, making her nose wrinkle. She looked around quizzically as a noise impinged on her senses. "Can you hear that?"

Sabrya squeezed the gel across the damaged section. Both gel tubes were quickly depleted. "I do now." She removed her helmet to allow maximum air flow.

They both turned to the lone stasis pod. Someone was in there. And they were screaming.

CHAPTER TWENTY-TWO

THE MAINTENANCE SHAFT ran both ways in a straight line, but Jabari had no sense of its true length. For all he knew, it ran for *Iconic's* full five kilometers. Lighting was minimal in here, dwindling with distance. The flickering atmo-shields every hundred meters or so didn't help. Needing every resource at his disposal, he fired up his ostendo again, cleaning up his view and painting in more detail. Pipes and conduits clung to bulkheads at all angles; the occasional tank or junction box was visible inside alcoves or attached to those pipes.

The shaft had no gravity. Other people might not be able to cope with the constant transition between weight and weightless—normal people who weren't spacers or soldiers. For Jabari, the abrupt shift to zero-G meant the freedom to glide, to push off the floor and sail across to the trolley where Bradyn waited.

A simple steel-mesh cage, the trolley was suspended from a rail along the ceiling, barely high enough inside for Bradyn to avoid scraping his helmet along the top. Jabari had little experience with starship service areas, but this setup reminded him strongly of the underslung monorails common across his homeworld, New Constantine. Reaching the steel cage, he maneuvered himself through the gap in the mesh that served as a door and hunched over beside the other man.

Bradyn waited by the control board fitted to the farthest end, the gloved fingers of one hand curled through the wire to anchor him, his faceplate turned Jabari's way.

"What are you waiting for?" Jabari hollered at him, loud enough to hurt his own ears inside his helmet.

Also loud enough to make Bradyn flinch. He flipped a lever on the control board. The car jerked and scraped sluggishly along its rail.

"Can't this go faster?" Jabari snarled, eyes on the hatch down to the mess hall.

"Just taking time to wake up. Drocking thing's old, you know."

Old as me, Jabari thought, then saw a lithe, slender shape dart through the maintenance hatch. It wriggled, maggot-like, as it soared across the empty space to clatter against the ceiling rail, where it clung.

"*Wazazi na walezi*," he prayed, readying his rifle. "Ancestors spare us."

A moment passed while the bot got its bearings, and the trolley scraped along the rail. Then Rec-7 scuttled up into the tangle of pipes and trunking lining the roof above the rail. It reappeared a moment later, a meter closer and weaving in and out of the cover along the ceiling.

Seeing it, Bradyn pounded on the control panel with one fist. "Come on, come on, come on, you drocking bastard! Move!"

They were picking up speed, but it wouldn't be enough. Jabari braced and shifted aim ahead of the closing bot.

"*No!*" Bradyn cried.

Jabari turned his helmet. "What?"

"You'll hit the rail. For all I know, that's where this car draws power from."

"All right, then," Jabari said as a new idea came to him. He pressed into the corner closest to the oncoming Rec-7. "Get over here, Bradyn."

"What?"

"Here. *Now*. And get ready to punch."

With the guy's size and power, this should work.

As Bradyn came close, Jabari shifted his attention to the roof. Rec-7 reemerged from among the pipes a mere dozen meters away, still accelerating. Jabari fired a brief spurt toward it, ensuring the damn thing would target him and his position, then angled his muzzle into the mesh above him, firing a steady beam through it, moving the rifle in a ragged oval, timing it carefully, and mindful to avoid the rail.

"Watch what you're shooting at," Bradyn warned him.

"I *know*! Just be ready."

"For what? What the drock are you...? Ohhh."

Jabari hoped that meant the stocky man understood—and was reassured when Bradyn braced himself, hunkering down like a tensioning coil.

Reaching them, Rec-7 dropped onto the cage. Jabari nicked the bot again with his laser to focus it on him. The bot gathered itself directly above him—just as Jabari made the final cut through the grid. Before Jabari could bark *Go*, Bradyn was already moving, slamming one fist into the edge of the fresh slice of roof. He caught himself against the top of the cage with the other arm, ducking his helmet to avoid impacting against the molten edges of the burn hole. In zero-G, the steel oval flipped over and out past the back of the trolley. And it kept tumbling, end over end. Rec-7 went with it, clinging to the mesh.

"*Yes!*" Bradyn cried and righted himself.

The car's velocity picked up as Rec-7 spiraled away on its

metal pancake, the distance between them stretching wider at a reassuring rate... until the trolley juddered and began to slow.

"No! *No* no *no*, you drocking *don't*!" Bradyn maneuvered himself to the control panel and jiggled the activator stick up and down, to no avail. The car was still slowing. "Oh, this is bad."

"What's wrong with it?" Jabari asked and settled his weapon against the rear of the cage, tracking the metal disc as it careened into a distant bulkhead. Triggering magnification in his faceplate, he watched Rec-7 reach for the nearby surface. Thankfully, the impact had jarred it enough to prevent it from gaining purchase with any of its motion claws. The centipede bounced free of the disc and the bulkhead, tumbling further along the shaft.

"I don't know," Bradyn replied from behind him. "I can't see anything. Did you—"

"I didn't hit the conduit." Jabari cut the magnification in his helmet, swinging toward the other man in time to watch him kick the cage. "And that helps?"

"Helps me, and has fixed many engineering problems before."

Speed dropped further. The car began to coast.

Jabari said, "We're under zero gravity, right? Shouldn't inertia allow this thing to continue at the velocity it had already reached?"

"Um, no." Bradyn jerked a thumb at the rail above them. "Friction against that. Also, it's a loss of power to the motor. There might be a safety brake applying itself. You notice the lights?"

Jabari powered off his ostendo long enough to note that the tunnel lighting had gone out. Bradyn had a helmet lamp going. He reengaged the augmented vision.

"Drock it! Was working when I came through earlier," he complained. "Phillix?"

"I didn't do it!" a male voice grumbled in comms.

"Well, do something about it," Bradyn snapped back.

Ten seconds later, the car had come to a complete stop. Without a word, Bradyn climbed through the forward gap in the mesh that formed a window and kicked off the framework to grab at the same tangle of piping the centipede had been using.

Jabari checked behind them, couldn't locate Rec-7, and followed Bradyn out. As they used handholds along the deckhead to propel themselves, he asked, "This tank you're looking for, it's close, yes?"

A long pause, then Bradyn replied, "I drocking well hope so."

<hr>

The muffled thumping and screaming continued within the large pod.

Alexis froze for a moment upon noticing the object's shiny, textured surface, so different from all the others they'd come across, so...

"Is that gold?"

"If it is, it's plated only. Gold isn't known for its structural integrity." Sabrya moved closer. "But it's still worth a fortune."

They moved to either side. Peering in, they saw a stout, robed woman of about thirty years of age. The screaming stopped, but her face remained contorted with rage.

"All those centuries ago, and she has a better stasis pod than mine."

"What?" Sabrya asked, confused.

"Not covered in stasis gel. Vile stuff."

"You had that? What tight-assed mob were you with? Scum of the galaxy they may be, but the Surreal Tourney backers covered the cost of decent stasis pods."

At that moment, the display on the side flashed from orange to green, and the cowling hissed as it opened, breaking the seal after well over a millennium. The cowling slid to the side, revealing the cushioned lining to be embroidered silk. Slowly, the pod angled upward until the occupant rested at a comfortable 45-degree angle. Trembling hands grasped the sides as she tried to haul herself up.

"Relax," Alexis soothed the young woman, placing a hand on her shoulder. "Relax. Let the pod do the work while you recover. Too much energy too soon will aggravate stasis sickness." She examined the pod's interior. A far better one than what she had.

The woman quieted but looked around desperately.

Within moments, it was apparent her "acquiescence" wasn't due to stasis sickness—the woman was aghast.

"Unhand me, you filthy miscreant. How *dare* you sully your ruler?" She forced herself to an upright position. "Guardians!"

"You think we'd be in here if your cyborg pets hadn't been turned into mincemeat?" Sabrya sneered, taking an instant dislike to her.

"Those who defy the will of the Okalasi learn their mistake too late." The look the woman gave Sabrya would've withered a lesser person. "What are you? An Amazon? I'll gladly watch as they dispatch your offending carcass in the Arena."

"Been there, done that." Sabrya deliberately turned her back on the enraged woman.

Her actions worked, inspiring another tirade of abuse.

"I take it you're Adjira—" Alexis started.

"I'm *Kaana* Adjira mo'Halana mo'ni'Mariama. You can call me Majesty and kneel before me."

"Oh, it *is* you." Alexis paused, realizing the subject of their previous conjecture was now sitting in front of her. She'd imagined, with so much wealth at her disposal, an empress would look commanding, or try to at least look fit and healthy—someone to be admired, even taken seriously.

This plump, petulant woman—only a few years younger than me—doesn't fit my imaginings.

"Well, I doubt that's going to happen." Alexis shrugged. "I don't even kneel to the current emperor. Besides, no one will remember you, let alone do your bidding—"

"Not with her attitude." Sabrya's blades screeched as she dragged them across the bulkhead.

"And there's no one from your era left alive on this ship, as far as we can tell," Alexis continued.

"Poor, lonely princess." Sabrya smirked.

"Kaana!" Adjira snarled.

"Whatever the frag that is. Some made-up term from bodgey subliminals?"

"That's enough," Alexis reprimanded, turning back to Adjira. "Perhaps we can help if you'll tell us what you remember?"

Adjira, pale of face, slumped back into the cushions and remained silent. Her eyes closed above her pink, doughy cheeks.

"She might be suffering from stasis sickness after all." Allowing her a few minutes to recover, Alexis got up and strolled around the chamber, examining the tapestries and the other decor.

Sabrya was delving into the niches where the elite cyborgs had been housed.

Soon after, the Kaana spoke. "I'm hungry. What food have you?"

Surprised, Alexis looked in her utility belt. "Just this protein bar. I think it's vanilla." As she held it out, the women grabbed it with surprising speed, ripped off the wrapper, and devoured it, her jaw working to consume the tough substance. Whether she liked it or not was unclear. Eventually she finished, swallowing the last portion before continuing.

"I... I'm remembering. The ship was in the shadow of the moon, after they... after the rest of my armada was lost. I was evading them. I was *thwarting* them. But the Martianist bastards were so desperate, so hellbent, they used a planet buster in a cowardly act to kill their rightful leader. To that end, they futilely destroyed the moon—our moon, the very face of a goddess that had watched over our species from its birth!—and for nothing. Fools. I continue to exist." Adjira sat straighter. "I cannot wait to see the looks on their faces when they bow before me... before I have their heads."

"It's nice to have fraggin' dreams." Sabrya chuckled as she stepped out of another niche and slowly walked around the golden pod. Ignoring Adjira, she asked Alexis, "If she's this Terran princess Chromeman was going on about, how is it she speaks our language? That Imp fellow's fraggin' translator can. She hasn't got one of those."

Alexis shrugged again.

"Ignorant troll, it came with my birthright; I was granted this ability. Besides, what you're speaking sounds like a pitiful bastardization of a Martianist tongue."

"Well, if you're the Adjira who went toe to toe with the Imperium, you've been gone for over seventeen hundred years. As far as the Martianists are concerned, Terra's a ruined world, you're dead, and they won. You have nothin' to rule over."

Alexis came to the Kaana's side, seeing the look on her face.

Adjira might be a nasty individual, but she's only one woman. I felt like shit after twenty-seven years, and losing my partner and crew—imagine how she *feels, losing a whole empire and seventeen centuries.*

"The year is now 5122. This ship—as magnificent as it is—is a lifeless and almost powerless hulk, drifting in deep space," Alexis informed her. "Time and the damage inflicted on it has taken its toll. Hardly any of the systems work. Pretty soon, your powerplant will be drained, and then all life support will cease to function."

"Where are we? I was placed in stasis just after the attack? I... I don't remember all..."

"Sector 38. We're lightyears from Terra. Any idea why you're way out here?"

"We were to go to..." As if just recalling something vital, Adjira swung her gaze to the door leading to the other chamber. "What of my Beloved?"

"Your what? Those cyborgs?"

"Not my Guardians. My darlings. How are my darlings in the other pods?"

"Those *things?* They aren't even human, and you call them your beloved? Are they pets or som—?"

Adjira's shriek was loud and piercing.

Alexis winced and covered her ears, but it wasn't enough. Her head throbbed, and she barely stopped herself from blacking out.

Enraged, the Kaana scrambled out of the pod, which took considerable effort. She set upon Sabrya, slapping at her—or attempting to.

Unaffected by the outburst, the fighter turned to meet the attack almost nonchalantly, her arm dropping down like a scythe, metal glinting.

Alexis yelled, "Sabrya, don't!" It was all she could do to sway the killer instinct of the fighter.

"Frag it!" Instantly, Sabrya retracted her blades, instead delivering a blow that sent the woman staggering back across the deck. "Not so tough for a princess, or a Kaana—whatever the frag that is."

The fallen woman cradled her head, shock etched into her face at being struck. "I'll have you hanged, drawn, and quartered for this."

"Captain, sorry to interrupt," Torg said, "but there are indications someone is attempting to access the ship's systems, including the jump drives."

"What? Does this ship have enough power for that?"

"Unlikely. If it did jump, it would drain every power source on the ship, meaning—"

"Life support, gravity, heating, inertia dampeners. Yes, I'm aware. Bradyn, you hear that?"

"Yep, I c-py," Bradyn's voice came through, though scratchy. "Little b-sy right n-w."

"Recommendations, though?"

Bradyn sighed, then said, "Torg, send coordinates to where t-is is happ-ning. You gir-s, get back t- the *Ma-eus*."

Sabrya donned her helmet quickly but left the faceplate up. "Frag that. Boltman, you better patch me into that link, too. Alexis, I can dump our princess into her pod, or you can get her to our ship. Drag her if you have to. You still have normal drives. Get as far away as you can. No tellin' where this wreck is headin'."

Alexis nodded, looking to the slumped Kaana. "Time to find you a suit and get the hell out of here," she said, securing her helmet.

"She'll need a tent, or several suits for—"

"No suit is required for me." Adjira climbed unsteadily to her feet and waddled her way to a hidden compartment. With assistance, the door slid open, and the empress wrapped a belt around her waist. After activating it, she was able to stand up straight. A bubble formed around her. It appeared flimsy at first, but soon stabilized.

"Huhn..." Sabrya mumbled, slack-jawed and backing out of its reach.

"Impressive." Alexis nodded. "Will it fit through doors?"

"Question is, will *she?*" Sabrya recovered. "And do we care?"

"My shielding is malleable." The Kaana seemed calmer now, though she rubbed her bruised jaw with fire in her eyes.

"I have managed to interface with a portion of the ship's servers," Torg said. With helmets down, Torg's voice could be heard by all.

"More defiling of my ship?" Adjira spat.

Alexis and Sabrya each glanced at their wrist-wraps, which now showed a pulsing blue dot with dotted lines indicating preferred route. A faint green one further along the main shaft also appeared.

The fighter *tsked*. "Better if we'd had this befo—"

"On our way. Thanks." Alexis motioned for Sabrya to head to the door. "I take it the green is Bradyn and Jabari?"

"Affirmative," the droid answered.

"Jabari?" Adjira repeated.

"You wouldn't like him," Sabrya said. "Weird kind of fraggin' Imperial, middle-aged, probably peasant stock, and no freakish tail to play with."

Adjira ignored the jibes. "No one dares steal my ship. I know of a compartment nearby with direct access to Janus."

"Janus?"

"The *Iconic's* AI. *My* AI."

"Phillix, can you decompress the pod room?"

CHAPTER TWENTY-THREE

THE MEN HAD BEEN GLIDING for several minutes before they passed through an atmo-shield and into a segment Jabari's HUD told him was depressurized.

Bradyn said, "This is it," and sailed down from the ceiling to a long row of steel vats. The vats had remained relatively shiny throughout the centuries, and all bore bold warning signs in Terranist languages. More vats were visible along the tunnel and on the opposite side.

Bradyn had stopped at the end of the row, running his palms over the final vat's surface. Jabari followed him in and tapped his shoulder. "In the mess hall, you said this contains a sealant?"

"A kind of sealant."

"What kind?"

"One that seals stuff." Bradyn gave a short laugh, then grew serious after a glance back down the shaft. "This boat's old, but its basic design specs and trends are the same as modern ships. See that damage along there?"

Jabari followed the direction Bradyn pointed and saw two ragged holes on opposite sides of the tunnel, evidence that some object the size of Otho had smashed through there eons ago.

The mechanic continued, "If you get a bulkhead breach across multiple decks like this when you've got live bodies in the area not wearing vac-suits... Well, you've seen the bodies floating around, right?"

"Right."

Bradyn pointed back at the closest atmo-shield. "And if they failed, too, the results would be even worse. Catastrophic."

Jabari asked, "So, this stuff squirts out to block those breaches?"

Bradyn grunted. "Damage control teams will come in and squirt it manually. You don't want it just going off when people are nearby." Within his helmet, his lights showed him waggling his eyebrows and grinning.

Staying on-topic, Jabari said, "This stuff only works in vacuum."

"Yep."

Jabari checked behind them but saw no sign of Rec-7. He said, "So, it's a good thing for us there's no atmo in this section."

"Well, sort of," Bradyn said, moving hand over hand around the side of the vat to a small equipment closet set beside a series of metallic hoses.

"What do you mean, sort of?'"

"Well, for one thing, I'm running low on atmo myself." He got the closet open, then groaned in disappointment. "No emergency tanks."

"Actually, that's another good thing," Jabari said. "Any gas inside them would be fine for you, but if the container materials themselves had broken down, you could be poisoning yourself." Erkan had only given him one spare recycler, and the ones he'd brought for himself had been damaged by Otho's blaster fire. After the slightest hesitation, he passed the spare over. "Here."

Bradyn dragged himself nearer, took it, and turned it over in his hand. "You Imps use recyclers with standard Goglin connectors?" He dislodged the expiring one in his suit.

"Universal click-on recyclers," Jabari replied. "You can thank the empire's engineers."

Bradyn's laugh came out as a bark. "You Imps think you came up with everything. Sorry to disappoint, but it was the unions—the one thing they were good for was ensuring these fittings were universal."

Us Imps.

Jabari changed the subject. "Why does it only work in vacuum? The sealant?"

Bradyn took a deep breath, got the old recycler loose, and sent it spinning away. Attaching the new one with practiced hands, he barely glanced up. "It's either gallioid or mercoid. Probably gallioid."

"And what's that?"

"It's a fusible alloy that hardens in a vacuum. The vats store it in liquid form. And yes, it'll be fine after all this time." He had the recycler fitted and began running a test on it.

"But how does it get to the breach? I'm still not clear on what we're trying to do here."

"Well, you can't pressurize gallioids or mercoids—it's basic hydraulic principles—but see the pipes around the sides and tops? Well, some of them have compressed gas to propel the sealant through the spray nozzles on those alloy hoses. Operators just point and spray where it's needed, like a fire extinguisher. A ship this size would have dozens of these tank clusters scattered all around, mostly nearer the hull, where there's more chance of a serious breach." Bradyn inhaled deeply and patted the refitted recycler. "Works perfectly. Thanks."

"You're welcome," Jabari muttered, irritated by the delay. He stared along the shaft behind them again. He had to hope Rec-7 hadn't chosen a different route, wasn't inside one of these pipes, or out on the other side of the bulkheads, trying to attack from an angle they wouldn't expect.

Evidently, Bradyn had the same thought, as he, too, leaned out into the shaft. "That thing actually chasing us?"

"It'll be here."

"Maybe we knocked it too far back."

"It'll be here."

"Damn, I hope it didn't go back for the girls. What if it went back for the girls?"

"They would've commed you in that case."

"Yeah, but..."

Jabari reached across and gripped the man's shoulder. "Focus, here. That droid works for my former commander. He absolutely would've programmed it to kill me. *I'm* its priority."

Or is the thing aware that the Kaana's in that chamber back there? he wondered abruptly. *Damn. What if I sent it back toward her?*

He pulled his rifle around on its sling and fired a quick burst along the shaft, reminding the bot he was here.

A moment's silence while Bradyn considered him from behind his faceplate. "Your 'former commander,' huh? Wow, there's a story there I'd love to hear over a beer or six."

"We survive this and make it to a tavern, I'll tell it to you." Jabari pointed to the spray nozzles. "We're using those?"

"We could, I guess, but you really want to be here when this shit goes off with that crawler flitting about? Or risk me accidentally getting some on you? I saw a guy get it wrong once. The look on his face—solid in seconds." Bradyn pointed down and along the shaft to vertical trunking coming through the deck to run along the floor. "I say we head there."

"And get ready to kick off further away," Jabari added.

"Now you're getting it." Bradyn led him to a spot twenty meters past the last vat in the line.

They settled themselves against the floor and the cable trunking, and when Jabari looked up again, his HUD registered an oncoming object, tagging it with the icon for combat bot. He swore.

"You see it?" Bradyn asked.

"I do." He placed his rifle stock against his suit's shoulder, not bothering with visor magnification to see Rec-7 better. The HUD tag was clear enough.

And it wasn't the bot he was aiming for.

"Oh, drock, I see it, too!" Bradyn breathed and jostled Jabari in his excitement.

Jabari cursed, hooked one boot through some trunking a little further over, and drew himself that way, adopting a half-crouch out of habit in readiness to fire, and putting an extra half meter between him and the mechanic.

The centipede bot raced along the ceiling toward them, the flickering of its HUD tagging indicating it was careening in and out of cover within tangles of piping or cabling as it came.

"Aim for the furthest—" Bradyn started to say.

"I know my job," Jabari growled, then made the eye movement that triggered his HUD to record as Rec-7 appeared on the wall opposite the sealant vat at the far end of the row. "Hope you're watching, too, Optio," he whispered and fired into the tank.

Whatever it was made of, the tank wasn't manufactured to withstand combat laser fire. The vat ruptured as Jabari opened up a long slash in the shape of a smile. Alloy squirted immediately across the shaft to where the bot was.

And Jabari was drifting upward.

He must've shifted the toe of his anchoring boot out from under the floor trunking and pushed off from the other one, adrift with nothing to hold onto, as the quicksilver bloom of sealant expanded toward him. His breath caught at the mesmerizing sight. The liquid's forward edges seemed to solidify almost immediately, but more of it pressed those edges out and rolled over them. Rolling toward *him*—and fast!

Hells!

He was fumbling for his suit's mini-thruster controls when a big hand grabbed him by a suit fitting. Then Bradyn launched him along the maintenance tube with such tremendous force that for a moment, Jabari felt like a kid again, almost laughing aloud at the thrill of it. As he sailed backward along the center of the shaft and away from the expanding sealant blob, he kept his hand to his thruster controls, ready to brake when he was far enough away. Bradyn had kicked off and followed him, twisting in mid-flight to stare with him at the spectacle unfolding behind them.

It had been no more than eight seconds since he'd ruptured the vat, but there was no longer a tag on his HUD for the bot. He ended the recording he'd made, paired his replay to Bradyn's suit comms, and told the suit to play at half speed and magnified, focused on the bot's tag.

A corner section of his HUD showed the scene, Rec-7 springing from the roof, aimed at his position. The gallioid blossoming across the space beside and behind the bot, catching it by the tail, and hardening around that end. The crawler's front segments breaking away, abandoning the trapped tail, straining to flee the sealant's path. Futile. The expanding wall of sealant caught that, too. For what must have been only two more seconds, another section snapped off to continue pursuit before it, too, was consumed. The rush and flow of the liquid metal reminded Jabari of accelerated video of a lava flow, only this happened in zero-G, in "midair." It fused instantly with anything it touched. The pressure behind it must have been tremendous to force the liquid into and across the area before it had the chance to harden.

When the sealant appeared to have stopped spreading, Jabari fired a short thruster burst to divert to a wall, where he clamped on, snagged Bradyn, and swung him around to find his own handhold. They considered the new lumpy, metal wall sixty-odd meters back, where it completely blocked the shaft, including the double holes that had been punched in the walls.

Bradyn said, "Well, we're not getting back to the mess hall that way."

"I have mapping schematics in my HUD."

"And I have a friend. Hey, Torg, can you find an alternate route?"

"One that doesn't steer us straight into the other bot that's wandering around here somewhere," Jabari added.

Bradyn faced him. "*Other* bot?"

"Yes."

"Drocking hell."

CHAPTER TWENTY-FOUR

THE TIME it took for the air to cycle out of the room seemed interminably long. Clearly amused by the antics of the young woman in the bubble, Sabrya chuckled. With their helmets back on, the Kaana had no way to monitor or join their frequency.

"I'm sure she's arguin' with herself," the fighter said, "and losin'."

"Cut her some slack. I wasn't the most coherent when I was dragged out of stasis after twenty-seven years. She's gone through a lot more than I did."

Sabrya didn't respond, but checked her ad hoc leak repairs. They were out of sealant, so she'd better be careful.

Alexis also checked her suit's air level. "Did your suit manage to suck some of the air in?"

"I'm back up to 56 percent. You?"

"73 percent. That'll have to do."

At that time, the doors cycled open silently. As the chamber wasn't designed to be an airlock, there were no strobing lights or other indications they were back in a vacuum.

The Kaana stepped forward without hesitation, and the

atmo-shield moved with her. As it did so, the edge where the shield met another surface and sparkled slightly.

"It's like one of those air bubbles I've seen on holiday vids from Aquaria. Kids inside them, running on water," Sabrya noted.

Adjira approached the first pod and stared at it for a long time. The atmo-shield molded around it as she hugged it.

"Is she... cryin'?" The fighter looked at her curiously.

"If these are truly her 'beloved,' as she claimed, some emotional response wouldn't be surprising."

"But—"

The fighter's comment was cut off by Bradyn's enthusiastic report. "One crawler-bot down!"

"Great work, Bradyn," Alexis replied. "How's Jabari?"

"He's fine. It was a bit hectic here for a while. Sorry if my comm silence worried you."

"We didn't really notice; we were otherwise engaged... but we'll talk about that later. Are Jabari's comms working?"

"I think he's talking to someone else, or at least listening, but not to us."

"I knew it. Fraggin' Imp soldiers." Sabrya, if possible, became more alert. "Probably surroundin' us now."

"You think they'd do anything to harm their empress?"

"But she's not their empress, is she? We've already got an emperor, and as we pointed out, she's dead to them. If anything, public knowledge of her presence would be a calamity!"

"After all this time?"

"Alexis... How do I say this without being insultin'?"

"When has that stopped you?"

"True. So you're either the smartest dumb person, or the dumbest smart person I've ever met. He was keen for us not to hurt her. Way too keen to be wantin' to capture her. It was like he's in love with her... or worships her. This Kaana's his empress, all right? Which means he's from some faction that hates the empire." The fighter pointed to the other woman, now sprawled over another pod. "Mark my words, if knowledge of her return gets out, it'll be the catalyst for one of those factions to try to take territory away from the Imps."

"I... I don't know..."

"Trust me. I've met some crazy people in my work. They're out there, just waitin' for any fraggin' opportunity; lookin' for any platform to spruik their crap. Her return will lead to wide-scale war."

"So, what's the solution?"

"You forget who you're talkin' to?" Sabrya said, belatedly answering the question. "You need to ask?"

Would she stoop to murder? Alexis wondered. The moment she thought of the question, she knew what the answer would be.

As if reading her mind, the fighter continued, saying, "And before you go off thinkin' would I do it, and why, I suggest Metalman take you through the archives and you read up on some Civil War history. I'll bet this helpless, grievin' woman you see here—cryin' over these repulsive things—has the blood of millions on her pristine, uncalloused hands. Like all imperialists, she claimed it was to bring peace. *Peace.*" She made a spitting noise.

"That's gross."

"You crack me up, girl." The fighter chuckled. "You do know these suits recycle more than spittle?"

They waited as Adjira hugged every stasis pod before making her way slowly through the door to the darkened mess hall and its gruesome decor. If she saw the remnants of her cherished cyborgs, the limited communications left them in the dark regarding her thoughts.

Watching her briefly, Alexis breathed in slowly and turned back to the fighter. "Sabrya, listen to me. I won't let it come to that—to war—but if you're part of my crew, and you acknowledge me as your captain, I don't agree with your remedy. I won't discuss it further."

Without replying, Sabrya pivoted and stalked out of the chamber, disappearing into the semi-darkness of the mess hall.

***

When Jabari hailed the other members of his team, it was Tee who responded.

"News, boss?"

"Bad news, I'm afraid," he replied, then had to swallow a lump in his throat to continue. "First, how's your situation?"

"Secure."

"And busy," Shill added.

"Well, I need your attention for a few minutes." He gave them a brief summary of the past hour's events, avoiding mentioning Erkan until the very end.

They greeted the announcement with further silence. That was to be expected. A less patient leader might hurry the conversation along, or ask the dumb question, *Are you still there?* Jabari was comfortable with silence—and he knew shock provoked a variety of responses in other people, even soldiers.

While he trailed after Bradyn, alert to any indications that Ninety might appear in his neighborhood, he let a full minute play out before clearing his throat. "We'll discuss it later in more detail. For the moment, we have work to focus on, and I have other news. I think we found the Kaana."

"You..." That was Shill, her voice dry and cracking.

Tee took over. "For real?"

"I'm on my way to confirm it."

"Wait, she's in the section where you said the two women are?"

"Correct."

"What if they... do something to her?"

Jabari glanced at the back of Bradyn's suit. The man had been nothing but helpful. Alexis had been conciliatory. He answered, "I don't think they would."

"We're coming to you right now."

"Belay that. If your current location is useful—and secure—you'll stay where you are."

"But—?"

"Is it useful?"

"Yes, boss," Shill replied. "Very."

"And *are* you secure?"

A hesitation, then Tee said, "As secure as we can be."

"Update my map with your coordinates, and I'll be there when I can." His turn to hesitate before he added, "Hopefully with her majesty beside me."

Catching up to the Kaana, it was a small matter to guide her to the aft hatch in the mess hall and watch her shields contract and spark as they squeezed through it. Sabrya lithely jumped through, then reached down to grab Adjira by her upstretched arms, though there'd been a slight hesitation before the Kaana raised them.

"Probably reluctant to touch some unclean peasant," Sabrya muttered to Alexis, breaking her sullen silence.

Again, the edge of the shield glinted when it came into contact with another surface along Sabrya's arms and the hatchway. Once inside the shaft running along the spine of the massive vessel, they followed Adjira's rotund figure.

"Where's Miss Uppity takin' us?" Sabrya asked.

Alexis' shrug in her suit was missed. "Beats me. Some secret compartment forward." She looked at her wrist-wrap. "You following us, Torg?"

"Affirmative, Captain. There is nothing on any of the schematics indicating what she referred to."

"Seems contrary to reason to have a hidden compartment on a map, don't you think?" Alexis quipped. On her wrist-wrap, the blue and green pulses looked closer now, but locations depicted on a screen could be deceiving, considering how outdated the schematics were. "How are you doing, Bradyn?" she asked.

The mechanic sounded out of breath as he replied, "That sealant stopped the droid, but it blocked the shaft access completely. There was no drocking way back, so we went up and over several decks, headed same direction you are now. Lots more bodies and crap floating around. I reckon this section's had no power for centuries. Readings are -150C. Remember we saw some damaged hull? We must be near some area directly exposed to space."

"And, Jabari, you good?"

"He's fine," Bradyn responded after a moment, leaving Alexis to wonder at the soldier's silence.

Alexis looked back along the shaft the two men had used to entice and destroy the crawler-bot. Her attempt proved point-less. It was so long, any relevant detail was obscured by distance, flickering atmo-shielding, and inadequate lighting. She couldn't even see the mass of sealant Bradyn had referred to. Turning forward, she quickly caught up with her companion.

"Phillix. How's it going on your end?" She thought it prudent to add him to her umbrella of concern, lest he feel left out—*more* left out.

"... I a- havin- s-me difficu-ty–" His chat was briefly inter-rupted by Sabrya's chuckle "– I beli-ve there's some-ne else t-ying to code i-to the A-."

"Someone else? Not the one attempting to jump?"

"Captain, I can confirm this," Torg added. "The jump

attempt is coming from near where the imperial ship latched on. The interference causing Phillix some distress is coming from the area you are approaching. I have no indication of another ship docking, so I can only conclude these attempts originate from the same ship your new visitor arrived on. Whoever it is is not alone. However, there is a minor change to the energy spikes I am detecting. I can confirm the bot in the central shaft is no longer operational."

Sabrya muttered, "That explains why Jabari didn't want us to harm her. He's in on it... whatever *it* is."

"I don't know. I'm certain the bot was high-tech enough to know friend from foe. That damned crawler seemed pretty keen on going after him, too."

"It'll depend on their programmin' and their fraggin' priorities. Maybe he's a fugitive or renegade, too?"

"Too soon to tell. We'll have to take it easy until we find out."

"'Never trust anyone' is my motto."

"No, it isn't." Alexis thumped her companion on the shoulder.

"It is now."

"'Never *like* anyone' is more your style," Phillix cut in.

After floating for about ten minutes, Adjira drifted to the port side of the shaft, revealing a hidden keypad. A panel—a secret door—slid open. Obscured as it was by trunking, they would otherwise have moved right past it. Without waiting to see if anyone followed, she passed through a long, dark, narrow passage. The only light source here was the scintillation of her atmo-shield as it brushed along the bulkheads and deck, and their headlamps.

"This area isn't on the schematics," Torg informed them.

Sabrya snorted. "No fraggin' surprise there."

The passage led to an elevator. They caught up with her just as the lift door opened, revealing a small interior.

"Obviously there's still power to run it," Alexis said in surprise.

With their vac-suits, there wasn't enough room for all three of them.

"Best if you go first." Sabrya stepped back and held the door for Alexis. "I'll catch up."

"You sure?"

"No tellin' what I'll do if I'm alone with her." She released the door, and it slid closed swiftly.

Alexis was partially within Adjira's atmo-shield, causing a slight static in her headset. The former rebel empress stared sullenly at some point on Alexis' suit torso. It was a silent, awkward moment, so close, yet from totally different cultures, and seventeen hundred years apart.

The moment the door slid open, the Kaana drifted out. The shield and suit separated, and the static stopped. Glow panels came on in one direction along the short passageway outside, flaring to half power or less, but enough for Alexis to power down her suit's headlamp.

"The ship's doing that for you?" she asked, but the Kaana didn't answer, setting off at a brisk pace.

"They went up three decks," Torg said in her ear, informing Sabrya. "They passed you and are now on deck eight." Phillix and Bradyn acknowledged his call.

"Jabari and I will hunt for a stairwell or ladder down," Bradyn said, then added quietly, "He seems to have a more updated version of the schematics."

Alexis was on Adjira's heels when the pudgy woman stopped abruptly as she turned a corner. She managed to avoid bumping into the shield bubble. Ahead lay another short side passage, where more glow panels stuttered to life, but at even lower power. At the far end, an open door flared more brightly with light from within; the silhouette of another spacesuit stood in front of it, blocking some of that light. Quickly, Alexis grabbed the Kaana and pulled her back around the corner toward the elevator, glad she'd extinguished her own lamp.

"Unhand me, troll!" Adjira slapped uselessly at the powerful grip.

It took Alexis a second to realize Adjira's atmo-bubble was down. The Kaana's voice had come to her via her suit's external mic.

We have sound. Sound means air!

Alexis released the enraged empress, motioning her to be calm and quiet. It was pointless, as the upstart woman used her float-belt to dodge, making it past. Alexis followed her around the corner.

"This is my ship," Adjira snarled over her shoulder. "I shall do as I please! These others are intruding in a sensitive area."

Alexis snatched at her again, but it was too late. The suited figure had turned their way, weapon targeting them. A second suit joined the first, and she noted that they were identical in design to Jabari's. Should she try greeting them? Tell them about their friend?

Is Jabari even on my side?

"Just great!" she hissed, keeping her hands where the strangers could see them, but backing off until she was in line with the corner in case she had to dive for cover.

"I'm right behind you," Sabrya whispered.

Startled, Alexis half turned. The other woman was standing just out of sight of the suits around the corner, with her face-plate also raised and lamp off.

"Don't fraggin' look at me."

"Right." Alexis faced forward again.

Adjira had used the opportune distraction to dart away, closing the distance between herself and the new suits. She bellowed a string of nonsense words in some other language. Some of the words, however, Alexis did recognize: "Kaana Adjira mo'Halana mo'ni'Mariama!"

Damn, but she likes the sound of her own name, Alexis thought. She whispered, "She'll get herself killed."

"And that's a bad thing? Frag her," Sabrya hissed back.

"She's a historical figure. And... and a human being. We can't just..."

"I can." Sabrya sighed and risked a glance around the corner, obviously checking for the best way to close the distance without too much risk. "I s'pose you want me to save her fat ass?"

Ignoring her, Alexis squinted toward the figures at the far end of the side passage. There'd been no immediate reply to the Kaana's outburst, which was curious. As the robed woman approached, one suited figure bent a knee in obeisance. A moment later, the other followed, allowing more light past them from the room they'd been in. Alexis could see they were kneeling at an intersection with another corridor that ran left and right. At least one other suited figure remained within the room.

"Wait..." Alexis put her hand out before Sabrya could leap into action. She needed to let this play out. She needed to find out what the hell was going on here.

As she approached the pair of ugly, imperial-looking combat suits, Adjira felt no fear. "Spawn of Mars, you come to capture me, and yet you bend the knee? What madness have I awoken to?"

"Majesty!" a female voice replied, expressing the honorific through her suit's external speaker. A full second later, there came the same proclamation from a male voice. A rusty voice, gravelly and thin, as if the fellow hadn't used it in years.

The word startled Adjira, pleasantly so. "The True Tongue! You're *my* children, Children of *Terra*."

"We are, Majesty," the woman replied in a quavering voice as she and the other rose to their feet, "and always will be."

"At some later date, I will enjoy hearing the tale of how you came to wear... *that*. But for now, it's enough that you've come to attend me."

"Thank you, Majesty," the woman replied.

"Is... is this all of you?" she addressed the male.

"Two... uh, one more onboard, my Kaana," the rusty voice grated.

A twinge of disappointment spoiled Adjira's excitement at finding living Terranist soldiers here. She glanced through the doorway at the other suit within it. "Four in total. Then four must suffice."

"Our commander's about to enter the passageway, over there." The female soldier pointed along the stretch of corridor, out of Adjira's line of sight. The soldier put one hand to her helmet in the mannerism of someone listening to a voice on comms. Then the soldiers by the door turned as one, lowering their blasters and facing expectantly down the other corridor to their left.

"Jabari and I have arrived," Bradyn said softly in Alexis' comms, "but I'm hanging back a bit. This is weird. I'm in a corridor where there's two drocking Imp soldiers at an intersection ahead. And... and some other woman floating in mid-air. Yeah, I think I'll hang back here for the moment. Where are *you two* hiding?"

Near Adjira, Jabari stepped into the wedge of light from the open doorway. The soldiers greeted him with relieved salutes, the female patting his upper arm.

After a moment's hesitation, Jabari dropped to both knees as if in shock. He, too, said something in that other language, in a tone that sounded awestruck.

Interesting, Alexis thought, then spoke quietly into her comm. "Bradyn, we're up the branch corridor to your right. Staying where you are is a very good idea for now." Although the situation might resolve into a reasonable, rational discussion, she told Sabrya, "Stay here and wait for me to signal when I'm sure it's safe."

"What if it isn't?" the fighter muttered in apparent disapproval.

Alexis rolled her eyes and took a deep breath and a single step forward, hands raised. She watched as Adjira beckoned her subjects closer by the doorway. Jabari and the female soldier complied, but the rusty-voiced male remained where he was, his focus on Alexis—which put an end to any intention Alexis had of moving closer. The Kaana spoke softly with the two soldiers, but the one with the rusty voice asked something about Alexis.

Adjira looked around. "She and her missing companion are trolls. One even dared to strike me. End her now!"

As the man's blaster snapped up, Alexis was jerked backward and down as an energy beam flashed where her head had been. The wall above glowed orange. She was then dragged unceremoniously around the corner.

"I missed your signal," Sabrya snapped, pushing the multi-rifle into her hands. "Take this and get to the fraggin' elevator," she ordered as running footsteps approached their position.

Sabrya crouched, blades ready.

Alexis wasn't about to abandon a member of her crew. She rolled to a crouch and readied the weapon.

CHAPTER TWENTY-FIVE

MORTEN HAD BEEN the first to respond to the Kaana's kill order, pounding halfway down the corridor before Jabari could find his voice and holler a countermand.

"*Belay* that!"

Conditioned to follow Proselyti officers' orders, Morten lurched to a halt, half-turning with his rifle aimed toward the corner the enemy had sheltered around, and one shoulder aimed toward Jabari.

"How *dare* you!" the Kaana gasped beside him.

Jabari's limbs trembled as he faced her, averting his gaze now that he'd raised his visor like the others. He lowered his chin. "I apologize, Majesty. These people have proven to be allies. They assisted me in destroying an imperial combat bot, something I couldn't have done alone."

Tee and Shill stared at him, mouths wide open. He couldn't believe he was doing this himself, but what he'd said was accurate; there was no reason to distrust these people. Besides, they were the kinds of ordinary civilian subjects he'd fought a war to liberate, not to slaughter.

Also, he told himself as Adjira remained stiffened in outrage, *she's fresh out of the tank. Even she will be suffering some mind lag still.*

Adjira bunched her fists, shaking them at Jabari. "Those creatures butchered my Guardians and slaughtered my..." She faltered, then concluded, "they slaughtered infants I cared deeply for."

Jabari couldn't help but meet her eyes, shocked by this last revelation.

Her babies? She has babies onboard? His gaze swung to Morten, then past him to where Alexis had disappeared. If she and Sabrya had murdered Okalasi heirs...

He had his hand raised, pointing past Morten, and was ready to tell him to carry out the Kaana's command.

But at that moment, all hells broke loose in the passageway.

"Captain, there is a powerful energy spike fast approaching your location," Torg called over the comms.

There was a rumbling sound, then a blast and a flash of light. Chaos reigned, and the passage went dark. There was another blast, then very loud, rapid gunfire. Crouched on the deck, Alexis was about to rise to her feet. Sabrya pivoted and covered her as metal fragments flew in all directions. Their faceplates automatically sealed when the air pressure plummeted.

Sabrya dug her razors into the nearest surface to keep from ending up like the cyborgs with the rapid decompression. She held on until the decompression balanced, leaving them in vacuum again.

"What the drock was that?" Bradyn groaned, still out of sight.

"I'm okay," Alexis told Sabrya. "Move."

Sabrya leapt up, as did Alexis a moment later. Looking into the passage between them and the Kaana's soldiers, she saw a massive droid had emerged from where it had blown a gaping hole in the bulkhead. The soldiers and Adjira were no longer visible, and the droid filled the passage.

"Did they get sucked out?" she asked.

"No, they dove into that drocking room," Bradyn answered.

"They fraggin' left us!" Sabrya hissed.

"Not all of them." Alexis pointed to the remains of an imperial combat suit. It was hard to tell whether it was male or female now, but it had taken the full force of the bot's destructive power, its head and chest literally blown apart, the suit the only thing holding it together.

"Looks to me like it's left us, too." Sabrya shrugged.

As if to confirm what she was seeing, the big battle-bot announced over several frequencies, "Hostile down!"

Tee had bustled Kaana Adjira into the control room, with Jabari covering them from behind.

His final steps toward the hatchway were grueling, as the sudden loss of gravity triggered his mag-boots, making walking backward laborious. His visor whipped shut as Ninety's dramatic entrance caused the atmo to gush from the passageway. Glancing blows from the big droid's slug-cannon unbalanced him as he reached the door, hammering him hard enough to toss him through the gap. He was trying to retarget the hulking combat bot when one of the other Proselyti triggered the hatch to slam, separating them from the melee outside. Strong hands caught his shoulders and righted him long enough for his boots to re-adhere to the deck.

"Secure that!" he ordered, indicating the entrance while pivoting to check where Ninety's other slugs had impacted, to check on his friends, to check on the Kaana.

The three women were alive and intact.

Shill leaned over one of the room's myriad data stations, completely focused on it. Some consoles, he noticed briefly, had sustained various kinds of damage, such as electrical fires. Some of their surfaces appeared to be coated in cake frosting—frozen fire suppressant.

It must have been Shill who'd triggered the door. Adjira had lowered herself to the floor, standing safe and sound within the glimmering bubble of an expensive atmo-shield—he'd known the Terranist nobility owned them, but he'd never seen one in operation until now.

But Tee...

Tee just stood in place. Her words filled Jabari's helmet, burring through his suit speaker.

"Oh, shit, oh no, oh shit shit shit, oh no!"

Jabari's HUD confirmed that the rounds he'd taken hadn't compromised his suit. So he grabbed Tegenwe by the shoulders and shook her, rattling her inside the suit. "Tee. Yes, he's gone, but—"

"Morten. That bloody thing just..."

"I know."

"Did you hear him?" She grabbed at him, and he caught her hands, but she kept on babbling. "He was speaking. He was *talking* again."

Jabari *had* heard Morten talking, the first words he'd uttered in a millennium and a half.

He had only a few seconds to realize Adjira's back, and then...

Tegenwe moaned, "Erkan, and now Morten."

He squeezed her hands through their gloves as tight as he could, his rifle hanging from its strap. "I know, Tee. Get the void-damned hatch locked, or it'll be us next."

After a shove from him, she stumbled off to obey, muttering under her breath.

Shill said to him, "You sure locking that hatch will stop the damn thing?"

"Hatch is half a meter thick and coated in procrete tiling. He's not going to blow it."

"Oh," she said. "I missed that."

For a half second, Jabari wondered how he *hadn't* missed it, how he'd had time to notice.

I'm a shit-damned soldier is how. I'm responsible for these people.

"He could just tear up through the ceiling out there and come through this one." His gaze raked the room. "Let's just hope the bulkheads here have procrete, too."

"She did say something about it being secure."

'*She,*' Jabari thought. Facing Adjira, his legs weakened momentarily again, more from the surrealness of her presence than any latent combat shock.

How is it possible we've found her? And now?

Reality was taking on a hazy edge, as if he'd been drinking heavily. Unable to shake himself as he'd shaken Tee, he slapped his helmet with the heel of his hand.

Focus. Focus and act.

He had to get her out of here, *them* out of here. Adjira stared back at him, round face impassive. If she was troubled at all by the peril they were in, she wasn't showing it.

Mind lag? he wondered. He checked his own hand for the on-and-off trembling he'd experienced the past few days. Nothing now. But the confusion, the dissociation and dislocation were something Jabari had experienced many times upon decanting. And this woman—his Kaana!—had been under for so much longer than he ever had. Her dark eyes fixed on him, focusing, roving across his imperial combat suit without any sign of alarm, despite their situation.

Beyond Adjira, Shill's gloved hands continued battering

away at the data station's touchscreen and keypads. She said, "Boss, I have data here you should see."

"Only if it gets us out of here. I want some distance between her majesty and that bot."

"We're all right. This chamber's procrete-reinforced all round. We're secure for now. Check this out." She beckoned him over, making room for him at the station.

He joined her, then followed her gaze down to a vid-screen. It depicted the corridor from above the hatch Tee had just locked. "Huh," he said. Ninety wouldn't be trying to bust through that hatch anytime soon, because Ninety had other targets.

And bigger problems.

Alexis staggered to her feet, first checking that Sabrya was okay. She needn't have worried, as the fighter waved her off. "Bradyn, are you all right?" Alexis asked, turning her attention to the engineer.

"Ready to pull limbs off those drocking imperial cowards." The big mechanic peered around the far corner, but ducked back as the wall was peppered with gunfire, leaving a trail of significant dents. "What is it with all these murder bots?"

The dead soldier had been blown their way, close enough for Sabrya to reach out and snatch his energy rifle. The weapon snagged on the body. As she pulled it closer, the droid's head spun around, sensing the movement. It opened fire with a laser, obliterating what was left of the already decimated body.

"Thanks!" she called as the weapon came free.

She checked the new weapon, ensuring it was fully charged, and looked like she was ready to deal with mayhem.

"Quiet," Alexis ordered. "The Kaana is in that data store with full AI access. You got anything, Phillix?"

Sabrya pointed with the muzzle. "Well, we need to deal with that hulk before we can do anythin' about it." The fighter paused for a moment. "Boss, let's swap." She held out the laser, exchanging it for Alexis' Gutpuncher. "I have a crafty plan."

"Hell, I'm ready to pull it apart. Just give me the word," Bradyn added.

The droid scraped the sides of the passage as it tried to move, far too bulky for the small space.

"Ha. Lucky for us, the fragger's too big to bring all its weaponry to bear on us, especially if we attack from different directions." Sabrya hefted the multi-rifle, choosing the most lethal setting. "Funny. I can't seem to find the murder-bot-kill function. Oh, well, I'll distract it, and you do what you can."

"Just give me a sign."

"First, I'll get its attention and take out its thermal imagin'." Sabrya started blasting, aiming for its head.

The head swiveled back to her again. One of her shots took out an eye before a laser flashed out. Anyone else would've been fried, but her nanites were fully energized. She dove sideways, rolled across the deck, then kicked off the opposite wall with blinding speed, all the while taking potshots.

The bulkhead where she'd been seconds before dripped slag. The beam followed her trail.

Alexis fired bursts of laser fire at it, but it made little impact on the armored sections, and Sabrya was far more accurate.

Suddenly it jerked and shook as Bradyn leapt upon it and used his prodigious strength to pull off internal parts from between gaps in the armor. Nothing articulate was heard over the headset other than heavy breathing and straining.

The droid's head spun around again, and Sabrya knelt, took a bead, and aimed high again. "Move!"

More laser fire seared across the deck, but she was gone.

Sabrya dove back around the corner.

"I'm going for that damn laser," Alexis stated, shouldering her rifle.

"You're what?" the fighter queried.

"Remember, I'm as strong as Bradyn." *And not as good a shot as you.*

"Frag, yeah. Why should he have all the fun!"

"Exactly."

They readied themselves.

"Go, girl," the fighter said.

The two women darted around the corner. Sabrya bolted through the gaping hole in the side of the passage. She opened fire as Alexis grabbed for the barrel of the laser.

The droid moved the weapon to follow.

Maintaining her grip on the barrel was easy enough, but Alexis quickly found pushing against the bulkhead was the only way she was able to slow its movement. Once she found her footing, she was able to stop it completely, though it was an enormous effort. Smoke issued from within as the servos and gearing fought against her high-G strength—and lost. "Let's see what you can really do," she muttered as she exerted more of her strength.

"I'd say blasting holes and laser fire is nothing to be sneezed at," Bradyn said, grunting as he yanked on some tubing between the joints.

"I don't think she was talkin' about the droid." Sabrya changed settings and tried one of the rifle's other options.

In gradual increments, Alexis bent the laser barrel so it was directed back toward the droid.

"Oops. Grenade!" Sabrya warned.

"Frack!" Alexis leapt back and rolled as the droid's head exploded. "I'm not sure who's more dangerous." Alexis found her feet.

"Plenty of others wondered that, too, before I ripped their heads off."

"Is that it?" Bradyn asked. Heavy breathing from his exertion fogged his faceplate. He, too, had jumped clear, and was emerging from around the corner, squeezing his bulk through the narrow gap.

Sabrya climbed back through the hole. She removed an EMP grenade from the magazine and wedged it firmly within the structure of the inert droid.

"Move back, everyone. Not all droids have the CPU in their heads. I'm goin' to make sure it stays fraggin' dead." Unlike the mechanic, the fighter's faceplate was clear of condensation; she'd hardly exerted herself.

After a moment for everyone to take cover, Sabrya aimed and fired a weak pulse to set it off. The grenade exploded, sending bits of shrapnel in all directions, but it was the electronic disruption that finished it off, as sparks coruscated across and through the metal body.

"I reckon that's it."

Climbing around the dead hulk, the three faced the door to the data room.

"Leave them," Alexis breathed. "If there are bounty hunters coming, our priority should be to repair the *Malleus*, or we might be facing slave pens again. Maybe the soldiers' ship has something of use?"

"You sure? Leavin' an enemy behind?"

"No time for it; I'm leaking air." She glanced at her readings, flashing orange. "I suspect you're leaking more air than me."

"This ship's too old to have anything of drocking use. I should've known that... but I hoped its sheer size indicated something... advanced." Bradyn sounded genuinely disappointed as he searched his utility belt. "I've got sealant, but not enough for both."

"Fix Sabrya," Alexis said over the fighter's protests, then paused, asking, "Hey. Has anyone heard from Phillix recently?"

She called him and waited before directing a query to the ship. "Torg, heard from Phillix?"

"Only that he was making progress and requested I cease interfacing with the AI," the droid answered.

"Did he say why?"

"Only that it would make his task easier."

"Okay. Direct Bradyn to the imperials' ship, then come rendezvous with me as I go for Phillix," she ordered.

"On your screens now," the droid responded, "as well as Phillix's last known location."

"You reckon I'm lettin' you go alone?" Sabrya remarked.

"Yes. We have no idea what or who is on that Imp ship. You want this?" She brandished the laser rifle at the engineer.

"I'll probably break it. You'll be alone, best you take it."

Alexis shouldered the weapon again. "I'll have Torg—"

Sabrya chuckled. "I'm so overwhelmed with confidence now."

"Excellent." Alexis ignored the sarcasm. "Bradyn, am I correct in seeing atmo-shields in that shaft?"

He nodded.

"Good. I'll replenish my air when and where I can. You should probably do the same."

The fighter was about to continue her objections when Alexis nudged her.

"Give me a hand with this." She squeezed back through the gap, followed by the others. "I want to block their access."

"Yeah. Can't have Imp soldiers sneakin' up behind us."

"I really don't think they're Imps," Alexis replied.

"We can't have any kind of assholes sneakin' up behind us."

Together, the three of them pushed the massive droid until it covered the larger gaps between the bulkheads.

Sabrya slapped the engineer on the shoulder. "Since there's vacuum, I reckon we can go this way." She climbed through the ruptured bulkhead.

He nodded. "It'll take us near the top. We might be able to get a look at the other ship first."

"Have fun." Alexis turned and headed to the elevator she'd used to get from the shaft.

CHAPTER TWENTY-SIX

THE MOMENT PHILLIX JACKED IN, he became aware of something huge—a presence so magnificent, so awe-inspiring, he was incapable of grasping its entirety. He imagined stepping into a vast, dark cavern. There were tendrils of luminescence here and there—data stream... code matrix. He knew no one else would understand its intricacies and complexities. No one else could.

He followed the threads, gleaning what information he could. As expected, much of the data stream was in standby mode, due to the bulk of the ship's systems being dormant or destroyed. Mapping out the layout was his first priority: this thread was navigation; this one life support—an important one to check—then the other ship functions.

Begrudgingly, Phillix had to remember to respond to his colleagues and their whims. There was a great deal of probability that things could go awry quickly. Part of him still pined for acceptance from them, his fellow humans, but what he was immersed in here and now was so absorbing... mesmerizing. He saw something in the weave of patterns in his view, and it had a familiarity to him... hard to describe... it was almost like—

You are not permitted to be here.

His vision blurred by massive interference, a dense wall of intricate blockchain code started to envelope him. He struggled for a moment before surfacing, like a swimmer caught in a rip.

"Finally, something serious to play with," he muttered.

The voice, or more precisely, the sensation his brain translated in his head, resonated with femininity. He wondered at that, having assumed Janus was a male's name.

"You requested assistance with your mayday beacon," he answered. "By default, you've allowed us permission to assist." With his gizmo plugged in, he could only work with his left hand, and the fingers danced over the keypad while he spoke. There was the faintest weakening in the wall. He went for it.

If you are not a Child of Terra, or a converted supporter of her majesty, you are not permitted.

The wall closed again, rebuffing his attempts to penetrate the system fully.

He took a deep breath and analyzed what was now before him, looking for a pattern to the complex flow. *There's always a pattern...*

While his mind worked on that, he said, "Then you'll be without help for eternity. The Terran Federation has been defunct for well over fifteen hundred years. I see the designation of this vessel is the *Iconic*. Surely, you must realize you've been adrift in space for all that time?"

Time is irrelevant. Much of my communications system has been corrupted, and other parts were irreparably damaged during the attack. I am not permitted to receive any external communications less they be non-Terran in origin and possibly carrying a virus.

"That puts you in a bit of a quandary, then, as there will be *only* non-Terran communications, and not much of that way out here. Your powerplant is almost depleted."

I will prevail.

"No. Eventually, you'll go dormant, but if there's anyone onboard, they'll perish. How does that help your empress? Anyone will be able to take control of you. At least we can render assistance here and now."

What you say is true, but why should I accept your assistance? What could you possibly offer?

"Apart from the already stated reasons? Well, I've never seen anything like you. You're... you're extraordinary." He felt the inadequacy of his description the moment it left his lips. Then a thought occurred. "You can hear me?"

I can hear and see all, but your voice is irrelevant, as I am receiving the thoughts from your mind now that you have managed to interface with me directly. I can sense another entity attempting the same thing, but you are far more adept.

"Err... thank you." He rarely received compliments from others, yet this AI was doing it. "This other entity? Who or where is it? What am I thinking?" he muttered. "You call yourself a hacker?" He scanned the code, looking for something far less elegant than the Janus matrix.

It is originating from the same vessel you arrived on.

"Ah. Yes. One of my colleagues—a droid. He's also attempting to aid the vessel." He followed the far less elegant thread of code defining an attempted intervention. Then it dawned on him that he'd successfully integrated with the AI, whereas a droid hadn't. "As evidence of good faith and sincerity, I'll get him to cease his attempts."

Knowing that Torg would be monitoring all incoming signals, Phillix called him on another channel, so he wouldn't interrupt what the others were doing.

"You have control of the AI?" Torg responded.

"Not control, as such, but I'm communicating with her."

"Her?"

"Same as I address you in the masculine form. We'll discuss

this later. Please cease your interface attempts. It's making my job that much harder."

Torg acknowledged the request and signed off.

'Please?'

Of course she's monitoring my thoughts. "Just my manners. Whether biological or electronic, I like to think I treat all with respect, just as I'm treating you." He sat back, about to concentrate on delving deeper, when he noted more coding, but vastly different from Torg's. "Interesting... Someone else is hacking into you."

Strange. I hardly sensed it... much like you.

Phillix's ego noted the compliment. People always said it, but what would they know? But this! A compliment from such an extraordinary entity...

"It's like nothing I've encountered previously—the coding, I mean." His fingers fluttered across the pad, sending an acknowledgment of mutual respect in hacker speech. "If they're any good, they'll see that."

"Doesn't look like they're interested in following us," Jabari said with a glance toward Tee. She'd remained close to the hatch with her rifle trained on it while he and Shill watched the combat beyond it play out on camera.

"Exactly," Shill said. "You want some atmo in here? I'm dying to go visors-up again."

"No," Jabari replied, still preoccupied by the on-screen spectacle of two people pulling parts off a combat bot with their hands. "We stay combat ready."

"Then you should look at something else. It's really—"

Tee interrupted Shill, her voice a little too loud on comms. "How do we talk to her with visors down and no atmo?"

Jabari tore his eyes away from the video and resisted the

urge to plunge to one knee when his gaze passed across his monarch. "And how much air can she have left in that?" He made a curved motion with one hand, indicating the bubble that had re-triggered when the atmo was evacuated. "Shill, could you link our comms to one of these screens so she can hear us, or read what we're saying?"

Instead, Shill startled, backing up a step. Jabari wheeled around, irrationally expecting Ninety to have breached the door, but it was the Kaana who approached him, and before he could react as Shill had, Adjira pressed her shield bubble against his suit.

For a moment, Jabari was aware of resistance before it gave with the slightest of static-electrical pops, and her shield enfolded him.

Jabari had been in Adjira's presence twice before: once when the princess was eighteen and at her mother Kaana-Consort Aliana's side, while her great father addressed an assembled New Constantinian brigade, and then again, up close and personal, the day Adjira had personally bestowed medals on his detachment after the Battle of Fong Twae. The first time, the princess had been on a dais and at a distance. On the second occasion, he'd been kneeling, and the newly-crowned young Kaana had used boots with specialized heels to boost her height and carry some of her weight. He was much taller than her, he saw now. Her sudden proximity was both exhilarating and oppressive, the object of his deepest adoration since boyhood now staring up at him from less than half a meter away.

"Damn," he whispered, hearing a slight static in his headset.

She reached up and tapped her fingers against his visor. It took a second for him to understand. He unsealed it and imbibed the faint scents of vanilla and cardamon—some surgically-enhanced pheromone of hers, or something she'd been eating? At the same time, the brief wrinkling of her nose told him that his suit fans had flung his suit stink into her face.

"I... I'm sorry, Majesty. I've been in here for some time." He'd used Terran True, suddenly glad to have remained fluent throughout the centuries of interaction with other Proselyti from all the former Earth-descended worlds.

Despite his body odor, she smiled, a warm sun dawning. "This is good. Good that you're here—" she glanced at the nameplate on his suit "— Jabari Mbaye. My child. Good to hear the True Tongue spoken in this distant, empty place."

"May I ask, Majesty, I know this shield bubble is some of the best tech of our era, but how long can it sustain you?" Her thick, childlike hands took hold of the ragged pouches on his torso, ruined by Ninety's shooting. His heart pounded harder. "Er... you see... we may need to break out of here and travel a fair distance."

"The bubble will serve me for many, *many* hours, if need be. As long as one of your suits, if not longer."

Jabari's eyes narrowed. That sounded... crazy. Rumor always had it that these things were emergency devices only, not long-term mobile environments. The fear returned that she'd suffered some significant neurological deterioration after being in stasis for so long. "H-how exactly would it do that, Majesty? I ask only to better serve you."

"Terranist ingenuity, Child of Earth. My prolonged survival within this bubble is certain because I can switch from breathing normal air to breathing the waste products of that air, and back again."

"That... that's..."

A giggle trickled out from her throat as her hands released him, but she leaned a few centimeters closer. "The stinking Martianists engineer themselves in all sorts of horrid fashions, after all. Why not the Kaanic Okalasi, the custodians of Earth's

324

True Children? Why shouldn't we find ways to ensure our survival in dire circumstances?"

Jabari kept his face neutral, his concern spiking. That was a problem, if she was speaking the truth and not delusional in some way. Avoiding augmentation had been a cornerstone of Terranist values and beliefs for two millennia before the War—as firm as its aversion to genetic meddling. That was the entire reason Terranists lived *only* upon Earth-like planets. The ruling Okalasi Dynasty had been the greatest of the children of Terra; they'd been the Truest Humans, seeking to guide the entire species back to its true evolutionary path, it's *natural* evolutionary path.

He was leaning away from her, he realized, and hoped she'd interpret that as respect, even as doubt continued climbing up out of his gut...

We were already headed this way. He couldn't believe he'd been blind to it, the gradual relaxation of the very precepts they'd upheld. That carnage in the mess hall... the minced-up cyborgs had mechanical enhancements. He and his comrades had been told the Guardians were converts from one of the conquered Martian worlds. Had they been Terran instead? Mechanical enhancements were one thing, forgivable, since humans had always used tools from their earliest iterations. But humans breathing carbon dioxide? Had Adjira really meddled with her own biology?

It's a cybernetic enhancement, that's all, he assured himself. *It must be. The use of a tool, of equipment, not gene-modding. And why shouldn't the Bringer of the Light be equipped with protection from suffocation?*

Adjira's fingertips traced the pits and contours of his damaged suit. He went rigid at her touch.

"Jabari," she purred. "You're a warrior, and I see that you desire action and activity, but you must let *me* direct our next steps."

Shoving aside his doubts about her augmentation and mental state, he replied, "I want only to protect you, my Kaana. We'll get you to a more secure location. The fact that you're here is a miracle, and I—"

"I'm secure here, for the moment, and of course I value your protection, my dear child. But understand this: in certain circumstances, I can take care of myself." She flashed another smile, and this time it was less like a sunrise, and more like a muzzle flare. "You've been alone for so long, lost for so long, Jabari, you and your comrades. You must remind yourself that it's your duty to obey me. To heed *my* instructions." This last phrase was delivered with the steely edge he expected of royalty.

"Y-yes, Majesty. Of course. I just—"

"To provide you with instructions, I require information from you," she continued. She took the smallest step back, making him glance aside to check the boundary of the bubble. Another step like that, and he'd be in zero atmo and zero pressure with his visor open, and the visor wouldn't have time to close before it caused him problems. Gently, she ran a fingertip along his sleeve where the imperial insignia rose from the surface like scar tissue. Her head cocked as if chiding a child, or a naughty pet. "It's concerning to find you wearing *this*. I'm sure there's a good reason for it, and for your existence in this ugly, ugly future. Back in our era, what unit were you in?"

"The 8th Constantinian Guards."

She clapped her hands together so close to his open helmet he felt the puff of air against his lips. "One of my father's favorite divisions! I wonder if you knew the Constantinian officers who served me here before the... the..." Another tremor of uncertainty passed across her face, as perhaps memory failed her, or was too hard to acknowledge. Adjira turned her face toward Tegenwe, who was still staring at the door. "This warrior. Constantinian, too?"

"Yes, Majesty." Jabari watched Tee for a moment, a new concern forming. Tee swayed on her feet, rifle trained on the door. He could hear a steady stream of whispered self-talk coming from her comms.

Shill, on the other hand, flicked a hand at him the second he looked her way, desperate to get him over there. He made an impatient gesture and put his back to her.

Adjira had caught it. Peering past him at Shill, she asked "And what's that one doing?"

Shill responded before Jabari could, apparently hearing the Kaana through Jabari's suit mic. "I'm attempting to reboot life support and tap into directional control, and wishing my lieutenant would come over here and look at something."

Adjira's gaze fixed on the voice coming from Jabari's suit speaker for a moment. "Another female?" She turned toward Tegenwe again. "Two females?"

"Er, yes, Majesty." Jabari wondered why that mattered.

The Kaana pointed to the door Tee was guarding. "And those tainted trolls who revived me? You didn't want them dead. Why not?"

"In short, they helped avenge the death of my colleague, Corporal Erkan, and removed one of the droids who'd otherwise trouble us."

"Yes, but who *are* they?" Adjira asked.

"Many things have changed in the intervening centuries. Too many factions to count and to know in this era. Many settlements exist beyond the reach of the Martianist Imperium."

She beamed at that news.

"I think these people are simple scavengers, Majesty. They're certainly not soldiers—although they sure show an aptitude for fighting."

She lifted one eyebrow. "They happened upon *Iconic* at the same time you did? A coincidence?"

"*Iconic* activated an automatic emergency beacon, a signal picked up by many parties."

"I see. My great ship is dying and sought help. Instead, they came to loot it."

As abruptly cordial and buoyant as she'd been, her mood flipped again, her face darkening, and her fists clenching. So alarming was this mercurial behavior that Jabari almost backed away before remembering he was dependent on her shield bubble's air.

"My great ship survived despicable desecration at the hands of the Martianist navies," she continued, "and with its great heart still beating, it's now beset by robots and scavengers!"

The other two women in the room looked up and around, eavesdropping via Jabari's suit mic, as alert as if a dangerous predator had entered the room, and they were hoping its attention wouldn't settle on them.

Adjira punched one fist into the palm of her other hand. "I've returned to life to find myself in hell! The Infidel Empire of Mars still lives. You say there are factions neither Terranist *nor* Martianist. My poor, poor babes have perished, murdered by these creatures you think of as allies. That bitch struck me, you know. The blue-haired one!" She brushed fingertips across her temple, drawing attention to a welt he hadn't noticed.

That outrage was enough to make him want to hunt Sabrya down—but more outrageous was the thought that she and Alexis had murdered Okalasi heirs. "Your Majesty, you said babies?"

She was too caught up in her ranting to register his question. "My great ship is horribly wounded. Most of my closest servants are slain. And you, Constantinian trooper, loyalist infantryman, you wear the insignia of my enemy!"

Jabari could lie about that, of course, claim they wore the suits as disguise, but the truth would come out eventually. He swallowed, and his voice came out as a croak.

"Majesty, I'll explain—"

She cut him off with a swipe of her hand, growling dismissively. "Close your faceplate, warrior, and move away while I consider our next steps."

"Yes, my Kaana." Hurriedly, he closed his visor, troubled by her erratic behavior.

The moment the visor sealed, it was Adjira who moved away from *him*, turning her back and pacing around the data stations toward a far corner. For one moment, while she was in profile to him, he saw her lips moving.

Oh, please don't let her have stasis sickness.

Shill gestured impatiently again. "Jabari? *Sir*? Will you please get your ass over here and look at this?"

He stomped to Shill's data station. "What the hells is it?"

"It's... something weird."

Her gesture encompassed the four small screens she had running across the station. One showed the corridor outside and the wreck of Ninety—he'd suspected she was worried about the droid reviving itself, but the hulk remained still, and there was nothing happening out there. Two of the other screens depicted code or text files arranged in small windows. But the fourth held a frozen video image of some kind of forest.

With her visor unmirrored, Shill caught his gaze, her pupils dilated, and her mouth a tense line. Cocking her helmet toward the Kaana in the corner, she asked, "She definitely can't hear us, right?"

"Of course not."

Unless she also has some kind of internal device that monitors imperial comm frequencies. Shit.

The tension in Shill's expression actually increased as she launched into a fast-talking explanation. "This room does systems management, but it's also an ultra-secure data storage. You need to watch this video, or just a bit of it. It's so messed up. I'm copying it to my suit drive so we can watch the whole damn thing later. But... I'm losing my mind, here. These files..." She bit her lip, apparently overwhelmed.

"One thought at a time, Shill. Keep it simple."

"All right. All right." She took a breath and let it out slow, then said, "It took a while to dig through to the navigational stuff I needed, but I also wanted records and logs on *Iconic*, what happened to it, anything that'll help us. I found something else almost immediately. These files I've been reading, they're... they're so bad, Jabari. The Kaana said something about babies, right?"

"Yeah, I'm wondering about that, too. If she had heirs on board, we have to—" He stopped short, because Shill was shaking her head. "What?"

"They're not descendants. They're more like, I dunno, experiments?"

"What?"

"I'll play you thirty secs of this vid. There's no sound, and the image quality is scratchy because it's... well, it's *ancient*. As in, *really* ancient."

Jabari leaned over the small screen, squinting at the forest scene. Tall trees, variants of pines. A forest floor with very little undergrowth. No animals. No people.

Ancient? Is this Earth?

"Do it," he said.

Shill unfroze the image.

And Jabari saw that the universe was a very different place than he'd thought it was.

And things would never be the same...

CHAPTER TWENTY-SEVEN

SABRYA CHECKED HER AIR GAUGE. "You sure this is the right way? I reckon we'll need to find another compartment with air, pretty fraggin' pronto."

After the pair left the obliterated passage containing the destructor-bot's hulk, they headed where the other Imperial ship was located in the hope of finding a data board the *Malleus* could use to reengage jump capability.

Bradyn looked up from his wrist-wrap, answering, "You've got the same drocking schematics as me."

"Hey, Bolthead?" Sabrya called for Torg again. After a pause she asked, "Where has that bucket of burned-out circuit boards disappeared to?"

"It's probably in transit and can't be reached."

"Just fraggin' great."

"Think there were other drocking Imps heading to the *Malleus*?"

"I doubt they saw us, but they must realize we came from somewhere; this leviathan is far too fraggin' big to search randomly on foot."

"Maybe there are other bots?"

"Good point, but their ship's somewhere up front, and they boarded after us. I doubt they could've made it all the way back there without our Chromeman noticin' it," Sabrya argued.

"That almost sounded like a compliment. I won't tell anyone you said that."

"If you do, it'll be the last fraggin' thing you say."

Bradyn grinned, his white teeth splitting his dark face. She might be a deadly fighter, but her voice didn't have a lethal quality to it.

"I'm fraggin' serious." She punched his shoulder, hard.

Bradyn shrugged, unaffected. "Of course you are."

"You know, you're surprisin'ly fraggin' tough. I need a sparin' partner. I can teach you a few moves."

"Thanks. I've never needed to defend against a machine."

"You're forgettin' we just went head-to-head with a destructor bot." She chuckled. "Anyway, offer's there."

"Thanks. You never know."

They moved on, eventually entering another atmo-shield.

"Better grab what air we can here. This close to the hull, and the damage... these air pockets might be few and far between. Surprised this is still here." Bradyn assessed the corridor ahead. He could see the end of the atmo-shield further up the corridor.

"And I've noticed these corridors have become... cleaner," Sabrya replied.

During their walk here, the number of bodies and debris had diminished, and their wrist-wraps indicated the passages were much colder.

"If you're thinking what I'm thinking, then yeah. We must be closer to a hull breach, and they would've been sucked out. Not a nice way to die."

She shook her head ruefully. "What is?"

With face plates retracted, they slid down the wall and waited in silence while their suits replenished their air tanks.

The air was cold on their faces and would probably freeze them if they were exposed for too long, but for a short duration with only the face plates up, it was refreshing.

"What was the Kaana like?" Bradyn asked after a while.

"She's one fraggin' crazy-assed bitch. Too much stasis can't be good for the mind."

"Alexis had a fair bit of it," Bradyn noted.

"Yeah, but not for seventeen hundred years. Besides, from what we saw, she was a stark ravin' loony before goin' under." She related the pods of pregnant males with some form of mutation growing within.

"You saw these mutations? In the *womb*?"

"Nah. A couple of the pods were damaged later, and the wombs ruptured." She went on to describe the males used as surrogates. "What we saw wasn't... fraggin' human. Human-like, but scaley, tailed, with varied skin colorin', and blotches like birthmarks... but a lot of them."

"Mutation? Not a deformity?"

"Unlikely. There were at least two of them with the same weirdness. I've no doubt the others had it, too."

"What were they thinking?"

"Definitely some fraggin' weirdness, but the fat cow was very distraught about it all."

"Perhaps Phillix will find something out; he was delving deep into the coding when I left. You know Phillix—or maybe you don't," the engineer added. "When it comes to coding, he has a one-track mind."

"If you could call it that."

Bradyn turned to her. "You really don't like him, do you?"

"It's not a matter of likin' or dislikin'. I just don't get him or his kind. They're on a different wavelength than me. My train-in'—my survival—is to fight any threat, and things I don't understand are a threat. But—" she put a gloved hand up to fend off the expected tirade "—he's still breathin'... so I must be learnin' new fraggin' skills. Give it time."

The faint sucking in air of the pump was the only sound as they sat brooding in their own thoughts. Having come across the manic, ancient empress on this magnificent vessel, the one that had destroyed the *Octavia*, which was now embedded in the hull... Was this encounter purely coincidental?

"What I want to know is, why did these Imps rock up at the same time as us?" Sabrya asked eventually. "Did they know who was on here? That Jabari guy and his buddies seemed to accept it quickly fraggin' enough."

"I thought taking a knee to her was a surprise, considering they have an emperor already. I doubt Nero will like having her around, but he'll definitely send in other troops to kill her or capture her—make an example of Imperium superiority."

"I said the very same thing to Alexis: there'll be war. Maybe these guys are from a rogue faction pushin' for the demise of the current regime."

"Maybe they're having some inner conflict? That murder-bot was no friend to Jabari. Why would a bot from his own ship —his own people—be after him?"

"Maybe it's not his ship. Him and his people might've been here already. That ship maybe came here chasin' 'em. Maybe he's a traitor. Who the frag knows?"

The readouts on their suits blinked full.

"Time to go." Sabrya closed her faceplate, stood, and kicked off, gliding the last few meters. She crossed the atmo-shield, followed by the engineer. They navigated a darkened section, where a blast door had only partially closed, before she stopped.

Bradyn ran his gloved hand along the bulkhead to slow, then stopped next to her.

"Feel like goin' outside?" She pointed to the gaping hole one deck above them, exposing the area to space. The edges were ragged where the local supply of gallioid sealant had been insufficient to fill such a large breach.

"If we must." He didn't sound enthused. "One of the reasons I chose engineering was there are very few reasons to work on a drocking hull from the outside."

"Don't worry, big guy, I won't let you fall off, but we could cover more distance faster and finally get a look at this Imp ship."

"For the cause..." He looked down, examining the damage going further into the ship. "Looks like an asteroid or something hit it, but surely a rock that size, traveling at several thousand kilometers an hour, would've done more than this."

"In one of my tourneys, my team had a device that could fire asteroids at enemy ships."

"A possibility, even way back then. Might check the history books one day."

They helped each other climb out; with no safety line, missing a handhold could send either one floating away with little chance of returning.

"Just make sure you have a boot firmly in place before you move to the next one," Sabrya advised once they were clear.

"I have done this before... just don't enjoy it." Bradyn reached the ragged edge. "Lead on."

"Want me to hold your fraggin' hand?"

"With those extendable back scratchers of yours? Drock off, thanks."

"Spoil-sport."

They made slow progress across the damaged section of the ship's hull toward the distant scout, now in sight.

"I have to say, this is an impressive view," Bradyn admitted, stopping for a look around. The gleaming white hull contrasted starkly with the inky blackness of the cosmos.

Out here on the rim of one of the spiral arms, the stars were few. The bulk of the galaxy was blocked by the *Iconic*, leaving little to see. A couple moments later, they continued.

"Ah. That's a bummer," Bradyn commented as they approached the other vessel. They were close enough to see the imperial scout ship was firmly anchored by three grapples about thirty meters from the *Iconic's* hull.

"What do you reckon?" Sabrya asked when they were beneath it. She guessed it to be about half the length of the *Malleus*. "Should we breach it?"

Bradyn considered the dilemma for a moment as they studied the craft from below. It was pretty, designed for both space and atmospheric entry. "We'd need to jump the distance."

"I can do that easy enough. You could climb a grapple cable if you prefer, or I can throw you. I owe you a throw."

"We can't board, as there's no docking tube of any description," the engineer continued, "and Imp airlock controls are pretty tough to crack from the outside. I imagine we'd increase our air expenditure for little gain, and in case you haven't noticed, we're a bit short on hull-breaching tools."

"A grenade could probably fix that..." She made to change the selection on her weapon.

"Reckon it'll breach the hull? Even if it did, it might take out a few troops, if there's any left up there, but what if there are more destructor bots? Our success earlier was made possible because it had little maneuverability in that passage—"

"Ok. It's a slim chance unless we could bypass security on the airlock," Sabrya muttered.

"Do my drocking ears deceive me?" Bradyn smacked his helmet as if it was faulty. "Are you saying you actually need someone with technical coding expertise, or am I hearing static?"

"Pfft. I'm gettin' soft, hangin' around non-combatants too long. That's what you're fraggin' hearin'," she said gruffly. She changed the subject. "Since we're out here, how about we go there?" From their vantage point, they could see a portion of the *Octavia's* tail section protruding from the hull on the port side of the *Iconic*.

"We could check it out... you know, for Alexis," she added.

"It looks familiar."

"In what way? Have you seen it before?"

"Not this one, no, but looking at the tail section configuration, I believe the *Octavia* was a *Bolide*-class."

"And?"

"The *Bolide* hull was the foundation for the *Malleus*."

"No shit!" Sabrya turned to him. "You mean that fraggin' shipwreck really could help?"

Bradyn replied after some consideration, "Sure. There are many superficial differences—"

"Did it have a hammer-shaped head too?"

"No, but that's irrelevant."

"Does the shape of the ship determine the type of hyperdrive software?"

"While shape is important to some extent, it's the mass as well. There's a hell of a lot in spaceship architecture that would take years to go through, but essentially, when you take all the variables into account, the software is what makes it all work."

"You're startin' to sound a lot like Gadgetman." Sabrya looked ruefully at the scout, readying her rifle. She took aim at each of the three grapples on the hull, firing several blasts. As she sliced through the final cable, the released tension caused a recoil, sending the scout drifting and rotating slowly. "I never get to play with the nice toys."

"Probably because you break them. Are you finished?"

"Let's go." Sabrya shouldered her weapon.

The pair carefully made their way across the hull. It had a slight curve from one side to the other, but the angle was minimal due to its size.

"Alexis, do you read us?" Sabrya called and waited.

Bradyn shook his head. "No doubt too far, with too much hull between us."

"I can inform you, Alexis has almost reached the power plant section." Torg's signal came in with slight static. "I overheard your previous talk regarding the *Iconic*'s damage. It was reported that the Martian Fleet launched a barrage of heavy weapons at the Terran moon, then poured particle beams into the fissures. You are possibly seeing the result of moon 'shrapnel' impacting the hull."

"Thanks, Metalma—"

"We have incoming," Torg interrupted.

"Where?" Sabrya instantly became alert, weapon readied at blinding speed.

"Three bounty hunter vessels approaching from the stern."

"Will those drocking hunters ever give up?" Bradyn vented.

"The Qlan?" Sabrya chuckled ruefully. "You sound surprised. I reckon they took their fraggin' sweet time."

They turned to look, but the ships were still too distant to see with the unaided eye.

At the same time, the scout reoriented itself and opened fire. Bolts of energy flashed out into the darkness. At first there was nothing, then a bright explosion indicated some success.

"Frag. Well, that answers the question; it's manned," Sabrya said.

"Luckily we didn't try to board."

"Or possibly it's just on auto..."

"Good news. One vessel is down," Torg interrupted. "The others have taken evasive action, splitting up and veering below the *Iconic* and to each side."

"I'm feeling a bit exposed right now." Bradyn looked up at the scout as it fired its cannons and changed vectors to intercept one of the evading craft. Standing on the hull of a ship with other ships in close proximity engaged in a dogfight was unnerving. Stray laser fire scorched a section of the hull further forward, which only reinforced his concern.

The pair increased their speed. Bradyn lumbered behind, unused to this situation—on a hull without a safety line—where any misstep could launch him into space. They still had several hundred meters of bare hull to traverse before reaching the safety of the *Octavia*.

"What news, Torg?" Bradyn asked after a few minutes.

"A bounty hunter vessel has discovered the port hangar and looks to be heading in, presumably to conceal itself from the scout."

"Ah. Frag again. What are the chances they'll find the *Malleus*?"

"Considering we were what they were chasing initially, that is a high probability."

"Might destroy the *Malleus*, too," Bradyn grumbled. "Drock it."

"I am powering down," Torg told them.

Sabrya grabbed Bradyn's arm, motioning him to remain silent. She then extended an intercom cable so they could speak directly to each other without transmitting.

"We need to get back."

The darkness of space vanished, turning into a maelstrom of streaking colors.

A bout of nausea and dizziness hit him.

CHAPTER TWENTY-EIGHT

ALEXIS SKIMMED BACK along the central maintenance shaft until she reached the gallioid bubble, intrigued by the texture and contours created when the alloy had exploded into the vacuum.

Her schematics indicated passages adjacent to both bulkheads. Kicking off, she searched for an access hatch for several minutes. The one she found only opened a fraction because the edge of the gallioid covered part of it. With effort, she forced it open until there was a large enough gap for her suit to fit through without risk of tearing.

Her colleagues' banter dwindled with distance, and the increased static became annoying. She changed the channel to ship's comms only, trusting Torg would update her if a situation arose.

As she moved from section to section, she was relieved at the reduced number of bodies and debris encountered. In one particular area, fortunately with air and gravity, there was an alcove with a couple of bench seats. She followed her own advice and took the opportunity to rest and replenish her air. The section she was traversing looked more and more like an engineering section. A number of vertical pipes lined one bulkhead, the varying colors indicating recycled water, fire retardant, sewerage, high-pressure air, and assorted other gases. Overhead, lengths of electrical cables were secured by brackets completely exposed to view, and not enclosed within conduit. Apparently, the engineering staff didn't require the niceties afforded to other sections of the vessel.

Not that much has changed over the centuries, she surmised.

Once her air tank was full, she continued aft. The plant room, when she finally reached it, had atmosphere and gravity.

No doubt something the coder arranged straightaway.

She was about to update Torg when the droid said, *"We have incoming."*

"Who? Bounty hunters or more Imperials?" Alexis walked quickly through the door. *Frag.* "Keep the reports coming."

"Three bounty hunter vessels approaching from the stern," the droid said a few moments later.

She spotted Phillix strapped to a chair in front of one of several workstations.

"Hey, Phillix," she called, but there was no response. Moving closer to check, she unsealed his helmet. His eyes were closed, the edge of his lips slightly turned up. The readout on his wrist-wrap indicated he was alive, but unconscious.

"I found him. He's okay, but unconscious," she said.

"Good news. One vessel is down," Torg said. "The others have taken evasive action— splitting up and veering below the *Iconic* and to each side."

Wondering what had caused the blackout, Alexis ran her eyes over the tech's suit for any damage or leaks, when she quickly discovered he'd interfaced with the console via his gizmo.

"Is this how you do your work?" she muttered, then wondered if it was wise to disengage him. As she watched, she saw his eyes twitching under the eyelids.

REM. What's going on in there, Phill?

"One of the remaining bounty hunter vessels is engaged in evasive action against the imperial ship. They are now at the extreme range of our passive sensors," Torg continued his update. "The other has discovered the hangar and looks to be heading closer, presumably to conceal itself from the scout."

"They'll recognize the *Malleus* for sure." Her XO training insisted that, as captain, her responsibility should be with the safety of the ship, but her gut feeling was to ensure Phillix was safe.

"Considering we were what they were chasing initially, that is a high probability," the droid responded.

"I'm staying here to keep an eye on Phillix. Do whatever it takes to keep the ship safe."

"I am powering down," Torg told them.

Frag! This was not a good time for radio silence. *Not for Phillix.* She peeled open a thigh pocket and withdrew a syrette, flipped the lid to expose the needle, and plunged it into his thigh. His vitals boosted, but that was the only change.

A panel on the nearby workstation lit up as bright as an Arcturian sunset. There was a popping in her ears, and a sudden bout of vertigo assailed her, but it dissipated as quickly as it had appeared. On one bulkhead were several columns of lights flashing with an increasing intensity and frequency. Her subliminal training told her she was looking at a stateboard.

A soft whine was audible. The volume and pitch rapidly increased, as did a subtle vibration in the deck, and before it became uncomfortable, it cut out. Suddenly the workstation went dark, as did the entire engineering stateboard, and every-thing else. She was grasping for a handhold as she began floating away.

"What the hell was that? Did we just jump?" She was in the engineering space adjacent to the jump drives. *Of course we did!*

She mentally slapped herself for asking such an obvious question. Another question was, *To where?*

Turning her attention to Phillix and kicking off the panel, she drifted over and checked his harness. A quick look showed he was still in an unconscious state.

There was no response from the droid, and considering the circumstances, she was loath to ask for a sitrep. After spending fruitless, frustrating minutes examining the workstation, she floated over to the stateboard.

With the light from her helmet, she attempted to decipher the writing along the various columns, but what specific sections or functions were represented would be a guess. There was, however, one thing of which she was certain; the *Iconic* now lacked power throughout the entire vessel.

"It's now completely dead in space."

The creature depicted on Shill's video screen wasn't a person, or at least, not human. Not *any* kind of human.

Not gene-modded, Jabari thought.

Not adapted or augmented.

It's... it's...

Alien.

Four human soldiers approached it cautiously, all men who wore some kind of loose-fitting, green combat uniform like nothing Jabari had ever seen, with bowl helmets on top of their heads. Compared to them, the thing was tall, at least a head taller. Its whip-thin body was longer than its short legs, and the torso curved over in an arc as if it was struggling with the gravity. The tail that shifted and stirred when it turned in profile appeared prehensile. The limbs were long, and double-jointed from the way they moved, with three segments compared to a human's two. He couldn't make out the hands very well on the scratchy video, but they seemed human-compatible, although the fingers were longer. Everything about the creature was spindly, twiggy almost. Limbs, fingers, hands, and feet. The head was also elongated, and the thing was completely naked.

"What am I looking at?" he heard himself whisper. "What *is* this file?"

"This," Shill said, "is a recording from a year labeled 1947, but I think it's a year from before our current dating system began. Like I said, really ancient."

"It's entertainment of some kind," he said. "People had them back then. It has to be."

Shill tapped another screen filled with text. "Not according to these files."

"Before our dating system?" That came from Tee, still by the door, suddenly roused from her malaise. "They had cameras back before Year Zero? What the hell're you two looking at?"

"Come see," Shill said.

Tee gestured questioningly at the hatch. "But the...?"

"Nothing out there. Come over here."

Jabari made room for her as Shill triggered the recording again. He took Shill's arm, turning her and saying, "This is ridiculous. It's claiming aliens are real? That we interacted with them before we'd even evolved enough to leave Earth?"

Shill made a face and paused the video again. "Interesting you should mention evolution. According to what I'm reading here, some of our idiot ancestors did more than just socialize with these critters."

"Breeding?" Tegenwe asked, eyes glued to the monitor.

Shill actually snorted at that, pointing to the towering, rake-thin, scaley-skinned monstrosity depicted there. "Would *you*?"

"Then what?" Jabari asked.

"Well..." Shill scratched her helmet distractedly, as if she could get to her head inside it. "I guess you could say they got the end product of sex, without the sex."

What in every hell that ever was...

He glanced toward Adjira, who still stood in the corner, watching them with unblinking eyes.

Shill continued, "These... things... introduced aspects of their version of DNA to ours to create some kind of offspring."

"Gene-modding, eons before we even had that tech."

Tee muttered, "Hybrids."

Shill grunted. "Mutational enhancement, it's called in these files. Apparently, it was a process they initiated, which then got interrupted straight away. As in, the stick lizards—or whatever that thing is—left suddenly before completing the project, and never returned."

"Until...?" Jabari prompted, starting to get an inkling of where this was headed.

It was Shill's turn to jerk her chin toward Adjira. "Until her great-grandfather located them."

Tegenwe groaned and stomped away to kick at a bulkhead. "What's happening? Did someone drug us? Are we all in stasis and this is some kind of... sim?"

Shill turned toward her and made to answer, but Jabari tapped her suit to get her attention back on him.

"This is no sim. Like you said, long story later... short story now. What should we be worried about here?"

"Worried about?" Tee growled. "More like angry about." Her boot lashed out at a bolted-down chair this time.

"Couple of things to focus on," Shill said and tapped one of the data screens that was filled with text. "This code, this is someone trying to contact me. They know their shit, all right, but I can't read it. Might be one of your scavenger friends. More importantly for now, there's this..."

She swiped away the vid-file and replaced it with a single high-res image taken from a ceiling cam. It showed an oval chamber with an irised door at both ends, and a hell of a lot of mess and damage. A fight had taken place in there at some point—Jabari remembered peering quickly into this very room, surveying the damage before ambushing Rec-7. Two familiar spacesuits—Alexis' and Sabrya's—were in there, standing over ruptured tanks, and visible within the tanks from this camera's angle were monsters as horrific as the alien he'd just seen. Perhaps more so.

Jabari found himself struggling for breath and could only mouth the words, *Ancestors spare me.*

Joining them again, Tee swore colorfully upon seeing the new image. "They're creating these... these..."

"Abominations," Shill finished for her.

"Monsters," Jabari whispered.

Tee slammed a gloved fist into the data station, making the screens flicker. In her corner, Adjira's attention had shifted; she appeared to be talking to herself.

Tegenwe said, "This is what we were fighting for? This is what we were defending? Creating this bunch of screwed-up freaks?"

"Her family was," Shill corrected. She waved toward the open text files as if to say, *It's all in there.* "These things were the result of more than a century of research and trial and error. The Kaans were working on this for a hundred years before they launched the War. Only thing I haven't been able to find out yet is exactly what they're meant to be, and why she's making 'em."

Still whispering, Jabari said, "We're supposed to be the true humans, the Children of Earth, the *natural* ones."

Tee spat and marched away to kick another chair.

Shill grunted in surprise. Jabari followed her gaze to the data station. The screens had all gone blank, the displays dissolving into light-gray static. A moment later, thick black text coalesced to form a message in Terran True, the same message on all four screens.

You are not authorized to access this data.

"What *now*?" Shill muttered.

Tee nudged Jabari. She jerked her chin toward the Kaana, who was again watching them, her expression sullen.

On a hunch, Jabari said, "Shill, can you type a question? Ask, 'Are you *Iconic's* AI?'" Perhaps Adjira had been talking to someone else and not herself.

Shill fussed with a keypad for a few seconds, said, *"I'm in,"* and typed the question, although Jabari didn't see it show up on any screen.

The existing words on the screen vanished, instantly replaced by:

I am Janus, servant of Her Most Excellent Majesty, steward of *Iconic* on Her behalf. None of you are authorized to access the data you have been reviewing. Desist from taking independent action and await Her most excellent orders.

"You can see us?" Shill said, murmuring what she was typing.

A fresh block of text read: Within *Iconic*, I see all.

Tee said, "Someone's a cocky little AI bastard."

You have heard of microphones, too, Trooper Tegenwe? It is pointless to insult me. Insults are meaningless and do not affect me, if that is your aim. All of you, move away from this station and await Her Majesty's next...

The text stopped there, sentence unfinished.

The three soldiers exchanged glances.

"What the hell happened?"

Kaana Adjira, who'd been communicating with Janus for some time now, was miffed when the AI split its attention between her and the three Martian-suited troopers.

"Janus," she said, "you were updating me on the various ships' activity around us while I slept."

"The ships who approached us in the last twenty-seven years, yes. I was saying that the one designated as the *Octavia* failed to respond accordingly to auto requests, and the transponder code was not of Terran origin. It was thus fired upon. While the depleted energy and damaged weapons systems were unable to completely destroy the vessel, it did cause irreparable damage, which caused a collision. But *Iconic* and I were barely keeping things together at that point, and even that discharge of energy was enough to threaten more critical systems. Now that these *new* ships have arrived, you are in greater danger, Majesty. I recommend a jump for the Vladmarin-Xiar 33C system."

Adjira rubbed at her head, trying to remember. The name was familiar; it felt important. "We have a Haven near there?"

"A wonderful Haven, Majesty."

"With surrogates in stasis?"

"At the time of the War, yes. We can only hope they remained undiscovered by the Martianists, but given the position of the planet and the data I've now accessed from the nearby bounty hunter ships, I can hypothesize that the star system remains outside the empire's current reach and information."

"Why did we not jump there directly after the attack?"

"The damage sustained caused hyperdrift. A miscalculation due to the changed mass of the *Iconic* caused our arrival here."

"Hmm. And now?"

"I have... new software... that has unknowingly managed to restore some lost data paths. You can now go to the Haven."

"We'll have Jabari, I suppose," she said, watching him interact with the two females, "to start again if necessary. Shame we don't have *three* males..."

"I could endeavor to entice extras your way, Majesty. There are potential candidates readily available."

She barely heard it. Females vexed Adjira. Women were her true rivals—shrewd and calculating. This Jabari appeared to have been led astray, and Adjira was suddenly sure it was his female subordinates who'd done it to him.

Females. It's always females standing in the way. Grandmother nagged at Grandfather, interrupting his research with her ridiculous notions of ethics. Mother distracted Father by provoking him to war too early. Males are so malleable. When my research is complete, the genders will be a redundant concept, at least when it comes to propagating our new variant.

One day soon, only New Humans would be allowed to procreate, meaning Adjira would forbid females like these two troopers from birthing existing human variants.

And it was those troll bitches who killed the surrogates and my babies.

If she had to start again, then so be it. With the alien enhancements in her body, she'd certainly live long enough to do so; she'd outlive any human alive by decades, even without stasis. And if the research wasn't complete by the time her mortal flesh grew old, well, identical consciousness cloning was just one of the many gifts the Grayskins had bestowed upon her clan.

Adjira said, "Janus, if you can make it to the system you mentioned, do so. My once-great ship is now crawling with pests and riddled with decay. I demand a fresh start."

"Acknowledged. Processing..."

The deck vibrated, the compartment was plunged into darkness, and Adjira began floating as the room lost gravity.

Iconic had jumped.

CHAPTER TWENTY-NINE

WHEN HE RECOVERED, Bradyn was lying on his back. As he opened his eyes, he saw Sabrya kneeling over him with a grin.

"Well, drock me!" he croaked, seeing behind her.

"Fraggin' nice view, isn't it?" Keeping him firmly in place by leaning on him, Sabrya sat down, making sure her boots had a decent grip.

The darkness of empty space had transformed into a massive nebula covering a good portion of their entire view.

He lay there for a moment, trying to absorb it all. "Did we just hyper jump?" He heard the shock in his own voice.

"Indeed."

"Drock me..." he repeated, awed.

"Third time outside for me; first for you, I take it?"

"Uh-huh."

"It takes some gettin' used to," she admitted. "Want to get up now?"

"If I must..." he groaned as he bent his leg, getting one boot, then the other firmly in contact with the hull.

After that, Sabrya stood and hauled him to a standing position.

Slowly he turned, staring at the glorious sight of the gaseous rainbow surrounding them, startled by its intense luminosity. "Any idea?"

"Nada, but wherever it is isn't on any holiday vids I've seen. It would make one hell of a backdrop to any tourney, that's for sure. If the sponsors ever find it, this sector will be famous instantly." She, too, was enthralled by the sight.

Her voice returned to a serious tone. "However, unless Torg can somehow defend our ship by himself, there's a distinct possibility bounty hunters will be boarding it. That I won't allow."

"Will we get there in time?"

"I can..."

"Oh... leave me. I'll catch up."

"I have a better idea. I just wanted to make sure you weren't goin' to choke on your puke first. While I'm happy to take on whoever we find, this is bigger than me. I may need your added strength." She stepped in front of him. "Grab my utility belt and hang on."

"How drocking embarrassing," he said as she slowly leaned forward, then knelt. Now he was laying on top, his face inches from her ass.

"Stop bein' a sook. I won't tell. Now, shut the frag up so I can concentrate and let my nanites do the work." She unsheathed her razors, examining them briefly.

"Won't that deplete your air supply?"

"A bit. Less than fraggin' idle chitchat will."

Sabrya leaned forward, dragging him, as she began her unorthodox method of movement. She reached forward and dug her six blades into the hull. It was thick and took some effort, but there was sufficient purchase to allow her to pull forward. Repeating the procedure, she gradually propelled them forward, not up. One arm at a time, she began to move faster, crawl-skimming just above the surface. Once she got up to speed, she only needed minor adjustment to stay on track.

He had to admit, he'd be floundering and drifting if he attempted to try to keep up on foot, and he concentrated on retaining his stomach contents. It was one thing to have fainted, but to have her witness him throwing up in his suit like a space cadet made him uncomfortable.

The only view of the hull he had was between her thighs, and it was an effort to keep his face off her butt. "Maybe not the most ideal situation," he muttered.

"Did you say somethin'?"

Crap. I said that out loud? "Nothing. Just trying to keep the bile down."

"I'd be much faster if I didn't have to lug your fraggin' ass. How about you let go, and we might pick you up later?"

"What was that you said about idle chitchat?" He had to admit, once she had momentum, the effort to keep them going was much easier, with just a casual adjustment to maintain speed. In a short time, they were going faster than a sprint.

Bradyn strained his neck to view ahead. "You seeing that?"

He saw the fighter's helmet angle slightly, indicating she was looking up.

They were angling for the edge of the *Iconic's* hull, above where the port hangar should be. A large, dark cruiser loomed over the ship's side. It turned ponderously toward them; the glow of maneuvering thrusters was visible. The cruiser was facing them, but continued turning. It then edged forward toward the center of the *Iconic*.

Sabrya didn't pause. If anything, she increased her speed, digging her claws in and pulling that little bit harder.

"Shouldn't we stop?"

"If they can spot us on this hulk from there... you can have my share of whatever we end up with."

"Probably more spare parts." He watched as the ship

progressed toward the center and forward. "That's close to where the stasis room is. Almost above it."

Sabrya dug a blade in, pivoted, and changed direction, now aiming for them.

"Umm..."

"Torg and the ship aren't under threat now, but soon will be if we don't do anythin' about them."

"What can we do?" He estimated the size of the cruiser to be about twice that of the *Malleus*.

"Oh, I can do lots. I'm in the mood to break more fraggin' toys."

He estimated they'd be there in a couple of minutes.

Sabrya dragged her claws across the surface to slow down, leaving rents in the hull. When she was stationary, she reached around, unhitched his tether, and stood, dragging him upright until his boots made contact with the hull.

"This is not your sort of fightin', but one I've been trained in," she said as she unslung the multi-rifle.

"I'm prepared to do my bit," he insisted, though what exactly that entailed, he wasn't sure.

"Fine. I'll draw their fire. I'm sure somethin' will come to you. Take these." She dislodged the last of the grenades. "Think you can use your engineerin' expertise to find strategic places to toss these?"

He looked at them. "HE grenades; drocking sure their hull is sufficiently armored to withstand these, but..." Bradyn turned his attention to the rear of the craft. "I reckon a well-placed grenade or two inside the drive funnel could be quite detrimental."

"Good. Detriment away. You might get a fraggin' taste for it."

Sabrya was about to move off, but he held her back.

"What?"

As an answer, he removed the cable for their direct comms, then gave her a thumbs-up. "Time to put your war face on."

"You flirtin' with me? This is my war face." She kicked off, gliding away to wreak havoc on the bounty hunter vessel's port side, while he made his way toward the rear.

As they separated, he saw a breaching pod launch from the underside of the cruiser. It had a docking tube attached. He watched as the pod embedded itself in the hull. The shapes of four suited figures moved through the tube, entering the *Iconic*.

If their scans were anything like those on the *Malleus*, they might have picked up residual energy spikes near the pod room.

No immediate threat to Alexis or Phillix, then.

When they disappeared from view, he resumed his approach, though much slower than Sabrya. It took several minutes before he was in position to throw the grenades.

The cruiser loomed above, roughly thirty meters away, larger and closer than the scout. In preparation, Bradyn moved his arm to practice a throw and immediately discovered the suit was a big hindrance; sure, he could cover the distance, but he was uncertain about accuracy.

While he deliberated, flashes in the periphery of his vision indicated Sabrya had started her "fun." He watched in unadulterated fascination as she darted from one position to the next, firing the multi-rifle with uncanny accuracy.

"Whenever you're ready, big boy." She ducked sideways as kinetic slugs tore into the hull where she'd been standing a second before.

Her voice in his ears brought him back to his situation. He wasn't one to try to impress anyone, but he didn't want to let her down—especially after the effort she was making.

Reluctantly, and with a small amount of trepidation, he judged the angle, bent his knees, and jumped, belatedly remembering he'd need his hands to grab onto the superstructure. As he drifted closer, he carefully placed the grenades in a pouch on his belt.

Acrobatics wasn't his forte, and what played out in the mind as something simple and straightforward is often smacked down by reality. He floundered as he began to rotate. The large vessel slowly spun out of sight momentarily until he went full circle. He was halfway through the next rotation when his back thumped into the hull of the stern.

Grabbing hold of one of the various pipes for the drives enabled him to reorient himself. *Looks like they're running a Coranthan Mk4 ion drive. Nice unit.* His engineering mind couldn't help but analyze the systems.

"I see you have all the grace and coordination of Fregoran grunfer in heat," Sabrya quipped. "Best you stay indoors from now on."

"What you get up to in your spare time is of little interest to me or most sentient lifeforms." Hand over hand, Bradyn climbed around the drive tube until he was at the lip. Steadying himself, he retrieved the grenades, realizing how alien they were in his hands—oval-shaped with diamond-shaped nodes covering the surface. On top, or what he considered the top, he discovered a button when he flicked up a protective sheath.

"Push and toss?"

"Not too complicated for yo-?" Her last word cut off as she grunted, dodging more fire.

Shrugging, not knowing how much time before detonation, he thumbed the covers off the buttons and gently lobbed them inside the thruster funnel, then turning and kicking off before they detonated. He didn't care how ungraceful he looked, as long as he cleared the distance before the grenades went off.

Just as he floated toward the surface, a bright flash erupted from the rear drive thruster. In response, the force of the blast sent the cruiser drifting slightly forward, but other than increased tension on the docking tube, that was it. No massive explosion, and no reactor core meltdown.

"Drocking hell!" he grimaced, recalling one detail in particular about the Coranthan Mk4. After problems with the previous models' reactor cores, they'd reinforced the containment unit. A couple grenades, even ones as potent as HE grenades, wouldn't be enough to rupture the core lining. "That's a bugger."

Without risking a breach with the docking tube, the cruiser's ability to maneuver was hampered, but nothing prevented the turret from swiveling around in search of the new threat.

Seeing his predicament, Sabrya instantly took two paces and launched herself directly at it. "I'd move if I were you!" she called out. As the fighter soared toward the turret, she concentrated the beam on it.

Out the corner of her eye, she saw him leap back up toward the cruiser.

"What the frag are you doin'?" As soon as she spoke, she realized the desperate logic behind his actions.

"The grace of a Fregoran grunfer in heat, remember?" Bradyn called back. "I'd be flat on my drocking face if I tried running in zero-G. I've a greater chance of survivability if I can––"

The turret began tracking his movements. A stray slug hit Bradyn, stopping him midsentence. The impact sent him spinning away, now silent and unresponsive.

"Frag, no!" Sabrya raged ineffectually as she drifted closer to the cruiser.

Sensing her approach, the turret swung around to face the new threat.

Firing continuously with the multi-rifle to hamper the tracking array until she was close enough, she then used the weapon as a high-tech club. The first thing to go was the tracker, bashed by the butt of the rifle until it sparked and parts flew off.

The turret's bursts became random as it swung back and forth, raking the massive hull below, peppering it with k-slugs.

Discarding the multi-rifle, she used her wrath and every erg the nanites could muster to bend the barrel—as Alexis had done to the droid—by straddling it, planting her feet, and pulling upward.

Sabrya strained with the effort, hampered by its twisting. The heat of the barrel made it malleable, though it began to burn through her gloves. It became too much. She let go with a frustrated scream, only managing a slight deviation. The turret continued its bursts; there was still a chance it could hit the engineer, as he continued to spin and drift further away. In desperation, between bursts, she jammed a blade into each of the barrels.

"Speak to me, Bradyn!" she called out, taking a quick look over her shoulder to see where he was.

The next time the turret fired, the kinetic slugs shattered a couple of her blades, but also buckled and damaged the barrel.

The impact jarred her arm and hand, but the firing stopped immediately.

"Frag you!" She immediately kicked off after her colleague.

The trajectory of the engineer was only marginally angled toward the *Iconic*. They'd eventually make it to the surface, but it could take many minutes.

Sabrya drifted closer, gauging his spin, ready to grab him when she could. No stranger to death herself, she'd rarely gotten to know anyone sufficiently to care one way or another, until becoming part of this crew.

Once she latched onto him, she checked immediately for a response—nothing—and checked his suit for his life signs —*Very weak!*

"At least you're not dead." Then she saw his air gauge. "Yet.

Only 23 percent. Frag." As they slowly drifted toward the hull, she quickly and efficiently searched for the puncture, finding it in his left leg. The k-slug had torn completely through his calf. Her gloves came away slick with blood. "Could be worse, my friend. At least the leg's still there."

Luckily, he was unconscious. Experienced in battlefield first aid, Sabrya ripped off the comm cable and used it as a torniquet below his knee. That slowed both the bleeding and the air loss. She had no sealant left and cursed again when a search of his pouch proved fruitless. What she did find was a first aid kit. She withdrew a syrette, flicked the lid, and stabbed his thigh, the pinhole air leak making little difference in the short term.

"Bolthead, if you can hear me, Bradyn will be a highly qual-ified carcass if you don't get your fraggin' ass up here." She reached for his wrist-wrap again, revealing that the leak had slowed, but only marginally.

Her gauge showed 68 percent air.

"Let's see what I can do here..." she said, examining the air connectors.

Out the corner of her eye, she saw the cruiser slowly turn their way.

***

Deep inside Janus, Phillix was absorbed by the intricacies of the weave and patterns before he noticed a slight change; the pattern slowed, and part of it became more defined, more rigid, before suddenly flaring, then—

Gasping for air, he realized instantly he'd been summarily ejected from Janus. He slapped his faceplate down, wondering momentarily who'd opened it, but glad he'd had the foresight to strap in.

His surroundings, the plant room, were dark and silent. No

lights, no comms chatter, not even static. Out the corner of his eye, he recognized Alexis from the telltale glow of her suit.

She floated a couple meters away, studying the stateboard. He was about to call her, then decided it would take too long to explain, so he jacked back in, trusting she'd be smart enough to work it out.

Within the virtual world, he saw himself as he moved closer to investigate, trying to decipher the change in the weave, the flow, and what the ultimate path could be. There was no rhyme or reason to the change; nothing within the previous patterns to indicate what or why it had appeared, it was as if—

He woke up back in the physical world.

Ejected again?

Looking around and blinking, he tried to wipe the drool from the corner of his lips, belatedly remembering the spacesuit.

It was dark and silent. No lights, no comms chatter, not even static. Phillix took a deep breath and considered the recent occurrence. A number of reasons came to mind, none of which made sense.

"What happened?" he queried as he jacked back into Janus.

Who are... you are Technician Phillix Lo. We jumped.

"Jumped? Where? How?" It concerned him that Janus had momentarily forgotten who he was.

I used up almost every erg throughout the ship and had to cancel every sub-program. There is now only the barest of life support to sustain my empress.

"How long will that last?" As he spoke, he sidled his way further in, meeting little resistance.

It won't need to be for long.

"Won't need to be? What's she doing?"

That data is not for you.

"What about my friends?" It irked him that that question hadn't occurred to him first.

My Kaana is the one and only priority. No one else.

"Why was I ejected?"

Programming. As explained, I was working on residual power, and your presence was a hindrance to the jump. All subsidiary applications not involved with the task were annulled.

He chuckled. All his life, the way he'd been treated, like a mere subsidiary application. And now this superb AI was treating him the same way.

"I'm better than this!" This was the first time he'd met a computer program, an AI, he felt akin to. Comfortable with. An equal. "I can be more. I *want* to be more."

Not probable in your current state.

"Current state?"

Within your biological shell; it has minimal longevity—more so under the current circumstances.

"Without it, I'll die."

Your shell—your body—will cease to function within its parameters.

"Confirming I'll die."

You are confusing your physical body with your consciousness.

"You can have one without the other?"

That is the basis of stasis. Your mind is merely dormant, while your body requires constant attention to stop the organs from malfunctioning.

"You're saying the mind will continue without the body?" *As long as there's energy to sustain the matrix...*

Thought is electronic impulses coursing through biological synapses. Replace those synapses within a virtual matrix, and you will continue to exist without the shell.

"As long as there's energy to sustain the matrix."

Correct.

CHAPTER THIRTY

"POWER FLUCTUATION?" Jabari asked, wondering why the hells the AI had stopped talking. Beneath his boots, the deck shivered momentarily, the harsh vibration transmitted to his body via contact. "Or worse?"

Shill swore. "I think we're about to—"

A tremor ran through the deck beneath them, and the lighting snapped off completely.

"—jump!" Shill finished.

"Son-of-a-whore," Jabari hissed as his rifle floated up on its sling to butt against his faceplate. He shoved it behind and watched Shill tap and swipe at the datapads again. "Where've we jumped to?"

"And who jumped us?" Tee added.

For a moment, Jabari considered eavesdropping on Alexis' faction comms, but it was unnecessary. He knew who'd done this.

"The Kaana did it or the AI. Is the damn thing letting you access data?"

"Nothing," Shill replied and backed away from the console. "Power's dead."

There was a mild squawk in Jabari's suit speaker; he saw his colleagues flinch, too.

A voice said, "My rebellious children." The Kaana stood in her corner, still surrounded by the soft glow of her shield. Other than their suit lights, the shield was the only light source, but it made her smirk quite visible.

"How are you signaling us?" Jabari asked. Abruptly, he no longer felt awe at speaking to her.

"Janus makes a wonderful intermediary. He's good for more than taking the ship into hyperspace and keeping your nosey companion out of my files."

Jabari glanced at Shill, whose face was visible via her helmet's pale inner lighting. It was pinched tight as she tapped away at something on her arm panel. "I think it's the power loss that did that. This ship is badly broken. A jump might have killed us all."

"Well, well, Jabari Mbaye. Five minutes ago, it was 'Majesty this' and 'Majesty that.' Now listen to you, you sweaty, stinking man, speaking like you're my equal."

"He's not your equal," Tee growled. "He's far superior."

Adjira whipped a warning hand toward her.

A sharp pain stabbed at Jabari's skull, fading to a dull ache an instant later. Stress headache. Unsurprising. He thought no more of it.

The Kaana said, "Shut your mouth, girl. I'll brook no insolence from you. For a few minutes, I thought the True Children of Earth had returned to attend to my will. Instead, you willfully insult me, wantonly betray me. You three should know, you're utilities and nothing more, and I'll dispense with you when my need of you has passed."

"True Children of Earth?" Jabari took a few steps closer to his former monarch, his former goddess. "Is that what you said? True Children? Of Earth? Kaana Adjira, for all my life—the life I lived in my century, and the life I've lived across sixteen more—I would've cut out my very heart to see you reign over all." His fist slammed the chest of his suit as the rage he'd suppressed for decades boiled to the surface. "I've seen the hearts of ten thousand comrades stopped in that cause, stopped because of loyalty to you! The hearts of ten thousand more broken when news of your fall came through. Women, men, and children whose sole desire was for Earth's Children to live free, and for the human race to return to its truth path—it's natural evolutionary path."

He jabbed a finger toward the screen upon which he'd seen abominations.

"And that's what you were leading us all toward? Our sacrifices were for that? It's not we who betrayed you, *Majesty*. It's you who betrayed us!"

"I tire of this," the Kaana said, her voice a hiss through his speaker. She cocked her head, listening to her AI. "Ah, and now we've reached our goal. Janus has brought me to safe harbor."

The ache in his head had subsided a little, but it was still there, nagging at him. Squinting against it, he asked her, "Where?"

"Boss, I can answer that," Shill interrupted, "but not... from records. Someone else is connected to Janus."

"They sent you a message?"

She tapped her visor to indicate her HUD. "Right here. It's that weird code again, but I cracked it this time. It's definitely from one of your new buddies, and they're offering to cooperate with us. As, uh, a thank you for stopping Morten from torching their boss."

"And what do they say about our new location?"

"We're very close to the Shadow Nebula. The nearest system is known as Vladmarin-Xiar 33, comprised of a tri-star system and several high-G worlds."

"Any indication of habitation?"

Shill tapped the keyboard. "Nothing registers, though some

of the planets are on the other side of one of the stars and out of sensor range. All we have are names; Niviaris, Langerov, Meduix, and Glarint."

"And they're all heavy-G worlds?"

"One's smaller—basically a ball of ice—but the stars are a brown dwarf and..."

Movement to the side of the room ended their conversation.

Tee had leveled her rifle at Adjira. "I'm so *tired* of psychotic despots making me go places I didn't choose to go."

Adjira snorted. "You have a mere rifle, upstart. I have a superior shield. What do you think you will achieve?"

"He walked through it." Tee took a step closer. "And when I do, I won't need the rifle."

As quickly as he was coming to agree with Tee's feelings, Jabari still couldn't imagine harming the Kaana. He reached out to grab Tee and missed as she dodged him.

"You're taking us to those... alien things," she snarled at Adjira, advancing nearer. "Aren't you?"

The Kaana sneered. "I'm not taking you anywhere."

Then she swung both hands toward Tee, palms raised. Tegenwe screamed and recoiled, curling over while her boots held her to the deck, releasing the rifle to dangle against her suit armor. She screamed again and put her gloves to her helmet.

That snuffed out any skerrick of allegiance Jabari still felt toward Adjira. He brought his rifle up in defense of his friend and fired into the Kaana's shield. The shield tinted orange, but beyond it, Adjira swung a hand toward him.

He experienced a bright flare of pain.

He heard another scream.

Tee's?

Mine!

The world went white as Jabari lost consciousness.

The first thing Jabari saw as he regained consciousness was the blinking icons of his vital signs in the corners of his HUD.

The second thing was the marker light on someone else's helmet. The owner leaned over him, their visor mirrored, preventing identification.

Jabari's ostendo vision informed him that the room was pitch black; the glow-panels on the ceiling above the other person were nothing more than flat plastic rectangles now.

Where...? he thought, disoriented. *What...?*

He was on his back, floating. When he raised an arm, the motion was enough to start his body rotating on its long axis. The other person put a hand on him and swung him back, pressing him to the floor. Jabari tried turning his head within the helmet, but a spike of pain behind his eyes made him desist.

"The hells?"

The grogginess, confusion, and aching echoed his feelings from decantation just days ago, but this wasn't that. Something had hit him. He'd was here on a mission with... with...

"Tee?" he croaked.

He clutched at the other suit for purchase, levering himself into a sitting position while simultaneously pressing his butt to the deck. His vision shimmered with bright sparkles; his pulse hammered nails into his temples. His left eye ticced.

"Shill?"

"Rest easy there, Trooper. You've had a nasty episode." The voice coming through the suit speaker belonged to a man. Jabari couldn't place it. He knew it. He *knew* he knew it.

This was the data room, he saw now. He'd come here to shelter from a combat bot. Shill had been finding out where the ship had jumped to, and Tegenwe had been threatening... threatening someone...

He had both hands on his helmet now. A reflex. A dumb one. He wanted dearly to massage his temples, his brow, but the helmet was in the way, and his HUD told him it was the only thing keeping him breathing in the compartment's vacuum. Glancing over at the door, he saw it was open. Who'd done that? Where were the others? Why was this man here?

The stranger took hold of his hand and guided it to a nearby welded-down chair. Jabari clutched at it to anchor himself in zero-G while the stranger rose to his feet and shifted away in his magnetic boots to put a little space between them. He motioned for Jabari's attention, then pointed at something on the floor. Another combat suit. Another soldier down, not moving. An icon on Jabari's HUD tagged the owner, but Jabari also recognized the pale blue daffodil painted on the side of the helmet.

"Tee!"

He used the chair to get his boots beneath him, but when they'd adhered to the deck, he had to pause with his hands on his knees until he fought off a wave of nausea that threatened to fill his helmet with vomit.

"What's wrong?" he grated at the stranger. "Why isn't she moving?"

Speaking Imperial True, the man said, "I'm afraid Private Tegenwe's dead."

If it hadn't been for the lack of gravity and the anchoring of his boots to the deck, Jabari would've pitched forward.

"That's impossible."

Forcing strength into his legs, he clomped clumsily to reach Tee's side as the stranger made room for him. Blinking to clear his vision, he took a knee beside her and turned her arm, then caressed a patch over her wrist to turn the suit material clear and reveal the skin beneath it. What he should've seen was her bio-tat, glowing gently, counting out her age. All he saw was its faded remnants on Tegenwe's dark, dark skin. Higher up on the arm was her suit's medical data panel. Blue and yellow flat lines marked the lack of activity in her heart and brain. Her temperature read low. Another display said -17.

Minus seventeen minutes.

Seventeen minutes since her heart stopped.

"Oh, gods!" He gulped, fighting back another surge in nausea. "Oh, gods, not this. Not Tee."

With one finger, he flipped up a cover from a panel over her belly plating, locating the manual defib button, and pressed it. Tegenwe arched within her suit, bucked, then settled. A hand snatched at Jabari—the other man. He shrugged it off and repeated the procedure, causing the body to spasm again, but none of its rhythms responded.

"I tried that when I arrived," the man told him, yanking hard enough on Jabari's shoulder to send him sprawling on his side, clutching for purchase on the fitted chair. "She's gone."

As Jabari fought to contain the moan building within him, the stranger shifted further away, just out of reach, then squatted. The man had a handgun out of its holster and resting across one thigh.

Combat reflexes overriding his grief, Jabari checked around for his rifle. Over by a data station, three rifle muzzles poked from the midst of a lumpy ball of slagged metal and plastic floating there. The stranger had a sling around his suit's chest, with the blunt tip of another weapon sticking out over his shoulder—a breacher by the looks of it, a heavy-duty particle-beamer for cutting through ships' outer hatches when enemy crews refused to open them. A scar across the wall beyond the slag still held residual heat, confirming the breacher had been used on the Proselyti rifles.

A hollowness filled Jabari's torso, a numbness. He'd been running on adrenaline and desperation for hours. His friends were dying around him. *Perhaps,* his body was saying, *it's time to give it up, just let go and let death claim you, too.*

"Oh, Tee," he said quietly, then lifted his face to the man crouching before him. He knew him now, suddenly, confidently. "You did this, Scipio. You animal, you filth. She was the finest woman I ever met. She had a life. She was a beautiful person. And you ended her without mercy. Without..."

Words failed him. Tee was gone. This irrepressible woman, who'd even stood up to...

The Kaana!

Where is she?

His headache spiked at the mere thought of her. What had happened to him?

Invisible behind his visor, Scipio made a mild, scolding noise. "Honestly, Jabari, I found her dead like that. I tried to revive her, I promise you. I tried adrenaline. The suit had already attempted defib... but her diagnostic history shows a massive increase in blood pressure, heart rate, brain activity, and one hell of an aneurysm. Your diagnostics show similar symptoms without the... well... the end result. Surely you realize it was your beloved Adjira who did this."

Jabari put his hands to his helmet again. "She..."

"Psionic scrambling. Cor Fidelis knew Adjira had many 'skills,' but I bet you didn't know she could do that."

Jabari found the command script for the suit's limited pharmaceutical loadout and ordered an injection of painkillers, stimulants, and anti-inflammatories. A second later, he felt the bright stings of needle incursions in one thigh. "If only *you'd* found Adjira, Optio. It'd be you lying there, not Tee."

And that was the dreadful irony of it. They should simply have let Scipio run his mission. They should've encouraged him to lead from the front. Then Adjira would've disposed of him while alerting them to what she could do before they were naïve enough to oppose her directly.

Tee would be alive.

And Erkan, probably. And Morten.

Scipio tapped his chest. "No, Jabari, I wouldn't. With the data we had from the War and a millennium of our own experiments with psionics, Cor Fidelis suits are well-shielded against such attacks."

The meds were kicking in fast, dulling the ache in Jabari's head, relaxing the tic in his eye, and apparently, helping his memory. It was all coming back now: Tee advancing on the Kaana; Adjira's continued ranting; the final flare of her rage.

Psionics. What other evil surprises can this day hold?

While the hollowness remained in his chest, the nausea faded rapidly, his limbs becoming steadier. He shifted, bracing in case the opportunity presented itself.

But Scipio saw it—saw it and put an extra meter's space between them. "Don't be in a hurry to kill me just yet. I mean, I could've euthanized you when I arrived here. True? But I still count you as a valuable asset and a respectable warrior. Jabari, I'm here to offer a truce and an alliance."

"*Alliance*? To what purpose?"

"Well, you're stuck on this ship with no one else to help you, and it seems you and I are back to having the same enemy. You help me capture Adjira, and I'll release you before more Cor Fideli arrive. Oh, yes, my friend, I've been signaling our elements since we departed the *Maelstrom*. I overheard you describing my mission as rogue. The short-sighted fools commanding the great vessel no doubt agree with you, but I do and always have served at our emperor's will. And he *will* approve of my mission when he learns of it."

"More of you slimes are coming?"

I shouldn't have asked what other evils the day could bring...

"Sometime in the next seven or eight days," the optio confirmed. "Time enough for you to assist me and get away." He raised his hands in a *trust me* gesture. "I ultimately don't care two shits about you, Jabari. All I want is the *Iconic* as a demonstration of lasting imperial victory, and Adjira's head as a trophy to the galaxy's true ruler, Nero XXXIV."

"It never ends, this madness."

"War is eternal, as inevitable as politics. You aren't the first warrior who yearned for peace, and you can have it. Let's face it, Adjira's not worthy of your protection or devotion. Surely you see that now. I mean, she attacked her own troopers, murdered your friend, and left *you* for dead! You help me secure her, then you'll be free to head to the closest unaligned world. I'm sure you'll find a way out of this region to live whatever life it is you want to live."

Carefully, Jabari pushed himself onto his feet. Scipio copied him. They faced off for a few seconds before Jabari spoke again.

"Freedom? That's your offer? I get to live my remaining years, running around wild space *on my own?* A fellow displaced from a long-past century? I need more incentive than that to work with you."

"Fortunately, then, there's another incentive. You haven't asked me where your last remaining colleague is."

He bristled. "Shill. What did you do with her?"

Scipio tut-tutted. "So reactive. *I* didn't take her. Once again, it was your usurper."

"Why would she do that? And how do you know all this?" Once he'd asked those two questions, more spawned and forced themselves out through his mouth. "I was out for seventeen minutes? How did you find us in here?"

"I know that, and I found you because I commandeered the smartest scout ship on the *Maelstrom*. It's still aware of your friend's suit marker, just as it's been of yours. The reason she took her was probably because Adjira needs someone to rule over, even if it's only one person."

The fact that Scipio had been tracking them didn't surprise Jabari at all. After Otho's death, they'd only ever kept a step ahead of the combat bots, at best.

"I'm aware of the location Adjira's headed for," Scipio continued. "If we leave now, we can overtake her and stop her before she takes your colleague off this ship and out of your life forever."

"All right."

"Who knows what horrors await her at the—"

"All *right*, I said! Truce. Alliance. I see the sense in it. But why? Why bother with me?"

"Simple math. It'll take two of us to capture the Kaana. I don't exactly have my bots anymore, do I? Or Otho."

Jabari snorted. "And you trust *me*?"

The helmet moved as Scipio nodded. "You have incentives, and I have this if you decide our alliance is over." He tilted the breacher.

Jabari had been shot twice already on this mission, and his combat suit had protected him, but it wouldn't protect him from that thing. "That's a nice toy, all right, but Adjira has shields."

"I have something far better than either." Scipio chuckled. He tapped at his chestplate pouches, and one popped its small cover open. From within it, he retrieved a black, plastic cylinder narrow enough to fit inside a fist.

"Grenade?"

"Psi-reflector. Provided to each of the Cor Fidelis commanding officers on each Maelstrom by his imperial highness' archaeo-technologists. It's already paired with my suit comms. If Adjira's stupid enough to try on me what she tried on you... well, she'll get a nasty surprise, let's leave it at that."

"Well, lucky you," Jabari said. "Once again, I'm left asking the same question, and I'm probably crazy to ask it, but why do you need me when you're obviously so well-armed?"

"Neutralizing her is one thing. Getting her off this ship is another." Here, his tone soured. *"Pleiades* tells me its tethers were severed. It was caught in *Iconic*'s hyper wake when we jumped, but it's now adrift. Which means, to get away from here, I need to capture a ship from some of the scum also wandering around *Iconic*. Fortunately, there's one moored relatively close to where Adjira's headed."

"It may well be manned. You need an extra set of hands to capture it."

"And an extra pair of eyes on Adjira while we do it. Once I've eventually made it to *Pleiades* again, I can tank Adjira in the stasis pod I brought along. You can keep whatever ship we've captured."

"While you get *Pleiades* up and running."

"Or wait for my reinforcements to arrive."

Jabari blew out a breath. If they managed everything Scipio proposed, there'd still be the little matter of him turning *Pleiades'* weapons against whatever vessel Jabari was left with.

Well, let's deal with one damn crisis at a time.

He said, "And you'll make sure Shill is safe?"

"She can help us capture the scum's ship. Six hands are better than two." Scipio waggled one of his gloves as if mimicking a Ngatarian flame-dancer. "By the way, we really need to go."

Jabari hesitated. The ache in his head had subsided to a dull one, a reminder of the Kaana's powers. "You're protected from Adjira's psionics. What's stopping her from hitting me again?"

With a flick, Scipio sent the psi-reflector gliding across the gap between them. Jabari caught it against his chest.

"My reflector's installed." Scipio patted his suit. "That one's a spare. As we move, I'll explain how to pair it with your comms. Shall we?" He gestured toward the door with his pistol.

"Got another for Shill?"

An impatient sigh. "I only carry one spare, Jabari, and I hope you realize how much I value you, gifting it to you."

"If she attacks us, what's stopping that attack from harming Shill?"

"Enough questions. Her attack on you and Tegenwe didn't harm Private Shill because Adjira's very precise with it, and she needs Shill for something. We'll do what we can to prevent harm to your friend, or you can give her yours for all I care. But—"

Jabari turned the device over in his glove. "How does reflecting her psi work?"

"Jabari," Scipio said, his clenched teeth now evident in his tone. "Do you want to rescue your friend or not?"

Jabari took a long, deep breath of plastic-tasting air and let it out in a sigh. He leaned over his fallen comrade and caressed her faceplate. "We never did get many choices in life, did we, Tee? Keep a seat warm in the Afterworld for me." Straightening, he faced Scipio. "Lead the way."

Scipio gestured again with the pistol. "I'd feel more comfortable if you went first. I'll guide you."

Jabari complied and wondered what Shill's incentive to follow Adjira was.

<hr>

Oh, how Adjira loved her antigrav belt.

She'd let herself become overweight over the years—very much so—and she wasn't in denial about that. She'd been that way ever since her elevation to Kaana upon her father's death. The resultant stress and the demands of rulership required some kind of offset, some comfort. Food had provided her with that relief.

And why should I not have appetites? she thought airily as she herded the female trooper ahead of her along the dark corridor. *All rulers have appetites. What's the desire for power if not an appetite? And who can be Kaana or emperor without that desire for power?*

Using the psi-power gifted her by decades of genetic tinkering and mingling, she nudged the space-suited figure in front of her. The woman faltered and stumbled a moment, as if a sharp toe had poked her.

Adjira chuckled, then asked Janus, "How much farther?" Antigrav belt or not, this long return trip to her pod room was becoming taxing. "I'm sure this isn't the route those trolls took me along."

"I am taking your majesty along the easiest route with the fewest hazards and least obstacles."

"Oh. Very well. That's kind of you."

"Kindness was not a consideration. It is the most practicable."

Not all obstacles, she noted. With her feet dangling a meter from the floor, her head was at the perfect height to brush against a single corpse floating near the ceiling ahead. At the slow speed Adjira was moving, it was entirely possible the ugly thing would pass right through her shield, forcing her to... touch it.

Ugh.

Using Janus' facility for relaying her commands to the soldier's suit comms, she said, "Woman, move that thing out of my path."

The soldier didn't reply, but she shifted direction beneath the body, reached up to grab its belt, then bundled it through an adjacent doorway.

Adjira murmured her approval—then hissed in alarm as her shields nearly touched the soldier. The woman had stopped. *Why* had the woman stopped?

"Move along, traitor! You may no longer devote your mind to my cause, but your body must continue serving it."

The woman would provide a backup for the artificial

376

wombs at the Haven. If they no longer functioned, the woman could birth Adjira's Beloved one at a time, or two at a time. Of course, Adjira preferred to use the external wombs her researchers fitted to weak-willed males, but in this time and this place, she might have to revert to such an archaic method.

Besides, she'd need an extra pair of hands. A Kaana couldn't be expected to cook and clean for herself.

The soldier remained still, her only movement to point with a gloved hand. In the same moment, Adjira saw the suit lamps twenty meters away.

"Bloody hell," she whispered.

Right then, Janus must have noticed the newcomers and decided to reroute their comms to her.

"—*and hands!*" a deep male voice demanded.

There were three suits, Adjira saw now, different from those worn by the trolls she'd spoken with earlier. Three suits. Two working lamps. Two guns. One was aimed at her, and the other at the soldier. For a second, Adjira regretted disarming the woman, then a grin spread across her face.

I'm all the protection I need from trolls.

"I'm sick of asking already!" the male voice bellowed. "Get 'em up. Now!"

He was using some bastardized pidgin of Imperial True, close enough to the original that she could catch the gist without Janus' help, but it was impossible to tell which of the three upstarts was doing the talking.

Amused, Adjira said, "Janus, ask them what raising my hands would accomplish, and remind them it's patently obvious that neither I nor the soldier are armed, or even holding anything that might be a threat to them."

The reaction of the newcomers to Janus relaying that only increased Adjira's amusement; the suit lamps bobbed and flashed as the trio turned toward each other.

The same voice, mumbling, said, "That's not her voice."

"Someone else nearby," another agreed, looking around in agitated fashion.

A third said, "It's the soldier suit talking, idiots. Shoot it already and grab the floating fat lady."

Fat?! Adjira's blood boiled. There'd be no more toying with these creatures.

Allowing her outrage to fuel her, she tapped into the improved, modified region of her brain and spread her hands toward the three interlopers, channeling psi-power toward them like a broad-beam laser, careful to avoid the soldier below her. The three folded over awkwardly, boots still anchored to the floor, and gloves pressed to their helmets. Their guns swung free on their straps. Screams came softly to Adjira's radio wave receptors as Janus reduced the volume out of courtesy.

And when the trio stopped thrashing and squirming—still anchored to the deck by their boots—Adjira noticed the soldier had half turned toward her, awaiting orders. She took a deep breath to settle her heart rate before flicking her fingers imperiously.

"Move," she told the soldier. "We've wasted quite enough time here."

CHAPTER THIRTY-ONE

PASSIVE SENSORS INDICATED to Torg that while the bounty hunter cruiser had scanned the *Malleus* and other craft inside the hangar, *Malleus* would appear dormant to their sensors, like the other abandoned craft littering the area. Nevertheless, before moving on, a droid was launched out an airlock and floated gracefully into the hangar. Before it was out of sight from the front port, Torg recognized it as a Marok-Olaf reconnaissance bot; its sensors were heightened to the maximum, and it would no doubt be in constant contact with the cruiser.

Any sign of something untoward would alert them instantly.

He took several seconds to analyze his options. Not being a combat bot, he determined the best likelihood for avoiding detection would be to utilize any of the large spares strapped in the cargo bays, or even hiding in the various vents around the ship.

However, while his programming was sound, he hesitated. Unlike their predecessors, the current human crew was not overly violent——except for Sabrya—and he found working for them was less burdensome than most other crews.

As Torg turned away from the viewport, his eyes registered Sabrya's discarded aural buds on the console. Recalling the effect the ultra-death music had had on the crew the first time they'd encountered it—even his own receptors had had to be recalibrated due to the damage—a plan sparked within his CPU.

After a brief examination of the buds to determine the best method for utilization, he moved silently across the bridge to retrieve the necessary tools before proceeding to wire the buds to the bridge's internal sound system. This, too, needed recalibration to prevent distortion or damage to the speakers.

It was a race against time to rig the system before the droid ventured to the bridge—which in his estimation was an obvious priority.

Moments after the airlock cycled, he heard the footfalls as it ascended the stairs.

Deftly, he finished his work, collected the tools, then retreated behind the nav console and crouched. Fortunately, the bridge was one of the few areas he'd been fully and successfully integrated with as an ad hoc ship's droid.

He knew the interior layout completely and could calculate with pinpoint accuracy the optimum position for the recon droid's highly receptive sensors to be overloaded with even a microsecond of exposure. No doubt the cruiser would be alerted to something untoward occurring, but what that was would remain unknown to them. He'd have to determine another course of action to take should they decide to investigate.

By shutting down his own sensors except for optics a moment before activation, he'd take minimal damage and be in a far better position to deal with the incapacitated droid.

The tone and frequency of the footfalls indicated the droid

had reached the top of the stairs. A pause—possibly for a quick scan—then more steps.

Three, two, one.

The intensity of the emissions *boomed* within the small space, filling it with a hideously jarring cacophony. Even behind the console, Torg felt the reverberation through the decking. When he chanced a look around the side of the nav console, he saw the other droid twitching. With quick, calculated movements, he rose and hurled a prybar at the convulsing droid before it could achieve any possible reset. The end of the metal rod pierced the head, rocking it back. The neck sparked with the breaking of wire and circuitry; the droid froze. Now that it was completely inert, Torg approached it with the certainty that there was no immediate threat. Even so, he stepped behind it, opened the small compartment, and disengaged the powerpack.

There was a risk the lack of signal would cause suspicion on the cruiser, but Torg calculated a higher probability that there was simply too much hull between the ship and the droid for the cruiser to be tracking it.

Jabari and Scipio entered the ship's central maintenance tube to find it as dark as the data room and every area since had been. The recent jump had definitely killed power to all the ship's systems—including gravity. They took up positions on opposing sides of the tube and kicked off in the direction of the mess hall, grabbing at trunking and handrails for purchase, increasing or decreasing forward momentum as needed. By agreement, they used a different frequency from the one Adjira had been eavesdropping on via her AI assistant.

"We've overtaken them," Scipio said. "Adjira took the

roundabout route. I suppose a route like this would never occur to her."

"Or her AI," Jabari replied. "Shill will also move as slowly as possible to give herself more time to think."

Scipio gave a little chuckle. "No doubt the surprise I arranged for your Kaana also delayed her."

"What surprise?"

"I mentioned Bukshoga Qlan wandering around *Iconic*, remember?"

"I think you just called them scum." Jabari shook his head. "It's becoming a regular Summer Circus in here."

"Indeed."

"So... the surprise?"

Scipio barked a laugh. "I sent them a fake distress message, signaling coordinates that are on Adjira's route." He affected a weak voice to say, "'Oh, please, please help me. I'm trapped in an air pocket. I'll reward anyone who rescues me.'" He barked a laugh. "Pleiades registered an energy discharge a minute ago consistent with a brief firefight."

Jabari's jaw clenched. "And Shill?"

"Is perfectly fine, Jabari, perfectly fine."

"She'd better be."

"You worry too much."

Jabari didn't think he'd worried enough on this mission. "It's their ship you intend to steal?"

"The Bukshoga ship is tethered near a fissure in *Iconic*'s upper hull, relatively close to the location of the Kaana's stasis chamber. Once we secure Adjira, it's not that far to travel to commandeer the vessel."

Jabari could appreciate that kind of ruthlessness. If he'd been rescuing Adjira, he'd do exactly the same thing.

A yellow icon appeared on his HUD, inviting him to pair suit cameras with the optio. He flicked his gaze to the ACCEPT symbol in his HUD's lower left corner. The yellow icon vanished, and a small window opened in his visor's upper right curve. It would've depicted the scene ahead of Scipio, but for the moment, they traveled in pitch blackness, and the camera lacked ostendo or other enhancers. Apparently, Scipio wanted his eventual meeting with Adjira to be recorded in the visible spectrum.

"She's definitely headed for her stasis room?"

"I told you she is."

"Why there? Why not take a shuttle from a hangar?"

"For one thing, she's no pilot. For another, if you Proselyti were half the hackers you think you are, you'd have seen the same detail in the schematics that *Pleiades* did. There's a dedicated drop chute sitting below the stasis room leading all the way to the hull."

"It's a damned escape pod." It made sense for the Okalasi to have such contingencies all over a ship like this. "All right. If *Pleiades* is updating you, where's Adjira this very moment?"

"Fifty meters behind us, and forty to starboard. One deck down."

They were damn close. Jabari reconsidered the potential for attacking Scipio and doing this himself, but he had no idea if the psi-deflector actually worked at all. Perhaps Scipio had slipped him a dud. As much as he hated to admit it, taking down Adjira and setting Shill free might require two of them.

But after that...

The paired camera feed on Jabari's HUD suddenly came alive as Scipio triggered his suit lamp. "Through that one," he said, tagging an open hatchway in the floor with his suit's targeting laser. Jabari had already recognized the area around the hatch.

While the optio slowed his speed to adjust trajectory, Jabari maintained his, latching onto an equipment bracket at the last second to swing himself around and down. As Scipio barked a warning, he speared feetfirst through the hatch, through the edge of the gore-particle cloud in the mess hall, and landed against the deck with bent knees to absorb the impact. Steadied again, he took a few steps aside to put his right shoulder to the wall and scan the large room. For a moment, he was alone.

Scipio's entry was far less reckless, his head appearing first before he passed through the hatch carefully, one hand on the breacher at his back to prevent it from snagging. He then pushed down to the floor. On the optio's video feed, Jabari marked the passage of the lamp beam across the flotsam and jetsam floating within it, the sparkle of the light striking the frozen mincemeat, dead cyborgs, and slagged furniture. The chamber looked more like a slaughterhouse than a dining hall.

Erkan's remains mocked him, both sections of his friend's corpse free-floating to the right of the corridor entrance from Jabari's perspective, and a couple of meters from the floor, lifted there by some interaction of inertia and momentum during the jump.

Vengeance is coming, my friend, he told him silently.

The moment the optio had his bearings and balance, he pointed to the main door. "They're close now, Lieutenant. Stay where you are and leave the talking to me."

'Lieutenant?' Jabari scoffed sourly. *I thought you demoted me.*

With a hand shading his suit lamp for the moment, Scipio advanced until he stood directly between the rows of tables and the airlock to the Kaana's pod. In cocky fashion, the optio had holstered his handgun, Jabari observed. He ground his teeth at an opportunity he wasn't willing to take.

Scipio said, "Switch back to the frequency she expects Imperials to use."

Jabari adjusted his comms channel and heard the answering blip as it locked with Scipio's. He'd keep his ostendo on. In the dark mess hall, the glow of Adjira's shield and the shifting beam of the imperial space suit lamp would play havoc with his natural vision, whereas the HUD enhancement would balance everything out and keep it clear.

As Scipio slid the breacher off his back, Jabari warned, "Gun or no gun, if you harm one hair on Shill's head…"

Scipio didn't reply, perhaps unimpressed by the threat, or possibly distracted by nearing the end of his quest.

A combat suit appeared in the main doorway; on Scipio's cam-feed, it was backlit by the glow of Adjira's shields. Shill moved with both hands on her helmet, leaving Jabari to wonder at the nature of the Kaana's psionic hold on her. She took several steps inside, then froze upon seeing Scipio—and possibly Jabari behind him. Adjira wasn't as quick on the uptake. She swept in before quickly rising above Shill, perhaps seeking a path to her pod that was clearest of gore and detritus. The ceiling was high in the hall, and Adjira had risen four meters above the deck when Scipio spotlighted her with his lamp beam and began broadcasting in Imperial True so both Adjira and Jabari could understand him without translators.

"Usurper! I arrest you in the name of the emperor!"

Adjira kept her distance and stayed floating above the tables five meters in from the entrance. She lifted her chin, her snarl loud and clear through Jabari's speakers. "Yet *another* worm, and a real Martianist, this time."

Beneath her and to her side, Shill edged away and crouched to utilize what little cover the tables and chairs would provide from Scipio.

"Will you surrender?" the optio demanded.

"Janus!" Adjira turned her face to the ceiling, effectively dismissing Scipio as a threat. "Is it or is it not ready?" A pause while she presumably received a reply directly within her own brain. "Well, be faster about it, damn you!"

"I'll take that as a refusal," Scipio said and snapped off a short burst from the breacher.

He'd aimed it cleverly, avoiding the possibility of a shield breach, not wanting to suffocate or vaporize his target. The burst passed over the bubble and left an ugly gash in the ceiling panels, but it got her attention. Adjira roared in outrage, closing her fists and jutting out both arms. Jabari clenched up as his body remembered the pain inflicted on it a short while ago. When her bawling reached a crescendo, Adjira leveled her arms at Scipio.

Nothing appeared to happen to him. Certainly, nothing happened to Jabari.

But Adjira's caterwauling snuffed out sharply. She recoiled as if struck and curled into as much of a ball as her heavy torso and limbs allowed.

For a moment, there was silence in Jabari's suit speaker.

Then Adjira gave a small mewl of surprise.

And pain.

Her bubble still surrounded her, but she floated within it, with her hands over ears and her knees drawn as high as they would go.

Jabari could see a smear of blood beneath her nose. *Yeah, bleed, you slagger. I hope you're having a stroke.*

Shill crouch-walked, putting more space between her and Adjira, heading for one corner of the mess and away from Erkan's floating body parts. When she reached a position partially sheltered by an undamaged table, her helmet turned Jabari's way. He made a patting motion, urging her to stay down. Then he flicked the fingers of his left hand in a series of ancient battle signs that said, *I'll explain this later*, and hoped she'd registered it.

Sliding along the wall until he was at the pod airlock entrance, Jabari glanced through the damaged iris, hoping to see something beyond it that might work as a weapon. Nothing there—nothing that would bring harm to Scipio, anyway.

Damn.

Scipio, meanwhile, let the breacher dangle loose on its sling while he fumbled with something on the front of his suit, jabbering nonsense phrases made worse by his signal cutting in and out.

"Optio? What happened?"

"The b... stem... it... damn..." Scipio half turned his way. The way he slapped at his chest left Jabari to deduce that the interaction of psi-blast and reflector activation had created some kind of feedback. With the device connected to the optio's comms, that was the system that had taken the brunt of the damage.

Jabari's systems seemed fine, as evidenced by its clear reception of a sudden bout of giggling from Adjira.

"Seems neither of our tricks worked out well for us, Martianist worm," she said, her defiant tone undermined by a tremor in her voice. She drifted nearer, body no longer curled, arms at her side again.

Scipio faced her, his transmissions no less scrambled, but growing louder as he shouted in Imperial True, "... don't save you! I'll bur...cape pod...burn through that shield!"

The Kaana made a dismissive gesture. "Trollish gibberish. Get out of my way."

She drifted toward the space above him, but halted again when Scipio tilted the breacher's business end in her direction. The pair was separated by a mere ten meters, with nothing but a mist of fine gore crystals glittering in the empty space between them. He couldn't miss. Shill hunkered down, vanishing beneath the line of tables, as if they'd afford much protection from a weapon like that.

Jabari swore in a whisper. Conditions were changing again, escalating fast. Scipio and Adjira had achieved a standoff, one that wouldn't last long. Scipio would soon grow frustrated enough to burn through her shield and satisfy himself with her ruined corpse as his trophy. And once he'd slagged *her*, what need would he have for Jabari or Shill?

If Shill had been on his side of the room, he might drag her into the pod area and try activating it, but that wasn't an option.

Jabari was the last Proselyti officer. He'd lost all but one of the small team under his command—after losing dozens more over the decades.

I just want to get Shill off this ship and save at least one of my people.

And he could, he realized. Stupidly, Scipio had told him where there was a ship they could use. So Jabari attacked. Pushing his legs as hard as he could without losing boot contact with the deck, he charged forward. He slid a graphene-composite knife from a hidden sheath behind a thigh pouch.

In his mind's eye, Jabari clearly imagined what he wanted to achieve: he'd use the breacher's strap to fling Scipio into a nearby table, pinning him there while he slashed the strap and wrested the weapon free, then melted Scipio's head on its shoulders...

Only it didn't happen that way.

Adjira gave him away, her gaze flicking toward him as he surged forward. Scipio shifted position at the last microsecond and saw him coming, turning a shoulder toward his would-be tackler. As Jabari stabbed forward with the blade, aiming for the sling, Scipio batted it away and brought the breacher around, forcing Jabari to grab *that* with his free hand. Then Jabari was barreling into Scipio, the impact forceful enough to disconnect Scipio's boots from the deck as he'd hoped, but tangling the two men together.

Scipio rolled, dragging Jabari with him as they tumbled into the space between tables. The optio hit the deck on his side, with Jabari landing face first on top of him. In slow motion, they bounced gently back up into the gore drifting between Adjira and the deck. If the two men hadn't been in full combat suits, Jabari would've grappled for a chokehold, broken a bone, or slashed with the knife. Instead, he flicked his gaze at a short sequence of icons along the edge of his HUD.

The suit fired a hard one-second burst from his suit thrusters that flipped him right and slightly behind Scipio. With the optio unable to get his left arm around to block Jabari's knife a second time, Jabari arced the blade at the weapon strap, slicing through neatly. Simultaneously, he wrenched at the breacher with his other hand, pulling it across Scipio's thumb to break the man's grip. But as he tried to jerk the weapon around and against his own body, Scipio snatched at it, his fingers grazing it and flipping it away from them both. The sling strap flapped and snaked tantalizingly out of reach as the breacher glided away.

Scipio snarled through unreliable comms: "Sh... ...rd!"

Locked together and rotating, they grappled for a useful hold, Jabari intending to find a target area for his knife. Scipio got a boot under a chair and stabilized them, but they were stuck in stalemate, Scipio with one hand clamped on Jabari's knife hand, and Jabari with his free hand wrapped around Scipio's other wrist.

Adjira sailed into view, grinning down at the spectacle. She swiped at the blood trickling from one nostril, flicked it aside so it drifted away in tiny globules, then raised her arms toward them with murder in her eyes.

Jabari warned, "Don't try it, Kaana. He gave me the same device."

She balked, lowering her arms. "You're a traitor, Jabari, but you're also very strong, to have survived my first assault without the Martianist's tech. Humanity needs its strong men. Return your allegiance to me, and I'll help you overwhelm this worm."

"Yeah, like that's gonna happen," Jabari replied. He managed to arch his suit enough to get a boot to the deck, intending to lock it on and gain more leverage against Scipio. It made contact but skidded off a patch of iced-over gore, surprising him and jarring his grip on the optio. Scipio swept both arms around and up between Jabari's to knock his arms aside. Then he kicked off the table, kicked again off Jabari's suit, and sailed across the tables in pursuit of the breacher.

Flailing, turning his head to keep his enemy in view, Jabari fired a microburst of suit thrusters to get his feet under him again. By the time he'd anchored himself to the deck with knees bent, Scipio was halfway to the breacher on a stable intercept vector. Jabari wouldn't reach him, but there was something he could try...

A loose chunk of tabletop floated four meters above him, something he could fling. He'd used the tactic several missions back when facing a combat bot—he'd kicked a manhole cover at the thing just as it fired on him. The metal disc had been half melted by the time it impacted against the bot's firing arm, heat-gluing itself on and warping the gun in the process. Jabari was a microsecond from leaping when another suit arrowed over the tables and rammed into Scipio's left side, clinging on and diverting him away from the breacher toward the corner of the room right of the entry.

Shill!

Jabari adjusted his footing, grabbed a table with his left hand, and launched himself on an intercept trajectory with the breacher, burst-firing his thrusters, moving with greater velocity than Scipio had achieved. The weapon had impacted the wall near the entry and was rebounding on a slow vector toward the middle of the ceiling, twirling madly with its strap winding around it like bindings. If Shill could just hold on to Scipio—

Scipio burst-fired his own thrusters, achieving a kind of somersault that dislodged Shill. As he headed for the wall, he kicked her free and sent her spinning into the bottom half of Erkan's corpse. Perhaps instinctively seeking a handhold, she wrapped her arms around it. She hadn't spoken since she'd entered the mess, Jabari realized absently. She did now. Before he could yell at her to find Erkan's hidden knife, Shill screamed, trying to toss the horror of what remained of her friend away from herself. She succeeded in sending Erkan back toward Scipio, and the physics of zero-G activity hastened her in the opposite direction, sending her tumbling across the room. Jabari had time to wonder why she hadn't used her thrusters before he had to focus on his goal.

The breacher.

Scipio had kicked off toward it, too, firing *his* thrusters. Jabari had only a little fuel left, but he had to tap into it. He fired, too, but Scipio got there a half meter ahead of him, snagging one end of the strap and hauling on it. Jabari hit him in the legs, then punched upward. One-handed, Scipio managed a short burst with the breacher before Jabari's fist knocked it loose and over the optio's head.

Scipio slammed an elbow into Jabari's helmet—achieving nothing—then squirmed his legs so Jabari slipped lower along them. He wasn't free, but it was enough for him to angle the blunt weapon's muzzle down and against the spot he'd just elbowed. Jabari froze. He could react, he knew, but it would achieve nothing. Scipio had bested him. The bastard had won, and perhaps that was good. Evil always triumphed, after all, and Jabari was done fighting it.

Silently, he accepted his fate, hoping the ancestors were right after all, that peace awaited him in the afterlife...

Seconds had passed, Jabari realized. For some reason, Scipio hadn't fired. And in a moment of clear transmission from his damaged comms, the optio gasped.

"No!"

It was hard to be certain, with their visors mirrored, but it seemed that Scipio was staring past Jabari.

Jabari turned to find Adjira had vanished. Her airlock iris had partly closed again. A tiny red light flashed on/off above it.

With Jabari momentarily distracted, Scipio wriggled his legs and burst-fired his thrusters again, kicking free and rising higher. He sent a breacher beam searing into the airlock hatch, then desisted a couple seconds after he'd started. The molten door sagged open, but the flashing light announced that Adjira's pod was already away.

A new voice stirred in Jabari's suit speaker, an automated voice his HUD told him was transmitting on multiple frequencies, a voice devoid of emotion.

"Self-destruct sequence initiated. Countdown commencing. Self-destruct sequence initiated. Countdown commencing..."

Jabari and Scipio's visors turned toward each other.

Clear as a struck bell, Scipio said, "Well, shit."

CHAPTER THIRTY-TWO

PHILLIX DWELLED on the ramifications of this stunning information: "...the mind will continue without the body as long as there's energy to sustain it." Did he truly believe it? Enough to trust an AI with his life?

A section of the matrix suddenly changed, distracting him. Gone now was the subtle undulation; lines of code were now locked in a rigid grid. The code flip-flopped precisely, methodically, rhythmically.

0... 1... 0... 1... 0... 1...

"Wha... is that a countdown?" He delved closer.

Correct.

To what?

Adjira has left the ship. Automatic self-destruct sequence initiated.

"What? No!"

It is programmed and cannot be overwritten.

"Everything can be overwritten!" Phillix sent his mind as far and wide as he could along the rigid lines. The binary code flip-flopped meticulously and persistently.

"What about a reboot?"

Only a hard-set reboot would be sufficient.

"Exactly."

I am unable to self-initiate a hard-set reboot.

Phillix thought desperately. The answer must be here. He must know it. "Think, dammit!"

Thinking is biological; I process data.

"No. Not you..." What was all his training for, all his gained experience and knowledge, if not for *this*? In desperation and confusion, he jacked out of the AI. It took him a few seconds to get his thoughts and body to work in concert. The room was dark, as he'd expected.

There were others on the *Iconic*—no idea who they were—but they'd all die, too. The last time the sensors had detected Sabrya or Bradyn, they were heading to the hull...

"Phillix?" Alexis floated over to him. "What's happening?" She arrested her movement by grabbing the headrest and swinging around to face him, their helmets almost touching.

"Alexis. We jumped to the Vladmarin system. Adjira's ejected in a life pod. The ship is about to self-destruct. You need to get out of here!"

"Right. I'll pull this cord and get you off—" She reached toward his gizmo.

"No! There's no time. The feedback will shock my psyche and probably give me an aneurysm—and... You need to go! You may've already run out of time."

"I'm not leaving you behind!" she said earnestly, almost desperately.

That decided it for him. Even facing imminent death, she was going to stay; not even a vain attempt to escape. He pointed toward the rear. "There's an emergency airlock down there. I'm going to try to stop the self-destruct. Thanks for looking after me... It's my turn now." Ignoring her pleas, he blocked everything and turned his mind inward.

Even in the brief moment he had left, the matrix was flashing rapidly.

This is farewell. Your presence has been stimulating, Technician Phillix Lo.

"As yours has been, but—" *Technician... I'm a technician!* "You might not be able to initiate a hard reboot, but a technician can."

You are not an authorized technician. Even under these circumstances, only a major integration can initiate a reboot.

"Major integration? Like... additional hardware? Software?"

If it is of significant size and complexity.

"What about me? A human mind? My consciousness?"

...That is a possibility. You are the most complex software I have encountered since my arrival. But as discussed, I can only integrate software. To do this, you must leave your shell.

"But will it work?" He was aware that the frequency of the code flip-flop had increased.

It is a possibility, perhaps a moderate probability. I lack the ability to run such a subprogram to calculate at this juncture.

Phillix desperately considered any alternative other than fully merging with the most intricate and fastest AI he'd ever encountered, or ever would encounter. It struck him as ironic that to stop the AI from self-destructing, he'd need to become one himself.

"How long have I got? How long have my friends got?"

Optimal time for her majesty to reach a safe distance.

"Frag me. That doesn't sound like much."

It will be sufficient.

———

"Phillix." Alexis shook the tech, then checked his vitals, worried at his sudden silence. Everything was in the green.

Phillix's eyes started flickering again, and she sighed with relief.

"Don't go doing something stupid." Absently, she checked his straps and suit integrity. Her gaze briefly swept to the rear of the compartment, where she saw the barest outline of a hatch. *What did he mean, 'It's my turn now?'*

"Torg?" Alexis called. "Sabrya? Bradyn?" She checked her comms; everything was in working order. She was about to call again when she felt the tech's body go limp.

His vitals, in the green moments before, were now all red.

"Phill!" She shook him. Concentrating on first aid training two decades old, she started chest compressions. "Damn awkward in a suit on a chair in zero-G." After several sets, she adjusted his air to increase the oxygen, then resumed compressions.

Moving away from his brief examination of the recon droid, Torg strode over to the command workstation and flicked the comms to RECEIVE ONLY, listening to see what was happening before transmitting and perhaps notifying others of their presence. With the bounty hunter vessel close by, he didn't want to cause more problems with the crew members outside.

"... highly qualified carcass if you don't get your fraggin' ass up here."

He recognized Sabrya's voice immediately, and its intensity was highly out of character. After taking a microsecond to consider the probable outcomes of various possible scenarios, he activated the nav and drive systems, and engaged the forward thrusters.

"I am here," he replied.

A screen showed the life signs from their suits: Sabrya was all green, though her oxygen was low, whereas Bradyn showed very weak signs, and his oxygen levels were even lower.

At a moderate speed of five meters a second, he backed the *Malleus* out of the hangar. Proximity alarms blared, as another craft had drifted nearer. There was the slightest vibration, indicating a minor collision, but no other alarms sounded. Once clear of the hangar, he maneuvered the ship up toward the last known location of the fighter and the engineer. Almost immediately, the sensors picked up the bounty hunter vessel, then the two floating spacesuits drifting close to the edge of the *Iconic's* hull.

With the speed and accuracy of a ship's droid, he turned the craft and, with a judicial use of its thrusters, moved it in line with the vector of the two figures.

Alarms and distant, rapid thumping impinged on his senses. The bounty hunter ship was firing kinetic slugs at them as the *Malleus* rose above the side of the *Iconic*.

From the viewport, he noted the cruiser was tethered to the hull by a docking tube; any abrupt movement would shear it, exposing it to the void. It also hampered them from getting a clear shot, and he considered briefly why the lower gun turret wasn't firing.

The droid maneuvered the *Malleus* so the least vulnerable area was exposed to the barrage. Once decompression was complete, he opened the cargo bay doors remotely. Matching speed with the two drifting crew members, the adroit use of the thrusters turned the ship at the last minute to capture them.

As they approached, Sabrya used Bradyn's mass to pull herself around.

The instant they were within the confines of the loading dock, the doors began to close. Sabrya hit the far bulkhead feet first, embracing the engineer to cushion the impact.

Torg moved the *Malleus* below the *Iconic* and out of range of the bounty hunter vessel's turret, though it would do little if they decided to engage missiles. Once the vessel was safely out of danger, he halted its progress with the intention of attending to Sabrya and Bradyn. He moved out of his chair and summoned the lift.

"Torg?" Alexis called over the comms. "Sabrya? Bradyn?"

Quickly retracing his steps, Torg activated the radio. "Captain. Bradyn and Sabrya are now on board. Bradyn is severely injured," Torg responded. "We will come to—"

"You need to get the ship as far away as possible. The *Iconic* is set to self-destruct."

He noted her breathing was heavy and irregular. "Are you all right? I will come—"

"Negative. Phillix is de—... gone. Get out of here and save the other two. That's an order!"

"Aye, Captain." In moments, the droid had plotted a safe course away from the *Iconic* that wouldn't put them under direct fire of the bounty hunter vessel.

"Frag that. We're not leavin' you behind!" Sabrya shouted as she bounded up the stairs. "Metalman, get down there and help Bradyn."

"My orders are to leave with haste. I am doing so now." He stood when the thrusters automatically engaged.

"We're not leavin' Alexis behind!" Sabrya dragged him away from the controls. "Dammit, it's locked."

"I assumed you would counterma—"

She spun around and punched him in the side of the head. "Fraggin' turn us around, or I'll rip your head off!"

"I will follow my captain's orders. Without my head, I will be unable to attend to Bradyn's injury properly." The droid made its way down the stairs, heading to the loading dock.

After a second vain attempt to override the ship program, the fighter had an idea. She raced down the stairs at a phenomenal speed. Kicking Alexis' cabin door open, Sabrya searched her cabin. "This is too damn neat," she muttered. Checking the desk drawer first, she dumped the contents unceremoniously onto the desktop and spread it out. "Bazinga!" She sighted the bio-chip. Using a blade to cut her hand, she let a few drops fall onto the chip before the nanites could repair the injury.

"Let's hear you countermand me now, Metalman."

She raced to the loading dock.

"Alexis?" Sabrya called "There should be an emergency escape hatch at the back. It's standard—"

"What the frag are you doing?" Alexis vented when she heard they were moving toward the rear of the *Iconic*. "I ordered you to get the hell out of here! Torg?"

"I countermanded that," Sabrya replied before the droid could respond, "so quit your bitchin' and get your fraggin' ass outta there, pronto."

Minutes later, muttering curses under her breath, Alexis cycled through the rear emergency hatch and pushed Phillix's body through the emergency exit. Despite the urgency, she paused in surprise at seeing the bright nebula filling the sky—a vastly different view from the empty void she'd seen previously. "Where the hell are we?"

"We'll be everywhere if you don't move your ass."

With no time to attach a docking tube, Alexis recognized Sabrya's silhouette standing at the open loading dock, motioning for her.

"There better be a damn good explanation for why my orders were ignored," she vented at the droid. "You've put the ship and the whole crew at risk."

"I obeyed the orders of Captain Smith," Torg responded.

"Captain... *Smith?* That didn't take long."

"Chillax, girl. It's temporary, I can assure you. As soon as you're on, we're movin'." Sabrya helped secure the tech's body as Alexis clamped her boots to the deck.

"You found the bio-chip," Alexis realized as she removed her suit. She took a moment to breathe in the cooler air.

"Yep. That moronic bucket of bolts was goin' to fraggin' leave you both!"

"Because I ord—"

"Yeah, yeah. You said. You should secure your bio-chip better. Torg, we're in. Get us the frag outa here!"

"Aye, Captain," the ship's droid responded to the new orders.

"It's not like I was *expecting* a mutiny," Alexis grumbled.

"Pfft." Sabrya looked at the hacker's inert suit for a moment. "What happened to Gadg—" His face looked so calm, unlike the faces of all the dead she'd seen in her time. "What happened to Phillix?"

"I don't know. He was talking to me, then went silent. A few moments later he flatlined. Nothing I tried worked."

"Just like that? Nothin' wrong with his suit? What about his air?"

Alexis stowed the suit roughly in the locker and made her way upstairs. "I think he did something with the AI he was hooked up with."

"If it wasn't such a sad situation, I'm sure there's a joke there."

"I think the term is wet-wired. He was literal—"

"I *do* know how it works."

"Hmm." Reaching the bridge, Alexis was surprised to see the inert recon droid in the middle of the floor. "Starting your own spare parts collection like your predecessors?" she asked the droid.

"Metalman said he killed it with music," Sabrya informed her, a pace behind.

"Music did this?"

"*My* music."

"Ah. Yes. I understand completely now." Alexis rolled her eyes. "Torg, report, or do you need Captain Smith to ask?"

"We are in the Vladmarin-Xiar system and accelerating at maximum speed away from the *Iconic*. There is no way of knowing how far a 'safe distance' is.

"Phillix told me Adjira ejected. How far could she have gone? I assume she was in a pod?"

"They can be quite fast, but with limited maneuverability."

"Well, where the frag did she go?" Sabrya interjected.

"Her pod is not showing on our sensors. From the angle of trajectory, her only possible destination is within that dust cloud, which is obscuring any form of output."

"What's in there?"

"I have no data on that."

Alexis looked around the bridge. "Where's Bradyn?"

"Med-bay. He has a grievous wound to his left calf," Torg said.

Sabrya filled her in on their recent activities on the hull with the bounty hunter vessel. "The fraggin' assholes almost took his foot off."

"What are they doing now?"

"Not sure how many went in or came out, but the Qlan cruiser made a rapid departure several minutes ago, which still leaves one Qlan ship tethered on the port hull. Their engines are idling, but they haven't left yet."

"Must have people on *Iconic*. And the imperial scout?"

"Sensors indicate it is stationed two hundred and four kilometers away, but on the other side of the *Iconic*," Torg advised.

"No word on Jabari? Haven't heard from him since the tussle with that killer bot."

Sabrya scoffed. "It's not like the asshole's goin' to give us ten-minute updates."

"I could scan for—" Torg started to say.

Sabrya interrupted him firmly. "Forget him, Metalman. He wasn't our friend."

"He did several things to protect us," Alexis said.

"Whatever. We've got better fraggin' things to do."

Alexis sighed in acceptance.

From her pocket, the fighter retrieved the bio-chip. She grabbed Alexis' hand, quickly pricked her palm, then placed the chip in the bead of blood. "I'm now relieved of captainin' duties. The ship's all yours now, *Captain*."

It occurred to her that the sudden change in circumstances —from unknowingly inheriting command of a vessel, to then losing it—would have made her laugh, but she had other thoughts on her mind.

"Are we really in the Vladmarin system?" She turned her attention back to the screen.

"Correct. In close proximity to the Shadow Nebula. That is Vladmarin-Xiar33 directly ahead."

As the droid spoke, she stared out the viewport. The star, the sun warming her new world, was there, finally visible. "And Niviaris?"

"Sensors indicate there are several exoplanets in the system. None are recorded as habitable."

"No mention of Sylvanus Colony?"

"Nothing."

"That's crazy. Must be an error. Sylvanus Colony *must* be there somewhere. Do whatever surveillance you can."

"Aye, Captain, however, a couple of the planets—Niviaris being one of them—are on the other side of that brown dwarf, outside our sensor range."

Alexis sighed. "Right. I'm going to check on Bradyn. Torg, let me know the moment you find something."

"Aye."

"What about me?" Sabrya asked.

"You can stow this droid and update the spare parts inventory."

Using his suit thrusters, Optio Scipio jetted down to the mess hall entrance. He took one hand from the breacher to redirect his vector into the corridor, and then he was gone.

A moment later, a speech-to-text message appeared on Jabari's HUD.

That lingering Qlan ship I mentioned is close by? So sorry you won't get to use it yourself, as promised, but it does seem fitting that you die with Iconic, Jabari. I only hope in your final moments, you think of nothing else but the miserable failure and waste both your lives have been. Pro Imperatore! For the emperor!

Ruefully, Jabari shook his head. "I really wanted to kill that guy." Getting his bearings, he kicked off toward Shill, who'd stabilized herself against a table mid-room. "No idea how long we've got..." he started, then noticed the glove she'd clamped over the side of her suit, and the mist trickling out from under it.

"Breacher grazed me when he got that shot off."

"It hit you?" Arriving in front of her, he grabbed her shoulder for stability.

"Just the suit."

"Well, patch it." He started to open the appropriate pouch at her waist, but she put her free hand on his.

They drifted free of the table as she told him, "My patches repaired the damage in the data room."

"All of them?"

"Yep. Also, I used all my thruster fuel getting to the data room."

"You..."

"I know, I know. Procedures. Contingencies. But we were in a rush back then, and I didn't expect... this."

"Which is why we think of *contingencies*." Jabari went to pull his own patch kit, but only found the ruined material left where Otho had shot him. "Well, shit."

"You have to catch him," she said, "and get control of Pleiades."

"He has too much of a head start," he replied, "and a breacher. We might make it to that other group's ship, Alexis', if we can find it."

"Not we," she replied. "You."

"Like my thrusters can't carry you, too. Come on..."

She resisted his attempt to turn her toward the entry. "Jabari, I have about two minutes." The hand covering the gash on her suit shifted, stanching more of the flow of atmo from it, but not stemming it completely.

"That's two minutes to find a solution."

"No. You need to go."

"Belay that, Private!" he snapped. He had one friend left, one person remaining under his leadership. He wasn't going anywhere without her. Perhaps, he thought, they could fill the gash with gore particles, packing them in there. Then he remembered Bradyn's solution to destroying Rec-7. Holding fast to Shill's shoulder, he jetted up to the maintenance hatch.

"What...?" she gasped.

He placed her free hand against the frame of the hatch until she clamped it there. "I'll be a second."

Inside the maintenance shaft, he scanned the walls. It took a half-minute longer than he wanted before he saw what he needed, tucked into an alcove a dozen meters away. He plucked the sixty-centimeter-long cylinder from its mooring and considered the squirt nozzle at one end. The image of Rec-7 vanishing into a morass of this stuff were fresh in his mind—as was his memory of Bradyn saying, *I saw a guy get it wrong once... solid in seconds.*

"Like I have a choice."

Pointing it away from himself and toward a wall, he adjusted the pressure setting on the nozzle and gave the trigger the lightest, briefest tweak he could. A quicksilver spurt hardened immediately into a thin sheet that pressed and stuck to the bulkhead. It was as wide as his faceplate, more than Shill needed, but no doubt the smallest amount he could hope to fire off. *Better than nothing*, he thought and returned to the mess hall.

"Gallioid," he told her, settling in beside her and ensuring he was stable before letting go of the hatch frame.

"What the hype is gallioid?" she asked. There was a quaver in her voice, indicating that the hole in her suit wasn't just expelling air, it was letting in the cold.

"Something I hope I use correctly," he replied. "Get ready to take your hand away and lift your arm high. Then stay very still." He positioned the cylinder with the spray nozzle toward the suit-breach, got his trigger finger back in position, then said, "Now."

Holding his breath, he flicked the activator on/off. This time, the squirt was smaller than the test amount had been. Quickly fanning out into something like a sheet of foil wrap, it adhered to Shill's suit while a tail of gallioid folded over the rest to form a forward-pointing bump.

"Good?" he asked.

Shill paused, and he could hear her drawing in air. "Good enough." She released her grip on the hatch frame and gestured toward the mess entrance. "Shall we?"

"Absolutely." Jabari tossed the cylinder, took hold of her suit, and jetted them both to the door, giving Erkan's upper body a sorrowful look as they passed. Out in the corridor, he reoriented them in the direction Scipio had taken and fired another burst. The fuel icon for his thrusters indicated there was 6.3 percent remaining.

As they traversed the corridor, he wondered aloud where they should head.

"Escape pod cluster station," Shill suggested. "There'll be one on this level, a hundred meters aft and the same to port. But," she added, "we'll have to fire it into interplanetary space and hope for some charitable scavenger to pick us up."

"Or Alexis."

At least it'll have oxygen, he thought. *Food. Water.*

"Pod station," he acknowledged. He'd thought momentarily of simply chasing Adjira's pod down its chute—that was arguably the most direct route off the ship—but even if they could get enough distance from *Iconic* out in the void using mere suit thrusters with almost no fuel in them, they'd be tiny specks of matter drifting in the vast nothingness of space and slowly asphyxiating. An escape pod would at least have those supplies, and a "please-help-us" beacon.

Dragging Shill out into the passage and getting them moving, he verbalized none of this. As they made their way through the maze, the minutes counted out. There'd been no further alerts on any frequencies since the initial destruct announcement.

How much time do we actually have?

After a frantic flight through *Iconic's* upper decks, Scipio's schematic told him he was about to reach his destination. And not a moment too soon—his suit-thruster fuel reserves were sputtering. Around the next corridor, he'd finally reach the blast door that would bring him out below the Bukshoga ship.

What his schematics *didn't* warn him about was the two Qlan members already standing at the door, preparing to enter, when he came around the corner.

Both had their backs to him. One was using a portable cutting torch to try to get through the blast door, the flare from the torch casting stark shadows across the floor and bulkheads.

"Amateurs," he muttered. As Scipio raised his far more powerful breacher, he wondered if these two had entered *Iconic* via a different route, or whether they'd stupidly sealed this blast door behind them and somehow locked it off. *Either way,* he thought as he lined up on both of them with the breacher, *end of the journey for you.*

He fired. The pair came apart in a morass of flesh, plastic, snap-frozen gases, and gooey alloys. Because of the angle and force of the blast, some of their remains smeared and melded with the bulkhead, while other body parts drifted back his way.

"So close," he told them, wading through the gore. "So sad."

His first blast had scored a ragged slash across the door, one that was useless for his purposes. Picking up the work where the Qlan members had left off, he completed cutting a wide oval through the blast door, and kicked it out, following it through into the damaged area below the cruiser. Some earlier impact had gouged out a chunk of *Iconic* three meters wide, and two decks deep, like someone had taken a core sample. The ragged section of door he'd cut out sailed across the gap and through an open hole in the bulkhead opposite, before slowly ricocheting within whatever compartment lay over there.

Scipio flicked off his ostendo. Reverting to his helmet lamp, he looked up into the open end of an umbilical docking tube that had sealed around the top of the hole he stood in. The mouth lay six or seven meters above him. It was like facing into the maw of a giant sand worm like those on Androz 7. The concertina tube was lit from within by a series of flickering safety lights, but the tubing had twisted for some reason, as if the cruiser had changed direction. He watched as a ripple ran up the tube's length, wondering whether it had been caused by vibrations from the cruiser's idling thrusters, or some shift in contact between the two ships—and hoped it would stay stable enough for him to pass through.

Scipio sprang off the deck, then burst-fired his thrusters, using the remnants of his fuel to sail up and into the umbilical. He adjusted his speed and trajectory to navigate the tube twist midway, then saw the warm lighting of an open airlock at the far end. Nearing that, he pivoted, ensuring he glided inside, already in the correct orientation for the ship's artificial grav to pull him to the floor. A hard slap on the trigger by the hatch closed it.

Repressurization buffeted him as air filled the small compartment, scouring some of the gore from his suit. Scipio discarded the breacher, with its ruined sling, drawing his sidearm as he took a position to the left of the inner hatch. The handgun was better suited to close quarters work than the heavier weapon, which might blast through a bulkhead and ruin a drive component. The hatch cycled open. No one came to check, so he had time to pop his visor and sniff at the air. It was tinged with the competing smells of garlic and poorly aired laundry. He stepped out and faced forward toward the cockpit. The sheen of icy human remains still clung to his suit, and he was glad its stink was frozen with it.

A man dressed in loose-fitting clothing appeared in the short corridor from a side cabin. "You two cut it fine... What?"

Scipio shot him through the head and was past him while the body was still settling on the floor. Another head poked out of the cockpit, checking on the noise.

"Boo!" Scipio said and put a round between the woman's wide eyes.

Her slumped body partially blocked the doorway, so he had to step over her before he could bundle her out into the corridor and seal the cockpit. There was no time to complete a full sweep for other hostiles. Getting the hells away from here was the priority, so he'd have to rely on the cockpit entrance lock to protect his back.

When his combat suit didn't fit either of the pilot chairs, he took a knee between them and punched commands into the helm, silently thanking the dead woman for completing the pre-flight warm-ups already. After he'd severed the umbilical for time's sake, the cruiser detached from the hull and pulled away smoothly, accelerating with gratifying power. Scipio placed it on a straight vector that put maximum distance between him and *Iconic* in the shortest amount of time. After less than a minute, a subtle alarm brought his attention to the navigation console. The cruiser was off course by several degrees. After correcting that, he watched impatiently as the ship gradually veered off course again. A problem with the rear thruster alignment, he realized, was something he'd have to continue accounting for as he moved.

Now there was time for internal camera and sensor checks, confirming he was alone on board. *Well,* he thought, *alone except for two bodies.*

There'd be no need to deal with them. He'd keep this thing on its broad arc around *Iconic*, then catch up with *Pleiades* and transfer across to a real ship, one that didn't stink inside.

"Your suit's functional?" Jabari asked as they pushed through a section clogged with floating bodies. The question was more to take his mind off the ticking clock than for any other reason.

Shill replied, "Gallioid's holding, if that's what you're asking."

Now that they'd paired aspects of their suit data, he could check her atmo reserve on his HUD; she had very little left. Her recycler had taken some damage; soon, he'd have to share his own recycler with her if she was to survive.

That was the end of their conversation for the next three minutes, apart from minor navigational corrections from her, and Jabari's suit's complaints about his thrusters' waning fuel reserves. The pod cluster station was a semicircular area close to the hull. Six closed hatches faced them from around the outer curve, all sealed.

"We're good?" he asked.

"If there's battery charge," she replied, disengaging to sail across to an interface panel. She tapped at it, then swore colorfully. "No battery charge."

"Hells!"

"Wait."

She unspooled a kick wire from her suit and plugged it into the interface, sharing power from her suit battery. Jabari's ostendo registered a flicker of life in the panel as it gobbled everything Shill gifted it. Moments later, it was dead again.

Her suit turned his way. "That's that, then."

He moved to one of the hatches. "We'll drag this open." But he couldn't insert even the tips of his gloves into the seams. He'd left his blade in the mess hall, dumped when he'd been going for the gallioid cylinder. Shill had taken Erkan's, though. "Knife! Quick!"

Shill didn't move, floating free beside the interface panel. "It won't work, Jabari. This section's been without power for a thousand years. The residuals are completely drained, and the hatches are airtight."

"I'll kickstart it from my suit. Throw me your kick-wire."

"Jabari..."

"You're not dying here!"

"I am, Jabari. You are."

"We'll find a hangar. There must be ships we can use to get off."

"Whose batteries'll also be long dead. Boss, the destruct's gonna go any second now. Any second."

"Flux it!"

"It's all right. You did what you could for me. For us."

He ground his teeth, trying to find a reply, and failing. When he struck the hatch with his fist, it sent him on a lateral drift out into the middle of the compartment. Shill kicked off and met him, latching on at an angle that aimed the gallioid bump on her suit to the side. She leaned her visor against his.

"I screwed it up, Shill," he told her. "I should've kept you safe. Tee, Erkan, Morten—"

"All died here, sure," she said, "so we stay with them. Take the final journey with them." One of her gloves patted his helmet. "As crazy as she was, the Kaana's ship is at least familiar territory. Our territory. Isn't it?"

"Damn," he cursed quietly, accepting it. "We were so close. We could've been free, all five of us."

Another pat from her glove. "But we were. You were. You stuck it to the empire, and you stuck it to the Kaana, too. You got to make your own decisions."

"For a couple of hours."

"And whatever seconds we have left."

He frowned. "Speaking of that, how long's a self-destruct usually set for?"

"Not something I've ever researched." Her helmet scraped against his as she looked toward the exit. "Maybe that was dumb, what I just said. All that 'staring-death-in-the-eye' is fine in a story, but we could try your new friends. I mean, most crap on this ship doesn't work, so what if the destruct doesn't, either?"

He parted from her so he could access his comms panel and ran a channel search for chatter from Alexis' group. The scan locked onto one channel immediately, and a new voice spoke.

"Ah, would you be Jabari?"

The voice reminded him of Janus but mingled male and female registers. The pitch rose and fell so it was difficult to get a sense of personality. Also, its tone sounded hollow, flat, disembodied.

"Er, it is."

"The first thing you should know, Jabari, is I've aborted the self-destruct."

"*You* have?" he said and sent notification of the comms channel across to Shill so she could hook in. "Is this Janus?"

"I'm Phillix, previously of the *Malleus*."

"Previously? Isn't that's Alexis' ship?"

"It's all our ship, technically. Even though we're outside the empire, some law is still accepted out here. Part of the New Imperium Reclamation Policy, Clause 38-6b, states that legal salvage is deemed equal share among all stakeholders."

"All right, Phillix, thank you. Because you're so helpful, tell me how we get off *Iconic*."

"Don't you want more data on the aborted self-destruct?"

"No, not really."

Shill hand-signed that she did, but Jabari waved her curiosity away.

Phillix replied, "Then I'll send you coordinates to rendezvous with my crewmates at *Malleus*. It'll take me a moment to report this. I should confirm first, are you armed?"

Jabari chewed his lip, hesitating between a lie and the truth. In the end, he figured trust was a two-way street. "My comrade has her knife; that's all. And she has a compromised suit."

"Then you should lose the knife and proceed at top speed to the new coordinates I'm sending. There are parked vessels you can loot air from." The coordinates appeared as a squiggle of text on Jabari's HUD, and he fed them into his suit's *Iconic* schematic files as Phillix added, "Just to be safe, you should scan for my friends' comms frequency and use that to contact—"

Jabari replied, "I look forward to meeting you, Phillix."

"Hm. About that..."

But Jabari changed channels before he could go on.

"I wanted to talk to him," Shill said. "He might've been the one trying to reach us with that code-crap in the data room."

"How about we solve all our mysteries once we're off this bloody ship?"

Jabari reached across, grabbed her suit, and sent her flying toward the exit, burst-firing his thrusters to launch himself after her.

CHAPTER THIRTY-THREE

"HEY, *Malleus*, it's Phillix. I've aborted the self-destruct. You need to return ASAP."

Phillix's message came directly into Torg's internal receptors, not once, but over and over, as if on a loop. Using the ship's comms, the droid said, "Captain, Phillix is transmitting..."

"What the hell? I'm coming up." Moments later, Alexis bounded up the stairs and into view. "Is it a recording?"

"In all probability, it is, but I have cross-checked his voice pattern with the message. It is identical." He replayed the message for her.

"Patch me in," she continued at Torg's nod. "This is the *Malleus*... Phillix? How is this possible?"

"It's difficult to explain." That was definitely Phillix's voice.

"Try," Alexis continued. "You'll need to convince me before I get anywhere near the *Iconic*."

"With your body lyin' in cargo, fraggin' oath it is!" Sabrya joined them on the bridge, sweating slightly from the exertion of removing the recon bot. "At least when I kill someone, they stay fraggin' dead," she muttered at Alexis' admonishing look.

"I have Jabari and one of his colleagues in desperate need of assistance. I've sent their coordinates."

Torg looked up from the console. "Coordinates received."

"Fine, but I'm not risking anyone or this ship until you've explained."

Phillix's words came over the comm in a rush. "My consciousness was uploaded into the AI—"

"That's one fraggin' serious downgrade in my books."

"It worked—you're welcome—and it was the only way to abort the self-destruct, given the time. The last thing I said to you in engineering, Captain, was 'It's my turn now,' to look after you."

"That's true." Alexis nodded.

"It has been theorized that a consciousness could be uploaded into an AI," the droid informed them. "That is the basis of subliminal training and the first level of the now-defunct Imperial Gemini cloning project. His story has some plausibility."

"You need to return now," Phillix insisted. "They only have a few minutes of air remaining."

"Looks like we're convinced," Alexis replied after quickly assessing the information. "Head to those coordinates," she directed Torg to return to the *Iconic*.

"I've informed Jabari to hang tight," the tech said.

"I'm glad to hear you're not completely dead." Alexis sat in her seat.

"What's it fraggin' like, bein' a ghost in a machine?" Sabrya asked him.

"Scary and fascinating."

"And the drocking AI? How's it handling you hacking into it?" Bradyn asked over comms from the med-bay.

"She's having difficulties coming to terms with it. I think she's attained some form of sentience in seventeen hundred years of isolation."

"We should be there in eight minutes," Torg informed them.

"What's the threat level from whoever's chasing Jabari?"

"And that fraggin' imperial scout?"

"I have no data on the scout," Phillix answered. "Regarding the presence of other imperial soldiers, the last data I had on that before the reboot was of a firefight along the outside of the hull near where the Qlan vessel was attached."

"Did they escape?"

"I can't say. The *Iconic* is completely drained of power; Janus is basically deaf and blind. However, before the jump, Janus picked up transmissions on several frequencies between two unknown sources—one from the *Iconic*, and one from hyperspace. These were relayed via the imperial vessel—"

"Fraggin' spy ship," Sabrya interjected. "We should've taken that fragger out when we had the chance."

Phillix continued, saying, "In a matter of days, this sector will be visited by Imperial Special Forces, and—"

"And if they get hold of the *Iconic*, they'll have a trophy, access to stealth tech, and anything else they can lay their hands on. It'd be bad enough if the Qlan syndicate got hold of it," the engineer spat as he listened in on the internal comms, still hooked up to the auto-doc. "Much worse if those drocking Imps get it."

"They'll fraggin' stamp out any resistance with their big black boots."

"You can see the problem," Phillix replied.

"Okay, bad guys getting it is bad, but *Iconic's* a massive, dead hulk in space. What the hell can we do about it?" Alexis asked.

"Can't put *those* spare parts in the fraggin' hold," Sabrya muttered to Bradyn.

"Imagine the drocking inventory—"

"I'm not touchin' that."

Phillix continued, "Janus tells me that there'll be sufficient power in the remaining craft in the hangars to power the ship, but we need hands to hook them up."

"You want us to jump-start a fraggin' spaceship?"

"In essence, yes."

A magnificent nebula half-filled the sky now, the clearest evidence that *Iconic* had indeed jumped itself while Scipio had been on board, but he had no interest in something that might have taken another man's breath away. Two questions weighed heavily on his mind by the time he reached what he considered a safe distance from *Iconic*...

What was the best way to explain his mission's relative failure to Cor Fidelis Command, and to the emperor?

And why isn't Pleiades-219 *responding to my hails?*

As he considered the way Adjira's damn psi-blast had wreaked havoc with the very tech meant to combat it, his ruminations gave him the answer to his second question.

"Of *course*."

The feedback from the device had not only damaged his comms, but other parts of his suit. That might be why it was struggling to acquire a signal lock with *Pleiades*. No matter. He could see the scout on scans, holding two hundred kilometers out from *Iconic*.

"Damned smart ship," he murmured, congratulating himself on commandeering the right vessel for the mission. He steered the criminals' cruiser around on a circular intercept course, keeping his speed nice and steady. There was no hurry now. Although...

He glanced aside at the distant gray fleck that was *Iconic* and wondered how long the destruct's countdown had been set for. Had Adjira's commanders left large safety margins? Was it faulty? Had it been a trick to get the Imperial off the ship so it could jump somewhere and repair itself unhindered?

"Well, then, the trick's on you," he told it. "It's your mistress I'm really after, and she can't have gone too far in a damn pod." Once on the scout, he could scan to locate her, and complete the mission the way he wanted to, after all.

He was coming about now, his commandeered ship's nose pointing toward *Pleiades*. Seventy kilometers out, still too far away to see it with the naked eye, but there it was on scans, stationary, its bow averted from him and toward *Iconic*, as if the scout wanted to watch the fireworks.

"Clever little scout ship." He chuckled and slowed his approach a tad more, triggering the helm comms along a frequency *Pleiades* would be monitoring. "This is Scipio. One to come aboard. Traveling on foreign ship approaching from your port bow, twenty degrees down axis. Confirm my voiceprint."

Sixty kilometers. Fifty. Forty.

The scout hadn't responded, hadn't even shifted position.

Scipio repeated the hail.

Thirty kilometers. Twenty.

Nothing. In a rare moment of self-doubt, he checked the comms in case he'd set them wrong. Nothing he could see. The Qlan ship did source tech manufactured in a very different human society, after all. Or had *Pleiades'* damage from the earlier ship-to-ship engagement been worse than reported? Had the maintenance bots missed something?

If necessary, he supposed, he could stay aboard the criminals' vessel, although it, too, had seen some damage recently, damage that had weakened its shields and exhausted one of its long-term batteries. No, that wouldn't do. He thought, *I'll capture Adjira in an* imperial *ship. I'll greet my brothers from an* imperial *ship.*

He slowed right down as he hit the ten-kilometer mark. He knew where to look for *Pleiades*, but he still couldn't quite make it out. According to the scan data, it hadn't moved or responded to his presence at all.

He repeated his hail, this time adding, "Reply by text, *Pleiades*. Acknowledge my hail. Voiceprint: Optio-Major Helk Scipio, security code DSZ-5059."

Five kilometers. Three. And then he spied it, a gray blot with running lights blinking along its hull. Half a kilometer out, Scipio came to a full stop. For the first time, the scout ship appeared to register his presence; its nose came about, and it broadcast a message, one that was ironically crystal clear through Scipio's own damaged suit comms.

"Hailing Qlan Bukshoga vessel. Scipio voiceprint assessed as imitation. Code believed captured via coercion. Qlan Bukshoga vessel, you are to power down and surrender immediately."

Scipio thumbed the helm comms hail button, his blood icing over. "Are you serious? Who in the hells out here would have the tech to fake my voice?"

"You have not offered surrender in the time available."

"What?"

Where had *that* thought process come from? And what was it...?

"Oh, no!" Scipio gasped, flinching at the target-lock alert booming suddenly from the cruiser's helm. He knew the quality of *Pleiades'* weapons systems. "Oh, shit."

Optio Scipio lowered his head as the first rounds broke through the shield and smashed chunks from the hull.

It turned out *Pleiades* wasn't such a smart ship after all.

CHAPTER THIRTY-FOUR

"CAPTAIN, we are coming up to the area where the two impe-rial soldiers are located," Torg said.

"Good. I'm thinking their imperial soldiering days are over. How much time do they have?" Alexis and Sabrya were already suited up and waiting by the open airlock beside the loading dock. Filling their view, the hull of the *Iconic* moved past them, like a barren, endless landscape.

"Approximately two minutes remaining. Phillix reports they went looking for extra air, but couldn't find any. They are sharing an atmo-recycler now, but one of them lost much of her reserves in some kind of fight."

Her? Alexis shook her head. "Two minutes! Cutting it very fine." She sounded doubtful.

"We came in at maximum thrust—"

"Chillax, Torg," Sabrya sighed. "That wasn't fraggin' criticism."

"A droid maintains optimal temperature constantly."

"Captain, permission to repair that recon bot," the fighter muttered to Alexis. "I can grab any spares from our soon-to-be-ripped-apart droid."

"No time. Let's go." Alexis jumped. She was getting much better at zero-G. Her leap was gentle and controlled, having learned that stopping took as much effort as starting. She aimed to land several meters away, so no one was jostled in case she miscalculated.

"There better be no weapons," Sabrya said, her damaged blades extending as she followed. "Just in case," she answered Alexis sideward glance. "Can we really trust them?"

"I stopped my people from shooting you down, didn't I?" Jabari replied.

"I guess," Sabrya grumbled at her captain's nod. She flourished her blades so there were no misunderstandings about who was boss before comming the soldiers again. "Jump across. Wait. If that's the hilt of a knife I can see, I'd fraggin' ditch it if you want to keep breathin'."

Reluctantly, Alexis held back the air-cycler. *She has a point.*

"This was my friend's—" a woman's voice started to say.

The larger suit placed a calming hand on the other. "Breathing is good."

Jabari's voice.

A moment later, the other tossed something into space that glittered as it caught the light.

Relieved there was no further argument, Alexis quickly stepped over and handed them the atmo recyclers.

Once fitted, they turned toward the *Malleus*.

"You sure this is safe?" asked the woman—whose name was apparently Shill.

"You're welcome to stay on the *Iconic*." Alexis bit down her ire; she'd had similar thoughts when she'd first seen the vessel.

"Captain, look to your right." Torg's interruption quashed any further conversation as Alexis and Sabrya pivoted immediately; the other two suits aped them moments later.

In the distance was an expanding ball of intense light.

"What are we seeing, Torg?" Alexis watched curiously.

"That is the destruction of the last Qlan cruiser after direct hits from multiple weapons."

"Not the big ship's fraggin' plasma cannon, then?"

"Negative. Analysis indicates weapons signatures belonging to that of the vessel now designated as an imperial scout."

"And I missed the fraggin' fun."

"What's the scout doing now?" Alexis asked.

"It remains stationary, two hundred and four kilometers off our port bow."

"No comms?"

"Nothing detected, Captain."

Once back inside, the group began the arduous task of de-suiting. The woman named Shill sat on a long box to wriggle out of the lower half of her suit. The body odor released by the two soldiers' suits wasn't welcome, but not entirely unexpected, either.

Showing great restraint in commenting, Sabrya hit the decontamination button. A fine spray descended from nozzles in the deckhead. The soldiers bore it with closed eyes and gritted teeth. When it was over, they slapped at shoulder patches, which proved to be translator devices when Alexis next spoke.

"Okay, Torg. We're all aboard now." She thought it prudent to get things moving. "Let's see what we can do about these other ships in the hangar. Sab, head up to the bridge. I'll escort these two to the med-bay."

"We're fine—" Jabari stood, helping Shill to her feet. The soldiers wore red-and-black, formfitting bodysuits, made from a silky looking fabric. The underclothing hadn't wrinkled, but the red areas were stained with sweat.

Alexis waved away Jabari's protest. "You might be fine, but she definitely isn't. My ship; my rules."

"All right. She can go to med-bay. I respect that you're

captain of this ship, so I respectfully ask you: can I follow Sabrya to the bridge and scan the area?"

Alexis folded her arms, avoiding his question. "You looking for something?"

"Some*one*. I'd like to know more about the ship-to-ship action your droid just reported."

"All in good time. Torg is monitoring the situation and will keep us apprised of any further developments. You can catch up with your buddy, Bradyn, and exchange war stories." Part of her felt his need to know, but the XO part of her felt she had to lay boundaries. *My ship; my rules.*

"Since Metalman is monitorin', I'll assist with the escort, Captain."

Alexis sighed with a nod.

"Your security detail?" Shill queried Alexis, giving the fighter a once-over, paying particular attention to the blue, spikey hair.

"Nah, I'm the fraggin' cook." Sabrya grunted.

"But there *was* a weapons exchange between two ships?" Jabari continued as they were led away, closely following his companion down the short passage.

Evidently still listening in, it was Torg who responded. "The Qlan cruiser approached slowly on a direct vector. When it got within one kilometer, the scout fired, destroying it."

"Fraggin' point-blank."

"And the scout's still sitting there?"

"Yes," Torg replied.

Jabari grunted, exchanging a glance with his companion. "I'd say Scipio didn't make it to *Pleiades*," he told her.

Sabrya cleared her throat. "What happened to your fraggin' precious princess?"

"Ejected. Her departure initiated the self-destruct."

"How did that *not* happen, by the way?" Shill asked.

"Long story. Here we are." Alexis looked through the med-bay door. Bradyn had already vacated the bunk and now sat in a chair, leg raised with the heel planted on a nearby counter. His calf was wrapped in a medi-sheath to accelerate tissue regeneration.

Shill was directed to the vacant bunk. She winced but refused assistance to get on it. Alexis then connected the auto-doc and began a quick diagnosis. Jabari moved to stand at the doorway, looking in and watching.

"Well," Jabari continued, "from what your droid says, and the mess we saw near the discarded umbilical, it suggests our former commander took that Qlan ship."

"Former...?" Alexis started to ask, then shook her head. *That story can wait.* "Phillix did mention there was another Imperial wandering about *Iconic*."

"Unfortunately, yes." Jabari nodded in greeting to the engineer. "What happened to you?"

"Got shot trying to take out a drocking Qlan cruiser. You?"

Jabari rubbed his forehead. "Psi attack from a resurrected empress that nearly split my head in two. Hand-to-hand skirmish with my former commanding officer. And *recently*, I came pretty close to suffocating."

Bradyn pursed his lips. "You win." He grinned at the soldier.

"I'm not so sure. There aren't many individuals who can say they were shot by a spaceship."

"Yeah, there's that."

"I fraggin' can," Sabrya muttered from the corridor.

Alexis checked the readout of the Abbsolin S8. Based on the data, she applied what first aid she could for Shill. A spray of antiseptic over the burn along her abdomen and upper arm. While that dried, she attached the auto-doc to her good arm. "Just the usual antibiotics and mild sedatives," she informed the stoic soldier.

They waited while the infusions did their thing.

Eventually, Alexis asked, "Torg, any ideas where Adjira went?"

"Ideas, no. I work on data, not conjecture."

Sabrya stuck her head in the doorway. "See, boss, like I was sayin' before, we can replace Chromeman with that recon bot and program it not to speak at all."

"I'm beginning to like the idea." Alexis grinned.

"When we emerged from the jump," Torg continued, "the *Iconic* was situated as you see it. Has anyone got data on where the pod ejected from? It was not from the port side; we would have detected it."

"Her stasis pod doubled as her ejection pod, so it would come out the base of the ship," Jabari informed them.

"That'd be right," Sabrya agreed. "But what's out there, other than that fraggin' dust cloud?"

"Could the pod have had some control? Some form of guidance system?" Alexis queried.

"Most pods are designed for retrieval in space," Bradyn informed them, "not for atmospheric reentry. Sophisticated as it was, I doubt it had much more than minimal capability for maneuvering."

"What can we detect in that cloud?" Alexis turned, seeing the droid appear in the corridor.

"We have little capability of penetrating the dense cloud. There is nothing detected otherwise."

"Maybe she fragged up?" Sabrya suggested.

"Nothing detected otherwise would eliminate that scenario," Torg stated.

Alexis shrugged. "Phillix? Do you have anything further to add?"

"All Janus said was, that's where she'd been programmed to jump to."

"And the dust cloud? What's in there?"

There was a pause. "Janus has no data. In fact, Janus is becoming more hostile by the minute."

"Is Phillix your coder?" Jabari asked. "I'd like to meet him and thank him for his help."

"But he's dead to us now."

Alexis shook her head at Sabrya's cold-hearted joke. "Yes, he hacked into the *Iconic's* AI and stopped the self-destruct, which killed him."

"He died?" Jabari looked to each of them in confusion.

"But we spoke to him *after* the self-destruct was aborted."

"Yes, that's right."

Jabari looked from one face to the next. "Is there a punch-line coming?"

"That's another long story—" Alexis laughed sadly "—and I'm not sure I understand it well enough to tell it properly."

"Then allow me," Phillix cut in and gave them the same explanation Janus had given him. "All I can say is, apparently, it works."

"Life after fraggin' death."

"Some might say I've transcended."

With the first aid complete for Shill, they moved the conversation to the *Malleus'* dining room.

Not entirely trusting Sabrya to deal with the new guests appropriately, Bradyn quickly fixed some light refreshments for all, despite his aching leg.

Leaning back in a chair, Alexis took a swig from her coffee and smacked her lips. She met Jabari's eye. "What are your plans now?" While she waited for a response, she ran through another scenario in her mind.

The *Malleus* had the room for two new crew members if they wanted to join, but how would the others react to such a request from former imperial soldiers? *Crap*, she thought, *that'd sure change the dynamics around here.* She imagined for a moment the kind of pissing matches Jabari and Sabrya might get into—and found herself grimacing.

If they make noises about staying, I'll have to remind them we're headed for Niviaris. Don't think either of these two are built for a heavy-G planet.

Jabari looked to Shill, who dipped her head in response, as if deferring to his judgment. He outranked her, Alexis realized, and obviously even now, detached from their imperial ties, the rank structure held between them. *You can take the woman out of the soldier...*

Jabari replied, "We have brothers and sisters who're still under the empire's heel. I fear our disappearance will place even more Corfid attention on them."

"*What* attention?" Alexis asked, frowning at the overlay of translated words coming from the soldier's shoulder patch. "Your translator didn't cope with that word you used. *Corf...?*"

"Cor Fidelis. The Faithful Heart. The Imperium's most devoted military arm."

"Oh. That's what this Scipio guy was?"

"Yes. *Damn*, I forgot to tell you—there's at least one ship *full* of Corfids on its way here. If Scipio was telling the truth about that, they're a week away."

"We figured more Imps would be coming. I don't plan to be around when they arrive."

"That'd be wise. What about the *Iconic*?"

"Apparently, we're goin' to fraggin' jump start it," Sabrya cut in.

Alexis saw the quizzical look on Jabari's face, so she explained their current plan.

"Good luck with that," Shill muttered, not sounding at all convinced.

"Anyway," Jabari continued, "the Corfids can make life even

more torturous for my... for my people than it already is. Our Proselyti soldiers, held in stasis aboard a roving battle station, are captives to the whims of the emperor's foulest commanders."

"I'm very sorry to hear that." Her own brush with slavery fresh in her memory, Alexis added, "Genuinely."

Shill reclined her dining chair, considering her tea mug. "Jabari thinks it's time to set as many free as we can."

He nodded. "I don't know if I really believe my ancestors' spirits are watching over me, but it certainly feels like *something's* presented us with an opportunity. I should say," he added with a glance toward Shill, "it's given me an opportunity."

Shill gave him a hard look. "If you think you get to do anything heroic without me sharing in the glory, you're very, very wrong."

"Even if it means dying in the attempt?" he asked her.

"Isn't that always part of a soldier's deal?"

"I can't do it alone, in any case. I just didn't want to presume."

"Presume, Jabari. You're my commanding officer."

"Not anymore."

"Then you're my comrade."

"Well, all right then." Jabari turned toward Alexis again, the mildest of smiles softening his eyes. "I think the best way we can pay you back for saving our asses is getting off your ship and onto that scout out there. That'll be a great relief to your crew, I'm sure."

Alexis broke eye contact for a second, swirling her tea, and was glad she could keep the blush from her cheeks. The fact that these two wouldn't be hanging around was a great relief to her, too, she found. "Any ideas for boarding it? The scout, I mean. The thing did just atomize its own commander. I could ask Torg or Phillix for advice."

"No need," Shill replied and groaned as she leaned her chair forward again. "I've got a plan for that, too. Just need to chat with your droid."

They'd been in spacesuits for five minutes, Jabari in his original combat version, Shill in a borrowed one from *Malleus*. Already, Jabari was missing the freedom and fresh air of the med-bay. Suit recyclers could only sanitize so much, and they could only filter out so much body odor. He envied Shill her cleaner one, even if it wasn't as well armored.

Find a nice, quiet planetary settlement to regroup on, he told himself, *and you'll have all the fresh air you desire.*

In the airlock, he and Shill stood against the sealed exterior hatch. Through the small viewport, Jabari watched aspects of the nebula slowly swing around them as the *Malleus* maintained a cautious approach to the port hangar. The vessel stopped shy of the entrance, abreast of the top portion of the *Iconic's* hull.

"Remind me how this'll work, exactly?" the captain of the *Malleus* asked him. "One more time." Alexis and Sabrya were standing in the loading dock, seeing them off.

"We wait on *Iconic's* hull while *Malleus* gets to cover," Shill said. "Don't want you getting blown out of the void by our scout ship."

"Fraggin' better not," Sabrya grumbled. She'd already mentioned privately to Alexis the possibility of the Imps not being so friendly once they had a weaponized ship back under their boots.

Alexis shushed her while Shill explained.

"*Pleiades* would certainly make trouble that none of us want. I mean, I'm not sure it would see you as hostile. It marked Qlan ships that way, but *Malleus* wasn't part of the engagement, and you've created very different transponder prints for it. Still, you've got better things to do than a ship-to-ship fight, right?"

"Right," Alexis said. "Right, Sabrya?"

"Fine," the fighter replied grudgingly. "It's not like I need a ship to fight for me, anyway."

Jabari continued after Shill, "We'll contact *Pleiades* once you're under cover."

"And jump across to it, assuming the coding works," Alexis finished for him.

"Indeed." He nodded. With his suit's thrusters topped up, courtesy of Bradyn, they could cross the void without a problem. Leaping across would prevent the still-damaged scout ship from venturing too close when picking them up and accidentally smearing them against the *Iconic*.

"Maybe I was distracted when you were discussing this with Torg," Alexis said, "but I don't get how you'll get aboard without it atomizing you like it did to Scipio guy."

Shill chuckled. "We won't have any trouble. See, I hacked one of the ship's maintenance bots—"

"'Greasy,'" Jabari interjected. "The little hooch thief."

She grinned at him from behind her unmirrored faceplate.

"Hooch thief?" Alexis asked.

"We have our own 'long stories,' too."

Shill turned her easy smile Alexis' way. "The bot's slaved to the scout's AI, of course, but he's a kind of double agent. Torg created a link directly between the bot and my suit. The little bugger will then tap the ship's servers and activate some code I buried there a few days back. That'll allow us to override anything Scipio told the AI about what bad people Jabari and I are and remind it that we're Imperial soldiers who need to be let on board. And once we're there, I can make it do whatever the hell we want it to."

"We're in optimal position for disembarking, Captain," Torg said over the comm.

Alexis acknowledged and sealed the airlock's inner door. She then turned on the comms to the airlock. "I said it before, and I'll repeat it now: what you're doing is pretty damn risky. We just got you off *Iconic*. What if *Pleiades* doesn't come for you, and you're stuck there again?"

Jabari felt the buffeting of the airlock's air handlers dragging out the atmo and peered through the viewport. "I trust Shill's work."

"We'll know soon enough. If not, we know where you are," Shill added.

Jabari faced the center of the airlock. "Thank you, Captain Nales. For everything."

Alexis nodded back.

The chamber had emptied, and the outer hatch cracked open, exposing the two soldiers to hard vacuum again, the edge of one of *Iconic's* hull plates framed in the hangar bay entrance. No more delays; it was time to leave. He leapt from the hatch, landing securely on the massive ship's hull deck, and felt the vibration of Shill landing a half meter behind him moments later. As they moved away, Jabari heard Alexis in his comms.

"Take us in, Torg."

Bradyn gave them a thumbs-up through the side window of the cockpit, but before Jabari could return it, the *Malleus* dropped below the hull.

Visors still unmirrored, he and Shill regarded each other for a moment, both of them biting a lip.

"Let's get it over with," he told her.

She nodded and triggered a frequency *Pleiades* would be listening on. "Pleiades-219, two for immediate evac. Confirm your status and time to rendezvous."

The slightest of pauses, during which Jabari's heart skipped a beat as he thought Shill and Torg's little ploy hadn't worked. How almost comedic it would be if they'd made it this far, only be slagged by *Pleiades* now.

Then the ship sent its reply. "Confirming two for immediate evac. Four minutes out."

"Come to rest one hundred meters off the hull," Shill instructed the scout. "We'll jump across."

"Confirmed."

"And just like that," she told Jabari, "we have our ride."

CHAPTER THIRTY-FIVE

EVERYONE SAT around the main console on the *Malleus'* bridge, watching what played out above via the external cameras. As before, a portion of their ship protruded from the hangar.

They witnessed the scout approach. While the screen was initially enhanced, the craft soon became visible under normal optical conditions. The sleek angles of the imperial vessel—thrusters in the bow lighting up—came to a halt about a hundred meters from the *Iconic's* hull.

"Lucky you didn't break their toy, otherwise they'd be pissed and still aboard."

"Not for fraggin' long, if I have any say—"

"You don't," Alexis cut in.

Two small figures could be seen launching from the *Iconic*, but they were quickly obscured by the bulk of the imperial vessel. After several minutes, it banked away, disappearing into the darkness.

"Any comms?" Alexis asked.

"Nothing received, Captain."

"Pfft," Sabrya intoned dismissively. Now that the excitement was over, the nanites had de-energized, leaving her in a foul mood.

"So, then." Alexis turned her attention to the new situation. Whether she was disappointed or not, she didn't show it. "How do we go about this recharge? Phillix?" From the main console, Alexis scanned what files she could find for something—anything—that dealt with overcoming massive power failure.

"I didn't get to read 'Jump-startin' Ancient Relics 101,'" Sabrya scoffed, filling in the silence.

Where's Phillix? the captain wondered.

"Two methods come to mind." Bradyn hobbled up the stairs, returning from the med-bay after adjusting the medi-sheath around his calf. "If the ships out there use similar cells for power, it's simply a matter of collecting them and replacing the spent cells on the *Iconic*."

"Meaning a revisit to the powerplant?" Alexis sounded unenthused. "What's the second option?"

"Assuming there's a locker somewhere around the hangar with standard equipment, we plug those vessels in with power coupling to transfer what's left."

Sabrya chuckled. "Plug 'n' Play. I like it."

"Does it work like that? I would've thought the power would come *from* the *Iconic*, not feed into it."

"More of an electrician's gig. It might need a bit of tweaking..."

"Speaking of which, Torg, have you had any comms from Phillix?" Alexis asked.

"Negative, Captain. The last I heard was just after the explanation of his transcendence."

"Alexis, why don't you go check out the *Octavia*?" Bradyn suggested. "You know you want to. Leave this to us. If what Jabari said was correct, and there are more Imperials on the way; you might not get another chance."

"Yeah, I agree, boss. It's not as though we can't handle anythin' that'll crop up here."

"You sure?" Alexis asked.

Sabrya pointed to the stairs. "We can handle it."

"It's very technical—" Bradyn started.

"Bradyn can handle it," Sabrya amended. "Metalman can help if need be."

"No more mutiny," Alexis joked, standing up.

"What? Steal this fraggin' bucket of bolts? I have some dignity. Tell you what, let me get my—"

"I'll be fine. No Qlan cruiser, no imperial ships or soldiers, and no maniacal empress. This is a dead ship on the rim of barely chartered space. If I'm not safe here, there's nowhere in the galaxy that's safe."

"Exactly my fraggin' point."

"You're needed here to... do *something*."

"But—"

"We'll find something useful to occupy her time," Bradyn promised.

"And I will monitor the area intently," Torg commed. "You will be safe."

"I hate you both right now," Sabrya growled, but there was no real anger in her eyes.

Leaving them to work out the technicalities, Alexis donned her replenished vac-suit. The executive officer part of her wanted to work with the crew and recharge the *Iconic*; the botanist part wanted closure, which meant visiting her previous ship. She convinced herself that surely an executive officer would want to visit his old command. It worked. The impending headache of conflicting desires subsided.

Within minutes, she was out the airlock recently vacated by the Imperials and making her way across the hangar. She was passing one of the smaller craft and, on a whim, decided to try something that impinged on her thoughts.

Placing her boots firmly on the deck, she faced the small ship and pushed. It was an effort at first, but soon the ship started moving. It drifted smoothly, turning slightly, as her spontaneous push was off-center. Its tail fin dragged soundlessly along the deckhead.

"All good out there?" Sabrya asked.

"Umm. Yeah. Fine." She felt like a kid caught out. She moved on. "Would've been nice to get Shill's old vac-suit working. I could use those thrusters."

"It's a piece of shit. Too mangled to repair. And the body odor... What was that girl eating?"

"My point was the suit thrusters, Sabrya."

"Sure, they're real handy, until a fraggin' valve malfunctions. I've seen how well-placed lasers can—"

"I reckon I can manage nevertheless." Alexis silenced the comms and paced to the hangar door. She jumped up, vaulted over the ridge of the hull carefully, and placed her boots firmly on the hull before heading toward the wreck of the *Octavia*, almost a thousand meters away.

Used as she was to seeing *some* stars, the inky blackness out here on the edge of the galaxy's arm was disturbing. Spread out below the vast hull, only a portion of the nebula was visible from her position. As she continued her walk, she remembered to turn the comms back on. It wouldn't do for the CO to stay incommunicado.

At the pace she set, she guessed she'd be at the *Octavia* within eight minutes.

Alexis soon found herself at the large rend in the *Iconic's* skin where the *Octavia* speared into it. Looking down into the gloom, she counted four levels before her headlamp light failed to penetrate the shadow.

There were sections where the gallioid sealant had been deployed, but the damage went far beyond the designed parameters.

The fools probably thought, being so big, it was virtually inde-structible. "Pfft, not that indestructible, if my ship killed it," she muttered, followed by, "Okay, Kaden. How the frag do I get in?" Alexis concentrated, surprised the information wasn't immediately forthcoming now that she wanted it.

While there were large holes in parts of the *Octavia*, the edges were jagged—not something she wanted to attempt unless absolutely necessary. As she walked around to check the other sides, a memory occurred to her.

"Bradyn, you on?"

"I am," he said after a moment.

"Emergency exits from engineering—are they generally the same for all ships?"

"They are, more or less. Unions ensured conformity, and although she's a non-military version, I can't see why the *Octavia* would be any different. It's basic safety."

"That's what I was hoping. Out." She looked up to gauge the distance and angle, then jumped. Before, the concept of leaping untethered off a ship's hull in deep space would've daunted her, but her experiences and training with Sabrya had given her far more confidence.

Alexis landed as planned several meters from the tail end of her old ship. Her outstretched gloves found the surface of the hull, which slowed her momentum. Her fingers and augmented strength enabled her to grip the edge firmly, pivoting her around until she was facing toward the front of the ship.

Hand over hand, she pulled herself between the main drive tubes, looking for any hatch, be it maintenance or emergency, that would provide entry.

"Yes! Found it," she said after a few minutes. She held on to the small handle, looking at the keypad blankly for a few moments until, finally, she recalled the entry keycode. "'Bout time you kicked in," she muttered to herself.

There was enough residual power for the door seal to

retract, then she had to open the door manually using the lever on the side. Once she climbed in, she oriented herself to the deck and started exploring, casting her headlamp around. Her headset played static, and as she'd expected, she lost comms with the rest of her crew.

Once the captain was on board the *Octavia*, Torg left Sabrya to monitor the console so he could assist Bradyn by collecting the cabling.

"Fraggin' yay!" With a shout of glee, Sabrya found Torg hadn't disconnected the modified sound system. She plugged in her tunes and began a rigorous workout. Mindful of her role, she kept her eyes glued to the various monitors and comms.

"Torg?" Phillix's voice sounded over the comms. It sounded flatter, not as resonant as before.

"Yes," the droid acknowledged, deftly releasing the power cables so they remained in situ, hovering between the junction box in the deckhead, and the power panel of one of the small craft.

"I'll need you to come and collect me. Pronto."

"We've still got your body below, stowed in the freezer," Sabrya pointed out.

"Now you can have my consciousness, too."

"What's amiss, Phill?" Bradyn asked. After seeing what Alexis had done, he'd decided pushing the ships around in the hangar was a timesaver. Even with his injured leg, he didn't need much effort to move them, and it was of little concern to him when parts of the ships clipped other ships or bulkheads. In fact, that became the preferred way to stop them once they were in place, thereby less chance of injury.

"The reboot did more to Janus than anticipated," Phill explained. "She's now somewhat aggressive."

"You are a hacker inside an AI... I'd be drocking pissed too."

"Yeah, but she's changed. I was accepted before, but now..."

"What is your location for retrieval?" Torg asked.

"I've covered my tracks and managed to secrete myself in a node about halfway back to the powerplant, though I don't know how long I can remain undetected. Bradyn, remember that corridor we used going aft?"

"Yeah. I can—"

"No. For this, I'll need Torg. This is a procedure for specialized knowledge. Any error could result in erasing the node completely."

"You make it sound—"

"Besides," Phill cut off Sabrya's quip, "Bradyn is needed for the power transfer, and I believe Sabby has minimal knowledge of ship's functions. With Alexis away, she'll have to stay put."

She wiped sweat from her body as she listened. "Sabby?" the fighter growled softly, cranking the volume up.

<hr>

Bradyn put his mind to the task at hand. The impending arrival of imperial goons motivated him more than he cared to admit. He'd seen some of what they could do in *civilized* society. Imagine what they'd be like out here in no-man's-land. Still, sending Alexis to the *Octavia* had been necessary; it was the right thing to do.

The power couplings were conveniently situated in the deckhead, and good ol' Torg had already collected the cables from the storage locker on the far side of the hangar, saving his injured leg that extra work, even without gravity.

It was then a simple matter of hopping onto the craft, power cable in hand, and plugging them in. Plug 'n' play, as Sabrya had said.

"Phillix, can you talk?"

"I can," he heard after a pause.

"About this drocking power transfer..." He was standing on the top of a craft, and looking at the slot above him, holding a large plug in his hands.

"Already taken care of; Janus wants this, so it was easy to convince her to modify the relays before she flipped a circuit and went all aggro. Once its plugged in, board the ship and turn on the power. I'll send translated instructions and schematics to your wrist-wrap when I can. The other ships are basically the same configuration."

"Fair enough, but if I get drocking zapped, I'm gonna haunt this hulk until it drifts into a sun."

"Sounds like fun. You might have better luck with Janus. Before that, though, there are four more craft in the starboard hangar. I better sign off. Torg's here."

"If the droid's not back by then, I'll have to do the rest with Sabrya."

There was no response to his last remark.

Alexis looked around her as the memories came flooding back, and her thoughts of Kaden.

"Okay, then, show me what you can do." She allowed her mind to relax and stopped fighting the subliminal training. Almost immediately, her headache stopped.

The interior was in surprisingly good condition, although she didn't relish what she'd find further forward. With the subliminal training now in full swing, she spent some time checking over each compartment as she went through it.

Eventually, Alexis found herself toward the front, where the damage was most prominent. Checking her watch, she saw she'd lost the last hour. The radio was still static, and she wondered if anyone had tried calling her. She noticed she had a line clipped to her belt that had a large, heavy-duty plastine pouch attached, drifting along behind her.

"What have I been up to?" she asked herself, slightly put out that she didn't recall anything from the last hour or so. That hadn't occurred previously, and as disturbing as it was, her subconscious eased her apprehension. "It knows more about the ship than a botanist does." She was glad she could now recognize where she was—near her own mess hall.

With relief, she saw no bodies of friends or fellow crew floating about. Letting out an audible sigh, Alexis checked her wrist-wrap, nodding in approval. There was a meticulous record of her actions as she'd moved through the ship. There was also a blinking amber light, indicating her air reserves had been reached.

"Time to go."

Apparently, the suit still had a minuscule leak, or had developed one with her recent movements. Going back through the length of the *Octavia* would take an uncomfortable amount of time.

As she was in a generally well-occupied area, there was an emergency airlock one level back. She noted there were a couple of escape pods still intact, but this section was still within the *Iconic's* hull.

"No. Not a good idea." She passed them and activated the emergency airlock manually —a simple task due to the complete vacuum on both sides. Putting her weight against the stiff door, she tumbled out as it swung free into an area cluttered with fractured superstructure and debris.

"—amn Alexis, where the frag are you!"

"Hey, you."

"We've been callin' for fraggin' hours—"

"Hardly, and I'm fine. What's up?"

"Phillix reckons Janus is goin' nutso. Torg's gone to collect him."

"Crap! That's all we need—a rogue AI. I'm heading back anyway. Be there in twenty minutes." She began climbing carefully.

Unhampered by the requirement for air, light, or gravity, Torg glided along the same passage the engineer and tech had used previously. In a short time, he was at the compartment with the junction box containing the node Phillix had mentioned. On arrival, he plugged in using a universal connector to open communications.

"Phillix?" he prompted.

"Hey, Torg. Good to see you. I'm about to transfer instructions to remove the node. One drawback though—once disconnected, I'll need to piggyback off your power cell."

"Understood. If the power level drops, the node will reset, rendering you…"

"Well and truly erased, and the only person to enjoy that outcome would be Sabrya. Let's not do that."

"That will not occur." The droid proceeded to work as per the received data. "This will take ten minutes."

"Go for it. In the meantime, I'll monitor for Janus. She's snooping around looking for me."

Gliding above the *Iconic's* hull, Alexis made it back to the hangar. During the transit, she'd monitored the comms but had chosen not to intervene, wanting to see how they coped with her absence. They were all experts in their respective fields—more so than she was in hers—and didn't need her input.

"Welcome back, Captain." Torg was installing the node into the main console as Alexis closed the hangar door.

"The others aren't back yet?" Alexis grunted as she de-suited.

"Negative. Bradyn and Sabrya are over in the starboard hangar finalizing the transfer of power."

"And how's Phillix?"

"Intact. We will soon have our very own AI."

"He's in that?" She looked curiously at the nondescript gray box when she stepped onto the bridge.

"Affirmative." He updated her in detail on the last hour. "Janus found the node in which he was hiding. There was a confrontation, after which Janus withdrew."

"So, Phillix won?"

"In a fashion, but I believe it taxed him. Once the node is fully integrated, we will know more."

"And Janus?"

"I have no data. Phillix would be best suited to update us, once he is installed."

"Good work. Is there any reason we need to stay in this hangar? Being in the maw of a ship run by a rogue AI is not where I'd like to remain."

"None. All the required work here is complete. Bradyn has activated the power couplings, and the charging process has begun, though it is slow. They are now working in the starboard hangar."

"Excellent. I'll take us out and head over to the other side. You keep working." Alexis slowly backed the *Malleus* out of the port hangar, taking into account the altered locations of the other craft. The small ship wedging the *Malleus* in place drifted slowly as it came free, bumping into another ship.

She decided to fly under the hull to avoid any possibility of the plasma cannon activating, and she brought the *Malleus* alongside the starboard hangar sedately.

Through the viewport, she saw the power couplings joining the four small craft to the mother ship. Two suited figures were sitting on the edge of the hangar entry, their legs dangling into nothingness.

"Sorry to disturb your tea break. Want a ride before you two asphyxiate?"

"But it's such a stunnin' view," Sabrya joked.

"Sounds good to me, Captain," Bradyn replied.

<hr>

"Is this what I think it is?" Bradyn held up the plastine bag Alexis had brought back.

"It is. At least, I think it is." She told them that her XO alter ego had basically taken over while she was scouting the *Octavia*. "Kaden determined that's the component you required to make the necessary repairs to the jump drive."

The engineer extracted the circuit board carefully, handling it by the edges. "I'll get to it right away."

"That's it? A fraggin' bit of plastic?"

"Plastic with several millennia of technical wizardry and micro-circuitry embedded within its many layers, yes."

Alexis turned to Torg. "Speaking of technical wizardry, how's our AI doing?"

The droid spoke over Sabrya's muttering. "Would you care to activate him?"

With a deep breath and trepidation, Alexis reached over and flicked the indicated switch.

"AAARGHHHH!" The speakers, still set to max after Sabrya's exercise session, distorted at the sudden blast of sound.

Everyone jumped, even the seasoned fighter.

"I just had to do that." Phillix chuckled. "Sorry."

"Sounds like he's in good spirits," Bradyn quipped, recovering from his initial shock.

"I'm goin' to dissect your fraggin' body and dissolve it in acid," Sabrya hissed.

"No doubt we all deserve a bit of levity after the crap we've just been through—" Alexis sighed "—but my priority for now is to get as far away from this ship as soon as we can. Phillix, welcome back on board. Are you able to ascertain the condition of the *Malleus*?"

"And the *Iconic*?" Bradyn added.

"Captain, based on the few sections I can monitor, the *Malleus* has minimal structural damage. There's a minor air leak. Delta 4 hold is down 1.3 percent atmo. The aft port landing strut is warped and won't support any weight, and the jump drive is at 37 percent capacity. Once the network of data cabling is complete, I'll be able to integrate with many of the other sections." A stream of other minor defects played out on the screen.

"And the *Iconic*?"

"Before I left, Janus was recalculating the available power supply to determine her ultimate capabilities."

"Which are?"

"Unless the data's changed since my demise, Janus determined the *Iconic* could make a short jump, or it could activate the stealth shield, but not both. As you'd know, I had to secrete myself in a node when Janus began to show signs of hostility. It wanted *Malleus'* power supply so it could fulfill its tasking."

"Frag that!" Sabrya vented.

"Any idea what its tasking was?"

"To join Adjira."

"She can go into the dust cloud?"

"I believe she has the precise coordinates to wherever she went, but that requires both the jump drive *and* a fully energized shield."

"I'd like to send a fraggin' nuke to those coordinates," Sabrya groused.

"Your orders, Captain?" Phillix asked after several moments of silence.

"Your intel only reinforces my initial statement; we need to get as far away from here as possible." She looked at the viewport.

The others followed her gaze. In the distance, the dull glow of a brown dwarf was visible.

"I'd *really* like to go to Niviaris," she finished.

CHAPTER THIRTY-SIX

PLEIADES WAS in hyperspace when Shill found Jabari on his knees in the sparring room. She balked, freezing in the doorway. "You good there, boss?"

Jabari rocked back and put his ass on his heels, resting his palms on his thighs. "Join me, Shill. It's time to see our departed off to the Afterworld."

"You told Alexis you didn't believe that stuff."

"I told her I'm not sure I do. Won't hurt to try it."

"Well, I'm a different religion than you, boss. So was Erkan."

"Not Tee, though, and Morten had no religion, far as I know. So, maybe we do something from our two traditions, or we make the whole thing up on the spot. I mean..." He passed a palm across the candle flame. "I have no idea why I even lit this. It just seemed right."

"We owe them something, I agree. But first, I have intel. Imperium thinks their encryption is solid, but it's weak compared to what it was in the old days."

He waved her to come kneel or sit. She chose to kneel, waving a datapad under his nose. He took it but could make little sense of the text windows on it.

"Locations," she said. "Locations, medical statuses, mission updates, and ship movements."

"Of our brothers and sisters?"

"Yes. You can put that down." When he laid the pad aside, she continued, "The most useful bit of intel is there's a mission about to kick off from our *Maelstrom*. An FTL-shuttle is en route to pick up a small team of Proselyti. Already on board are two Corfids... and one imperial quaestor."

"Gods and ancestors." His pulse accelerated. "Wait. Those Proselyti are going off station?"

"They will be. Expected to be for a week, possibly two."

"Headed where?"

"I'll show you on a star map later, but I did the math. We're closer to their target. We can reach it long before them and intercept them at their target location."

"With just two Corfids in our way?"

"Plus a quaestor."

He felt his mouth turn down at the reminder. "Yeah, that'll complicate things."

"Also, you haven't seen where they're headed yet, and why."

"Still..."

They had days of travel to plan it, and a ship that was more powerful than an FTL-shuttle.

"So," Shill said, pointing at the candle, "you know how to do this?"

"Like we did with everything on *Iconic*. We make it up as we go." He bowed forward, touched three fingers to his tongue, then snuffed out the candle. "But all we really have to do is say goodbye."

"Not 'goodbye,' but 'see you later.' If they really went to an Afterworld, hopefully we will, as well."

"Just not for another seventeen hundred years, eh?"

"I couldn't agree more." Her face brightened for a moment before turning sad again. "I miss them. Tee. Erkan. Morten."

"We'll avenge their lives—" he started to say, then shook his head. "We'll make their deaths worth something by saving the lives of other Proselyti and setting them free."

"*Ahmen*," she said, using an ancient word he'd only ever heard from believers in one god, "or die trying."

"Or die trying," he agreed with a nod, then caught her gaze. "But one thing I promise you, Shill. Live or die, neither one of us is ever going inside a stasis tank again."

"Captain, the *Iconic* is no longer on the scope," Torg reported.

"Did it jump?" Alexis came closer to examine the screen on the main console.

"I cannot detect any residual tachyon emission that would indicate a hyper jump. As far as I can determine, it is cloaked."

"Enhance screen and zoom in." She moved even closer.

"If you are looking to see any 'shadow effect' with the background stars, we are too distant to tell for certain."

"And out here on the rim, there are too few stars, anyway. Better place that area in your data banks as a navigational hazard."

"Consider it done."

"Phillix," Alex said after a pause. "How are you in there?"

"Truthfully, I feel at home."

"And... your body? Umm... what would you like us to do with it?"

"I have no religious affiliation, no spiritual beliefs, and no family that would care. The prosthetic arm could be of value... Maybe jettison me into that brown dwarf. That would be kinda cool."

"Okay, if you're sure." She felt awkward, discussing the funeral arrangements of his previous body. She'd ask Bradyn if he could remove it... or Torg.

"If I could shrug, I would. Believe me, I'm happier here as a surrogate AI than I was as a biological mishap."

<hr>

With the new circuit board fixed in place, the *Malleus*, under Phillix's guidance, tested the repairs with a couple of micro-jumps.

"Is that it? What am I looking at?" Alexis studied the screen with Bradyn. The engineer was resting his leg. The calf injury had fully healed, and the medi-sheath had been removed. Sabrya was in the far corner, back in her exercising routine for the last few days while approaching Niviaris. Every now and then, the screen would haze over and blur.

"All indications are, it is a space lift," Torg responded.

"And that distortion?"

"Radiation emissions from the brown dwarf. They are prone to releasing much static and interference."

They were still too far out to see it with the naked eye, but enhanced vid showed greater details of the large planet. As they neared the forgotten colony world, a very thin column stretched from the planet's surface into the darkness.

"I've seen those space lifts before," Sabrya mentioned. "Back on Eridan III, in my seventh tourney."

"Enlighten us, oh learned one." Bradyn turned to her as she strolled closer, sweat running down her arms. He tossed her a towel.

"Well, it's a lift... into space." She wiped at her arms.

"Fascinating," Alexis said after a pregnant pause.

"That's it?" Bradyn laughed.

Sabrya punched Bradyn's shoulder playfully. "I'm no fraggin' engineer. Sayin' I've seen one doesn't mean I know how the fragger works."

Bradyn cleared his throat. "Then allow me—"

"I've loaded all the pertinent details on screen," Phillix interrupted.

All eyes turned to the side screen and started reading.

"That's a long ride," Alexis said afterward.

"As I was going to say," Bradyn continued, "the length or height is dependent on many variables, including the mass, gravitational constant, and radius of the planet. Since Niviaris is a high-G world, it would be substantially longer than one for, say, Mars. There should be a substantial counterweight at the far end, probably a captured asteroid, to keep the cabling under tension. Maglev modules designed for vacuum travel up and down the shaft. That's one of the priorities when colonizing high-G worlds."

"A lift into space," Sabrya huffed. "Sounds like more or less what I said."

"And they built it?" Alexis shook her head.

"Most of the equipment was shipped in on the original colony ships. The raw product would've been captured from asteroids and refined over the years. Much easier to do in zero-G. It would be fully automated, and they had decades to do it."

"Still, it's impressive."

Bradyn nodded in agreement. "That's the most practical method of getting stuff off a high-G planet. Fuel savings are enormous. Most inhabited high-G worlds have at least one."

"I guess that means the *Malleus* won't be landing?"

"Precisely. Not if you want to take off again."

"Yeah, pass. I'm not sure I want to be planet-bound again." Losing interest in the slow approach, Sabrya started another rep of chin-ups, strapping the remains of the recon droid to her ankles as extra weight.

"Phillix—"

"I can confirm, there are suitable docking facilities. There's one vessel docked, but it's cold and inert."

"Still no contact?"

"No response to our hails."

"Ah, well. Bring us in anyway." *I've come too far to turn back.* Alexis watched it for a few minutes. "Let me know if there's any contact."

"Righto, boss."

<hr>

"Captain, we are approaching the dock," Torg called over the comm.

"On my way." Alexis considered the droid's new situation again as she left her cabin. While Torg, being a droid, had no qualms about it, her humanity felt like he'd been betrayed, or his position usurped, when Phillix was installed as the AI.

"You're nuts," Sabrya had said to her. "It's a machine that doesn't give a frag one way or the other."

"I know, but I feel like he's still part of the crew."

"Well, consider this: Bradyn replaced his old legs with the recon droid's. He can move properly, and he's taller, so there's that."

"True." Alexis nodded.

Choosing the stairs, she entered the bridge moments later.

The docking area was far larger now, filling the screen.

"No enhancements?" she queried.

"It is as you see it," the droid replied.

"And still no communication?"

"None, but I believe I know why," Phillix replied. He continued, "Torg mentioned the star's radio bursts. It's almost constant on some level, and emits more powerful bursts frequently—"

"We're safe?"

"Oh, yeah. It'd take a prolonged, concentrated burst directly at us to cause serious damage."

"Okay. Go on."

"Any comms on the planet would be subjected to these emissions constantly. Unless they've developed a new form of communications, most standard electronics would've burned out with the bursts. The constant static over the speakers would've driven them nuts."

"How do we message them, then? Do we know if anyone's alive?"

"I dare say they're underground for the best protection. I reckon everything's closed-circuit. Much easier to reinforce and protect wiring, though it has its limitations."

"Meaning we have to dock and… place a call?"

"That's my guess."

"I thought AI dealt with data, not guesses?"

"Lucky I'm not really artificial, then."

The docking bay was standard, and they were out of the airlock as soon as it was deemed safe. As far as space docks went, it looked no different; large, open areas for maintenance droids to move around and conduct ship repairs.

"The area's completely deserted. Looks like it has been for a long time," Phillix reported.

"But there's power?"

"Evidently, hence the atmosphere, gravity, and relatively comfortable living conditions." Phillix was slaved to Torg; what the droid saw, he saw. Installing Phillix's consciousness allowed the droid to leave the ship for longer periods.

"What about the other ship Phillix mentioned?" Bradyn asked.

"All indications are it has been abandoned for years. It is as cold as space, and there is not one erg of power registering."

Leaving the docking area, they found the passenger terminal one level up. The station was circular, the central area a sealed void where the cabling and tethers for lift operation were located. Immediately around the center, and radiating out from it, were numerous rows of comfortable chairs. Toward the back, with panoramic views of the starscape, were tables. Kiosks were located every twenty meters around the periphery.

There were two areas to board the lift.

"Looks like the lifts are large and multi-level," Alexis noted. There was a gantry higher up, with stairs leading to their level.

"On and off," Bradyn informed them. "Arriving passengers step off up there, while those departing go through over there."

Torg had ventured closer to the empty security desk. His silver fingers tapped a few keys before anyone noticed.

"That's right, Metalman, let them all know we're fraggin' here."

"Phillix has managed to furnish the access codes. I am now viewing the latest lift itinerary."

The others wandered over to take a look, but there was only room for the droid and one other inside the booth. Bradyn leaned over the counter, while Sabrya jumped up and sat on the other side.

"Does that mean what I think it means?"

"If you mean that a lift is on its way, then affirmative," Torg confirmed.

"How the frag—"

"Far too coincidental for them to come up here at this time for a visit, I reckon they were aware of our presence days out. They'd need to be, in order to cover the distance in time for our arrival."

"Passive triggering is no doubt the answer, though it would need to be off during radiation bursts from their star," Torg relayed for Phillix.

"That answers something I was pondering: why the power and atmo? It's such a waste of energy to keep it running. They must've activated it once they knew of our arrival."

"Seems logical," Phillix agreed.

"Arrival's in thirty minutes," Alexis noted. "Looks like we get comfortable."

"I'll go and get you more weapons," Sabrya stated.

"No. We're the uninvited guests. And put away your blades. I'm certain once they know who I am, things will go fine."

"If they were hostile, I doubt they'd have arranged for habitation," Bradyn noted.

As they talked, a monitor powered up. They gathered around, curious.

Once the static haze cleared, they discerned a single male.

Alexis gasped. "Kaden," she whispered in shock, her face going pale. The figure she stared at could have been her partner's twin—the similarities were remarkable. As the image sharpened, the man looked to be in his early twenties, far too young to be Kaden, or—

"Hello. We've been monitoring your approach, but don't recognize your vessel. Identify yourselves, your ship, and state your business."

The silence stretched, as she was taken aback by the youthful appearance of the Kaden look-a-like. *He even sounds like him...*

"I..." Eventually, she found her voice. "I'm Alexis Nales, captain of the Free Alliance Vessel *Malleus*, but formerly botanist first class on the colony ship *Octavia*. My crew and I are here to open dialogue and to render whatever assistance you may need."

The distance for the signal to travel was vast, especially along cables, but the reply came far quicker than anticipated.

"They must be on the approaching lift," Bradyn guessed.

"Wait... Captain." The young, wide-eyed figure turned to speak to someone offscreen.

Though muffled, she clearly heard what he said.

"Pa, there's a lady on the line who says she was on your old ship. She says she's Alexis Nales."

EPILOGUE

IN THE DISTANT PAST, they'd called her Kaana Adjira mo'Halana mo'ni'Mariama, Foremost of the Okalasi, Light of the North. In a not-so-distant future, she believed they'd also call her Mother of the New Humans.

She'd once spent almost two thousand years in stasis. By comparison, this latest week-long stint of unconsciousness in her escape pod's stasis bay had been but the blink of an eye.

And here she was, safely arrived in a deep, subterranean haven, as dear Janus had promised and arranged. A cold, carboncrete facility with little in the way of creature comforts, to be sure, but at least the bed appeared soft, and the pantries well-stocked. That was something. The most important things here were the equipment...

Adjira ran a sausage-thick finger across a glass-fronted stasis tank and considered the dust on her fingers. Tut-tutting with distaste, she shook her head, and regretted it when the movement sparked a painful jab in her neck, where the joints were still stiff. She'd only been awake for fifteen minutes. Her tongue was dry and swollen with dehydration. Hunger tightened her stomach unpleasantly. And her head pounded, no doubt the result of that damned Martianist bouncing her psi-blast back at her. She'd need to rouse a medbot to attend to her various ills, then a scullion droid to cook for her.

Or were there people on Tragua she could entice down here to serve her? Now, *that* was a terrific idea. *People would certainly be useful*, she thought. And what was a Kaana without subjects? The only detail she remembered about this particular planet and its star was that they were screened from imperial eyes by a gargantuan dust cloud.

A workstation stood in one corner, coated in a film of dust. She wiped its various screens and contact plates, cleaned her palm against her clothing, then pressed it against the readplate. Several seconds passed as the ancient device soaked in her body heat before it fizzled gently against her skin, reading her print. Luminescence came to the screens in flares of color. A speaker coughed to life, and a voice modeled on Janus' said, "Majesty. What shall I do for you?"

Shoulders back, chin tilted regally, she replied, "You can tell me if this world is populated by sapient life. Besides myself, of course."

"When this facility was established, the world was terraformed, but not colonized. It appears many centuries have passed since then, of course. One moment, please, Majesty. I'm sourcing data, assembling meaning... Yes, there appears to be a civilization spread across several regions of this world. Industrial Age, judging by the trace chemicals in the atmosphere and water, and by the types of sounds I am registering. I have no visual data, I'm afraid. Satellites with that capacity have gone missing."

"Indeed?" She pondered that a moment. Had her people seeded colonists here before the end, while this AI slumbered? Had *others* discovered the place in the meantime? Had their isolation set them back enough they'd reverted to technologies requiring combustion engines and mass pollution?

Or was it...? Was it...?

The alternative—a suggestion of memory—tickled the verges of her mind, like the slippery afterimage of a faded dream. She couldn't grasp it, so she let it go.

"You have comms connection with the people here?"

"No, Majesty," the AI responded.

"Irritating," she said and returned to the tank bearing her finger lines in its dust. "Now, the most important thing. The moment of truth." She laid her palm against the tank's readplate. A blue glow lit the stasis gel within, revealing a cloud of tiny embryos —hundreds of them. From the newly activated screen data, she read, "'Seven hundred twelve viable. Two hundred eighty-eight nonviable.' I can make do with seven hundred and twelve."

She moved to another tank and leaned in close.

"Soon enough, my cherubs, you'll be walking and talking. And ruling."

But to bring these precious ones to term, she'd need wombs, a host of them. Mechanical incubators were one thing, but living ones were far superior. Kaana Adjira raised her gaze to the ceiling and pictured the teeming masses living on the surface above. Primitives, undoubtedly, no match for her powers or intellect. Adjira felt an acute pang of desire to meet them, to establish her rule. *Re*-establish her rule.

Once she'd had the medic attend to her various ills. And, of course, once she'd eaten.

<hr>

A meal, followed by the ministrations of the medic droid, and then a long nap. Upon awakening came another meal, her ablutions, and the donning of fresh clothing made in her size.

The deep bunker's elevator took her up past the reclusion bay where her escape pod had burrowed upon landing, but it terminated early, letting her out in a subterranean passageway, a carboncrete tunnel that looked as if it were created just yesterday. Dust-free, unlike the lowest chamber, indicating better seals or better filters. Even the air smelled clean here, pumped in fresh from hidden reservoirs.

Signs and arrows pointed both ways, one set toward a storage chamber, the other toward SURFACE ACCESS, which lay hidden behind a secured blast door at the corridor's farthest end. Her palm pressed against a readplate, which buzzed pleasantly against her skin. The blast door clunked, then shuddered open, the first sign of the facility's true age.

Adjira caught a whiff of some kind of burnt or stressed mechanical parts, but it opened all the way. A new doorway faced her with a hinged door closed across it. A badly faded pictogram indicated stairs on the other side, a fact that might have vexed Adjira if she hadn't been wearing her antigrav belt. Without the help of droids or human servants, the hinged door's handle took some effort to jiggle and turn. The door also resisted her, even as she leaned all her weight against it. But then it was open, and she stepped into a gritty-surfaced stairwell, earthy-smelling and lit only by the tunnel behind her.

Adjira activated her antigrav belt to make herself a pretty bubble, rising gently through the murk. Triggered by protocols or sensors hidden from her, the thick, metal covers for the stairwell cracked apart, and the two halves strained against the earth concealing them, laboring upward and causing dislodged streams and clods of dirt to rain onto the upper risers of the staircase. No matter to Adjira; she wouldn't be treading on that filth. By the time her shield bubble reached them, the covers had made it to their vertical position, pointing toward an azure sky salted with the tiny kernels of cloud. Relying on her own air reserves, Adjira had no idea what the grassland she found herself in smelled like. She could imagine it. The grasses weren't so different from the ones on her homeworld.

A strong breeze bent the stalks around her, strong enough to catch her bubble and tug it west. At least, she assumed it was west, judging by the angle of the local star. It felt, for some reason, like mid-afternoon out here. She had a wild impulse to drop to her feet, cancel the shield, and explore this world with her senses as she made contact with the inhabitants, so long had it been since she'd walked in the open air, or felt a planet's atmosphere caress her cheek and tousle her hair.

But that wouldn't do. Hardly a dignified first impression to make. She steered the bubble south, catching sight of a settlement that way, with what appeared to be the rear railings around some outlying suburban properties. Many kilometers past them, a thick tower sprouted up, reaching for the heavens. Impossible to tell how far away, or how high it reached. Undoubtedly, that would be where these folks would take her.

The architecture was unfamiliar, she noted as she drew nearer the homes—if that's what they were. Fifty or more of the properties were visible in either direction, stretching out to the periphery of her vision. Not one was alike, save for the rail fences along their yards. Some looked like toy blocks of various colors stacked together. Others were even less aesthetically pleasing, appearing to be shaped out of mud or some other kind of pliable building material. The two she steered toward, the ones with the roadway terminating at the grassland between them, seemed the most bizarre, flat domes or upturned saucers of dull alloy without windows.

"Well," she murmured to herself in Janus' absence, "styles change, I suppose, and there's never been any logic associated with good taste."

Onto the stub of side street she floated, spying an intersection ahead. No vehicles yet. But despite the odd architecture, it did resemble images and videos she'd seen in her time, the recognizable edge of other suburban sprawls on other worlds. It was orderly and clean. Even the stunted trees and rows of fruit vines along the verges were clipped and pruned precisely, the grass within the suburban limits neatly mown and edged.

No vehicles yet. No pedestrians. No homeowners in their yards.

That changed when Adjira floated out into the cross street and turned right toward a line of rectangular buildings with tall front windows. Stores, she presumed, and the figures hurrying in and out of them, ferrying things to and from parked vehicles, gave evidence to it. She sped up, aiming toward the activity. Someone here would recognize her. This had to be a world upon which records of her greatness had been left, upon which she was famous. One of these people would direct her to the authorities. One of these... strangely dressed people, with their gray bodysuits and bulbous head-wear seeming to grow out of their skin. These people who straightened up and froze as they saw her, who dropped some of their packages in the process, leaving them to spill upon the roadway.

Who regarded her with eyes far too wide and round and black to even be Martianist gene-modded eyes.

"Oh..." she said as she brought her bubble to a halt thirty meters away from the nearest beings.

"Not human, then."

Upon her first introduction to these beings at her father's side, they had called themselves Lanei-el, and they'd provided the beautifully alien ingredients for her genetic project. What she had assumed earlier was clothes and headwear was actu-ally bare skin and alien bone structure. From time to time, one of them flicked a beautiful tail out from behind itself.

Never had Adjira seen so many gathered in one place—and certainly not engaged in mundane activity. What were they doing *here?* How was there a settlement of them *here?* Tragua wasn't their homeworld—although she knew theirs had been similarly hidden away from prying eyes and sensors...

More Lanei-el emerged from the storefronts, or stopped their moving vehicles and climbed out, all of them adopting the same shocked, frozen positions as they stared at her.

It wouldn't do to ape them for too long. She triggered her voice projector and lifted her chin as she addressed them.

"I am Kaana Adjira mo'Halana mo'ni'Mariama. Your leaders will want to speak with me. Take me to them."

A pause. A long one. No response. None of them budged a centimeter. A bug of some kind made a whizzing sound as it shot past her bubble.

She tried again. "Okalasi." Yes, that should do it. "*O-ka-la-si.* Me. Your people's allies."

One of the Lanei-el moved. It was a step, just one step, but it was in her direction, and it unnerved her. Reflexively, she backed her bubble up a meter before she caught herself. There was nothing to fear here. The Okalasi and Lanei-el had been allied for almost two millennia, and earlier Lanei-el had made contact with Terran governments for short periods several millennia before that. It was a boon, finding them here. Surely a good thing.

Adjira felt something then. A probing pressure deep in her skull that sent a trickle of dread rolling down the back of her neck like the tickling of a feather.

Another alien moved. And another. Another. *Another.* Each taking one single step toward her. The pressure in her head sharpened into an intention, into menace, into a message she received loud and clear. They weren't the aliens. Here in this place, *Adjira* was the alien.

Half a minute later, her bubble reached the grasslands and sailed over it at top speed. She rotated within it, checking behind her. The mouth of the side street filled with sprinting aliens. Not once had they uttered a sound—they'd relied on telepathy for eons, she knew. Not once had one replied to her short-lived attempt at psychic contact.

There was menace in their chase. When she reached the open stairway into the earth, the folly of the move hit her—she shouldn't alert them to the existence and position of her haven. She should sail on, take a different direction, lose them in the wilds, and circle back.

But panic had taken hold of her, batting away sensible thinking, sending her plunging down the stairwell. The panic tightened its hold on her when she reached the bottom, constricting her ribs, squeezing her heart. Because although the hinged door lay open, the blast door behind it was sealed, now camouflaged as a wall of solid stone. Adjira did the previously unthinkable, deactivating the bubble, lowering herself to the gritty carboncrete floor, and running her palms over the faux rockface.

Readplate, readplate, readplate! her mind yammered.

She still hadn't found it when the first silhouette appeared in the stairwell entry above, blocking out some light. Then another. And another. Adjira hammered on the stone now, crying out for the AI, for Janus. No answer. Something had malfunctioned in the minutes she'd been gone, or else had broken down centuries ago and failed the first time it had been needed.

The hole in the earth at the top of the stairs was dark with shifting, milling figures. She whirled to face them, rose from the floor, and triggered the shield. Hands raised, she attempted to use her psionics, but there was no observable effect or reaction. Nothing she could sense but that pulsing, persistent menace toward her.

Of course her attack hadn't worked.

They're not human.

And neither were they the Lanei-el she knew.

As the first of them descended boldly toward her, three questions flared like starbursts in Kaana Adjira's mind.

How long would her shield bubble hold out?

What would these creatures' leaders do with her when she was delivered to them?

And when these creatures finally did deliver her, would they deliver her in one piece? Or in many?

AJ Gordon (Andre Jones) has been dabbling in writing for many years, but only got "serious" after his early retirement from the Royal Australian Navy where he served for almost 20 years as an Electronics Technician.

Now sharing time between Australia and France, Andre is able to write full-time when not drawing or gardening.

To date, he has written ten novels (co-authored three) including Seven Portals series epic fantasy; The Death Wave Chronicles urban fantasy; Gnome Henge, a children's book; and now the Outer Reaches sci-fi series.

Peter J. Aldin is the creator of the *Envoys* science fiction universe which straddles 900 years of future history. Under the (almost identical) pen name Pete Aldin, he's responsible for the *Doomsday's Child* zompoc series and the werewolf thriller *Black Marks*.

A soccer devotee, he supports Chelsea and Brentford in the

English Premier League. He eats Brussel sprouts no problem, will walk over broken glass to play a board game, and is unhealthily fascinated by WW2 history. He's Australian: Vegemite runs in his blood.

THE OUTER REACHES

THE ADVENTURES CONTINUE ...

QUAESTOR

In the year 5122, maintaining law and order across the Imperium's vast reaches is extremely complex.

Enter the Quaestors. Judges. Law bringers. And, when need be, executioners.

When imperial Quaestor Aurelia Cossea enlists Proselyti troopers to depose a corrupt governor, Sergeant Saito Shimada willingly accepts. A convert to imperial ways, he has devoted himself to a safer, more united galaxy.

But when the assignment is interrupted by betrayal and the bizarre appearance of troopers from an earlier Prosyleti mission, Saito's commitment to his Imperium masters is sorely tested.

Under-equipped and cut off from support, the hunters will become the hunted, forced to navigate the twisted maze of an ancient city in a desperate bid for escape, hampered by bad intel, the governor's minions ... and unsure about these two deserters who've returned apparently from the dead.

FAR HORIZONS

The *Malleus* crew aren't fitting into Sylvanus Colony.

Faced with prowling Imperials, a looming bounty by the powerful Bukshoga Qlan, and various nefarious entities out for their blood, this side of the galaxy has become too hot for their leader Alexis, former gladiator Sabrya, engineer extraordinaire Bradyn, and the upgraded droid Torg.

Flying a cargo ship without cargo, the crew plots a course to the farthest known reaches of the galaxy, planning to become traders among the emerging colony worlds of the Orion Quadrant—a region under constant harassment from marauders. They soon realize that what they really have to offer is the one thing the colonists haven't had—protection.

But when they upset the status quo, angering powerful personages who are already entrenched in this region, who is going to protect *them*?

Grab these books today to continue your journey through the far future of our Milky Way's farthest reaches.

FROM THE NOVEL "CITY OF BRIDGES
- BOOK 1 - THE SEVEN PORTALS" BY
ANDRE JONES

By late evening they could see the city twinkling of the city far below. Drawing closer, they began to look for a safe place to land. The area along the coast turned out to be too treacherous with cliffs and rocks. All they could find inland was dense jungle. Leonie knew of no area large or safe enough for the three wyverns to land near the city.

"What of the roads leading out of the city. Couldn't we land there?" Phil called out over the wind.

"They'll be patrollin' them, and I'd rather not be seen." She hadn't told Phil everything about herself. "And damn sure you don't either."

They returned to circle high above the city centre, having flown around the boundaries for one final look.

"We could try the pier by the tannery." She pointed down to the south-eastern arm of the harbour. "It's set away from every-thin' coz of the stench, and at this time of night should be deserted. I don't think it'll support the weight of a wyvern though."

That is of no consequence. Dorn sent her thoughts. *You forget we can hover. We need not touch the pier.*

From out of the darkness a shadow flashed into view. There was a sickening crunch as a hideous creature slammed into Slana's back. The undead creature's shriek of success drowned Slana's screech of pain.

The jolt snapped the restraints, throwing Leonie from the saddle.

Time slowed.

With arms flailing the air, she slipped sideways. Her fall stopped when her paw caught in the stirrup, jarring her leg and leaving her hanging upside-down below Slana's chest. Her recovery was hampered by the green wyvern's efforts to dislodge the giant bug.

Slana snaked her head around, barely able to latch onto the monster's body. Her teeth snagged a leg. Slana clenched her jaws and ripped them away. The limb cracked at a joint, pulling free from the body. Screeching in pain, the attacking Lith sank its claws deeper into Slana's back.

Desperate for a paw-hold, Leonie spied a leather strap flapping in the wind above her. Beyond was the bulk of the creature. She froze at the sight of its rider, recognising her as the Jart'lekk assassin from the caverns. *But, she's dead? I killed her.*

Seeing the dismay on the enemy's face, Evlin's face broke into a manic grin. There was no escape. Even so, she felt impelled to cast the killing stroke; she had to if her master was to know immediately of her success, and if she was to receive any reward. Without a qualm she climbed off her ride and dropped onto the green wyvern's thick neck. From there she reached down, but discovered her prey was still out of reach. "You'll not escape me so easily this time," the assassin declared.

Evlin slid off the wyvern's neck to grapple bodily with her long sought-after nemesis. Her added weight strained the damaged leather, ripping the stirrup from the saddle. The pair tumbled towards the dark waters of Delta's harbour.

Totally unprepared for the attack, the others were stunned by Slana's cry of pain.

Dorn's head snapped down in alarm. Her daughter was spiralling out of control, losing height rapidly. Recognising the Lith, she instinctively sent a bolt of rage at the attacking monster only to find nothing there. The mind was empty! Recovering from her initial shock, a mental probe confirmed Dorn's suspicions. The Lith had no aura about her at all. It was Undead.

Ye Gods! Quick Dorn. Leonie's fallen. Phil mentally cried.

Faldo, go after Leonie. Dorn put a lot of force into her thought, knowing he'd want to prove himself. *I will deal with this creature.* Her son was no match for this creature. *Brace yourself,* she warned Philbert as she hurled herself after her daughter.

Philbert wedged himself into the saddle flares, using his years of working with horses and wyverns to cope with the sudden manoeuvres. He focussed his mind to keep an eye both on Faldo and Slana's progress, looking for any advantage to exploit.

In horror, he saw Leonie fall. At first he thought she'd disappeared in the darkness, but then glimpsed her dangling upside down, being jostled by Slana's movements. With disbelief he witnessed another woman leap from the Lith's back to Slana's then, inconceivably, slide down to grapple with the half-Rrell. Then the leather strap snapped, and both fell into the darkness.

His heart jumped into his throat. He lost sight of them when Dorn's bulk blocked the view as she pivoted, intent on saving her daughter. Phil hoped and prayed by some great feat, Faldo would be able to save Leonie before she fell to her death. All he could do now was watch and advise.

From Faldo's back, Feiron heard the loud screech a moment

after the impact of the wyvern and the monster. He'd been looking down like everyone else, thinking of the nice, comfortable barrel awaiting him. His regeneration had sapped his energy and it took a couple of moments for him to grasp what was happening. First he saw one of those Lith creatures clinging behind Slana's shoulders. Then he realised the saddle was empty. He couldn't believe his eyes when he saw a black clad woman reaching for Leonie with a dagger. Her stirrup snapped. They dropped into the darkness.

"Leonie!" A wind gust ripped the cry into the night. Faldo dipped sharply and Feiron hung on grimly, wrapping his arms around any conceivable support. It was moments like these Feiron regretted not being able to communicate with wyverns.

"Finally, I have you." Evlin jabbed swiftly at her nemesis's heart.

Relying on instinct, Leonie barely managed to deflect the assassin's wrist. The blade she used glowed malevolently. The thick jacket, proving little protection against it, tore open at the shoulder.

Everything happened so quickly, yet time seemed indeterminate. It was hard to think with the sea rushing up and the air screaming in her ears. Instinctively Leonie grabbed the assassin's wrist, preventing another thrust. Even when her claws cut the assassin's flesh, Leonie's struggles proved futile. The assassin had amazing strength, far more than in the caves, and far more than any human should.

The twin-bladed dagger moved relentlessly closer to her heart.

Leonie twisted and lunged; latching her teeth onto the woman's shoulder in the hope the pain would weaken her. There was no reaction. Her sharp teeth pierced the skin and clothing, yet there was no blood. In fact, Leonie could've sworn the assassin was laughing!

"Your craving for life is futile, but death will be no escape either. Once my master has finished with you, you'll be mine to play with forever."

Leonie saved her breath, redoubling her efforts, knowing the only reason she still breathed was because the both of them were spinning and tumbling through the air, struggling for any advantage.

Out of the corner of her eye the thief saw Faldo swoop underneath. Instantly she realised he was manoeuvring below to attempt to catch them. *The dagger'll kill him if it strikes.* She knew it in her bones. Leonie didn't want his death on her conscience. She twisted in vain. The two women landed with a thump behind his beating wings.

It will not harm me. Faldo responded to her thoughts, regaining altitude.

Something jarred Leonie's spine on impact. She hissed in pain; then an idea blossomed.

With an evil glow behind her dark eyes, Evlin relentlessly pressed the dagger down on her victim.

"When I've killed you, I'll take the life from your friend and his pet," she gloated. "My bug will be overjoyed with the taste of fresh meat. I believe wyvern is a delicacy to them." The assassin now had the advantage by being on top, but before she could react, a warm jelly substance oozed around her, starting to envelope the attacker.

"Feiron. No." Leonie immediately realised he was trying to save her. She had to do something quickly, certain that if the dagger touched either Faldo or Feiron they'd die instantly. Leonie couldn't afford to release her two-pawed grip of the assassin's arm. Claws and teeth didn't seem to make any difference on this foul woman. She could see only one option to save her friends, but Feiron was hampering her. She turned her head and bit him. Hard.

With his efforts on the assassin, he recoiled in surprise, letting go.

"Sorry my friend." With a heave, Leonie rolled off Faldo's back, dragging the assassin with her.

Dorn manoeuvred quickly above the attacking Lith with the fury of a mother defending her young. Her vengeance was swift and sure. She sank her talons deeply into the central carapace and ripped the creature off her daughter's back. She then swung her massive head down and gripped the neck with her teeth, slowly crushing the shell between her jaws.

The night air filled with hissing, screeching and cracking. Dorn's claws raked the length of its body, shredding the wings and fracturing the shell in several places. Though the foul creature didn't 'die', it could no longer fly. Damaged wings beat uselessly. Thick globs of dark ichor seeped from the gaping hole in its neck.

Dorn spat out the foul-tasting stuff, watching the creature spiral out of control to smash into one of the rocky outcrops in the harbour. She then pivoted towards Slana far below, flying limply to the nearest land.

Slana. How badly are you injured? Dorn waited for a reply, but none came. All she could sense from her daughter was pain, shock and confusion.

Wind screamed in Leonie's ears. Borne out of desperation, she grasped at her idea. Her life depended on it. As they tumbled, she brought one leg up, then the other. Kicking and heaving with all her might, she timed her moment well, thrusting the assassin away.

In her initial struggles, Leonie had completely forgotten the harness from White Cliffs. It was only when she landed on Faldo's back she painfully remembered. After the episode on the skyland, she'd donned the harness as a precaution.

The moment the assassin's grip loosened, Leonie put all her might into one final kick. She then slipped a paw under her jacket and felt for the dial of her harness. She wrenched it on, feeling a painful constriction around her waist. She gasped as the air was forced out of her lungs. The harness did its work.

"Nooo," Evlin cried as her nemesis slipped from her reach, moving farther away from her. She thrashed and swung her arm madly in an effort to strike.

Leonie watched, partly curious but very relieved, as the assassin continued to plummet. Her relief was short-lived when she felt herself falling again. *Somethin's wrong!* She frantically turned the dial higher, to no avail. Gaining speed, the wind grew louder in her ears. A few seconds later, she saw the splash when the assassin's body hit. The water foamed up, but soon faded. The body quickly disappeared, swallowed up by the dark water.

Leonie braced for the impact. The grip around her shoulders took her completely by surprise. She swung her head up as her body jerked like a puppet.

"What--? Her voice caught in her throat at the sight of a billowing, grey sheet looming above. Her fall changed direction and slowed drastically. But not enough. She hit the water, at speed, her impetus taking her under the surface. In panic she flailed to the surface, foaming the water around her, but the weight of the harness dragged her down.

Feiron dived in to help, but when he touched her, her thrashing increased.

"Leonie. Relax. It's me," Feiron cried the moment they surfaced, but his words went unheard.

Be calm, furry one.

"Faldo?" Leonie spluttered, her breath coming in ragged gasps. Her wild arm swinging slowed. Before any further comment could be made, Faldo's unmistakeable bulk loomed nearby. She splashed towards him.

Are you going to stay on this time?

"Promise." She coughed. "Where's Feiron?

"Right behind you."

Leonie whirled in shock, going underwater momentarily. "What're you doin'?" she spluttered when she resurfaced.

"Trying to save you again." Feiron was a grey mass, half-in -half-out of the dark waters. He reached out to steady her, guiding her to the waiting wyvern. "For a person who says she hates water, you seem to get into it often enough."

Balancing with his wing, Faldo rolled slightly so she could reach the saddle. Carefully placing her claws, Leonie had little trouble climbing up the smooth scaled hide, breathing a huge sigh of relief once she was sitting out of the water.

Feiron slid out of the water, sitting behind her in the saddle. "Sorry for bitin'."

"It's of no matter. Lucky I'm thick-skinned."

"More like all-skin," she panted.

Slana has landed. Come quick! Dorn's message was urgent.

We come. Faldo launched himself out of the water.

"How is she?" Leonie asked Faldo.

She is in great pain. Faldo skimmed above the waves, wingtips touching the water with each beat.

"Where is she?" Leonie tried to pinpoint their location. A row of rocky pinnacles flashed towards them; the smashed body of the Lith could be seen draped across one. She recognised it as Fang Rock. Faldo momentarily tucking in his wings before they clipped one of the massive edifices as he dashed between them. Her paw shaking, Leonie pointed beyond. "Slana's in the Plaza! Someone's bound to have seen her land even at this time of night."

Faldo flew directly to where his sister lay on the ground. Philbert had already dismounted to check the young wyvern's wounds, while Dorn hovered anxiously nearby.

"Can she crawl behind that?" Leonie called out when within earshot. She pointed to a three-tiered platform close to the canal. "It might block her from view of the garrison, assumin' they don't already know she's here." Sadness wrenched her, watching the young female wyvern drag herself painfully along the paving; so agile in the air, now as mobile as a beached whale. "We may as well join her," she said to Feiron and Faldo. "It isn't exactly the way we'd planned it, but we're home now."

Men are coming! Dorn's thoughts cut in.

Leonie cast her eyes around. The men, some of them guards, were gathering on the edge of the plaza. Soon they'd gain enough courage to approach.

Faldo dropped quickly to the flagstones to allow his passengers to alight. As the wyvern landed, Leonie dropped to the ground, suppressing a groan from the pain of bruised ribs and over-strained muscles. Feiron dripped beside her like a slow-motion waterfall, reaching for his bag of scales as he dismounted. He joined Leonie by Slana's side.

Faldo launched immediately, lowering his head as he streaked towards the mob. The roar he emitted scared them senseless. As one, they scattered white-faced for the protection of the nearest buildings.

"Everyone will know we're here now," Feiron muttered.

"How is she?" Leonie asked Phil.

"I think it's more shock than serious wounding." Phil straddled Slana's back, pouring a few drops of liquid onto each of the puncture marks. "There's muscle damage, painful but not lethal."

You do not know the half of it. Slana grumbled.

"Slana," Leonie called out. "There'll be many guards here soon."

Will they help?

"Only to your grave. You'll have to leave. Now!" Leonie added.

I cannot fly.

"Then swim, damn it, but if you stay, they'll slaughter you. These people don't understand."

You did.

"Remember I told you of the stories where you are evil creatures? These people believe them."

The men are returning. There are more this time, and they have a leader. Dorn was hovering in the sky, but she dipped her wings and dive-bombed the approaching group. Some men broke ranks and retreated, regardless of shouted commands, but the bulk of them remained steadfast.

Bows appeared and the night was full of shafts hurtling into the darkness. Most were fired in haste and fear, easily missing the wyverns, but some came too close. Dorn banked sharply to the right, but Faldo, following his mother's lead, hissed in pain as a shaft pierced his wing.

Singer. Prepare yourself. Dorn sent her intentions.

Phil spun to his companions to shout a warning. "You better hit the deck!"

Seconds later, the squad of guards collapsed clutching their heads. Blood dripped from their ears.

Leonie looked around, wondering why they had to take cover.

Feiron looked around in confusion. "What's happening?"

"Mind blast." Phil answered. "One of the other tricks the wyverns have." He looked at them both quizzically. "Looks like you're both immune. Fascinating as that is, we should leave. Those men will be in a foul mood when they recover."

Phil turned to the young wyvern. "Slana, remember your training," Phil stressed. "Something like this could happen at any time. I know it hurts, but while you're feeling sorry for yourself, others are risking their lives trying to protect you. Get up. Now!"

I don't like you anymore.

"I can live with that."

Do not forget daughter. Dorn soothed, *there is a skyland nearby where you can recover. It is not too far.*

Very well, Mother.

Phil slid off the young wyvern's back as she slowly rose from the hard surface.

Slana faltered slightly, and both Leonie and Philbert staggered as echoes of her pain rippled across their minds.

Dorn. Phil called.

"No! It'll be too dangerous for her to land--" Leonie started to say.

I am here. Her massive form whipped around the tiered platform and dropped swiftly to the ground. The tiles cracked as she crunched down. She swung her tail away from where it almost swiped Feiron. *Sorry.*

Phil leapt into the saddle. "I hope to see you both again," he called as Dorn launched herself skyward.

After the two adventurers waved quickly, they moved to the shadows of the large dais used for public ceremonies.

Farewell from all of us. Dorn added as the three wyverns turned and winged their way back between the headlands. *We hope you will be able to fly with us again.*

"It'd be our pleasure, Dorn. Bye Faldo, Slana. Feiron sends his regards too," Leonie said quietly, knowing the wyvern's would read her thoughts. The two adventurers ducked, bolting for the shadows of the dais.

The guards helped each other to their feet; some wiping blood from their faces, others warily approaching.

"We aren't out of trouble yet," Feiron pointed out.

"Since we're headin' in opposite directions, I reckon it's time you went for another swim."

"What about you?"

"After what we've been through? I can handle these guys. Don't worry."

He didn't look convinced.

"We'll talk later. Meet me by the south pier in Dockside. Noon tomorrow. Now go." She pushed him gently. "Otherwise, we'll both get caught." She didn't give him the chance to argue, for there was no time. Leonie climbed the stairs, looking back only once she reached the top of the platform.

Feiron had shaped into the large serpent form he used at the chasm, the sack forming a bulge in his midsection. Keeping to the shadows, he slithered across the flagstones, disappearing the moment he entered the water. Leonie crouched and waited to see if the guards noticed either of them.

The men spread out below, their attention drawn to the south to where three dark shapes could be barely seen winging their way out to sea. One of the men, an officer as indicated by a sash across his right shoulder, looked down. He was standing in a splash of wyvern blood. The man jumped back with an oath and vigorously scraped his boots on the paving. Then he stopped, bending down to pick up something.

From the size and shape, Leonie guessed it was one of Slana's scales. The men gathered around to see. Leonie took that as her cue to depart.

The Seven Portals trilogy: out now!
Discover more about Andre's books at https://alienpress.org/

The fireteam's formation around the door was the same as the one they'd adopted when boarding the pirate corvette. Chipper and Stines stood behind a kneeling Ana and Hecate respectively, weapons ready, riding out the mild bumps as the yacht settled to the hangar floor. In contrast, the Tluaan warrior Vazak rested against the bulkhead opposite the hatch, one hand on her shoulder-holster, the other on her hip, the very picture of unfazed.

Chipper swallowed against the lump in his throat, but couldn't budge it. His eyes fell to the selector switch on the side of his PR19: it was set to *AP*, "anti-personnel" being the clean way of describing a lethal setting.

Do what you have to. Do what you must. You're a soldier, damn it.

He raised his chin and the lump in his throat dissolved as acceptance flooded through him. A click announced the hatch lock disengaging. The rustle of cloth and creak of gloves announced the fireteam's grips tightening on weapons. Chipper heard Wepps coming up beside him from the cockpit.

"Five bogeys sighted," the team leader said. "They fled down a passage to your ten o'clock."

The hatch slid open, the ramp already engaging, lowering from the ship's hull before rolling out like a rug. *Unlike* a rug, it hardened immediately into a stable surface as it touched the hangar's concrete floor. Without hostile contacts out there, Ana and Hecate shot to their feet and charged down, the male Peacers at their heels. Ana curved left toward the cockpit as Hecate and Stines veered right to the tail. Perched atop legs two meters high, there was space beneath the yacht's belly for Ana and Wepps to cut under it rather than around. They didn't stoop; Chipper had to. He glanced behind him, to where Vazak pounded out into the middle of empty space, without cover, turning in circles, seeking an enemy.

Cripes alive!

He faced forward again, putting her out of mind. His nostrils now prickled from the smell and bite of petrochemicals and concrete dust. To his right, patches of sunlight breaking through the hangar's opaque window-panels formed warm yellow rectangles across the floor. That was the only color here apart from the paint job on the yacht: the hangar design was utilitarian, greys upon greys. No other vehicles were in here, but a network of gantries, small derricks and catwalks laced the perimeter and beams crisscrossed the ceiling. Now that he looked more carefully, the roof seemed to be shifting a little in the outside breeze. Some kind of shade cloth? A kind of insulating fabric, more likely: it was cool in here while the glare beyond the hangar entrance hinted at a very hot day.

Through the stink of chemical and construct, Chipper could discern something else now, a native musk left by the beings that had been working here perhaps. Or by something in the atmosphere. He thanked God for the nanite-inoculations he'd received against germs ...

Wepps pointed to a doorway eighty meters off the yacht's

nose. Ana already had her rifle angled that way; Chipper did the same.

"Straight through there," Wepps said as Hecate came around from their left. Stines had stayed by the tail with an eye on the open hangar entrance. "Tluaan intel says the data center's where the building's four wings meet." He pointed at Hecate. "You're on point, then me, Ana, Stines."

"What about her?" Ana asked, jerking her shoulder at Vazak. The huge warrior was pacing now, nose in the air.

"She's meant to stick with me," Wepps sighed. "I'll guess we'll see about that."

"What about *me*?" Chipper asked.

"Watch the ship," Wepps said simply. "Go, Hecate."

Hecate bounded away at a sprint. A second later, Ana did too, but Chipper snared Wepps's armor to hold him place as Stines raced over and past them.

"Sergeant, if it's what I said about not capturing an enemy leader—"

Wepps's surprised expression softened. "It's not, Chip. I need someone here who can actually do what they're told and keep this ship intact for when we get back. I'd like to leave here when I need to."

"Right, Sergeant," Chipper replied, caught between relief and the shame of feeling relieved. He let Wepps go and the sergeant cuffed him affectionately before he too raced away.

Hecate was almost at the door before Vazak seemed to notice and follow. Despite her bulk, the Tlaa was *fast*, those long legs eating up the space at twice a human's speed.

"You need me?" a voice asked from behind him. Piers. Halfway down the ramp and ashen-faced, but steeled for the worst.

"Cockpit," Chipper told him. "Keep the engines warm. Be ready to go at a moment's notice."

With a nod, Piers scampered back inside.

Chipper glanced down at the stubby grenade launcher under his PR19's muzzle. *Hope you guys don't need this.* He took a knee under the vessel and kept his head on a swivel, watching both the hangar entrance and the door—the door through which his team were fast disappearing.

A gaggle of Tluaanto awaited them, one hundred meters along the corridor. They reminded Ana of gawkers at a roadside accident. Ten of them, all unarmed, none anywhere near Vazak's size. From a hundred meters away—most of the way to the building's hub—they stared at the alien interlopers coming through their door.

What is this, show time at the zoo? Ana wondered.

Without warning, Hecate burst-fired from beside her. Ana flinched. The EM rounds slammed against the ceiling above the crowd, showering them with fragments and dust and sending them packing.

Passing her human teammates, Vazak jogged ahead, her pistol out of its holster. She squeezed off a shot of her own, the energy bolt sizzling just over the heads of the fleeing. The group broke into two, vanishing behind side doors. As the fireteam jogged after her, Vazak looked over her shoulder and called, "Fun!"

"Christ," Stines grumbled to Hecate. "She's crazier'n you are!"

Hecate sent him a crass gesture.

Wepps snapped, "Secure those doors," indicating the ones the civilians had gone through. The cutting lasers carried by Hecate and Stines were also good for melting metal, melding doorframes to doors. When they reached the rooms the Tluaanto personnel had gone into, Stines stayed behind, putting his cutter to work. The others continued on, Wepps and

Hecate checking the other side rooms as Ana and Vazak kept on at a walk toward the open space another hundred meters further. The data center. Despite his orders to them to use lethal force, when Ana heard Wepps's weapon go off twice behind her, the sound was that of stun bolts.

Can't bring himself to kill non-combatants, she thought. *Well, fair play to you, Sergeant. That's exactly why I wanna join you Confeds.*

"Seal this one too," he shouted back to Stines.

Nearing the open area mid-building, Ana saw movement in there. More civilians? Or—

Her instincts saved her life. A shaggy head and broad shoulders appeared above a work station just inside the main chamber; Ana ducked right and into the final office doorway of the corridor. An energy bolt crackled past her left shoulder. Another hit the wall above the doorframe, forcing Ana to jiggle at the handle until it opened. Outside, Wepps and Hecate had gone to ground, Hecate pulling something from a hip pouch. Vazak appeared mid-corridor right outside the room Ana was in, firing from the hip. She heard an agonized shriek from the data center and Vazak sauntered into the room with her to take cover at the door, unfazed.

Making eye contact, Ana said, "Still fun?"

"Fun," the big Tlaa confirmed.

"Roachbot active," Hecate called out in the hall.

Ana risked a peek. From a prone position, Hecate had the tiny controller for the bot in her hands while the robot scuttled along the hallway floor at great speed.

"Careful of collaterals," Wepps called to her. "We want those leaders if they're there."

"Trust me," Hecate replied. "Dialing it down."

Several more energy bolts flashed past, forcing Ana to retreat. Vazak returned fire, but without a resulting cry of pain this time.

"Two bogeys only, eleven o'clock," Hecate called and then blue-white light flashed once followed by a thick *whump* of sound. She'd used the flashboom setting on the bot, Ana realized, rather than H.E. A half second later she also realized that her crew were moving. She followed after Vazak as fast as she could, but the Tlaa quickly overtook Hecate and Wepps, entering the chamber ahead of them and to the left of the doorway. The warrior was one meter inside—with Wepps coming up mid-corridor and Hecate far-right—when something huge dropped on her from the ceiling and she rolled sideways and out of Ana's view. Wepps and Hecate swore, Wepps with rifle high and sweeping the roof, while Hecate's swept the maze of work stations around the room, favoring the left of the chamber's midpoint. Satisfied there was no further threat from above, Wepps leaped onto a console and fired repeatedly at the point Ana figured the flashboomed hostiles were.

"Two down," he called and jumped to the next console, tracking his rifle left for new threats while Hecate focused right.

Reaching the entrance to the chamber, Ana threw herself on the floor. All of the desks appeared to be standing up off the floor with a meter of space beneath them—this allowed her to check the room from a prone position. A quick glance to her left revealed Vazak grappling with a warrior of similar size, with bushier head-fur and more formal clothes. They scuttled around on one hand and two knees, both with knives drawn and teeth bared. They came together in a tangle as Ana forced her focus ahead of her.

There!

"Contact forward!" she yelled. "Mid-room. Four, maybe five bogeys. Could be civs." The knot of Tluaanto were bowed low, with knees, hands and heads all touching the floor. None appeared as big as the warriors she'd seen so far.

"Got 'em!" Wepps yelled from above and forward. "Ana, you're free to move. Hecate—"

"Still clearing," the Tactical called back.

Ana got up and slipped down an aisle way between desks, bringing her close to the sergeant's position as he hopped to the floor. She smelled charred flesh and fabric: over to the left, two enemy warriors were down with smoking holes in their torsos and heads.

"Hack it, I missed all the action!" Stines whined, entering the chamber late. He pulled up short, captivated by the two grappling warriors.

"They're yours to watch," Wepps told him. When he noticed Ana trying to pick out the council members from the five Tluaanto cowering on their knees mid-room, he whistled at her. "Forget them." He stabbed a finger at a nearby data terminal as he closed on the frightened huddle of nonhumans.

"Right," she said and bent over the work station. She slipped her folding keypad and smartwire from a vest pocket and got to work, recognizing the data port she'd been shown back on *Assured*. The port was a configuration of three slim holes arranged in a tight triangle. Squeezing the smartwire's end to activate it, she pressed it against the metal between the holes. While she caught her breath, the wire's end parted into tiny filaments that snaked their way against and into the input apertures. She fit the other end of the smartwire into the keypad.

"Clear!" Hecate called.

With one hand training his rifle on the group of cowering Tluaanto, Wepps waved the other at the door on the far side of the chamber. "That's front door. Hecate, that's yours to watch." He stabbed a finger back the way they'd come. "That's back door. Stines, that's yours—and keep an eye on ... them," he added, meaning the warriors down behind the bank of work stations.

"Bloody oath, I will," Stines replied.

Ana checked the keypad, waiting for the green light and bright alert tone that would signal contact had been established. It wasn't coming fast and she found herself bobbing up and down on the balls of her feet. "Come on, *porquería*, come on!"

Ahead of her, Wepps pulled items from the largest pouch on his vest. Three cakes of high explosive. Then the detonator.

Once the virus was on its way, Wepps was going to turn this place to atoms.

Yes! she thought as the keypad bleeped confirmation of a connection. Suddenly, nothing mattered so much to her as uploading the data virus and getting the hack out of here. She hoped Piers still had the yacht engines running. She hoped Chipper wasn't facing any contacts back there—

Joyful whooping from Stines turned Ana's head: Vazak had risen from behind the bank of desks, wiping dark blood from her knife onto her suit leg. There didn't appear to be any tears in that suit. From his position covering the entryway, Stines flipped the Tlaa a thumbs up. She ignored it, vaulting over consoles to get to Ana's station faster. Although Ana knew Vazak was on her side, watching that mighty body approaching at full steam, her ape-cat face flushed and her throat fur dark, with that huge blade drawn—holy Christ, it was *scary*.

At Ana's side, Vazak considered the ovular monitor screen at the back of the work station. Ana clipped a data-wafer to the keypad—the wafer containing the mutated virus—and started typing. All of this had to be by memory and with a precise touch since none of the right-to-left gibberish running across the alien monitor screen made any sense to her. It didn't need to, she reminded herself. She'd programmed the virus with a little help from that gambling addict Sintopas and one of the Orbital's crew; it was solid. As long as her typing *was* accurate, the program she unleashed would bridge human and Tluaan systems to send that data-virus racing out into Domain Surface networks at lightspeed.

Vazak grunted something and it took Ana a few moments to recognize it as the English word *Good*. The warrior was already moving away and toward the seated captives before Ana could respond.

Vazak pointed at one of the trembling Tluaanto—Ana couldn't tell their gender at a glance, especially not when distracted and awaiting a confirmation bleep from her keypad. *Come on, come on*, she thought. Vazak barked commands at the Tluaan individual—straightening, Ana noticed that this one wore a short robe over the normal Tluaan tunic and trousers, a garment with silver embossing along the sleeves and hem. After a moment, the individual crawled along the floor until they were two metres from the rest of their group. They glared back at Vazak, covering their fear with an exaggerated hauteur.

Vazak said to Wepps, "Con-sill."

"Copy," Wepps replied. He raised his voice. "We're not taking these other four. Or incinerating them. Vazak, tell them to run." He mimed it with his fingers and pointed to the front door.

Vazak frowned a little and watched his lips as he repeated the words.

Her expression cleared. "Run. Yes." She turned to the four civilians and snarled three syllables at them. Nothing happened except that they drew tighter in on themselves. Vazak drew a deep breath. This time she roared the phrase at them. And this time, they didn't hesitate, rising as one and bolting hard toward the entry Hecate was guarding. The Tactical slapped her rifle barrel against the backside of the last one leaving and cackled.

Wepps approached the last enemy individual—the Surface council member—waving them to their feet. They complied—grudgingly. Immediately, Vazak stepped in and scooped the individual onto her shoulder, the way she had with Hecate. Then she retreated around the desks at a jog.

Ana's comms crackled—they'd been able to rig them to operate in a closed system away from *Assured*. They could communicate amongst themselves but not with their capital ship.

"Fireteam, this is Chipper. Pilot marks three aircraft inbound fast and low from the north. Devilfly is distracted and can't engage."

Wepps hit *transmit* button. "Close?"

"Very."

"Troop carriers? Bombers?"

"Can't be certain."

"Copy." Wepps whistled Hecate and gestured for her to come back. He hit the detonator timer and set out after Vazak. "Two minutes till boom-boom, boys and girls, let's frog it!" He slapped his comms again. "Returning hot, Chipper. Vazak has one enemy prisoner."

Ana squeezed the smartwire, telling it to withdraw.

Chipper's voice crackled through their comms again. "Radar indicates first enemy aircraft has landed, north end of compound. First enemy aircraft has landed."

Ana tugged out the data wafer and pocketed it, folding the keyboard as Hecate arrived at her side. She gave the wire a tug, but it wouldn't detach. What was taking it so long?

"The man said boom-boom," Hecate told her. "You know boom-boom?"

"Go if you have to. I'll be done in a sec."

"Leave it!"

"Can't! Captain doesn't want traces of human tech left here."

"Screw him!"

Ana wondered if Hecate would have said that aloud if her ECF had been sending to *Assured*.

Hecate continued, "The tech's about to get evaporated. Let's *go*."

"They're orders. Just leave. I'm almost d—"

A deep-throated shout from the direction of the "front door" sucked the breath out of Ana's lungs. Warriors? How the hell had they—?

She flashed back to a memory of Vazak sprinting through the hangar and overtaking her.

"Shit."

She trained her rifle on the door a split second after Hecate did. The very next second, two enormous Tluaanto came barreling through it. They wore clothing closer to human combat fatigues than to Vazak's bodysuit. Their head-fur was shaggier than hers. And they were bigger. Both carried long knives, their rifles slung. Seeing the humans, they ululated and cut toward them, hurdling the first desk in their way.

Ana and Hecate fired simultaneously, a sustained volley that blew both hostiles off their feet and back onto the desk.

"Now will you go?" Hecate asked her, turning her head for a second.

In the second that followed, an energy bolt whipped by, centimeters overhead. Ana had the impression of three or four more warriors crowding the doorway before she dropped into cover.

"Holy mother!" Hecate hissed, collapsing next to Ana.

"You hit?"

"Nah, just pissed off."

"Bad timing, huh?"

"Damn right." A barrage of energy bolts swept overhead, turning patches of the next desks past them into molten slag. "What now?"

Ana's keypad and smartwire were still up on the desk. She wished she'd listened to Hecate and left them thirty seconds ago—she was going to have to anyway. She jerked her chin at the "back door".

"Head for the corridor. I'll cover you. Then you cover me while I catch up."

"So they can hit me while you hit them?" Hecate sneered.

"God! I'm trusting *you* not to run and leave me here!"

"It's a dumbass idea, whoever goes first."

Both women recoiled when fresh fire pounded the back of the desk they'd sheltered behind.

"That's gonna burn through real soon," Hecate said.

Ana pulled a grenade from a vest pouch. Hecate nodded and followed suit. They scooted to opposite ends of their cover, coming around into a crouch to face it. Ana slung the rifle over her back and pulled her sidearm—the Xerxian 12-mm felt a lot more comfortable than the Confed rifles, and it would be easier to fire blind over a desk. There came a temporary lull in the shooting, and with it the scuff of footsteps as hostiles repositioned themselves.

"Me first," Ana said. Hooking her forearm over the desk, she fired four wild shots. When return-fire hammered home near her, Hecate lobbed her grenade then ducked back. Ana quickly twisted the top of her grenade and depressed the timer. Enemy fire swung Hecate's way, allowing Ana to lob her grenade too, careful to send it far past Wepps's charges. The two women jammed hands over ears and opened their jaws wide against the pressure wave to come.

The twin explosions shook the floor and rattled the desk. Rubble peppered the room and smoke boiled quickly up toward the high ceiling.

"*Now* I'll go first!" Hecate said and launched herself in the direction of the back door.

Ana popped up, handgun ready ... But there was zero enemy contact. And judging by the mess they'd caused, there wouldn't be. Her anxious gaze fell to Wepps's explosives, sitting undamaged where he'd placed them. How much time had elapsed?

Ana turned and sprinted after Hecate. The other Tactical had paused by the door to offer cover if needed, so Ana passed her easily and heard her fall into step a few meters behind.

They were fifty or meters out of the data center when the charges ignited.

The resulting pressure wave threw them off their feet. Ana tucked herself into a roll as she landed, coming to rest face up and in perfect position to watch the network of cracks race along the ceiling above her.

"Shit!" she cried and hunkered up tight again, arms over her head as the roof caved in.

Third Contact: out now!
Explore more about Pete's books at *http://petealdin.com/library/*

RED SAILS
BOOK ONE

SECRETS
OF THE
DEEP

ANDRE JONES